ROAD TO JUNEAU
BY
LIAM QUANE

Beaten Track
www.beatentrackpublishing.com

Road to Juneau

First published 2021 by Beaten Track Publishing
Copyright © 2021 Liam Quane

Hardcover ISBN: 978 1 78645 474 4
Paperback ISBN: 978 1 78645 452 2
eBook ISBN: 978 1 78645 453 9

Cover Design: Holly Dunn

Beaten Track Publishing,
Burscough, Lancashire.
www.beatentrackpublishing.com

For my brother Adam, my father Anthony, my brother Lee & my mother Rita.

Without you, I wouldn't be.

So, by that logic, the following is your fault.

How was God supposed to defend Earth
from the Monster, when the Monster
knew Earth better than God ever could?

Chapter 1

8:08 A.M. That's what my clock says as I burst out of my covers. I must have fallen out of bed again. I know this because I'm staring at it from the other side of my room. There was luck to this particular tumble, however—I'm only sixteen minutes behind! I wheeze as I lift myself up, kicking the sheets from my ankles like a half-swaddled baby. The same old tapping returns, persistent and loud, and I walk over to my ground-floor window, lifting it dramatically in an effort to shoo the seagull pecking at the pane. The blunt-billed bird squawks as it flaps away. I slam the window closed, keeping the cold morning air off my skin for a few more minutes.

My shower was lukewarm and my breakfast fictional. This is the best I can hope for on Tribute day at my place of work: Montage Tower. The building may be taller than most, but the work is still lowly. I lock my bedroom door out of an irrational precaution; my roommate is still upstairs. It's his third day off this week, and it's silent, but I know he's awake because his door is slightly ajar. If anything were to disappear from my room, he would be blamed for it, regardless, as either a successful thief or a failing watchdog. I collect my earbuds, phone, and wallet combo and silently make for the exit. As my door card reaches the scanner, a magazine bricks the window, launched from the top of the stairs where Sam now stands.

"Almost hit you, Dan!" he shouts down to me in his usual excitable manner.

"What is it this time? I'm already late." I almost don't reply.

"Page twelve—the blue *chaise longue*!" He points at the once-airborne catalog, which now sits crumpled in my hands.

"I'm not *dragging* a chaise longue home for you!"

"It's not for *me*, it's for Shanty," he says, partitioning himself from the blame.

I spin the catalog around and read the cover. "Scratchwork Furrrnishings."

"It's only small—twenty-five by sixteen." He holds his hands out like a puppeteer.

"Can't your hamster just sleep in your bed with you?"

"No. He has an erratic sleeping pattern."

A silence lingers.

"Fffffine," I reluctantly sputter, throwing the catalog onto the floor in a sulk.

Sam giggles and retreats back into his lair of aspen shavings and lavender. I finally scan my door card, which sounds a cheery beep of freedom.

Do you remember the colors of your life? How it used to feel before you became *responsible* and *independent*? Everyone does, I guess. Three shades usually cocoon themselves around the memories: the *Blue* Stage, the *Purple* Stage, and the *Gray* Stage.

I am at *Gray* and dreading what comes after. The Blue Stage is the oldest. It consists of the memories of when you were a child. An only child. Not specifically *you*, but *me*.

I forget how to separate myself from the situation sometimes, Sorry.

Anyway, *my* childhood could only be described as glowing. Mom and Dad were always here for me, breakfast-table mornings and dinner-table evenings. They both worked interesting jobs, each excelling in a separate creative field. My mother was a software programmer; a good one too. The start-up she worked at grew from a hole in the wall to an admired business. Similarly, my father was successful in his career as an architect, not of towering superstructures but of small, respectable buildings in which families could live happy lives. Those homes are gone now.

I was around thirteen years old when I realized I'd never heard my parents fight. In fact, I hadn't seen any anger from them at all. Not toward each other. Not about work, or money—something which we were never without. Eventually, as my teenhood set in, I attributed their constant state of bliss to a secret drug habit, hoping to one day join the gang. But I was wrong. I found this out soon after Purple reared its ugly head.

My life as a teenager was a lot slower than when I was a kid, and that aforementioned *blissful family atmosphere* quickly started to crack. Dad's work hours increased. Taxes were the same, but he wasn't, not with the stress he carried to keep the family "secure." The same could be said for Mom. The company she originally worked for was poached and absorbed into a much larger company named Hourglass Industries—the place that now owns the building I work in. I think I repressed the name of the original, probably for the best.

Mom's place of work was reduced from a company into a department practically overnight. That department was nicknamed the "Hamsters," with their keyboards taking the place of an ever-revolving running wheel. Each operator acted as a tiny part in the company's development effort to incorporate full-stack artificial intelligence into everyday technology, paving the way for a new age filled with pre-programmed vending machines, facial recognition in cell phones, and even software made for monitoring agricultural growth patterns. Naturally, that software was rerouted into the war effort, bringing more autonomy to the war drones than had previously existed. After that, Mom grew more restless and pricklier as time went on. Maybe it was out of resentment for Hourglass forcing her into a box, maybe it was her age, but a deep-seated disdain slowly rose over the years, and it was aimed at Dad, though only acted upon when she thought I wasn't watching.

★

My wireless earbuds boom with the music of an old British band—
Pennylands. Yes, it *is* a strange name if you look at it now. We don't
use pennies anymore, and the British no longer have "land." This is
their last prewar album, so I'm not even sure they're making stuff
anymore. That is, if they're alive. The metro still hasn't been rebuilt,
so I'm walking to the office. It's only a short distance, but it's a
tricky trek. I hop off the still-fractured sidewalk, cautiously avoiding
the early morning traffic. Sidewalks are being fixed neighborhood
by neighborhood, as opposed to the roads, which were initially
re-paved en masse. Sleep was difficult over those four months due to
the noise of the colossal paving vehicles dragging along like sloths
with a mission.

I gaze up at the quaint metropolis that surrounds me, polished
knives of business and pleasure pointing toward the sky, all the blue
snuffed out by a huge smear of muted gray cloud which stretches
far and wide in every direction. The war took away a lot of what
was iconic about Manhattan: the Chrysler Building, Grand Central
Station, and the Empire State Building. The latter was quickly rebuilt
but is now only referred to as the *Empire Building* out of some odd-
placed respect for what stood before. The city is more like a pretty
scar of its former self. Madison and Park are still standing. The Sony
Tower luckily avoided disaster, as the one errant shell fired that way
flew through its open pediments, leaving no damage.

One of the good things that came out of the fighting was the
Housing Pledge. Social housing would be provided to a grieving,
downtrodden nation of *war heroes* and cowards for a discounted
fee, not that there were many buildings left to discount. I'm now able
to rent a newly built brownstone with Sam and Holly. Sam you've
met; Holly is my floor neighbor. Her room is above mine, though
she's hardly ever home. She's stern and hard-headed but smart and
responsible, a young, undecorated veteran of the war. Strangely, after
everything she went through, she doesn't seek a quiet life.

Holly is out of the house earlier than any of us, and we hardly
see her some weeks, the result of constant deadlines. She is an
intern at *Huble* News—like the telescope, apparently. I think there

was an error when they filed the trademark, an error Holly will never let them forget. *Huble* took her on the spot when they saw she had combat experience, only they don't have her writing anything remotely related to the war. Sam, on the other hand, is not so smart, not so responsible, and I can say all of this because he's my friend, not yours. He has a hamster named Shanty. Yes, Shanty is a hamster, not a cat, contrary to what I believed when we first moved in together. I learned that sane people have cats; insane people have hamsters that they treat like cats.

I finally reach work. "MONTAGE TOWER." The gigantic words scream at my eyes from a newly varnished metal sign at the foot of the steps. Behind the lettering on the logo stands an embossed hourglass, a universal symbol meant to be inviting and self-explanatory, but I try to avoid thinking about that meta-artistic bullshit and climb the church-like steps that are so deep I have to stride just to traverse them one at a time. The tower has been described as "modern" even though that term was blown to hell with the hourglass stamp that hovers around the company logo like the belted jacket of a falsely imprisoned sane person. As I make my way higher, I look skyward, past the tethered windowpanes that crisscross one another forming a mosaic-style curtain wall that runs halfway up the building like a skirt on a skeleton. I say this because the top half needs to be constructed first; it's only a rebar and rivets so far.

I enter through a garish set of double doors nestled under an enormous metallic arch. They give way to a fully furnished lobby. The walls are painted a harsh, cartoonish red; the ceiling is a natural cream, good for bouncing light around from the entrance. There are skinny halves of Corinthian pillars laid vertically across the walls like dado rails, four per wall. The designer was on thin ice; they were either creating a mythical palace or a very real, very intimidating whorehouse.

I reach the security desk. Attached to it is a full-body scan or, as the staff call it, the Sex-Ray because it sees every part of you. Behind the desk sits a yeti of a security guard whose name escapes me. I look for his badge. It shines at me from his barreled-chest.

It reads: "Hi! My name is Derek!" A *cheerful* badge for a security guard to have.

"Morning, Derek!" I confidently yell. My greeting bounces off the wide walls, echoing awkwardly. Derek looks around for the reverberations, then back to me, folding his face into a frown.

"My name is Andrew!" he says angrily.

I stare confused, grinning like a Cheshire Idiot at the angriest man in the world. "But your tag says——"

"I lost my tag! My name is Andrew, sir!" he interrupts with more aggression. "Sir" means nothing here.

"Then who's Derek?" I ask, flushed.

"I DON'T KNOW!"

I quickly lay my backpack in the box on the conveyor belt and swipe my card across the scanner. Andrew glares at his monitor, scanning my bag for a reason to hurt me. My name and title appear on the screen: Daniel Hardacre, Social Media Executive. I hate *Daniel*.

"Looks good. Go on through, sir," Der—I mean *Andrew* says in a more enlivened way.

"Thanks…you very much." I pull my bag into my arms and hurry to the elevators.

Social Media Executive. It sounds like a well-paying job with flexible hours and convenient perks. It is not. Now that the world has opened up its heart to the digital space completely, it's harder to actually find success within it.

BING! The elevator's arrived. I hate this part. Not just the cramped space but also the irrational fear of the journey never stopping. Can you imagine standing, minding your own business waiting to get to your floor, and then the floors run out, they stop ticking down, and you carry on climbing forever and ever? I never used to be like this. Maybe it's because I'll just be getting out of one box and into another. A drone will be brought in to rework the thing when the rest of the tower is finished, but until then, this is the only way up. The architect thinks stairs are *primitive*.

BING!

I rush out, dashing down a stretch of pale hallway and into the employee locker room, where I shove my backpack into the clinically colorless cage with a SLAM and head out to the main office. The room isn't especially small, but most of it is taken up by a grid of workspaces that make it a nightmare to navigate. The back of the room is lined with a huge window that looks out over Times Square. My light steps quicken as I get closer and closer to my cubicle and… I have a hand on my shoulder. I'm spun around to face my boss, Martin Nebrezza, smiling at me through his newly acquired teeth. His copper-colored skin and milky-white hair make him look like the *Cappuchpresso* I desperately crave. His rolled-up shirtsleeves beg me to respect and admire his easy-going managerial manner. I don't.

"Danny-boy!" he yells just loud enough to make a dozen heads pop up over their cubicle walls. Ana isn't among them. I can see her myself; she is still typing at her computer, trying to avoid the scene.

"What time do you call this?"

I check my phone: 8:45 a.m.

"I'm sorry, Martin. My housemate's hamster got out of the door when I was leaving, and I spent fifteen minutes trying to catch it." Shut up! I *will* blame the hamster!

"Shouldn't it be in a cage?" he asks like it's *my* hamster.

"It should, but my housemate likes to make me late for work."

Martin sits on the copy machine behind him, thinking to himself. He already knows what he's going to say, but he likes to perform.

"Danny, that's the kind of whacky balls-to-the-wall lifestyle we need around this place!"

That was not the answer I expected. The stress of leading is getting to him…I hope.

"Speaking of walls, look around you, Dan. Tell me what you see." His words are mint-encrusted, and his arms are outstretched making him more "T" than man.

"Cubicles?" I naively guess, assuming it's a trick question. He shakes his head.

"Walls?"

His face lights up with pure childish joy at my second answer. "WALLS! THAT'S RIGHT! AND WHAT WERE WALLS MADE FOR?!"

"Privacy?" I whisper hesitantly.

"TO BE KNOCKED DOWN! COME ON, EVERYONE, TAKE YOUR CHAIRS AND GET KNOCKING!"

The staff is unsure, but Martin enthusiastically raises his arms in reply, becoming "Y" personified. Everybody stands, lifting their ergonomic chairs above their heads, and *bang*, they smash the walls of their cubicles down like dominoes. The cheap panels hit the carpet softly while I stare in horror.

"GOOD WORK, PEOPLE! SEE WHAT YOU *MISSED*, DANNY?!"

"But...I was here," I say, recomposing myself.

Martin sympathetically tilts his head. "Yes...you were, and *now* you can go put these walls into storage. FIGHT THE POWER!"

I burrow through the shadows of the dusty storage room in an effort to *fight the power*. The shelves are littered with old computer pieces: monitors, keyboards, mice, and tablets. Next to them is a stack of water-cooler bottles and dozens of stationery boxes filled with things that no one uses anymore. The farther I get into the room, the more junk has reduced the space. That *feeling* comes back again. I change focus and search for the stepladder. One of the electricians must have it. I don't know why I think that, but I can picture someone fiddling with a faulty light switch in the corner.

Awkwardly, I heave the cubicle panels up onto the top shelf because, of course, the *top* shelf is the *only* empty one. I have to push one foot on the bottom shelf in order to gain enough height. One by one, I stack the walls higher and higher until I *fingertip* the last one in place. I hear a noise coming from the top of the wall stack—a soft scraping—and stretch on my tiptoes to see what the cause is. As I peer toward the back of the unit, a panel launches itself at my head, knocking me down. The wall falls after me, and I squint in defense of the blow that's about to come, only...there *is* no blow, and when I open my eyes, the panel is hovering above me...I *think*.

I roll out of its way and *crash*! It and the rest of the wall panels come tumbling down, barely missing me. In less than a second, I'm on my feet and hurtling toward the exit, trying my hardest not to touch anything else. Martin told me to put the panels in storage; they're in storage.

As I open the door, I am greeted by a short, familiar friend of mine.

"What was all that noise?" Ana asks, sheepish but concerned.

"None of your business." I slam the door behind me.

"Oh...okay." She lowers her head, ashamed. I *hate* it when she does that.

"Break?" I suggest, changing the subject.

"But...it's *only* ten thirty."

I pull a sad puppy face at her, but she's still looking down at her shoes. "Ana, please, I...just have to get some *air*."

She brings her head back up in horror.

We sit under the bare skeleton of framework, halfway up the building. We're not supposed to be up here, but as long as we're wearing safety helmets, the foreman doesn't seem to care. I finally have my *Cappuchpressoooooo*. The coffee sits in my hands, steaming in its little blue recyclable cup, the words "WE ARE HAPPY TO SERVE YOU!" written along the base in Greek-style letters. Ana pulls a water bottle out of her bag.

"Why always water?" I ask.

"Caffeine makes me anxious. I've told you this." She pops the bottle cap open.

"Oh...I forgot."

"Yes, Claustrophobia can do that to a person." Her sarcastic teasing is genuinely comforting. Her barbs are from a dark place, but it's a darker place than mine.

"That's not funny!" I retort, hiding a smile.

There's a loud screech above us—the sound of a retracting crane wire, and we peer up to see a group of drones sitting along the top of a metal girder, hoisting it all the way to the highest point of the tower.

Ana takes a sip of her water; the bottle is frosted, even on this humid day. "I can't believe I'm working under those things," she whispers.

"At least you don't have to sleep under them anymore. That's something."

"My mom's blow-dryer," she says between long swills, "wakes me up a whole hour before I have to..." She gulps the rest of the bottle down and drops it into her oversize clutch. "I'm not *punctual*. I'm rushed. Not that you'd know. You can't use that fake hamster excuse again the next time you oversleep."

"Alarms don't work on me, like coffee doesn't work on you," I reply. That word flicks a switch on in my brain: *Work, oh, shit!*

"Oh, shit! The Tribute starts in *three minutes*!"

Ana checks her watch and slowly lurches to her feet, like a *rushed* zombie.

We leave our helmets on two protruding pieces of rebar and make our way downstairs, where a crowd has formed at the huge back window of our office. We push through to get space to see. The flickering advertisements around Times Square have ceased, and a blank screen now plays in place of the usual fruity soft drinks and movie GIFs. It's not a happy occasion, but you have to appear interested otherwise you're just a dick. Martin is here, flustered; nervous even. He notices me staring and forces a smile onto his face.

"Eyes forward, son," he murmurs. I do as he says.

The crowd livens up as *The Aerostat* reveals itself: a massive electronic blimp fitted with fans at each side of the car to add a classic, cartoonish feel to an extremely depressing dirigible. Down the sides of the balloon are the names of every American soldier killed in action during the war, each one etched into the surface in tiny, painful lettering. They're difficult to make out, but I'm able to read a few:

L.Cpl. Charlotte Albrier, died age 28.
L.Cpl. Scott Alvarez died aged 35.
Cpl. Oliver Benson, died aged 32.
Pvt. Sara Lowcroft, died aged 22.
S.Sgt. Nathan…Nebrezza…died aged…

Oh God.

I turn to find Martin, but he's gone. I look to Ana, who nods, confirming the dark news.

S.Sgt. Nathan Nebrezza, died aged 19.

The blimps hover through the length of Times Square. The crowds below are still, frozen in time until the memories drift past.

I spend the rest of the day forwarding and re-forwarding emails between potential clients and management. I'm essentially advertising a building, something not listed on my job description. Ana steps up behind me in somber silence.

"I can't believe they wouldn't give him the day off," I say, but she shakes her head.

"That could be the worst thing for him. People find comfort in work." She drifts into deep thought briefly, and then snaps out of her stupor. "What's on your mind, anyway? I mean, besides Martin."

"Oh…nothing." A silence looms. "Ana?"

"It's just…I can't help wondering, what was that crash from before? I went to take a look after the Tribute—"

"I know. The walls…"

"And the room was empty," she finishes.

"That's weird." I frown. "Maybe the caretaker took them downstairs for space?"

"No," she says. "The whole room was empty."

We switch on the light in the storage room. She was right. There's nothing there. No computers, no tablets, but there is one thing—the stepladder, sitting in the middle of the floor, mockingly.

We slam the door to the haunted storage closet and flush the thought from our minds. As I do, my phone *buzzes* in my pocket: an alarm. Work is done!

"See ya Monday, Ana!" I shout cheerily. She doesn't have a chance to reply before I'm out the door. I take my backpack from my locker and charge into the elevator. I push my earbuds in, close my eyes, and wait for the sound...*come on...please...*

BING!

"Oh, shit!" The car muffles my accidental exclamation. I forgot I have to pick up Shanty's goddamned chaise longue! The doors open up, giving me freedom to run through the lobby. There comes a loud chanting that even my earbuds can't keep from annoying me. I pass the security desk without a word and make my way to the front doors; outside, I spy a whole troupe of protesters carrying multicolored plasterboard signs decorated with large, terrifying letters. I read a few at the front:

TRADITIONAL SOLUTIONS!
BUILT ON THE GRAVES OF MANY!
DON'T FIX WHAT'S NOT BROKEN...P****S!

You see? They're calling us "pricks" but in a polite way!

This group of protestors is called the Surtsey Signholders, named after some untouched island off the coast of Iceland, at least that's what every news site says whenever it wants to stir the peace pot. They stand in a messy cluster at the bottom of the steps. They spot me coming and all scream at me.

"I'm sorry. I only work in the building. I'm not—"

One of the group leaps in front of me, blocking my path of escape.

"*You work for the devil!*" the protestor screams, and a loud cheer spirals as the protestors completely encircle me.

"I didn't know he was in real estate—perfect time for it!" I retort. There is a brief pause before a torrent of anger broadsides me from every mouth in the vicinity. I try my best to get down to the street, crossing only to be blocked from the road by an ever-growing wave of angry bodies. I don't wait for the stoplight to change; I purposefully walk the group in front of a beaten-up old hatchback, which skids to a halt, blasting its horn. The protestors change target, surrounding the understandably angry driver who is now trapped in a small box of audible pain. I don't look back; I hurry away up the street toward the pet store.

Breathlessly, I burst into Scratchwork Furrrnishings. Hands on my knees: my shape's not good. I glance up at the store owner and her assistant, both glaring at me inquisitively. I address the owner. She has a down-to-earth grandmother quality about her, bifocals and all. I point toward the now-swinging door.

"Animal Palz are here!" I say, lying to her. The owner looks in horror at the uniformed young man across the store.

"Peter?" she calls to her assistant. "Those protesters are back! Get my machete!"

My face drops to shock, and she notices.

"You'd better find what you want and get the hell outta here!"

I lug myself up the road toward my apartment, backpack over my right arm, miniature navy blue chaise longue, size "35x20," under my left. That was the only size they had in-store. Look, Shanty doesn't need these trivial things. He would be pleased with food and warmth.

As I follow the cracked pavement back to my house, I'm sent back into my memories, of fear, heartbreak, excitement, anticipation, cowardice. I grow cold after seeing that even after a war, conflict remains. Even after the big three—Russia, China, and the USA—changed the face of the world. At first, the friction was remarkably difficult to follow, something about immigration rights, referendums, patriotism. Then after a few months, nothing could have been simpler. The world was at war, again. Here were no Surtsey Signholders or Animal Palz. There was hardly any protest at all. I thought there would be, but when a nuclear treaty was brought into play, the table was set, and humanity was at its own throat without complaint.

Every man, woman, and child had to be catalogued and categorized, and everyone of eligible age to fight was greeted at home by a large white *draft* envelope, marked on the back with the Great Seal of the United States to make them feel personal.

I never received one of those envelopes. I could have; I should have. But I never did. I thought of following up the order, mainly out of fear. But then I realized how lucky I was after seeing mothers, fathers, daughters, and sons dead on the news, and I wasn't *eligible*. Part of me wanted to help, but a bigger part of me wanted to live.

Chapter 2

Goo, I knew I'd forgotten something. My phone sits on my nightstand buzzing like an excited dog in a bumblebee outfit. I don't even have to look; I know who's calling. I haven't spoken to him in about a month. It's usually at this time when he starts to worry, if he is capable of *not* worrying, that is. He isn't calling; he is just texting…a lot. Fast-paced, parental texts can really drive one mad early in the morning. I may as well have a woodpecker on my forehead. *Peck-peck-peck…peck-peck-peck…peck-peck-pe*—Fine! I'll answer!

Scraping myself up off my morning floor, I catch my reflection in the wall-mounted mirror above my useless bed. I look like a Flock of Seagull who has fought with an actual flock of seagulls. Instinctively, I try to flatten my mess of hair only for my brown spikes to spring back into *place*. I pick up my phone and read his latest message. It says:

> *Hi Son, I know what you're thinking: "Grrr! he's at it again!" But you know our agreement; reclusiveness is all well and good, but if I don't hear from you at least once a month then I'll assume the worst! Get back to me when you can. I know you're busy with work, and with your friends and with your life as a grown man ;P but if—*

I stop reading. I can probably guess where this is going. We keep contact. That was the deal. Every month seems to come around quicker than the last. It's such a hassle. I don't know whether I feel this way about him out of laziness or cowardice. Or resentment for what happened with Mom?

I text back:

Hi dad, sorry I didn't respond to your previous 13 [?] messages. I was sleeping, plus my phone was on silent.

He responds almost instantly:

LOL, no worries Son :D I'm just glad you're OK. Do you think we could, you know, meet up for a coffee today? Nothing 2 heavy. I just wanna hang out, you know? Hahaha.

I find no humor in this. Apprehensively, I hit reply. My mind says, "No, no!" but my fingers say:

Yes, yes, I do. Coffee sounds great!

I hate my fingers.

Ashamed of myself, I stumble out of my bedroom. The first thing I see isn't a thing at all but Holly. What time is it? She's sitting at the kitchen table, eating breakfast and staring at her tablet computer like a normal functioning adult. The clanking of her breakfast bowl keeps in rhythm with the ticking clock on the wall next to me: 6:32 a.m. Goddammit, I under-slept again! I tiptoe into the kitchen, hoping to pass by unnoticed—as if I could truly be invisible.

"Nice hair," Holly says sardonically, mid-chew. She hasn't even turned around to look at me; she just stays slumped in her Corn Flakes.

"I—thank you," I drowsily reply.

She manages to respond with a simple, "Mm-hmm!" A verbal nod, if you will. This grants me freedom from the mundane pleasantries of *friendship* and quick passage to the shower.

As the water heats up from inside the clicking unit, I make my way to the mirror on the other side of the bathroom to check my face for discrepancies. It's filthy—the mirror, not my face. Small spatters of toothpaste and shaving cream dot the surface of the glass, like drops of snow on a summer street. I stare at my reflection for longer than is healthy. I peer closer, and my face fades from my sight behind a silver cloud. I bounce back in shock. Am I turning invisible?

No, the steam from the shower has reached all the way over to the mirror. I shiver in anticipation and prepare to leap through a wall of fog into the warm waters beyond. Blessed relief!

I scrub the usual way: up, down, left, right, up above, *down below* and *far behind*. The shower is the one box I can stand to be in without the *feeling* twisting my stomach. I think it's because I can see the steam as it rises out of the top, like it's marking a path of escape for me.

I step out onto the dark linoleum floor, thick liquid footprints marking my territory as I shake the water off my skin like a wet dog, soaking the entirety of the room around me. A pang of guilt strikes my heart when I see the level of splashing that's hit the cream-colored, featureless walls. I approach the closest patch and swipe my hand through the beads of water. It makes more of a mess, but it's a prettier mess, like hundreds of tiny comets scooting past our toiletries. A cold coat of chill wind wraps itself around me like an old, dead friend, each droplet a little ice climber working its way down my body.

A rapid knocking strikes the door right next to my ear and seemingly covering one impatient bastard.

"*Yes*?!" I fire back, hoping my words break through the door and strangle the person on the other side.

"Can you hurry up in there?" Sam shouts. "I have to be at the market in a half hour!"

"Can't you just use the bathroom upstairs?" I ask.

Sam scoffs. "No! Shanty is in there—can't you hear his bell?" His voice is muffled by the door.

I roll my eyes, wrap a thick, gray towel around my waist, and reach for the handle. Then I remember. *Holly is in the kitchen.* This could be embarrassing. I take a breath and open the door, meeting Sam's guilty eyes. He takes my arm, and I'm thrown out of the bathroom, clutching my towel as I stumble back into the occupied kitchen. The door slams behind me, blocking me in with Holly and her stari— she's not looking. Why isn't she looking?! Her breakfast bowl is gone, but she is still tapping away at her tablet. I peer over at what she is working on. She slams the tablet down.

"I don't have any singles on me," she says in a low, frustrated breath.

"I don't dance because I'm paid to, Holly Wood!" (that's genuinely her name) I retort in a camp British accent.

"What is it, Dan?" she asks, unamused, leering up at me from her chair. The shadowy circles that line her eyes tell me she's had another rough night.

"Nothing. I was just wondering what you're working on." I seat myself next to her on the breakfast barstool, brushing the back of my towel down like a skirt. She yields, dropping her "work persona," and spins her tablet to me, revealing a **bold** title headlining a mostly blank page.

STOWAWAY? I'M ON VACATION!
How a Colombian donkey hacked the system,
gaining passage on a summer cruise!

"Wow," I whisper.

"I know!" she says, resting her face on my moist shoulder, exhausted. Then she springs back off with a retch, hand on her cheek. "Eww, you're all wet!"

I laugh. "Showers tend to do that to a person."

"You don't shower," Sam says, standing in the doorway between the bathroom and kitchen.

"Says the guy who sleeps with a hamster!"

"Awwww, where is Shanty this morning?" Holly asks in a rare display of affection. From the floor above us comes a soft ringing sound. It travels across the ceiling rapidly, the sounds of door slams following a drum of tiny, furry footsteps. The ringing turns into soft little bounces as Shanty hops his way down the stairs, drifts around the banister and speeds into the kitchen corner without acknowledging *any* of us. He finds his small bowl of food tucked in the corner by the trash can and dives headlong into it, spilling crumbs all over the floor.

"I put that out last night," Holly explains with a satisfied smile.

"He's certainly pleased." Sam laughs, watching Shanty dive in and around his food bowl like an asynchronous swimmer.

"So what's the headline for?" I ask Holly, getting back on topic.

"Oh, well, it's my report for this week." She's beginning to fluster. I was right, there *was* embarrassment.

Sam notices and chimes in, "At least you're writing. How long has it been since they've let you write anything?" I understand what he's trying to do, but I know it won't work with Holly.

"Too long, because I *can't* do it! I don't give a shit about a donkey!" See?

"Don't remind me!" Sam says, covering his eyes with his large hands.

"What's wrong with donkeys?" I ask.

Behind his fingers, Sam's expression squishes into a frustrated grimace. "It was the Animal Palz' logo back when I rolled with that group of phonies."

Holly plants her face in her empty cereal bowl while Sam continues his rant.

"We used to practice our chants on the animals we'd rescued. I didn't realize that counted as an animal-tested product. I left when they refused to accept my revelation. The only reason why anyone talks about them is because of their size—the world is size-biased!"

"You're six five!" I interrupt.

"The perfect height to see that there's a problem. Every building has to be tall...Pluto can't be a planet...all mountains are there to be climbed for glory. And no one looks out for the little guy!"

"Like Shanty?" I say.

"Exactly!"

"*You're not helping*!" Holly yells, exiting her hidey-bowl. "Guys, it's seven a.m., and I have to get this lump of fluffy, commercial garbage in my boss's inbox by *nine*!" The room grows quiet.

"*We're sorry*," Sam and I say in tandem, our heads down in shame.

"It's all right. Just...help me find a fitting way to make a donkey appealing to older readers without resorting to smut." She becomes embarrassed once again. I giggle, and she hits me in the stomach before winding up a rant of her own. "There has been a war, whole cities are being rebuilt, traditionalists mobbing the sites to keep them exactly as they were before they were leveled, veterans applying for their *first* jobs, and I'm writing about a stupid *animal*!"

Shanty pops his head out of his food bowl with an angry squeak, and we freeze. Like a child in a ball pit, he falls back into his food.

Soon after, I open my wardrobe and stare at my choices; the drawn-out stack of old, textureless shirts and identical blue jeans both folded and unfolded spell out the word *RUT*. They're all right, they're just...old. I could use some fresh air in my life. I haven't been on a date in a long time, and I gave up social media after I started working for it. I spend all my time going to work and staying home, and my weekends consist of quiet nights indoors with a specter of a journalist and a hamster-guy. We barely interact with our landlord, Mr. Emmerich. I think I've met him once, and that was the day I moved in. Either he trusts us way too much or he's an irresponsible homeowner. Then there's Dad and our forced play dates. I don't hate them; I don't even dislike them. But I don't respect him—I mean them. Not like I used to. I'm stuck in a rut, and he was the one who changed for the worse. After Mom left, I watched him descend into this broken, hunchbacked coward in horn-rimmed glasses. He used to be *The* Man. Alpha *and* omega and the life of the party all in one!

His friends all looked up to him and we adored him. We felt safe around him, like his big-bear arms deflected every problem the world could throw at us.

I was almost seventeen when Mom left, taking the life out of the house with her. Dad stopped eating, stopped working, stopped existing. He couldn't work freelance anymore; not when it was just the two of us. He eventually found a steadier, less fulfilling job teaching at a community college outside the city. I went there myself, but I didn't take his class. I majored computer science. It seemed like the right decision to me. I graduated, Dad missed the ceremony, and then I moved out of the house and ended up where I am now. The monthly meet-ups are always identical: same drinks at the same place. I hate the shaky, fearful hand gestures that accompany his needy questions. I hate the tea he orders for the table before I even arrive, almost as a payment.

I drag my feet along the sidewalk in long, lumbered steps as if the concrete slabs are warning me of impending doom. Because Dad's place is so far away, I try to make it easier on him, to meet him halfway. I can't really afford to take a cab the whole way there, so I split the travel between a long walk to the construction yard that houses the metro station and then I get a cab from there. I miss Grand Central. The attack on Manhattan came long after the war was declared; it was inevitable but nonetheless devastating. After Boston had come under fire from sleeper-cell militias, the threat was tangible, no longer just a headline but a sound, the sound of death and chaos and destruction echoing from miles away.

Then came the newsreels: startling images of Bunker Hill; a pyramid of dead bodies piled up next to the Obelisk, all the way up to the top. This obviously wasn't the only state attacked, but it is the image that haunts me the most. At least, that's the image I've settled on, the devil I know. You see, there was creativity to the killing, almost as if combat had become so mundane, so commonplace that the soldiers needed a project to stop it from becoming boring. The militia was made from a formed coalition of powers: China and Russia, Russia providing the weapons and China the manpower. But don't be mistaken;

this was not the only way the situation would play out. The world went to war initially when the powers of Europe turned on each other, a three-way shadow war. Right-wing governments led each country into a powerless state of ubiquity, with strict immigration laws and punishments, forced patriotism spreading across the lands like an infectious disease. Each carrier became an angry, bitter, and violent specimen, allergic to any threat of being emasculated by the effects of social humility. War is a novel, not a movie, so there are a lot of impactful events that have been forgotten way down the line. So, the specificity of the events that caused the war comes down to a couple of "big ones."

I reach the station, my feet burning and my breath short from walking! I sit on the sidewalk with the fear of not being able to get back up. Through the beads of sweat dripping from my eyebrows, I see the cab standing and a family of three hurrying toward it. It's the last one at the stand, and it'll be like ten minutes until another arrives. The passenger side window is open, so I take off my backpack and *hurl* it straight for the door. The bag almost moves in slow-motion, flying farther and farther and YES!!! It smacks the driver in the face. Before he can recompose himself, I'm in the back of the car. The family glare at me in angry unison through the rear window before stomping off in a sulk. I turn face front, and the driver locks me in his frightening sights. He's a big, bald guy in a tracksuit jacket, sweatpants, and bloodshot eyes, almost looks what used to be referred to as "Eastern European." He throws my bag back at me; it lands right where Holly hit me earlier.

"Will a bigger tip keep me alive?" I splutter.

"Only the biggest, you little shit!" he snarls back in a slow Californian drawl as he hunches over the steering wheel, rolling up his windows, I assume to stop any more luggage hitting him. His cab has an air freshener above the mirror as usual; it's a marijuana leaf, and it's powerful. The smell of burned tea surrounds me, and I'm stricken with a frightening thought. I'm in a hotbox with wheels. I'm surprised he even felt the bag hit him! As the car speeds out from the metro station, I regret having beaten that small child and his mothers in a foot race.

The cab arrives at the coffee house, and I see Dad waiting in the outside seating area. In a graceful display, my passenger window frames his head. The brake disks squeak loudly as the car grinds to a halt as my face falls perfectly into Dad's eye line. He sees me and smiles with pure joy. There's a downtrodden relief behind his wide, baggy eyes. He was in the middle of cleaning his thick-framed glasses when I arrived, so naturally, he waves at me with his cleaning cloth and then laughs at himself. I force a wide grin onto my face, no relief to be found. I pay the driver the $100 fare. As the cab speeds away, I find my way to Dad's table, at which he sits frozen in ecstasy. He hasn't taken his eyes off me since I arrived.

"All right, calm down," I tell him with a waving hand, but he jumps up to embrace me. His bear hug is unexpected and long, and his green windbreaker scratches uncomfortably at my chin. I pat his back a few times to let him know he's safe. He doesn't let go.

"Dad?" I say, patting him again. The signal gets through, and he pulls away, embarrassed.

"Oh, right, *Public*. Sorry, right. Sit, sit—please sit. Take a load off, champ!"

His words chisel through my bones like a dentist drill. I park my butt on the warm metal seat across from his. He has two cups in front of him—one coffee, one tea—and a small bowl of biscotto?… biscotti?…*cookies* pushed to the center of the rusted, olive-green table. The bowl has text printed around it which reads: ORGANIC! NUT FREE! GLUTEN FREE! FAT FREE! NOT FREE! (SORRY!)

"Mine?" I gesture to the cookie bowl.

"Of course! Eat up, you're looking a little thin."

Pettily, I retract my hand, leaving the cookies to go to waste in their bowl. After a short silence, a pasty look of horror rushes over his face.

"Green tea *is* your favorite, right?"

"Yes! It's perfect," I lie, stirring my passive aggression into the murky swamp-like tea. I spin the thin strip of balsa wood clockwise a few revolutions, then reverse the direction causing a mass of unevenly sized bubbles that spin in perfect rhythm, happily dancing in the presence of my misery. The smallest bubble pops, sending a ripple across the surface, while the rest stay put. I put the lid back on the cup and down the tea quickly, hoping the taste will bypass my tongue. It doesn't, and my face reddens with the change of temperature.

"Whoa, slow down there! Is everything all right?" Dad asks, panicked.

"Thirsty. It was a long, painful walk to the cab stand."

"Well, you know, exercise isn't working unless it hurts, right?"

"No pain no gain?" I rally back.

"Exactly!" He throws his boiling coffee down his throat, exhaling hard afterward. "It burns!!!" he gasps. This makes me laugh and, just like that, he has me. Here come the questions.

"So, how's everything? How is work? How's that girl you work with? She's pretty! Are the protests lightening up, if not, why, if so, how come?"

I pause to take everything in. He leans over the table, bouncing eagerly in his chair.

"Fine, Fine, Fine, okay? No, can't say." I sigh bluntly.

"Oh, that's good," he says, re-deflating. A short silence follows until, "Well, I've been busy! Really, I have! Class changeovers are coming soon, so I'm preparing to let my little ones go! It's so sad!"

I reel at his sappiness. "You're helping strange kids take the job you used to have."

He swallows my words like bitter cough syrup. He knows what I'm getting at. Solemnness then falls over him. "Look, Son, when your mother left, I didn't know what I could do..." The atmosphere dips like the Mariana Trench. "I had you, I had the house, I had a whole mess of clients breathing down my neck to *be creative* when I just wanted to *die*."

This takes me aback.

Dad picks up his cup in silence, swirling the last drop of coffee around in a dark circle. "Well, what can I say? It was like this black hole of shame and misery was dragging me away from actually *wanting* to do anything. Understand? And you...you were strong. Resentful, but strong. I felt pity coming through your afterschool greetings, the times when you refused to go out with your friends because you didn't want to leave me alone, when you minored in architecture just to make me happy. I love you, Son."

"Dad...I didn't minor in architecture."

A shameful surprise washes over his face. He brushes his long dark bangs on top of his head, flattening it down with sweat. "Ah... I must have missed that message."

I go to take a drink out of my cup only I see it's empty. I'm stuck. I have to give him something to work with.

"Dad, I...I saw the stress you were under with the deadlines and the constant phone calls and routine visits to the construction sites. There were so many people fighting for your attention that it made the whole prospect of having any career like that immeasurably unattractive."

"You did theatre, didn't you?" he asks, wiping a tear from his cheek. I feel an ill-timed smile trying to break its way onto my face at this incredibly awkward time. I don't want to smile; I definitely don't want to laugh. But it's coming, except he starts first, belting out a fit of loud, unmetered laughter. I let my chuckle out. The other patrons stare at us, grinning.

Dad removes his glasses and rests them in his empty cup. "You should have told me. I could have come and watched!"

"I'm glad you didn't!" I scoff, triggering a playful but loud defensiveness which takes over his tone.

"Oh, come on! What did you do? Did you write something? A play? A one-man show?"

"No. Our program basically consisted of finding a specific Shakespeare script we liked and adapting it any way we saw fit."

"And what did *you* choose?" he asks, resting his head on his hands in anticipation.

"*The Tempest*," I answer bashfully.

"I don't know that one," he says, rubbing his straining, red eyes.

"It's the one with the storm on a desert island, the wizard, a shipwreck, and fairies?"

He nods with a lack of certainty. "How did you do a storm?" He picks up a cookie and munches on it.

"We changed the show to be about robots on Mars. It was kind of a dust storm instead of a tropical one, and we just pretended it was there, covering our faces, shouting. We practiced pushing heavy furniture to get the movement right."

He looks genuinely proud. "Okay, well, that's fun. *Creative* fun—your *own* creative fun—and that's what matters!" And I realize something. It *was* fun.

I spot a familiar face in the window behind Dad. It's Ana! She's standing at the coffee counter, leaning patiently against the pick-up desk. Next to her is a loomingly tall, dangerously tanned pink-haired lady about Dad's age. Ana looks up and catches me staring. This startles her. The woman she's with is muttering something, but Ana waves at me, ignoring her. The pink-haired lady looks out to see who has Ana's attention. She quickly spots me, and a large, cat-like grin streaks her face. I guess I'm the canary? Forcefully, she snatches her extra-large coffee cup from the countertop and begins to pull Ana by her arm toward the exit. Oh, no, I forgot! I'm not alone! Ana's going to meet Dad!

The door crashes open, and the pair shamble toward our table like a Siamese Hunchback of Notre Dame. Ana has completely retreated within herself and at this moment is a simulacrum of Ana, nothing more.

"Hello," the simulacrum of Ana whispers to me and my father, who looks confused but welcoming.

"Hi, Ana." I reply, concerned. She doesn't get a chance to respond as the pink-haired lady has already pushed her down onto the empty seat next to mine.

"Hello! My name is Lillith! I've heard so much about you, Daniel!" Did I mention I hate Daniel?

I nervously return the greeting. "N-n-nice to meet you, I've heard a…lot about you—from Ana, of course!" I didn't even know Ana had a mother.

Lillith turns her attention to Dad. "And you must be his father! What do I call you? Daniel Senior?" she asks, completing her joke with a loud chuckle.

For a moment, my *father* sits like a deer in the headlights of a hunter's truck. He flips back to reality, mirrors her laugh and sticks out his hand in a robotic way. "Good one! My name is Henry—Henry Hardacre, and you would be right. I'm a kind of Daniel Senior."

She takes his hand; a giant purple stone hangs off her pinkie finger, blinding us both. She holds on for an uncomfortable amount of time. "As charming as you are *handsome*, it seems."

Oh dear God! She takes the seat next to him. As the panic sets in, my father kicks me under the table. It rattles the cups and biscotti bowl. A vehement clanking ripples through the seating area. The noise gives Ana a fright, and her neck snaps back upright without her saying a word.

"What on earth was that noise?" Lillith asks me and my injured leg.

"The table isn't held down properly!" Dad answers, saving me. The pink-haired lady sees her opening.

"Well, if we all sit with our elbows on the table, it won't be too much of a distraction." She puts her head in her hands, inspecting him as if he is her middle-school crush. The table springs up again, but this time I didn't feel a kick. I look to Dad, whose face has turned a shocking white. He missed my leg and hit Ana! She snaps out of her anxiety coma and does not look happy.

"Mom! Dan and his father live on opposite sides of the city. I'm sure they have a lot to talk about. Isn't that right, you guys?"

Our savior! We nod in tandem like two terrified Drinking Birds.

"Oh my! I'm so sorry! Let us get out of your hair! After all, you don't need a couple of chatterboxes like us getting in the way of your catch-up!

I look to Ana with relieved thanks. "Aw, so soon? Well, it was lovely to meet you, I'll see you on Monday, Ana!"

"Hopefully even sooner," Lillith chimes.

I don't get it? As I turn to see if Dad knew what she meant, Lilith plunges her vibrantly painted nails into the bowl of cookies. "Now, boys, you can't sit with a bowl of biscotti and not share! So rude."

We let out a nervous giggle. She's not kidding. She genuinely takes one of our cookies! Ana turns the table and pulls Lillith by *her* arm. They swerve around the front of the seating area and away from the building.

"So, what was all that about?" Dad asks, breaking the calm silence in the aftermath.

"You were almost lunch, that was what that was all about," I say.

"Oh, come on, it's not even past breakfast!" he protests, checking his watch. "Say, after this, do you want to go catch a movie or something?"

I hesitate to answer.

"Never mind. I've already taken up enough of your time. You probably have a lot on your plate." He reaches around for his windbreaker.

"No, no, it's fine. A movie sounds great."

He stops shuffling and turns to me, beaming with happiness like he's just won the Powerball. This is good. I haven't been to the movie theater in a long time, and I don't think Dad has either. He takes a little "Now Showing" pamphlet out of his coat.

"Okay, so there's the superhero one, the space one, the other superhero one, the other space one, the other—"

I stop him mid-stream with a smile on my face. "Your choice if you're buying."

"Sure, no...problem." Dad is too excited, flicking through the pamphlet to question the price. He grows quiet as a loud clomping of footsteps rush their way toward us. It's Ana again. She's alone and has tears in her eyes.

"Dan, call someone! My mom needs help. She's collapsed... she's not breathing!"

Chapter 3

Lost for words at the sight of a shaking and panicked Ana, I look to my Dad. He is in deep, pressing thought. His nerves have left him, as have all the useless platitudes he hides behind. He places his hands firmly on Ana's shoulders and gazes steadily into her eyes in an attempt to rope her to earth.

"Ana, look at me. You have to calm down and tell me where you left your mother. Where is she?"

"I-I-I…" Ana stutters. Her eyes dart around, wobbling behind tears. She is trapped between a memory and the present.

"*Ana*! *Where is your mother*?" Dad shouts, shaking her firmly by the shoulders. She points past the corner of the coffee shop. Dad takes note and splits his attention between Ana and me. "Don't just stand there, Daniel. Call nine-one-one! Ana, will you take me to her?" He grabs her hand, and they hurry along the street toward Lillith.

I dial and listen for a response…

"*Nine-one-one, what's your emergency?*"

"Sixty-year-old woman, collapsed near the Brown Fountain!"

"*Is this a joke?*"

"No! It's the coffee house on Broadway!"

"*Okay, sir, don't panic. Emergency services will be there fast as they can.*"

"Hurry! She's not responding!"

The call cuts off with a click, and I run down the street to find them. I hope everything is okay. I really hope she is okay. She was *only* being friendly. A bit forward, excitable maybe, but perhaps we were too reserved? We didn't stop to think about that, did we? Oh God.

I see where Dad and Ana have stopped, and my run becomes a sprint. Dad is kneeling over Lillith's body as if he has slain her. Quite the opposite: he's pushing on her chest with rhythmic CPR. Ana is standing stiff with her hands over her mouth; the shock hasn't left her. She moves to squat next to her mom, but my father holds out his hand, stopping her. He needs all the space he can get. A crowd is forming, and Dad yells at them to keep back, but they don't seem to want to listen. I huff my way to the gathering of people. One by one, I push anyone in my way out of sight until I get to the center.

"Dad?" He doesn't look up.

"What's wrong with her?!" Ana cries over the loud, jabbering voices of the crowd, who seem to be trying to guess the answer. Even the tan can't hide the color of Lillith's face. It's gone from chestnut brown to a swollen blood red; same with her eyes.

"The ambulance is on its way," I assure the pair. Ana nods, relieved, but Dad isn't as heartened to hear this. He thinks to himself for a precious second and finds a change of plan.

"We don't have much time. I know a guy who lives a block or two down West 96th Street. He has a car and can take us straight there. You two wait here for the ambulance—jump in with them and meet us there." My dad tucks his arms under Lillith and hoists her up into the air in a bridal lift, one arm under her legs, one under her back, and one of her arms draped lifelessly around his neck. His tattered glasses fall out of his breast pocket and hit the sidewalk. I bend down to retrieve them, but Dad's first step crushes them underfoot.

"Leave them. Just get everyone away!" he shouts with gruff urgency.

Ana and I begin to push through the crowd, making an opening for Dad and Lillith. There are too many people, one of whom shoves me from behind. I almost fall into Ana, who keeps me on my feet with her elbow and swings a fist past my head and into the shover's face. He goes down, dragging a few bystanders with him—she's cleared a hole. Dad steps over the man, standing on his chest and hopping over a whole bunch of people he took to the ground with him. And...they're out! Dad picks up his pace with Lilith still in his arms and dodges down the nearest alleyway, out of sight. He didn't wait for us. He couldn't. We hear faint sirens buzzing farther along the street. The ambulance is almost here.

Soon after, we sit in the waiting room of Gesond Hospital. The place is almost entirely empty, which I would never have expected for a city ER. There's just me, Ana, and Dad, who is seated at the end of the chair fold, which rests against the pale, clinical, gray wall. The cold florescent light above us starts to flicker, but I'm the only one who notices. I'm not surprised. Ana didn't even get to see her mom go into the emergency OR. She'd been rushed in before we arrived. And there's no sign of Dad's friend. Maybe he left as soon as he'd dropped them off.

What happened to her? How had that ball of energy we met minutes before just collapsed after a small walk? She'd looked perfectly fine. Better than fine. She was excited, full of life. What caused it? Was it us?

Ana is looking down at her shoes, which swing impatiently beneath her chair. She's pale, locked in her own thoughts. Probably asking herself the same questions I am. Dad is stretched out, his arms folded rigidly across his chest. His unusually small eyes are shut tight. He's angry with the orderly for kicking us out of the room, but I guess they had no choice.

Ana lets out a quiet sigh, mutilating the tension. Dad and I both shoot up and give her our full attention. Dad puts his hand on her shoulder.

"Don't worry, sweetie. She has a fighting spirit. I could tell from the moment we met. She's not going anywhere."

Ana continues to stare at her cross-hatched pumps as they sway back and forth, under and out from her red plastic chair.

"Ana?" I mumble. She doesn't answer. "Do you want me to get you some water?" And, of course, her eyes start to fill up again.

"I don't know what happened," she whispers. "One minute, she was yelling at me for pulling her away so soon, acting as if I was embarrassed of her. Then she just stopped talking. I thought she was finished. I thought she'd calmed down and let it go quickly, like she always does. That was when it hit me—it *wasn't* like always. She couldn't breathe. If only I wasn't so embarrassed of...I..." More tears come, blocking her words, dripping from her lips. They fall into the silence.

"Ana, you need answers, not blame, okay?" As Dad says this, Ana pushes herself into my arms, and it startles me. I look to Dad, who gives me a small, understanding nod and quietly gets up to leave. I mouth at him to stop, but he puts a finger on his lips and makes his way along the corridor without a sound.

It's the two of us now. The silence has...changed somehow; it's become warmer. I hug Ana back, tightly. Her muffled sniffs sound out from beneath my arms as she rests her head on my hoodie-covered chest.

★

The door to the ER bursts open. A woman in blue scrubs walks past us, stops, and turns around to face us. She has a brown leather-bound tablet computer in her arms.

"Are you here for Lillith...Burnette?"

"Yes," Ana replies, jumping to her feet.

"Where is the man who brought her in?"

"He was here a second ago." Ana looks along the corridor.

I jump in. "I told him to leave. He was falling asleep in the chair, so I told him to go home." The doctor hasn't taken her eyes off Ana. She must know I'm not family.

"Well, I'm guessing you're her daughter. Tell me, does your mother have any allergies?"

"Cat hair."

"Was this because of a cat?" I ask.

The doctor keeps her eyes on Ana. "Anything else?" she quizzes.

Ana nods. "Nuts. She's allergic to nuts, but we were only out getting coffee!"

"Without an Epi-pen?" the doctor presses bluntly. Ana stiffens.

"As I said, we were only out getting coffee, there was no need! It's not like we were going to be attacked by a swarm of angry cashews!"

The doctor doesn't bite.

Ana thinks, then says, "She had a tall black coffee and...a biscotto from Dan's table."

"Hmm-hmmm, and who's Dan?" The doctor taps the details into her tablet.

"I am," I answer, trying to be as respectful as I can.

"Nuts in the biscotto?" she accuses.

"No. The bowl said they were nut-free."

"Well, evidently, the bowl was wrong," the doctor says, turning back to Ana. "I'm sorry to inform you, miss, but your mother was hit hard. She went into severe anaphylactic shock. We've managed to stabilize her, but it's not over."

Ana collapses back onto her chair.

"Can that happen?" I ask naively.

"I'm not speaking to you, sir," the doctor warns.

"Just answer!" Ana pleads.

The doctor sighs and brings her chart down to her side. "Yes. It's very rare, but it can happen. We had to perform a tracheotomy, but that wasn't enough, and I'm afraid your mother went into cardiac arrest. The lack of oxygen to her brain caused it to swell. Our best option to stem the swelling is to induce a comatose state."

Ana takes the news in without a word. She gets to her feet, and the doctor hands the tablet to her.

"Just sign at the bottom, miss. We'll get her up and out of here in no time at all."

I arrive back at my house, which is as dark as the night it sits in. It's almost midnight. I scan my door card and slowly push the door open. Surreptitiously, I creep toward the kitchen and find a dark figure strewn over the breakfast bar. It's Holly, still in the same place she was this morning. Her tablet is jacked into the wall; there's no blinking light, so it must be fully charged. I quietly unplug the cable, and drape the dish towel over Holly's sleeping shoulders. I don't know what else to do.

I go into the bathroom and silently lock myself in before I flick on the light. The dangling bulb above me buzzes, greeting me. I don't greet it back—that would be weird. Instead, I fill the sink to the top with cold water and slam my face into its freezing depths. My skin tightens with the cold, and I open my eyes a little to let the fluids mingle. After half a minute, I lift my head out and move to the drying rack; my stringy, dark bangs drip a single thin stream across the tile. Grabbing a plain orange bed sheet from the rack, I smother my head with it, pushing my hair into the shape it was when I first woke up. Dark spikes protrude skyward as if I'm being pulled from the earth headfirst.

I look at the now-soaked sheet in my hands. Maybe this will be better for Holly? No, stupid idea. Shut up and get to bed, you idiot.

CRACK! The light bulb splinters into a dozen pieces, raining glass past my shoulders, darkening the whole room around me. The *feeling* comes back again: I have to get out. I pull the door open and tiptoe-run through the kitchen. I must have woken Holly after all because she's not there anymore.

I speed-creep into my room and open the window unnecessarily wide. The curtains billow in a comfortable way above my bed and soundlessly fall back into place. It's a still night, the kind of still where there's nothing to stop outside conversations being completely audible. I hear two sets of footsteps, one clacking, one clomping—high heels and casual boots? The noises travel past the yard wall. Are they friends on their way out? Lovers on their way back? Either way, they're heading down the adjacent alley at a fast pace.

"Why can't we just meet at Justine's?" the woman asks. That's all I hear. I can't help but empathize, to imagine their story—where they're going, what they're doing. I wonder *why* they can't just meet at Justine's. I try to imagine who Justine is and why her place is a preferable destination for the event in question. Is she a good friend? The life of the party? The joker of the pack? The runt of the litter? I look at the clock on my nightstand. It reads: 12:04 a.m. Jesus, I really need to sleep.

A huge explosion jolts me from my cot. REM sleep is nice, but when you're woken during it, the heart goes crazy. It's an instant snap—resting one minute, gasping for air the next, like I'm drowning in a dream. My unit is gathered around me. Camo figures surrounding my bed should put me at ease, and I lie back to stare at the ceiling of the ref center. My dog tags rattle from my bed frame, swinging pendulously in the corner of my eye. We all hang them off our beds just in case the heat from a mortar blast fuses them to our chests. We're soldiers but not by choice, and dedication is lacking around the mandatory Marine Corps. We're lucky to have the beds we do. This isn't a military motel; it's an old refugee shelter. *"3D printed in 24 hours!"* That's what the commercials used to say. Good for keeping the cold out, but a fifty-cal will eat this place alive in a matter of seconds. It was already cleared out by the time we found it. Lucky for us, there were some supplies left behind—medical equipment, reading material, even an old TV. Not that there's anything broadcasting at this point.

My pants screech on the polyester as I twist my legs around in my cot. I cringe at the pain. The tactical pack does a number on your back, but I've learned to accept this. "Without the battle there is no victory," right? I can't remember where I heard that—school or church? I like little quotes like that. They're useful, defensive.

I think I'm the only one who slept some. The rest of the 32nd are all up and restless: L.Cpl. Albrier, L.Cpl. Alvarez, Pvt. Lowcroft, S.Sgt. Nebrezza—and me, of course. They call us the *Pantheon.*

I want to take that as a compliment, but those gods were known for causing all sorts of mischief, and we are a strange bunch. Nebrezza made staff sergeant before he was twenty! That's usually impossible, but he's special. You know when you think you're smart, but then a younger version of your "smarts" comes around and turns your greatest effort into child's play? That's S.Sgt. Nebrezza in a nutshell. He's reading some old book found in one of the content lockers: *The Drunk* by Arnold Marinos. It's clearly Greek, so it's local.

"Hey, Sarge, whatcha reading?" I ask. He holds up his book, cover toward me, without a word. "Yeah, I know *what* you're reading but…what's it about?"

He sighs and slams it down. "Murder. The four suspects are as follows: the baker, the fisherman, the crooked cop, and the drunk." He says all this in his droll monotone. "You'll never guess who I think did it."

"The fisherman?" I snark.

"Funny shit, Benson," Lowcroft fires back at me. "Aren't you a little young for that?" she asks Nebrezza, who drags his bewildered eyes up and over the pages.

"You're twenty-two!" he yells, to the amusement of Alvarez, who sits in the corner scribbling in his diary. Good old-fashioned notebooks, irreplaceable in times of war.

"Hey, where's Albrier?" I ask.

"She went out for gum," Nebrezza answers from behind his *Drunk*. I don't know if he's serious.

"In a warzone?" My hand is already on my carbine. Lowcroft spots this.

"Oh, put the rifle down, Ben. She's fine! She's gone to see a trader she met a week back. He used to own a Periptera, lost half his family, poor guy."

"What about that explosion?" I ask, well aware of how I'm coming across. I'm not scared for Albrier and don't want to be sitting in here if anything goes down. It wasn't our decision to come to this place, but we're together for a reason.

Nebrezza puts his book down once more. Clearly, he's losing his patience. He checks his watch. "That *explosion* was the door slamming behind her. She hasn't been gone long. Give her until dawn. If she's not back by then, you and Lowcroft go and investigate."

I slump back onto my bed, relieved slightly.

"Hey, guys, does this make sense to y—" Alvarez stops mid-sentence to correct his question's course. "Nebrezza, does this make sense to you?" He clears his throat before reading from his battered journal page. "*Your body is my Andes, your soul my oxygen tank.*" He waits for a patient, literary critique.

"Probably not," Nebrezza says, uninterested.

"Why the Andes?" Lowcroft asks through a trapped laugh.

"He's from Chile," I answer. Lowcroft knows how foolish she looks right now. Good. It's her turn for a change.

"Right—makes sense," she says and turns around in her cot to face the wall.

"What are you even writing that stuff for?" I ask Alvarez, as if it isn't obvious.

"Because, unlike you, I have someone back *home*."

Lowcroft jumps out of her shame as quick as silver. "He has someone here! Ooooooh, Albrier, you...sexy...German—is she German?"

"Alaskan," Alvarez says with a grin, urging her to continue what she's started.

"Thanks, Al!" I mutter. He holds his hands up in surrender and turns back to his writings as Lowcroft continues with her pantomime.

"Ooooooh, Albrier, my sexy *Alaskan* goddess. Get any gum in your hair, I'll help! Just let me shoot my lo—" She stops to listen out. "Footsteps," she whispers.

Rising from my cot, I grab my carbine and move to the side of the door. As the steps close in, I give the door a sharp kick, and it swings open behind me. Alvarez sits at the back of the room, his rifle aimed straight at the entrance I've just made.

"Lower your weapons, goddammit!" a familiar voice growls, and Albrier hops inside the center, a small paper bag in hand. Without looking at me, she says, "At ease, Corporal."

I let out a disapproving grunt, which Albrier hears as clear as a desert wind.

"Here!" She tosses me an item out of the bag. It's a candy bar, but it's not one I recognize. All I can make out are three letters *I-O-N*? Oh! Ion! Ion wafer...something. What can I say? I'm from Wisconsin, not Crete. Maybe best to name a place still visible to the naked eye. Oh, well, wafer is wafer. What did the others get? Gum, Gummy Bears...*Hershey's*? What the...?

"Hey half-screw, why does Nebrezza get the American candy?" The boy in question catches his candy with open arms and a smile, throwing the book out of his sight.

"Because I outrank you!" he says with already-filled cheeks. Lowcroft rubs fake tears out of her eyes at me. Alvarez jumps in, panicked.

"Guys, shut up!" You hear that?"

We pause and listen out.

"It's just the waves," I dismiss, but he shakes his head and makes the "door" sign with his right hand, taking out his pistol with his left.

I get back into position beside the door while the rest of the squad flip their cots into makeshift cover. The loud ringing of dog tags hitting the ground bounces around the building. I raise my hand and listen out; I hear them: sneakers gnashing against the sands outside, awkward steps, a third crunch—a guy with a cane? I kick the door open, and Albrier aims her rifle at the gap, pauses, then lowers it.

"CIV!" she shouts, and we follow suit, lowering our weapons. Albrier beckons to whoever it is. In hobbles a small, aging, bald man wearing a Jacob Marley T-shirt and denim shorts. He drops his cane at the sight of us.

"It's the trader. His name is Nestor," Albrier says, apprehensively holding out her free hand to the old man. Nestor takes an ancient Glock 17 pistol out of the back of his shorts and passes it to her. She removes the magazine and chambered round, seemingly prompting the old man to raise both his arms. He shakes his head and jabbers in Greek. Alvarez replies in the man's tongue, and he cautiously lowers his arms. I shut the door behind us, and he whirls around to face me, panicked.

"No, no, no, no! Beach...boat. *Red* boat."

"Russian or Chinese?" Albrier asks. Nestor thinks for a second then holds up two fingers.

"Sarge?" I say. Nebrezza stands quietly, but I can almost see the cogs turning behind his eyes.

"How far out are they?" he asks as he scrapes the fallen tags up from the floor.

"A quarter-click, south." Alvarez translates for Nebrezza, who looks to me and Albrier.

"Corporals, the boulders outside—can you roll them apart any farther than they are? About ten feet from the building?"

"Sir, that's unorthodox!" Lowcroft protests.

"We'll definitely draw their fire, so I want three targets instead of one."

"They'll probably have at least two mortars—a sixty and a hundred," Lowcroft adds.

Nebrezza thinks and then gestures to the group. "Al, get Nestor to the shed out back. Keep him safe and quiet. Lowcroft, set the heavy up at the south window. It's not like they won't have seen Grandpa here coming to warn us."

Lowcroft shrugs, lugging her M249 LMG over to the beach-facing window. Alvarez grabs Nestor's stick and leads him out back. Albrier whistles at him; he turns, and Albrier throws Nestor's now-loaded pistol over to them. Nestor catches it and cocks it unnecessarily.

"That's the spirit!" Alvarez says with a trepidatious joy.

Nebrezza drags the cots together and shoves our bags onto each side, creating a sniping nest for himself. He's not high up but it will have to do. He rolls into prone and takes aim.

"I see them. The...captain...is pointing *right* this way. Shit! There are two more boats behind him, He was holding out on us." He clicks at Albrier and me, indicating the door. We cock a round into our rifle chambers, duck out of the door and separate behind our respective beached boulders. Our comms light up, delivering Nebrezza's orders.

"Stay where you are. Don't bother pushing the rock—they'll pick you off before you even get it moving."

I nod, unsure about what I'm hearing. I look toward...who is she? Across from me: a soldier lady.

Where am I? I'm... Why have I got a gun?! I hear waves crashing onto shore far behind me. Why am I on a beach? I go to look over the boulder I'm resting my back against.

"Keep your head down!" a voice buzzes at close range. I have a strange, wireless bud in my right ear. What is going on? I'm...at the beach...with a rifle...next to a soldier lady...and I have a tattoo on my arm! Yellow text around a red badge, with a lightning bolt in the middle. The text reads: 32nd REG | THE PANTHEON.

When did I get a tattoo?! Why do I need a tattoo? The sleeve of my T-shirt has the same logo stitched onto it. Wait! Why is that important? When did I even join the Marines?!

I lift my head up to see the soldier lady. She has something written on her helmet: L.Cpl. Albrier. Lance Corporal...*Albrier*? Is that German? She's just sitting there, gun in hand, taking deep breaths with her eyes closed. It's like she's meditating.

I unsnap the helmet from my head; it has a name on it also. Cpl. Benson. That's not my name! My name's Dan.

"WHAT THE HELL IS GOING ON?" I shout over to *L.Cpl. Albrier*. She shakes her head at me and makes some weird hand gesture, past the rock she is leaning against.

My earpiece yells at me again: *"Benson, get your shit together, they've landed!"*

Who have landed? Aliens? I peek around the rock behind me; there's a small red dingy pulling up to the shore. It's full of soldiers in black uniforms. I see a symbol on one of their shoulders—Japanese or Chinese. I think it's the Chinese Navy. What are the Chinese Navy doing in my beach bedroom?

One of the soldiers jumps out the dingy and begins setting up a small funnel thing, like...*a cannon*?!

I wriggle about, checking my weapon. It's a rifle of some kind, with a glowing scope on top. I press the little button on the side, and the clip falls out. Shut up! I've never fired a gun before! I try to put it back in, to no avail. I flip it around, and it goes in with a loud snap. I pull on the...pulley-thing near the butt of the gun, and a bullet flies out the side. What do I do? An incredibly sudden *BANG* comes from the building in front of me. A real gunshot. It speeds between me and L.Cpl. Albrier and hits the cannon soldier right in the head with a loud crack. His helmet rolls across the sand as his body hits the ground. The other soldiers jump back into their beached boat, keeping their heads down.

There is a long silence. L.Cpl. Albrier is still meditating, mouthing something to herself.

"Hey! Lance Corporal?!" I shout across to her. She breaks out of her meditation and glares at me. Her gaze takes me aback; it's louder than the gunshot, but I manage to get my words out. "Wh-h-hat's the mission?"

Bewilderment takes hold of her. Without breaking eye contact, she points at the boats as if what we're doing is obvious. Sudden gunfire comes from the closest boat, rattling the small building behind us, denting the metal walls. A black rod slides out of one of the windows; through my scope, I see another soldier, and she's carrying the biggest gun I've ever seen! It's not got a scope on like ours, but I don't think it's built to be precise. A violent noise erupts from the window, and a huge flash of fire follows as a mass of bullets peppers the boat. Two soldiers are dragged back by the impact and fall out of the vessel. Their body armor did nothing; they're dead, only moving when stray rounds hit them by chance. The other boat pulls up behind the first, and the soldiers on board begin to fire, laying down cover for the others to get into a better position. My earpiece buzzes again.

"*NOW!*" the voice screams, and L.Cpl. Albrier begins firing at the second boat. Effortlessly, her first shot hits the captain. She fires slowly, one shot per second. I find a switch on the side of my rifle and set it to a single line—I hope that's right. I peer around the corner and fire a shot of my own. The recoil sends me onto my back and sand blasts into my face. I hurry back behind the rock, my precious rock of *protection*. The sniper starts up again from behind me, firing another three rounds at the boats. The third boat is still coming, but their captain falls off into the water. Nice shot! L.Cpl. Albrier gets up onto one knee and rests her rifle on top of the rock, aiming it at the sky, and *PLOMP!* She fires an odd-shaped bullet that's thick and visible, and *BANG!!!* The second boat explodes. She must have fired a grenade.

Screw this! I can't just sit here. I copy Albrier, steadying myself to a knee. I aim over the rock above the first boat that landed and locate the second trigger under my rifle: it's a grenade launcher built onto the gun! Cool! I ready myself for the kickback and squeeze the trigger. *PLOMP!* YES! My grenade launches, it flies, farther and farther, until *BOOM!* It hits the boat that Albrier just blew up. Shit.

"Sorry!" I yell across the beach.

"LOOK OUT!" she shouts back. The rock behind me begins to crackle. They're shooting at me! Why? I missed!

I look to Albrier for assistance. She growls and lets loose a hail of gunfire. The third boat lands without its captain. They have a gun like the one in the window.

"GET DOWN!" Albrier screams as she covers her head. I do the same. Thunderous gunfire comes from their side, and the window of the ref center is torn to pieces. The machine gun falls out, half-empty.

"*Lowcroft! Shit! They got Lowcroft! Albrier, you cover Benson! Benson, pick up her SAW—got that?!*"

"Her gun?" I ask, pressing on my earbud.

There is a short, disbelieving pause and then, *YES! GET HER FUCKING GUN!*" This guy is crazy! I'm not going out there!

Albrier lays down the cover for me, but I don't know what to do. I look over my rock to see a soldier from the first boat has set up one of those cannons. She's moving the joystick around below it. *PLOMP!* A grenade fires up into the air, and...oh shit, it's coming for—*BAAANG!* The rock explodes behind me.

My ears are ringing, everything seems slower, and there are splinters of stone in my cheek, but I don't feel any pain. I stumble onto all fours, in time to see Albrier launch another grenade back at them. The first boat explodes, taking half of the other boat with it. The machine gunner is ripped from the gun and out of sight. She did it! She's bought me some time. I scramble to the window and find the machine gun in the dirt below; its handle is slick with blood. Lifting it takes all my might—it weighs a ton—but I don't know what to do with it. The soldiers in the final boat are setting up another cannon. I lug the gun over to Albrier; she looks relieved to see me.

"I thought they got you!" she says.

"I...have rock in my face," I whimper.

"Well, it'll take more than that to stop me." She grabs my face and lays an unexpected giant kiss on my lips. I drop the gun and we embrace. Our sniper starts firing again, and the final boat explodes behind us, but we don't care. She pulls away from me and takes the "SAW" and begins to fire at the remaining soldiers, a deafening *rat-a-tat* that causes me to collapse behind the rock. The cannon fires just as Albrier hits the operator, and the house behind us explodes. I hear a scream in my earpiece before it fizzes to silence. Albrier grabs my arm.

"They got Nebrezza!"

Nebrezza? *Martin* Nebrezza?

Tears well up in Albrier's fierce warrior eyes, and she lets out a broken roar and fires every round she has. The hot shells rain down on my head. The PLF cannon fires back. Our rock explodes, and both of us fly across the beach. I crawl over to Albrier, calling for her through the loud hiss in my brain. I turn her around to see her face, lifeless, the fire gone from her eyes. She's gone.

I lie flat on the bashed-up beach. Smoke rises up to the brightening sky. I hear echoes of an unintelligible chatter in the distance. The final few soldiers are yelling at one another. One of them has the captain in her arms, screaming pain into the dawn. Another starts to fire in our direction. Splashes of sand shoot up past out bodies, covering us in a thick, brown mist. I roll over and take another look at the soldiers. They're all still, heads up, gazing into the gray clouds above. They point chaotically, astonished by whatever they're seeing. They drop their weapons. I hear a low, swishing sound; it travels over our heads. Is it a drone? A rescue chopper? Air support? All at once, the soldiers fall to their knees and bury their heads in their hands, trembling, not daring to peek.

I look up to see a shadowy figure hovering high above me, a god in the morning mist. A featureless, muscular mannequin shadow. It descends toward us, airborne without wings. I can't move my legs, but the shock hasn't reached my heart yet, so I feel no physical pain. I turn to Albrier and rest my hand on her cold cheek. As the pain sets in, I try to get words of comfort through to her, just in case. "Don't worry, you're going to be fine, you hear me? You're going to be fine." Even if she can't respond, I need to tell her.

Water splashes against my leg; the tide is coming in frighteningly fast. The soldiers are still. They're kneeling in the rising sea. It's up to their thighs, but they won't move.

The shadowed being lands next to my body. I see now it wasn't shadowed; it was *different*. Inhuman. Its smooth, faceless humanoid form, the color of lead, shines dully in the morning sun.

Gently, it tucks one arm under my legs and one under my back and lifts me like a babe to its chest. I hear the thumping of its heart. It's soothing. Without warning, the being floats up off the ground, lifting me with it, away from the battlefield, which has almost washed away. I can barely make out the heads and shoulders of my former enemies below. It won't be long before the sea claims them.

Albrier has disappeared, down below the waves. The flames are extinguished, and I'm past the clouds, away from the fighting, away from her. No! It's not fair! Why is it taking me? She was the hero! She helped me! She bought me time! Take her instead! *Take her instead!* I try to scream these words at it, but they refuse to come out. All I can do is let out a silent scream as if my lungs have stopped working.

The figure looks down at me with pity. It takes my weight with a single arm and holds a finger up to where its lips would be. I follow its instructions and quiet myself. I look down toward the shrinking beach, watching it get smaller and smaller until it fades behind the clouds. We move, faster and faster, and the beach becomes an island, and the island becomes a country, and the country becomes a continent, and the continent becomes the Earth, and then...the Earth itself shrinks from sight as we move deeper and deeper into the darkness of space, until I am surrounded by a cold, emotionless nothing.

I shoot up from my pillow. I'm awake, back on Earth. I'm drenched in an icy sweat and numb from the waist down. The figure is gone, and the scream has let itself out, untethered and unabated.

I can't stop.

I can't stop screaming.

Chapter 4

BROKEN sleep again. The curtains blow over my head, fanning my nightmare away. I don't know what happened. I've woken up from vivid dreams before, and I know they aren't real the second I'm back in the real world. But something's not right. It wasn't just vivid; it was emotional, physical, and sensational. Every fiber of my being was in that world. The smell of the ocean air hasn't left my nostrils, and the pain hasn't left my jaw.

I sit up and search my teeth with my tongue. They don't connect like they usually do; something doesn't belong. I reach in and pluck out whatever it is out of my molar. It's a small piece of stone, jagged and porous. Benson had stones in his cheek. Was this from the boulder we hid behind? I bite at it. It doesn't break; it's not a nut or a seed. As I inspect what is definitely a shard of stone, a quiet knocking taps at my bedroom door. I don't answer. The handle turns slowly, and the door opens. I make a fist, ready to fight whatever it is.

Holly pops her head through the gap. She looks uncomfortable.

"Are you okay?" she whispers. She must have heard my screaming. Sam's head pops in below hers.

"Are you okay?" he repeats as if he didn't hear Holly ask the same thing.

Swiftly, without a peep, Shanty runs his way into my room and hops up onto my bed, snuggling into my lap. He's warm as a toasted tea-cozy. I'd normally be scared for them to see me in just my briefs, but at this point I don't care. Something happened last night. I put the stone on my nightstand and wave the rest of them inside.

"You look a little shaken. Do you want me to bring you something? Cocoa?" Sam offers softly.

Those words are like music to my ears, but I have my pride.

"Please," I say. Screw pride. Sam hurries out to the kitchen—his primary domain.

Holly sits at the foot of my bed. She's lost in a memory. I wonder what of. "Holly? Are you okay?"

She buries the memory and turns to me, uneasy. "You were screaming for a long time, Dan."

"Sorry. I must have woken you first."

She holds out her hands as if to show they're empty. "No apologies necessary. Floor neighbors for life, right?"

I nod. A faint smile comes to my lips as I nestle my fingers in Shanty's fur. He looks so peaceful. His little red collar pushes his cheeks up, making him look more hamster-like than normal. I guess it's cute.

"Can I ask what happened?" Holly whispers. "You don't have to tell me, but…it didn't sound good."

I don't know how to answer. A small noise is easily explained, but I don't know how long I was screaming for. "I had a nightmare," I admit with some hesitation. She doesn't look satisfied. "It was about the war," I add. The wind blows the curtains above us, and they flail around distractingly. Holly gets up and closes the window, bringing the drapes back down to earth. The room grows even quieter.

"You didn't go to war, Dan," she says, sitting back on my bed, noticeably trying to figure out whether she should be relieved or offended. I sit myself up farther, giving her more space.

"I know, but…about fifteen minutes ago, I did."

"In a dream?" She rubs the sleep from her eyes.

"Yes, only…it wasn't me. Or it wasn't just me—well, *Corporal* Benson. It was Alvarez, Lowcroft, Nebrezza, Nestor, and…" Her face flashes in my mind. "Albrier," I finish. As I was saying the names, Holly was typing into her tablet. She reads them back to me.

"Lance Corporal Charlotte Albrier, died age twenty-eight. Lance Corporal Scott Alvarez, died aged thirty-five. Lance Corporal Oliver Benson—"

"Yes! Benson! That was him, I mean me! I was Benson, and we were…we were in this rescue center in Greece, and we were attacked by this group of Chinese soldiers."

"The People's Liberation Army?" she quizzes.

"Yes. We held them off for as long as we could, but it was no good. They overwhelmed us. They had these weird cannons."

"Mortars?" Holly suggests.

That's what they were! "Yes, *mortars*!" I try to whistle to add an effect to my story, but it doesn't come out. Whistling never worked for me. Holly stays serious, holding me on topic. "Anyway, we got a bunch of them, but in the end, they killed everyone…but me."

Holly shakes her head. "It says here that every member of the *Pantheon* was declared KIA at the same time. That includes Benson."

I take her tablet from her and put it on the bed. "I know. I saw their names on The Aerostat. But this thing—this lead-colored bald guy floated down from the sky and rescued me. He looked like he was textured from those smooth magnets I had as a kid, you know? The ones that ruined the TV if you held them close? Anyway, the soldiers dropped their weapons, got to their knees, and as the tide began to engulf them I was carried away."

Sam comes back in. I eye the tray of colorful mugs wobbling in his hands. They're painted with smiley faces. He bought them from a flea market not so long ago. Steam rises from them into the cold morning air, and my belly starts to smile.

Holly is still processing what I've told her. "Holly, I know how it sounds—"

She cuts me off. "Like a dream. It's okay. You're fine. He's fine, Sam. He just had a nightmare."

Sam smiles, relieved.

Holly turns back to me; her eyes shake as her computer-brain goes to work. I sense a speech coming.

"You feel guilty for dodging the draft, and your mind created a scenario for you using the names of the dead soldiers you saw on the Aerostat as reference. Am I right?"

I stare blankly. No, she isn't—is she?

"Sounds right to me," Sam cuts in, nose deep in his cocoa mug.

I don't know what to say. I can't really argue against them, but they weren't there.

Holly takes my hand, then Sam's. "It's not your fault you got lucky—both of you. You hear me?" Her tone has sharpened. Her words are rickety, and her hand is shaking on top of mine. I pick up the now-sleeping Shanty and lay him in Holly's palm. She caresses his fur, and the shaking subsides. Shanty belongs to Sam, but he has always brought comfort to Holly. I'm glad he's here.

I stand at my window with my cocoa. It's cold now, and I'm alone. Holly is working her sixth Sunday in a row, and it's back to the market for Sam. He'll be home at two p.m., but I don't think I'll be here.

Sam works for his parents. During the war, he and his family lived on the southern border above Niger with his mom's family; Niger was neutral territory. Africa kept to itself, as it had its own problems; there was never any worry of an overpopulation problem due to the low mortality rate of some of the poorer countries. A middle ground was attained, with as many people being born as there were dying. Droughts became more frequent, and religious abominations were promoted from atrocities to common occurrences, born of a desperate need to address what side of the balance you were on and tipping the scales in your favor by any means necessary. Blood-based capitalism. Even with all that, it was still one of the safest places on Earth for Sam's family to be.

Across from them, small parts of the Middle East were on China's side, seeing as China was the only part of the trinity of power that hadn't previously attacked the oil-soaked lands. The Middle East had a very simple job: aid PLA soldiers by granting them protected passage to the closest of the independent countries that once made up the European Union. Small, disconnected territories that were angry, stubborn, conceited, and ripe for the taking. When war was declared, no one thought the Earth would be standing after the first day. But, lo and behold, a miracle presented itself! The denuclearization declaration: an almost unbelievable bill which called for complete nuclear disarmament, and it was successful. The contest for attainable land was useless if the foundations were completely irradiated.

In an almost sportsman-like effort, China, Russia, and America banded together for the last time, ridding themselves of nuclear capabilities. The rest of the world complied, as if the smaller countries felt they'd gain more of a chance of victory, or maybe it was driven purely by survival instinct. I guess everyone just wanted to fight *that* much, but even boxers wear gloves. America was the last to disarm their close-to-a-trillion-dollar arsenal.

The sky outside is dark and ominous, the clouds pregnant with a couple of weeks' worth of rain. I'll need my hoodie today after all. There is an extra chill in the air, so I take a coat from the back of my closet: a gray, checked sports coat my dad got me last Christmas. I cut the tag from the collar and throw it on. Extraordinarily, it's a perfect fit. I pull at the shoulders, and the coat relaxes over my body. I exit the house and remember that the last cab I took to the Fountain cleaned me out. I should have gotten a rain check; it would have been perfect. I know: I'll go to the market, bum a transfer from Sam. I can see the store entrance from our doorway. The Dahra Range, it's called. He doesn't stray far from his nest.

I enter the market. A small bell rings above the doorway. It hangs from the collar of a carved wooden hamster...cute! I see exotic, overpriced organic...*things* in rows stretched out before me. I don't recognize most of what I'm seeing. It's either labeled in Algerian or it's an unrecognizable color. I can make out...dates...mint tea... couscous. They're on some sort on a sale shelf as "Damaged Items." They don't look damaged. Wow! Sixteen dollars for a fruit salad! Well, it's called "Fakya." Can a fruit salad even *be* damaged? Funny, I never see Sam making any of this at home.

There are a few customers, though no one in the store looks Algerian, so it probably has an attractiveness to the rich and bored. They all look rich and bored anyway. They drift in and out of sight, eyes forward like zombies pushing really, really tiny shopping carts. One puppy and that thing will be filled.

As I make my way down another aisle, I spot the top of Sam's head in the distance. He's on his knees filling shelved baskets with small loaves of bread that look like tiny baguettes. I approach him. He hears my steps and holds a loaf above his head like a baton. Relief washes over him when he sees it's me.

"Sorry, my mom keeps a close eye on me—too close if you ask me." As he says this, a can of chickpeas flies past his head and hits the wall. He shouts something to a short, middle-aged woman wearing a headscarf. I don't know what he said, but I can guess it wasn't good. Another can of peas flies past us, and the woman disappears around the next shelf in a huff.

"Are you guys okay?" I ask, afraid I might be stepping in some bad business.

"Yeah," he sighs. "We throw stuff at each other all the time. My mom finds it hilarious." His mom's laughing fades as she walks to the back of the market.

"I need money, please, it's an emergency," I say, quickening my words as I get to the end of the sentence to give the request less thinking time.

"I've only got my credit card. Sorry." Sam focuses on the bread, but I frown and push back.

"Well, can I *borrow* your card?" I did say it was an emergency after all.

He gets to his feet and towers over me. Don't forget your being kind to small things rule, Sam. He just steps past me.

"Dude, I'm kinda busy here. Ask Holly." He dismissively waves a baguette like a conductor's baton.

Oh, come on! He knows Holly never answers her phone, and he also knows I'm on the clock, but he doesn't budge. I angrily huff at him and storm out of the market empty-handed.

I start walking up 7th Avenue, arguing with nobody under my breath. I approach the metro, which is *still* being worked on! I take an impatient step onto the road to cross, and as I do a car screeches to a halt in front of me. The driver looks pleased to have almost killed me. I hold out my hands in question. The woman in the passenger seat playfully hits the driver in the arm and waves me across with a smile. The man lowers the driver-side window.

"Yes?" I ask in a sharp, perturbed way.

"Hi, there! Sorry about that. We're not from the island, and we're supposed to be meeting someone around here. Do you know the way to a coffee house called—" He pulls a card from his breast pocket. "—the Brown Fountain?" No way!

"Is this a joke?" I ask suspiciously.

He looks confused, almost offended. "No, sir. Why? We haven't been given wrong information, have we?" He looks to his passenger, who rummages through her purse. She takes out the same card and holds it up.

"No, that's the place, hon!"

I inspect the pair curiously. The driver is a business type—light-brown suit, dyed hair—and his wife (I think) is wearing cool-looking aviator sunglasses and a polka-dot neckerchief tied in a jaunty bow.

"Yeah, no. I *know* where it is," I say. "You won't believe this, but I'm headed there myself. Do you think I could ride with you?" My adrenaline from nearly getting hit has gone. I probably shouldn't be so forward, but I don't have time to wait.

The driver sits at the wheel, thinking to himself.

"Oh, now, Devon," his wife says. "Of course he can. We're not just going to leave him on the side of the road!"

He stops thinking and brandishes a big ol' smile. "You're right, sweetie. Besides, I know what your memory for details is like."

"Oh, okay, Mister I-don't-need-a-map!" she retorts in a gravelly, mocking voice.

He laughs and takes the child lock off the back passenger door of their typical family sedan that's suspiciously devoid of any children. I let myself in. The seats are so low that I practically fall into them.

"A seat belt is heartfelt!" the woman calls out, looking at me in the rearview mirror. My face paradoxes in the additional reflection of her sunglasses. I let out a courteous chuckle and snap myself in. There really was no need for a rhyme, but you know—friendly enough, I guess.

The car pulls away from the sidewalk, and we head toward the coffee house. I hope this is a good idea. There is a long silence met only by the sound of flowing wind. I try to make conversation, but the words won't come out. It's like I've fallen into a really cold river. The passenger-side window hasn't been shut since we spoke, and it sends a breeze right into my face. I rest my hand on the seat, and the wind stops. There's nothing now; no outside buzz, no choking air current overpowering my breathing; just a pleasant, warm silence. The woman in the aviators plays with the window button. Up and down it slides, but not a difference is made in the car.

"Strange" she mutters to herself.

I peek up, curious. "So…you guys like to be this adventurous on the way for a coffee? Make a left here."

The wife giggles to herself as the car slowly turns. Suddenly, a look of shock befalls her. "Oh my, how rude! Allow me to introduce ourselves. I'm Rhonda and this is Devon. You're…?" She's waiting for me to answer, it takes me second.

"Dan…iel. Dan Hardacre."

She stretches her arm backward over her seat, presenting her palm. I take it and shake it. It's unusual; the thumbs overlap, which throws me off guard and I hold on for a bit too long.

"Are you in town for business or pleasure?" I ask, pulling my hand away. Devon slips his driver-side visor down. In it sits a picture of a teenage girl. She's holding a bronze trophy with a golf ball on top. "Does your daughter play golf?" I ask pointlessly.

Rhonda grins with big pearly whites. "Sure does! Our little champion. She gets it from me—well, she gets the interest from me, but her skill is from somewhere else. I couldn't tell you where. She's at college in the north end of the city. Scholarship. Living out here is expensive, but we're lucky we're able to afford it. Did you go to college, Daniel?"

I nod. "Computer science—another left here."

At my answer, Devon perks up, and he spins the wheel in his excitement. The tires let out a small screech. "That's what I'm talking about! How's that for irony? What you working on now, son?"

I shudder at the question. I don't know why. The wind has stopped. "Social networking management for Montage Tower."

His eyes light up. "Oh, the big one they're building next to Times Square?" I nod. "That's exciting. Your parents must be very proud."

"Yeeaah." I change the subject. "So where are you guys from? You mentioned living outside the city?"

Devon looks at his rearview when he addresses me. "Syracuse. Jenny didn't want to go to a local school, so you can imagine how thrilled she was when she received the offer from Colombia. That's a great school!"

"Where did you go, Daniel?" Rhonda asks.

"NYU," I say quite proudly. "I always wanted to go there. Too bad it took me half my time before I realized what I wanted to do. I guess your daughter didn't have that problem, huh?" My pride dissipates. Devon laughs.

"No way. She was hitting balls before she could ride a bicycle!" he says into his mirror.

I'm startled by a scream from the front seat.

"JENNYYYY! WE'RE HEEEEEERE!" Rhonda shrieks joyously, pointing and waving to an incredibly tall, mousy girl who doesn't at all resemble the tiny golfing legend in the photograph.

I click the seat belt holster, and it snaps up jarringly, almost cracking the window behind me. "Well, this is the pla—"

Devon lets out his own long, high-pitched screech. I should laugh, but I don't. Jenny recognizes the car and starts to jump up and down on the spot, her excitement almost sending her airborne. She runs toward the car, stops at the curb and waves as we turn into the Brown Fountain's parking area. I try to get out before I intrude any further than I already have.

"Thanks for the ride, guys. Have a nice visit and good luck."

Devon looks disappointed. "Awww, you're not going to join us?" His head almost tilts off his shoulders.

"No can do, sorry. I'm meeting someone myself." The door clicks open, and I slide out. The wind hits me like a truck. My sports coat rises upward like a cape. I grab the bottom corners, yank it down, and button it up.

"Woo! Brisk today! Be careful, sweetie!" Rhonda shouts out of her window.

I wave goodbye and set off toward the front of the café, looking in each window as I do. It's packed. I don't see him. There are too many people, and he's not out front or else would have caught me on the way in. I head inside the building. It smells amazing. The aroma alone is enough to drive adrenaline through your veins. I hear a long, long, loud flush, and the bathroom door slowly opens. I see Dad. He's flattening the dark nest of hair down behind his ears. His glasses are fogged up and...unbroken.

The fog starts to fade from the glass. As it reaches the bottom, his eyes visibly adjust, widening as he catches sight of me. He starts to tear up. He runs over to me, arms out, wanting a hug...and he isn't stopping himself. Oh God, here it comes. His arms cocoon me like an embarrassing anaconda. I give him a pat on the back as usual. He lets me go.

"Look, I know you don't like it when I gush, but hell, it's a big day. We shouldn't have to hide!" His words are muffled by the ambience of the café, but I hear him clearly enough.

"What do you mean?" I shout back.

"WHAT?" he yells.

"Let's just go!" I say, ushering him out of the door.

Side by side and without caffeine, we walk down the street where Lillith collapsed a few days prior. I wonder how she's doing, and Ana. We stop at an ergonomic bench; I didn't see this during the incident. It has two cups on the armrests. No lids, both filled with... coffee? We sit quietly, and I sip at my drink; its soothing warmth encapsulates me. I look around at the deserted street—a far cry from yesterday.

Dad can tell I'm lost in thought. He clears his throat, getting my focus back on him. "So, what's going on with you? Me? I'm fine. The semester has come to a close. Another group of my lovelies are out the door to fend for themselves. But I don't hold it against them. I did the same thing. And let me say, that sports coat is *so working on you, girlfriend*! Speaking of which…have you spoken to that Ana girl? How is she? How is her mom? Sorry I left in such a strange manner, but I thought it would be better if you two could have some time together. She really relies on you, you know? She doesn't show it, but I can tell. Is that what this is about? I mean, it's not often we meet twice in one month. Aren't you going to drink your coffee—"

"Dad!" I interrupt. I feel a rising heat redden my cheeks. He stops and faces front.

It's been quiet for a while now.

In fact, he hasn't said a word in almost eight seconds. I look over to him; he's scared stiff, keeping his eyes fixed on the building in front of him.

Eight more seconds and still nothing. Guilt washes over me like acid rain.

"Sorry I…I'm going through some…stuff."

He slowly reaches over, resting his hand on my shoulder, and we sit in silence. A gentle breeze flows through my hair, soft and forgiving.

"Thank you for being so patient with me, Son," he says meekly. He removes his glasses and slides them into his breast pocket. His eyelids look heavy, now that I see them clearly. The circles around his eyes have been getting darker over the last year or so. He rubs at them, and my heart floats up to my throat. I don't like it being like this.

I rest my head on his hand. He's looking off into the distance, probably trying to keep from getting in my firing line again. The street remains surprisingly still, not a car or person in sight. It's like the city owes us this silence. Or maybe we owe it to ourselves? The apartment blocks along this street aren't open yet, but the glass has been fitted, and the door is uncovered. Modern red-stones, dark fire escapes—these buildings make up a village tribute act. They won't be empty much longer, but they are now, and from this angle, I mean that literally. The windows reflect the overcast sky from way down here, ridding them of their newly furnished insides.

At this moment, I can't help but think about Rhonda and Devon. They exhibited this warm, relaxed attitude. They were weird, sure, but they held nothing back. I don't know how they could keep it up. Maybe they were just having a good day, but even still, they should have been nervous, coming to see their daughter again. By the way they all screamed when they saw each other, it had been a long time. Like BFFs. I wonder how long their hug lasted. I wonder how many times Jenny has raised her voice to stop her mother showing affection.

Could that ever have been me and my mother? She was my rock, my protection, but I don't think I was ever hers. That was Dad's job, but...I don't know. How good of a job could he have done? He was always good with the both of us. Whenever I'd start fussing as a child, he'd find odd little tricks to perform to calm me down. Juggling was my favorite. He used to juggle fruit out of this small bowl we had on the dining room table. Oranges were his go-to instruments, tossing and catching like a citrus-circus clown. One time, he tried with two bananas and my sippy-cup. I don't know what came over him—maybe he wanted to challenge himself? Anyway, he almost broke the TV. My sippy-cup burst in midair and rained juice down all over Mom. She just laughed; it was infectious. As soon as she'd start, Dad would join her.

I'm sure she was happy. I know I was.

I wonder how much of what I remember is accurate. Or if a lot of the joy we remember is just an altered truth: free from boredom and tears and filled with airborne fruit displays.

Blue, Purple, and Gray: the spectrum seems to darken. Could Mom's memories have been the other way around? Could her life have been a darker shade from the beginning? Is that why she left us, to bring some color into her life? I don't expect her to even exist now;

the war took so many people from their loved ones. But mine were already gone. Dad said he was too old to join the draft, though he was only in his fifties. Maybe he *was* too old, or maybe he wished it away. Or maybe, like Rhonda and Devon, he'd gotten exactly what he needed at the perfect time. A gift from the universe.

"Dad?" I say, childlike and guilt-ridden.

"Yeah, Son?" Dad faces me with a patient yet worried smile. "What's been going on, Daniel? Is it your claustrophobia? Problems at work? Sleep?"

"All of the above," I say, smirking at my own bad luck. "I...had this dream."

"Oh?" He's listening intently.

"Yeah. I was a soldier in the war. I was on this Greek beach, fighting off a bunch of soldiers, and my unit was called the Pantheon.

"Like the gods? That sounds exciting."

I take a breath. "We lost. They were all killed in front of me."

"It was only a dream, Son." He's trying to reassure me, but he sounds like Holly.

"You have dreams, Dad. How many of them do you remember afterward?"

He thinks to himself. "Lots," he lies.

"Well, I didn't tell you, but...toward the end of the dream, I became aware I was dreaming. I was me, in the body of a soldier. I couldn't operate the weapons, and my team had to keep me out of trouble. Only at the end, I...I...we were overrun, and I watched the people who were protecting me die right in front of my eyes. A soldier, her name was Albrier...she went out fighting to her last round, firing this giant machine gun at a group of guys with these weird mortar cannons. One of them fired back, and our cover was blown away, as were we. I felt no pain, only sadness. I was drenched in an overwhelming failure, a feeling of complete uselessness.

"And then, after the mistake I made, after every life I had helped end, did I get what was coming to me? Did I lose my life at the hands of strange enemies whose language I can't even speak? No! They just stopped fighting. Stopped right where they were, got down on their knees and surrendered to this…thing, this shiny, metallic figure."

Dad's eyebrow trembles. It's quick, but I see it.

I continue, watching him like a hawk. "Well, it came down and picked me up in its arms and carried me away from the battlefield—the beach we were fighting on—and we drifted up to the sky. It had no face, no wings, but it was humanoid. Only it didn't act like a person. Its actions were more like a—"

"Valkyrie," Dad finishes my sentence. He is lost in a vacuum of fear. He takes his glasses out of his pocket and hangs them back on his ears. "Son, do you mind accompanying me somewhere?" His words are eerily calm and controlled.

"Where?" I ask.

"Washington Bridge. It's the closest one."

I give an uncertain nod. I can see the bridge from the bench—well, the top of the suspension towers anyway. They poke out above the buildings in front like horns on a devil, newly furnished and steady as a rock. We start walking.

I wish Dad would start talking again.

When the airstrikes became local, the bridges were the first things hit, probably to isolate everyone together. That would make for an easier target. Whatever the reason, it doesn't matter anymore. They've been upgraded. Glowing, touch-sensitive panels line the newly paved roads and crosswalks, lighting the way for vehicles at night. They have magnetic locks that halt cars in place, and they display colored messages: stop; go; turn; construction ahead. It's a neat system. Almost makes the damage worthwhile.

That's a dark thought. Let's pack that away in the "sorry box," shall we?

Cars have made themselves known once more, darting past us toward the bridge, crossing it in a hurry, too much of a hurry, as if the war has restarted. The sidewalk we're on tapers as we step foot on the path. The bridge's loose-hanging cables sway and creak, causing the road we're on to vibrate. What does he have to show me that requires such a presentation? I hope he's okay. It was a dream, fantasy, make-believe. There's no reason for him to react this badly.

As we get closer to the bridge, the wind picks up. It batters my eardrums with a hoarse rumble. A few of the cars blare their horns at us; Dad just carries on at his own pace. He looks up at the bridge's towers.

"Keep in close to the barricade, okay? The cables are incredibly loose up top! Shoddy workmanship." He tags that with a sarcastic thumbs-up. He can see surprisingly far for a man who needs glasses. He's lucky he has them on at this point; the wind bounces off them without trouble. I have no such luck. It's an uncomfortable way to move.

We get onto the walkway, and Dad looks back to see if I'm still following him. The creaks grow louder as the bridge cables swing violently in the rising wind as if they're waving us away. The newly fitted wooden boards rattle with each step. The traffic has stopped for now, though, strangely. It's more like a cemetery than a brand-new, state-of-the-art double-deck bridge, and the other walkway is also deserted. Where is everyone today? I know it's Sunday, but *day of rest* is a suggestion, not an order. Not anymore, anyway.

"Dad, where are we going?" I shout over a blast of wind, losing some of my patience.

"Not far now, Daniel. I know it's a drag, but it'll be worth it, trust me!"

I roll my eyes and stuff my hands into my pockets. A squawking sounds in the distance. A flock of seagulls flies overhead, their pushing against the pressure of the wind, giving the illusion that they're hovering, magnetically held in place between the towers. I'm starting to wish I could be a seagull, Sam once told me that they're incredible navigators. Dad could use that skill at this moment.

Finally, he stops. He is way out in front of me, about at the halfway point of the bridge. He pushes up over the safety rail so he can get a look at the river below. It's green and murky, a little like the tea

Dad usually gets for me. Those are starting to feel like simpler times. He drops back down. My heartbeat quickens.

"You're not planning to do anything weird, are you?" I ask.

He dumps his glasses over the side, and they fall out of sight into the river below. What the hell?

"Not anymore," he says, waving me over. My walk turns into a jog, and my heart really starts moving. What is he doing? He kicks at the safety rail, which flutters about in the wind and breaks off, following his glasses down into the water. I start to tremble. Dad puts his arm around my shoulders.

"Oh, this is going to be great!" he exclaims.

"What is? You just kicked the guardrail down. That's vandalism, Dad!" I'm panicking, and that *feeling* returns to my stomach, dancing about in steel-tipped shoes. Even all the way out here it still finds me. I start to feel dizzy, but Dad clicks his fingers and I snap out of it. He chuckles to himself.

"I told you, shoddy workmanship! Now, are you listening closely?"

The wind picks up.

"Barely!" I shout back.

Spinning me to face him, he rests his hands on my shoulders and looks directly into my eyes with his sharp blues, unshielded and steelier than ever. He nods as he starts.

"Daniel, I want you to do something for me." He's almost begging. "I want you to catch me. Okay?"

"I'm s-sorry? C-Catch you?"

He simpers, turning back toward the edge. From this angle, I can only see one of his eyes, like he is extending an ominous wink with his whole body.

"Oh, don't look at me like that, Daniel. I know you don't like me much." He glances up to the sky, taking the cold air into his lungs. "But I think we can remedy that...together. Okay?" He readies himself for whatever step of his mad plan comes next.

"No, I-I-I don't—" My whole body grows weak. I start to sway like the bridge cables and plant my feet in the ground, stopping myself, refocusing on Dad.

"Catch me." He jogs forward.

The wind pushes against me, like it did the seagulls before. I reach for Dad's coat.

"Catch me, Daniel!"

I miss.

Chapter 5

DAD jumps from the edge of the bridge and tumbles toward the dark depths below. I scream in shock-horror and instinctively leap off the bridge after my falling father, plunging toward the water, retracing his descent, but he is gone from sight. Waves fill my vision, growing bigger and bigger—

They stop. I'm no longer falling, I'm upright. I'm standing...on air. I spin myself around to see my father; he is doing the same thing—with a huge grin on his face. We're both hovering under the bridge. The screams of sea birds overhead are suddenly muted by the vortex of wind flowing around us. Dad stretches out his arms.

"Come to me," he calls, and I want to go to him—I need to. I push my head forward, nothing, my arms, nothing. I get a flash of Benson's dog tag, swinging from his bedpost like a pendulum, and I swing my legs back and forth, reach out my arms, and close my eyes. I start to feel something: a light breeze across my cheeks. I open my eyes to see that I'm drifting across the air. I look like an idiot, but I'm doing it. I keep swinging, verging closer and closer to my father, who excitedly reaches out to catch me. I ready myself and *WHOOSH!* I swing into a flip, hovering higher over Dad, who floats below, impressed by my kinesthetic development. He opens out his arms, keeping his eyes fixed on me. My grip on the wind slips, causing me to fall.

"CATCH ME!" I scream as my body begins to spin out of my control.

I'm falling.

I'm falling.

I'm falling.

And I fall, straight into his arms. His bones break my fall, digging into the bottom of my spine.

"Whoa. Easy as you go there." He slowly puts me back into the air.

I'm hovering once again, looking in terror at the raging Hudson River below. "*What is going on, Dad?*" I shriek with a fading breath.

"Context!" he declares with an open smirk. He propels himself farther up into the air, breaking the sound barrier behind as he soars under the bridge, up to the sky above and then swoops back over the bridge, looping it. He skids to a halt in front of me, looking particularly proud of himself. I can't blame him for that.

"Now you," he says.

I feel a terrible tremor move through my body—my mouth still hasn't closed since I took my plunge, and as I adjust to my surroundings, panic sets in. With no contact between my body and a solid surface, my pulse races in a waveform pattern from the top of my head to the bottom of my toes.

"Daniel, just think about my movements, how I held myself, my confidence, my feelings of familiarity. The wind is an old friend of ours, you've known him all of your life. Trust me!"

I grin, unsure, and hold out my hands to feel the breeze run through my fingers. I picture Dad pirouetting in the air, cordless and free. Soaring as he just was. The tremble begins again, only it moves to my hands. I push my palms out behind me and release. *BOOM!* I fire across the river and thread my way under the bridge, trying to outthink fear and relying only on instinct. When I've cleared the bridge, I turn my nose up, and I'm carried into the sky. The rumbling in my ears distracts me, and I let go of the wind, which sends me spinning farther than I wanted. The silvery city whirls in my vision, around and around it goes, when it stops, even—*STOP!* I think to myself, loudly, and that's exactly what I do, lying on my back in midair. I flip onto my stomach.

I see Dad past the bridge; he waves, not another soul in sight. I release the tremor again, sonic-booming myself back toward the bridge. I don't fly back under, however. Instead, I weave through the beams of the support towers, and a high-pitched whooshing slices at my ears every time I pass a gap in the framework. The cables on the left side of the tower are beginning to tear out of the wall—the force of my flight is what's responsible. Following the path I have just made, I turn to the falling supports, still flying the way I was—and crash right into Dad. We both spin for a second, but he takes control, bringing us to a halt. He then holds out his hand toward the bridge, and the metallic cables stop their descent. *Phew!*

Dad nudges me back, and as he flies toward them, I hear him shout, "WATCH THIS!" He corkscrews in midair, collecting the thick wires and threading them around each other. He does all of this without laying a finger on them. They all stop ahead in separated sections, and he slams each cable into the support, one by one, like snakes biting at the same giant piece of prey. He flies back over to me, leaving the cables slotted in different spots than they were before they fell. "Fixed it!" he exclaims cheerfully.

"So, we can fly? Is that what's happening right now?"

"Tip of the iceberg, Daniel." He smiles. A sudden thought hits him, and he holds up a finger to me—"In fact, give me a second, would you?"—and shoots into the air. A faint twinkle flashes from the space he exited and then nothing. Silence. I scan the sky to see where he could have gone. Not a speck of him in sight.

Hold on...I see a pale blob, brighter than the steely gray clouds. It grows bigger and bigger until it smashes into the ocean, washing a huge wave over me. I remain in the air, but I'm soaked. I look up to see Dad standing on a colossal chunk of ice.

"As I said, tip of the iceberg. I found the most famous one! This sank the *Titanic*, you know?"

"How did you get that?" I shout, nervously.

"Time travel! We can navigate space and time free and without harm!"

"Bullshit! That breaks the laws of physics!" I shout in a smart-ass way.

He holds his arms out at his sides. "Son, we *swim* the laws of physics." Those words stick to me like a paste.

I point to the iceberg. "Well...still...that thing will cause havoc to the sea level over here."

His eyes widen as if this didn't occur to him. I thought it was obvious. He floats away from the great shard of ice, reaches out a hand to it and *whoosh*, the jagged block springs out of the water and up into the air, speeding like a bullet farther out of sight.

"Where is it going?" I ask.

He follows the berg with his eyes. "The sun...in five...four...three—that was fast. It's gone!"

I can do nothing but laugh.

I swing my legs from the edge of the former Sony Tower (it still doesn't have a name). We're forty stories above Madison Avenue, and I'm sitting in the hole of the pediments—the same place where an errant shell flew through. Dad described this building as a "post-modern masterpiece; a furious concoction of culture and controversy." Fitting that it's the first place he's taken me to. He is perched on the opposite side of the roof; I think he has just spit off it. I ask him; he raises his thumb.

I'm tempted to copy, but I'll probably just hit my shoes. I like these shoes. Brown leather, an embossed dot pattern, almost like snakeskin coiled around my feet as tight as can be. I retied them when I learned I could fly. I don't think it would be a good first day if I accidentally made my shoe into a meteor. They're a bit formal for my jeans, but I'm glad I wore them now. Formal seems like an apt way of presenting myself today, not that I knew what I was in for. My jeans aren't ironed, but they still have their color. That reminds me...

I turn to Dad, who sits watching the world go by beneath us. "So, the dream I had—it wasn't just a dream was it?"

Dad stands up from his edge and saunters over to my side, resting himself down with a long sigh. "No. It was a side effect of your— I think the term I would use is *powerlessness*. You didn't know you had these abilities, so your body was trying to tell you. That night was extra stressful for you, and *obviously*, your body reacted in a different way in order to cope. This may or may not sound insane, but it seems to me that you unknowingly projected your consciousness across time. It found a home in that *Benson* guy, for some reason."

A light bulb appears above my head—not literally, but I guess I can now make that happen if I wanted to.

"They were the only names I could read on the side of The Aerostat when it passed on Friday. Maybe that's why they were chosen?"

He shrugs. "Probably. That's not the part I'm concentrating on, though. The thing that carried you from the battlefield— the 'Valkyrie'—that's not what we called it."

I'm confused. "*We*?"

"Yes, '*we*.' Your mother and me. You see, Son, there's a lot you don't know about the two of us." I shuffle with discomfort. "I'm going to tell you now—if that's okay with you?" His eyes are wide with courtesy, or apprehensiveness. Why is he even asking?

"Of course!" I say.

He puts a leg up in the tower and rests himself back on his elbows. "So...big news—your mother was the same as us. She could do everything we can do—maybe even more. She was incredible. She really was. *A soaring goddess, my adventurous companion, love incarnate*—there are so many things I want to say about her. But that *thing*..." An anger stirs up in his breathing; I can feel the energy radiating from him.

"One day, when we were at *our* spot in the system, a mysterious metallic figure made its presence known to us. It had no face, just like you described. It turns out it had been by our sides for a long time, watching, waiting for the right time to reveal itself—as a threat.

"We didn't take it too seriously at first. I guess that was our hubris. We decided to offer this thing its own part of the universe. However, an olive branch from *lesser beings* appears as hemlock to something so driven by self-love. It bided its time, formulating its strategy, and eventually, when our guards were down and our moods were high, it attacked. Think back, Daniel—a few days after your sixteenth birthday, what happened?"

My mouth trembles as I force it to answer. "Mom left us."

"No," he spits through his teeth at me. "She went to war...*alone*. Without telling me! And she paid for it with her life. I couldn't detect her presence anywhere. She wanted to keep us safe. She planted me here as a time capsule to usher you into godhood.

Godhood? That was an unexpected word. Dad gives me a moment to absorb it before he continues.

"As soon as I detected some inkling of cosmic power, I raced to its location as fast as I could carry myself, leaving you here for what felt like forever. But when I got there, the only thing waiting for me was the Valkyrie. It wanted me to find it...floating there, your mother in the palm of its hand, its lead-lined mitt wrapped around her head, her lifeless body hanging from its grip. Once I saw what it had done, I exploded, and so began a war behind the universe."

Tears run down my cheeks, break from my skin, and rain from the tower. "But I don't remember you leaving," I cry as the strings of drool fall from my lips.

Dad shakes his head, cold anger holding back his pain, welding it onto his words. "You wouldn't. We were so far from Earth, time moved much differently for us than it did for you. We fought without a break for what felt like centuries, small pockets of conflict specking the entire galaxy—the anger and hate reverberated throughout space. This war forced the fabric of reality to change. Black holes started popping up from nowhere, matter transformed into dark matter, gravity into dark gravity. The laws of physics were being rewritten. Earth was affected in a different way, but it still felt us. That was our bard's song.

"Eventually, I gained the upper hand. Early on, I had noticed the Valkyrie's metallic skin cracked from the heat of our sun. As our fight persisted, it managed to slip away from my sight for a short while. Days later, whole constellations began to disappear. The monster was destroying every star it could see, collapsing hundreds of them because they seemed to weaken it—how selfish evil can be. Finally, I banished it to AR Cassiopeiae—the multi-star system.

"Now, I ask you to imagine what the heat of *seven* stars could do to this creature if just one caused it to splinter. Rebuilding the ones the monster had destroyed informed me of their anatomy, so I shrank the seven stars of Cassiopeiae down to the size of golf balls, took them with my right hand, and with one strike, the monster shattered entirely—no friction to keep its ashes from floating away into darkness."

I'm a wet mess. I slam my head into his arms. He runs his fingers through my hair, softly stroking the sadness from me. I feel instantly better, I don't know how. It's strange. I was sad; now I'm...even. Tears still stream from my eyes, but I'm holding myself together. I can talk again.

I lift my head, and Dad's hand moves down to my cheeks. I feel warmth on my face, and the teardrops begin to evaporate. With the steam comes a frightening revelation. I sniff, hard, fearing the answer to my next question.

"Dad...if the Valkyrie is dead, how—"

"It *is* technically dead, Daniel, but because it existed at the time of the war, it remains alive, eternally in the past. It's like us—it still exists as a threat somewhere in the past. It seems it is taunting me through your subconscious—an act of benevolence from one so malevolent. What does that say to you?"

I think for a second.

"It wants to get to you."

He tucks his lips together and nods. "But it can't have me. It's too late. I killed it, and to illustrate the futility of its taunt, I can tell you that we're extremely difficult to kill. Natural causes have no chance.

Our bodies won't allow it. World War Three could do nothing to us. But that doesn't mean we can't be careful."

Dark clouds gather across my mind, covering all but the thought of the war. All-powerful, time-travelling beings, two dead, one free: how did the world almost destroy itself through war on his watch?! I feel the slow rising of rage deep within me at the very thought of having to ask such questions.

"Then where were you? Mom has the excuse of being dead, but you—you did nothing?"

"I—"

I won't let him interrupt me again. Even if he does look like he's on the verge of a breakdown.

"Nothing! The world on the brink of annihilation and—what, you had seen enough war for an infinite lifetime? We were nothing—mere mortals punishing this planet, and you could have ended it in an instant!"

"WE CAUSED IT, DANIEL!"

Everything around us stops; the very world grows silent. Cracks start to form on the roof we're sitting in, rattling the foundations of the world beneath us. Then Dad calms himself. One deep breath and the tremors subside.

"What do you mean?" I ask.

"What I said earlier, about our conflict resonating through the universe? It wasn't a metaphor. The violence the Valkyrie unleashed from me had an effect on life itself. As we raged cosmic battle with each other, the forceful waves of hate and anger present in our violence were weaving into the fabric of the universe. The energy of our pain—emotional, physical, spatial, astral, temporal—was affecting every living creature, but we weren't aware until it was too late. Time moved differently for us out there compared to how it moves for you here. Seconds for us was years for the Earth, so the effects were taking shape—parochialism, pauperism, patriotism, pessimism, predatism, and finally..." He waits for me to answer. I comply, finishing the pattern.

"Paroxysm," I say, almost out of breath.

"Exactly. I don't know how—maybe it was an instinctual reaction. These effects separated countries, closed borders, and eventually laid the foundations for another world war. All I wanted was for you to be safe."

"You were why I wasn't drafted—the reason for the Deactivation Declaration."

"Yes," he says, unashamed.

"I have to ask—if you could do things like that to protect me, why not just stop the whole thing?"

Dad slowly traces the pattern of the cracks around him with his finger, erasing them from view. "We can do so much, Daniel, but there are a lot of things I haven't been able to do. I can increase the dopamine levels in your brain, but that's only because we're connected as father and son, and we're wired the same. An entire planet, however, is a whole other story."

I take his answer in. It melts away my rage, but questions remain floating in the unstable goo of my soul.

"So, what do we do now?" I ask, like a child—which is apt considering I have almost been reborn today. August eighth: my *rebirthday*.

Dad steps off the building and walks on the air, hands clasped behind his back. Calm and sophisticated. It's a strange image, his ratty old windbreaker and his thinning hair blowing in the breeze under the pale evening sky. I follow him, stepping onto his path, except my foot falls through, almost hurling me off the building. After catching my balance, I look up at Dad. A smirk zips across his face.

"Watch your step there, Son."

"I can't even see my steps!" I scoff back at him.

"I can," he says.

I shrug like the smart-ass he just was. He lightly flicks with the wide front of one his shoes, from which a transparent, glass-like path forms, dashing its way under *my* feet. The path hits the wall of the building with perfect precision. "Yes!" he shouts, fist up in celebration as if he has bowled a 7/10 split. I step onto the clear bridge he has made for me. "Come on!" he calls over his shoulder. "Follow me to that building over there."

I look out to the building on 712 and fifth: that's where the bridge ends. I slowly creep across the transparent track. I wonder if anyone can see us down below. I doubt it; he's probably made us invisible to their eyes.

"Dad, are we invi—"

"Yes, like the bridge."

I gaze down through the walkway. It's strange: because we're up so high, the evening light is refracting through it, creating a sort of rainbow effect. I'm walking on a *rainbow*—this is insane! With each step I take, the city seems to move on its own, like I'm controlling the buildings with my feet. Small, colorful shapes drift down the road like ducks down a river, only they're cars on the road. Left, right, left. I look over to Dad and see he is on his hands…walking. He pops his head through his arms, lifts a hand and waves at me before he flips himself back up and lands with opened arms.

"TA-DA!" he shouts over to me. I give him a small golf-clap and then the finger, and he chuckles to himself.

I pick up my pace until I'm power-walking on the crystal catwalk. Like competitive tightrope walkers, we dangle on our prismatic pathway. I hurry up to my father's back and leap at him, spring-boarding over his shoulders. As soon as my feet are back down, he grabs me and throws me under his legs and back to second place. The race is on!

I clutch at his coat-tails. This weighs him down, but he simply wriggles the coat off his shoulders. I lift myself up, throwing the windbreaker behind me. He is gaining on the other building. I speed up and dart toward him, and as I do, small holes appear in the path ahead of me. I jump over each appearing gap like I'm in a video game. On the last one, I jump not over it but through it, and picture myself landing on the surface. Just like that, my gravity has been reversed. I look down to see Dad still speeding ahead on what is now the underside.

"*Hey, Dad!*" I yell.

As he turns around to answer, a horror strikes him: he can't see me. I whistle from down below/up above him. Yesterday, I didn't know how to whistle. A wave of relief washes over him, and he phases himself through the path and onto my level. He starts his run up again, but he's headed away from the end and straight for me.

"You reach that building behind me and I'll get you ice cream!" he taunts. Challenge accepted!

I raise my arms above my head, and an identical path appears overhead. I salute him just before he can lunge at me, but he does anyway. Relaxing my muscles, I rise, and with a quick twist I'm the right way up on my *own* bridge. I start to run toward the building as Dad skids to a halt below/above me. If only someone could see us. I hurry toward the finish-building, stepping over the St. Regis below me. The sound of footsteps gets quicker and louder; Dad is hot on my heels, and my path in front is starting to unravel toward me, retracting like a frog's tongue into its mouth. I squeeze my eyes together and keep going. And I'm still running. I am running on thin air.

"I'm doing it! I'm doing it!" I scream behind me, a mix of excitement and fear coursing through my nerves and veins. I open my eyes and see fireworks screaming past my face; I stop and look on as they flash above me. Colorful sprinkles dance, lighting up the evening sky. The city is a rainbow beneath my feet, the light from the rockets soaking the city in bright hues of green, gold, red, and blue. Car horns blare at once-crossing pedestrians who stand frozen in wonder. They'll never know.

I step onto the roof of the finish-building, but Dad is nowhere to be found. The sun has begun its descent, painting the sky the softest of pinks. Suddenly, through the warm August air, a small swishing sounds from above. I look up to see Dad hovering majestically; in his hands sit two of the fanciest filled ice cream cones I've ever seen. He has a smile on his face. It's so warm I fear for the safety of the soft-scoop. Vanilla—I know, it's boring, but it's the safest bet when choosing for a relative. You can't know everything.

Dad steps onto the gravel of the roof. He levitates the cones from his hands and holds out his arms, I lean in and give him the hug he wants. He lets out a small, joyful guffaw.

"You were wonderful. I barely recognized you out there!" His face is lit up like one of the fireworks.

I grab my ice cream from the midair and poke my tongue to it. The taste fills my mouth, my nose, and my heart.

"This is amazing!" I say, surprise ringing in my voice. "Where did you get it?"

"Oh, you know, there's a small diner I like across the street…in Naples." He is fully aware how cool that sounds. I reply by sticking my face into my cone. The ice cream is all I need now; everything else can leave me alo— Oh, it's gone. I was hungrier than I thought.

"Goddammit," I sigh. Goodbye, my frozen friend. As if conscious, the cone refills before my eyes. I look to Dad through tear-filled eyes. He's busy carving a bird's head into his ice cream, I think trying for a swan, but it looks like a seagull. "You have no idea how much that meant to me," I cry happily.

"Sure I do," he says, quietly poking eyes into his vanilla frankenbird before it twists back to its original shape as if he has taken an eraser to it. Dad's eyes widen as he gets an idea. "Hey, hey, Dan… guess who I am!" He lifts off the roof, shifting himself toward the ledge on the south side of the building. Still facing me, he holds his cone up into the air, and he is perfectly placed at Liberty Island, where the lady herself used to stand.

"Lady Liberty was right-handed, Dad." I say to his chagrin.

"Oh, come on. It's a joke!" He throws his ice cream over his shoulder and off the roof. I wouldn't like to be down there in the next minute when it lands. I would laugh, but I can still see the statue crumbling to pieces whenever I think about it; the news showed orange flames licking the green paint from her face.

"She is still down there somewhere," I reply, humoring him.

He seems surprised. "Do you wanna go get her out? We can put her back together in the garage or something? Shrink her and fix her in the morning? What do you say?" he asks, filling my ice cream cone back up for the third time.

I shake my head and throw it away. "Nah, I just want to go home."

He nods understandingly. I'm glad he's being so patient with me. The world doesn't stop turning when my memories surface again.

"Don't worry about it, Son. I did a lot less than this on my first day."

"Oh, really?" I murmur, half-distracted by war-imagery. "What did you do?" Suddenly, the image of the sunken statue of Liberty turns into one of Dad, projected onto the roof in flashing Technicolor. He's my age and is confidently flying through sky that is thick with white, fluffy clouds. He twists his body, corkscrewing through the cumuli. Then he smashes into a cliff and the projection fizzes out. I can't hide my joy at seeing that.

"Oh, now you laugh!" he complains, acting as if he didn't show me this for that very result.

"Are you a cartoon?!" I mock, unable to hold back my delight over what I have just seen.

"Let's go then." He's already taking off.

"No!" I shout, and he hovers, confused. "Can we walk? I feel a little dizzy with all this flying around and walking on air, plus the ice cream gave me a headache."

He swoops down, puts his arm around me, and leads me to the edge of the roof. "Walking it is!" He pulls us from the ledge, and we rush toward the sidewalk, yellow blocks of light streaking past us until we crash—in complete silence. This side of the building happens to be traffic and pedestrian-free. I think it's been cordoned off by construction—I can hear the moans and groans coming from the other side of the street. Ah, New Yorkers, never change.

We're walking on East 51st. The dark, jagged towers of St. Patrick's Cathedral hang over us; there is a beauty in its decrepitude. Ironically, it was safe during the airstrikes: the taller buildings around it acted as a shield, absorbing the Russian Kinzhal missiles like cinder block bodyguards. Even the Venezuelan consulate was taken down. Funnily enough, the same drones that hit the city are also being used to rebuild it. It leveled its neighbors, however, and they're all still down. All that remains is a stumpy border wall highlighting the perimeter. It's been cleared of rubble and danger and is now as clean as a chalk outline of a murder victim.

Many more follow down the street, just brick boxes sticking out of the ground: a wireframe graveyard. There are still human workers, thank goodness, both in stores and on-site. But if life had progressed as normal, I don't think automation would be so far behind in its development as to allow humans the freedom of an active work routine, not that the drones themselves aren't following orders of crueler, lackadaisical men. Most of the machines were updated for war work, so only heavy-lifting can be filed under that category. I wonder if vending machines will be worshipped as gods in the future. Like…Autom-athena…No? Okay.

The Bells of St. Patrick are rearing to ring, but it's not time for them just yet. The night is starless for now, keeping us insulated as we happen upon our first crowd of people. Carefully, we wind in and out of mob with relative unease—eclectic packs of strangers, neighbors, artists, tourists, and workers. If they get in one another's way, too much conflict can brew, like crossing streams foaming at the contact point. Dad is trying his hardest to give me space; I'll throw him a bone. He did get me ice cream.

"Dad?" He looks at me with eyebrows raised. "What did you do when the fighting started?" Not much of a bone, I admit, but it's something I'm curious about.

"I was teaching," he says with a smile. "Why do you ask?"

"No, the *real* you—what were you doing? Were you even in the city, the country, on the planet?

He thinks to himself, but his thoughts are drowned out by the cluster of life around us. Their chatter, breathing, and bashing grow strangely quiet: it appears that he's lowered their volume. We can now chat in peace. Nice trick!

"Well, I was here for a while at the beginning. I was mainly laying foundations."

I don't think he means this architecturally. The silence is starting to feel very unnatural—eerie even. I reverse-engineer his crowd-controlling effect and raise the volume a touch. It's now a murmur as opposed to nothing at all. The tingling has gone from my spine.

"Thank God you did that," Dad says. "I was starting to get creeped out, but I didn't want to ask you to repeat yourself."

"So what did you mean 'foundations'? Like, physical or metaphorical?"

He smiles. "Both. You see, there are certain lines that can be drawn in order to deflect event paths, like the way the construction sites are cordoned off around the city. I cordoned off the areas I wanted to protect—I didn't have enough skill to layer the whole city, so I made sure that you could be comfortable if your powers came through, but they didn't. You couldn't have helped even if you wanted to, and that's not your fault."

"But I wasn't comfortable, Dad," I say. He looks spaced—you know the way adults zone out when they feel the need for a breather? I'll approach him when I'm ready; that's what he's doing with me.

"Thank you...for everything, Dad. I mean that." I see an excitement form behind his eyes, but he suppresses it.

"It's my job, Son."

I recognize him again: holding himself together was one of the ways he kept me feeling safe, like he knew he should only dispense excitement when it was warranted like...a vending machine.

"Hey, did you get my coat?" he asks. "Or did it fly away from the bridge during the race?" He's feigning nonchalance with his question.

"Sorry. I must have lost track of it in all the excitement."

"No problem."

As we approach the house, Dad turns to walk away.

"Love you, Dad," I say.

He stops, and a frame of pale light forms around him, overtaking his entire body, re-texturing it. His shoulders rise, his sides trim, his chest puffs out, his hair shortens and styles. The light then clears, revealing him. He looks different and the same, like he used to. Why be immortal if you can't look the way you want? His skin shines a faint golden hue, and his dark, knotty hair has lightened to a sun-kissed brunet. A long, dark wool coat forms on his person. It looks expensive. His face is clean-shaven and wrinkle-free. He looks over his shoulder at me like he used to, smiling his cool smile.

"I love you too, Son." He steps forward, clutching a colorful notepad in his hands, like a squirrel clutching a nutty gift. His face turns a bashful red. I walk over to him. "I forgot to give you this," he says, puffing up his cheeks. He holds the scrapbook out to me. It looks homemade. The text on the cover reads: "For DanIEL, My SoN. HaPPy ReBirTHDay! Love DAD."

Chapter 6

HALF-MOON shadows fill my room. The sun is up, but it is late summer, so the tone of the world takes longer to adjust. It's almost time for work. I sit up in my bed after the best night's sleep I have had in so long and pick up the guidebook Dad *gifted* me last night: an introduction to my "godhood."

It's scruffy and creased, bordered with pulpy gold paper, and every word of it is handwritten. In the center of the front cover, there is a printed photo of Dad, Mom, and me. We're all smiling joyfully at the lens, although Dad's eyes are closed—he must have blinked. We are pictured around a large buttercream sheet cake. The sixteen candles on the cake light the image with an orange hue. They were those "trick candles" that reignited the second they were blown out; however, after three blows, they refused to come back to life. I don't remember much more than that, but I think this might be the last photo taken of Mom before she left—I mean...before she...

There is a mottled red ribbon laced through the inside that acts as a bookmark, which is a strange level of *fancy* for a handmade scrapbook. The spine is bound with a dark strip of card and has the feel of velvet. The manual is not that short either, and I was too tired to look through it last night, so I just skimmed it. I turn to the exact center of the book, to the one page that stood out to me. It is entitled:

ABILITIES (SO FAR. :P)

ADAPTABILITY [LIVE, BREATHE, THINK, FEEL, COMMUNICATE, AND SURVIVE IN/ON ANY ENVIRONMENT]

TEMPERATURE CONTROL

CONTROL OVER EVERY ASPECT OF ALL PROPERTIES OF MATTER AND ANTIMATTER

CONJURING AND CREATION

ENERGY PROJECTION

FOREVER

FLIGHT

"HEIGHTENED" LEVELS OF INTELLIGENCE AND PERCEPTION

"HEIGHTENED" STAMINA LEVEL

MULTIDIMENSIONAL TRAVEL

TELEKINESIS

STRENGTH LEVEL ENOUGH TO TAKE THE WEIGHT OF MULTIPLE STARS

TIME MANIPULATION

TELEPORTATION

∞?

I put the book down and lay my head on my pillows, cautiously sniffing at the linen-covered foam. It smells like hair grease and dust. I stick out my hand toward my wardrobe. The doors fly open, and fresh, folded sheets slowly drift out. I hoist the covers off me, and they hover in the air like cotton clouds. The pillows follow, sliding up and out from under my head as I roll off the bed and onto my feet, giving the pillows room to fly. The buttons unclasp from my now-floating comforter, and I, with a wave of my hands, strip the cover off like it's the tablecloth at a magician's dinner party. Then the bottom sheet politely pops off my bed, and both it and the cover fly into the laundry basket in the corner of my room. Finally, like formerly gloved hands, the pillows are free from their covers. As they hover above me, I reach out and unfold the fresh pile without touching them, reversing the process. *Whoosh!* Comforter cover on. *Pop!* Bottom sheet snaps. *Boop!* Pillows covered. I let go, and they all fall onto my mattress at once. That was so satisfying I may faint. No, pull yourself together. It's time for work!

It's eight a.m. Holly is out again, and Sam's work hours and lifestyle vary. I don't hear Shanty the hamster, so they both must be sound asleep. Let's see if I can time this. I glide into the kitchen and slide three pieces from the $25 organic miche Holly bought a few days ago. She doesn't have time to sleep, but she has time to shop. I speedily jam the slices in the toaster, then pull the butter out of the fridge, skin three thin sheets from the top of the tub, and levitate them over the toaster—all without touching. I set the digital timer, and it's off to the races!

I slide into the bathroom. The shower is already running, rhythmically rattling like a cicada on a motorcycle. I lower my level of temperature resistance; it won't burn or chill regardless of what the temperature is. I phase through the closed glass screen and into the soft fog. My toothbrush makes its own way here, toothpaste already on the head. I have at myself with every one of my watered weapons—sponge, soap, toothbrush—all working away like the sentient mops in that magic movie. Rinse, repeat, and out I go!

As my feet hit the linoleum, I adjust my internal temperature. My naked body streams in the sunlight. I clench my frame, causing cells to climb on cells, unfamiliar patterns forming, softly filling out my skin with rolling hills last seen in the chiseled art of antiquity. My used toothbrush goes back in the cup, and I'm out the door. With a snap of my fingers, my clothes teleport onto me, and as I float through the space between the bathroom and the kitchen, the toast pops up, hitting the butter above, the bit-filled slices landing on a plate I psychically pull from the cupboard. Done and done!

I open my ground-floor window and launch myself out of it; the force of my flight rips the curtains from the frame, and the pole follows, plonking on my carpet. Whoops! I'll fix that when I get home. The whole street rumbles as I take off into the air, my tie streaming behind me like an airbrushed aerial advertisement. I soar higher and higher, flying straight toward the panel of unfurled stratocumulus clouds that blanket the city.

I stop when I reach the border and punch my fist into them. With a simple thought, I fire a shock wave from my hand, forcing an ever-growing hole into the middle of the clouds, dispersing them away from one another and bringing the blue sky into view. The sight is warm and welcoming. I open my arms and let my weight go, tumbling back down to earth, to Montage Tower. I slow down before I get inside the building's space. Checking my watch, I see I have twenty minutes until my shift starts. Why do I want to get into work this early? I'm going to have some fun before I start my day, thank you very much!

I land noiselessly on the highest tower and balance precariously on its tip. Out of nowhere, a small construction drone hovers up next to me. They have motion detectors and spatial awareness but no eyes, so I blend into the tower's peak. Gently, I pat the drone on its head like the good boy it is. It makes a small squeaking noise, moving its rotors up and down as if it appreciates the affection.

I look past it to my next target: the building site of Rockefeller Center, which looks to be nothing but a tall frame of what's to come. Launching from the tip of the tower, I leap over the smaller buildings below me toward the center's skeleton. As I draw closer, I see that one of the girders at the top hasn't been attached to more than the floor below it and stands pointing up to the sky. I hold out my hand and catch it in my grip; the forceful break spins me around it like a courageous stripper on a very unusual pole. I put my feet to it and hang off the side, no strain on my arm or legs at all. Another shock wave rattles the cold metal in my hands as I start my next leap, arching toward the newly constructed Music Hall. The bricks wobble as I hit the roof; I'm not stopping. Faint sounds of a jazz orchestra echo up from below, and it brings an excitement out in me. With this new surge of energy, I whoosh off again, but this time, I don't land. I stretch out my arms and legs and idly fly over all.

I peer down at the theater district; large, simple outlines now sit where whole buildings used to stand. They're populated with groups of people dressed for danger, who smash at large chunks of rock within low walls, sledgehammers beating away like the ticking of a clock. I think I'll continue on to the park—I haven't been in so long. It will be nice to see the greenery from up above. Obviously, they aren't the original trees; a majority of them were air-lifted here from upstate, where the greener areas were left largely untouched by the bombers. I corkscrew my way leftward while lowering my altitude and hold out an empty hand. In it, a small, recyclable cup appears, followed by a plastic lid that clasps around its rim. The cup gets slightly heavier and a lot hotter, and the steam from my newly conjured coffee filters out of the drinking hole at the top. This is indeed my life now.

I see the green hue of nature in the distance. Central Park: the precious emerald that sits as the heart of a crown of glass, metal, and concrete. I continue over the neighboring buildings toward the green patchwork paradise and slow my pace to a crawl. Looking down at the park, I take in the swath of iconic images, strange to see on a Monday morning: families lying out in the sun; dogs and Frisbees at war with one another; ducks splashing about in the yawning lakes. Young lovers lie on the grassy hills enjoying shared time in their own little worlds.

Swooping down, I land on the roof of Belvedere Castle; the lack of clouds really enhances the view. I make my way to the flagpole at the top of the main tower and rest against it, lying lengthways along the pole. There isn't any wind, so the flag, which was only aloft due to my flight, flops down over my face. I drop from the pole and twist the entire thing around as if I'm churning building-butter, allowing the flag to droop over the other side, and back up I go, perched and relaxed. I sip my coffee, which stays consistently at the temperature I like. I look down past the rocks below to see Turtle Pond. All this time I thought that was just a name, but to my surprise, skimming along the rippling water is a small family of slider turtles, a baby following its parents. It's adorable.

Oh, shit, what was that squawk? I follow the noise to a seagull, which is flying down to the pond, its beak open and aimed at the baby turtle! No! You leave Timmy alone! (Yes, I've named the baby turtle Timmy.) I throw my coffee straight at the bird, but it swiftly dodges my attack in a wild fit, changes direction, and speeds toward me! Like a diving falcon, the gull closes its wings and becomes a bullet of a bird—something I didn't know seagulls could do. I wait for the perfect moment, and as it draws closer and closer, I put my shoes on the pole and flip backward, up and over the flag. The bird crashes, denting the metal, and flaps violently. I look closer and see that its beak is caught in the flag. It rips away at the colored cotton, shredding it to strings.

"That's illegal!" I shout at the animal as it frets in the flag. It doesn't look so tough now. In fact, quite the opposite. It looks weak, lost in a symbol it has no understanding of. Oh God, I don't want to let it out. Why am I doing this? It tried to kill Timmy! What if it tries again?! In a flash, I get an idea! I open my hands and form a breakfast pastry in them, shaping it to resemble a turtle with shell lines and everything. I hold it out to the bird, and it viciously snaps at me, but I give it time to focus, which calms it down. Slowly, I unhook the strings of the flag from its beak until it has enough room to wriggle free. As it breaks away from its star-spangled snare, I hurl the pastry to the other end of the park. The seagull heads after it and away from Timmy and his family. I look down to see how they are, and they're gone, nowhere to be seen. I hope they're okay.

That's enough excitement for one day. I dust the flakes of pastry from my hands and shoot up into the sky, zooming my way back to Montage Tower. As I approach, I fail to notice a helicopter speeding past a high building to my left. It smacks into me, and I smear along the windscreen. I'm being led away from work. I peer inside and see the pilot is just terrified. I wave through the glass, mouthing at her to slow down because I want to get off. Her eyebrows arch above the frames of her sunglasses, and they're not coming back down anytime soon. From her mouth, which hangs cartoonishly agape, a small piece of chewing gum falls and lightly bounces off the instrument panel, and I realize I'm blocking the pilot's view.

Like a recently fished flounder, I flip myself around only to see that a tall, red building is speeding toward us. Since the pilot doesn't have control anymore—of the chopper or herself—I stick out my feet and take the impact, stopping the chopper in its flight. However, unless I can get her back on the stick, the weight will soon become too much for me. I can already feel the chopper pushing forward, bending my knees without my permission. I don't want to break the glass, so I have to keep its rotors away from the brickwork. Oh God, what am I going to do? How am I going to explain myself? *I was suicidal and you caught me mid-fall?* No, that…might work? No. Okay, how about *I was cleaning one of the high windows and I fell off my pulley-thingy?* No, I'm wearing a suit. Who wears a suit to clean windows?!????????

—

—

Okay, that's enough excitement for one day. I dust the flakes of pastry from my hands and shoot up into the sky, zooming my way back to Montage Tower. As I approach, I fail to see an errant arm sticking out from one of the buildings. I stop mid-flight. Dad swoops in and blocks my path. What is he doing here? He just hovers there in his new coat and perfect haircut. His hand is still out in front of me.

"Hey, Dad," I say, confused. "Is everything okay? I can't stay and chat. I'm on my way to wo—" Before I can finish, a local news helicopter speeds past us both. The pilot isn't looking where she's going; she's looking under her seat. Good thing too, otherwise she would have seen both of us up here. "What was all that about?"

Dad smirks. "A distracted pilot, that's all. She was trying to find her sunglasses. They fell off her face a few seconds before I stopped you."

I nod, meditating on that close call. "She should be more careful. She could have hit...well, not someone but something!"

"Right. Unforgivable behavior. Anyway, gotta go. See ya, Son, have a great day at work!" And with that, he shoots off across the city.

That was weird. Lucky he was there. I could have been hit by that chopper. Not that it would have done anything to me, but still, I can't really imagine what would happen if anyone found out what I can do. I'm not really up to doing a show-and-tell presentation yet.

It's 8:29, and my feet touch the paved canter of the building's framework. The construction crew hasn't shown up yet, so I saunter through the fire escape and down the stairs. As I reach the bottom, I am short of breath. Goddammit. Flying is child's play, but steps will never change. I walk into the office; it's still cubicle-free and a whole lot more communal. This is how it's going to be now, huh?

The place looks a lot bigger. While it's not empty, there does seem to be a lot more space when I'm on time. It's darker too. The giant red curtains haven't even been drawn out of the way of the glass wall-window—wait! Were those curtains always there? Whatever, I find my workstation in the dark and turn it on. It lets out a loud hum as if it's been woken from a deep sleep. I put my password into the little box (no, I won't tell you what it is!) and open my mailing list. In it is the usual Monday morning newsletter, pizza advertisements from when I registered using my work email for a new customer discount...oh, a staff memorandum? It's from Martin. It says we should stay off the roof while the workers lay the foundations of the next floor above. They weren't there when I landed, so I haven't broken any rules.

Getting up from my chair, I walk over to the window and pull at the golden drawstring to draw the huge, red drape out of the way. Sunlight fills the room, and my eyes begin to water, adjusting to the change of light. I hear a collective groan coming from the group of early bird workers who were sitting in the dark long before I arrived. I brush it off. I look out to see Times Square again; it's lit up with an assortment of reds, greens, and golds—like Christmas come early.

Suddenly from out of the static, my father's face appears on the biggest screen in the square. What is he doing? He waves over to me. I wave back, and his image laughs soundlessly. His students are on break for now, so I guess he is out having a little fun in the sun. I position my phone camera against the glass and take my fifty-eighth photograph of the screen-laden buildings of the square. As I lower my phone, I see that Dad's face has been replaced in the shot by another in an ad for *Bespoke Bifocals*. Nice touch.

I sit back down and plug my USB dongle into the system, which I should have done when I first got here. The USB finds my phone's signal wirelessly, and I transfer the photograph onto the Hourglass Industries' official company LensFriends account and upload it. I haven't graded it or adjusted it in any way because I'm not a professional photographer and I'm not being paid to do any of that stuff. Caption reads: "This is only the beginning!" I hope I haven't already used that quote, but I'm not checking. Next, I log into my company email, only to find the inbox filled with various pieces of hate mail from perturbed strangers, all claiming that "mONTAGE tOWER IS A SCAR ON THE FACE OF nEW yORK cITY!" Blah-blah-bye-bye. I trash the entire virtual stack.

A few minutes later, the office door is nudged open, and Ana enters the room, shoulders up and head down with her pale-auburn hair draped over her eyes like she's hoping to become one with the big, red curtains. She doesn't notice me, and why would she? I'm a half hour too early. She walks the long way around the desks, as there is a cluster of abandoned office chairs blocking the short way. She sits, making almost no noise at all. Finally, she slides her bag under the desk and begins to type. Ana is a database engineer, working on the intranet for a small, digital magazine company called Stower's; they're too tiny to afford this place for long. I wish them luck.

So yeah, we're not staying seated together forever, Ana and I; it's a temporary accommodation until the whole place is finished. It's much easier to make long-term decisions stick when you know how the place is actually going to be wired. At the moment, part of my job is to court potential buyers. There are some interested parties, but there are heavy negotiations happening between their money men and Hourglass's. Stower's has already been secured and will be moving upstairs within a couple of months. It's a significant risk, taking stock in a building that hasn't even been constructed yet.

A lot of companies have moved around the city to different locations after the high-rises—in which they originally set up shop—fell to the Russian drones. Many struggled to stay afloat—what, with big business having to take a back seat to more charitable efforts. Larger companies like SoCor and Zen & Neal had to close their doors. The only companies around here who remained standing were either tied to neutral countries or were particularly ruthless in their dealings with their staff and customers; "controlled by sociopaths" is a good way to describe the latter category.

At the moment, I'm between messaging a sycophantic local investor who is "new to this world" or a sycophantic foreign investor who is "looking to expand on new soil." I don't fail to see the insult in that phrase. Frankly, I don't want either of them to get it. There's no telling how many changes they will bring. The former seems to be an overconfident rich kid in need of a hobby, and the latter is likely to have their own team of engineers and technicians on hand so our jobs might be at risk.

Ana is in a particularly bad place with her personal business getting in the way of work at such a time. Shit! I forgot about Lillith.

I hope she's okay. I've not heard anything. Oh God, something terrible could have happened, and I would have been out gallivanting in the sky. How do I even approach this?

Ana's still typing, heavy fingers pounding quickly at the keys— what could that mean? She's usually slower, more controlled. Is she tired? Are worries keeping her up at night? Has it been a particularly rough morning? How am I supposed to know? I mean, I could always ask.

All of a sudden, Ana whacks her fists against her keyboard. Her face reflects a harsh, blue light from her unusually bright screen. That can't be good.

"Hi, Ana," I say quietly from behind my monitor. I hope my tone is okay. I don't want it to sound too—

"What are you doing here?" she asks, fist raised, loaded with her next swing.

"Me? I was wondering…"

"Yeah?" She seems slightly shocked, hand still up above her head, almost like a victory pose.

"How is everything? You know…with your mom?" I'm overly aware of my surroundings and grow quieter with the last few words to avoid anyone eavesdropping. I can't stand the level of idle gossip around this place.

Ana's hand drops to her side. "Oh! Well…she's fine. Well, she's unresponsive…to medication, I mean. But that's a good thing, I think? No response is better than a permanent response, so… she's hanging in there."

Cautiously, I point to her monitor. "So, what's the problem with this?"

She turns toward it. "Well, the screen turned blue, and punching it isn't helping. I'm going to have to call Todd."

"You called?!"

We swing around, wide-eyed and startled, to find Todd grinning enthusiastically.

"Ms. Burnette? May I call you Ana? What seems to be the trouble?"

Todd Ince: systems administrator. He is perfectly respectful—okay, he is a little *too* respectful. He's always on the lookout to be of help. Like some sort of costumed hero, he waits for the signal, and boom! He appears. Almost like magic, or maybe he never leaves the office, just in case he's needed. He means well, but any ray of sunshine can burn too bright at times.

Ana puts a finger to the blue screen.

"Oh, Nelly. We got a 'code blue'! I'm going to need some space to operate. Nurse!" he shouts over his shoulder despite nobody being there.

A shiver goes down my spine at Todd's ill-timed theatrics. But I guess he's not aware of Ana's family situation.

"I kid, of course. I *will* have to take the machine for now, but I'll have it back to you in an hour or so? I'll inform Martin so he can give you something else to do. Is that okay, Ana?"

Todd's smile never wavers, while Ana sits unresponsive. She goes through anxious phases where her speech becomes trapped, and no one really takes notice, but I can always tell. I owe her one for Friday, anyway.

"That will be fine, Todd," I say. "Just...do what you can for it." Oh, that almost hurt.

He raises a salute to me. "You can count on me, Mr. Hardcastle!" In an instant, he pulls the machine from the wall and disappears from the room.

"Thanks, Mr. Hard*castle*!" Ana says from beneath her bangs without missing a beat.

"Shut up," I mutter, and she giggles quietly to herself and puts her head on her arms. She shoots back up, though, when Martin walks through the still-swinging office door. He seems calmer today—more focused. He waves over at us.

"Morning, everyone! Daniel! A word in my office, if you please?"

I look to Ana, who shrugs, so I get up from my chair and follow him into his dim and dreary office. Except, when I open the door, he isn't here. I walk in and look around, perplexed. I'm sure I saw him enter.

At this point, Dad jumps out from behind the door, and I jump *back* in fright. Dad laughs.

"That's not funny!" I hiss angrily.

"Oh, lighten up, Son! How's work going?" He seems unaware of how weird this situation has become.

"Where's Martin?" I ask.

"Who?"

"My boss—the guy you were pretending to be?"

His eyes widen as does his smile. "Oh, him? He hasn't even come up here yet. I saw him in the cafeteria getting some coffee for his whisky. I wanted to see if you were up to doing something today. We had fun yesterday, didn't we?"

I stare at him incredulously for a moment before I manage to shake it off.

"Yeah, we did, but the weekend is over. I'm busy."

Dad puts his hands on his hips and inspects the room. "You don't look very busy," he says, nosily opening and closing Martin's drawers. I scoff at his cheek.

"As if you'd know! Look, I can't leave after posting a single photograph on a single site! I also have a bunch of backed-up correspondences to deal with and four major public profiles to update. I can't just take the day off!" I can almost make the cogs out, turning behind his eyes.

"Not even for a trip to the Moon?" he asks slowly, sliding the last of Martin's desk drawers back into place with a heavy thud.

I stop. In fact, the whole world stops. The Moon? Oh, shit, I have to say that out loud.

"The Moon? But it's…daytime!" I say in disbelief.

"It doesn't have to be *that* moon, but yeah, we'll fly up…two hundred…ninety-four degrees north-west, and we'll be there in a few minutes. If you're worried about missing a day then I can make all those correspondences go away and have the websites update themselves. Pictures, posts—anything you want will be updated and uploaded in a few seconds. We'll be back before you know it, if you even want to come back that is!" He chuckles to himself.

I need to think. I know it's irresponsible, but it's only one day. Plus, if he can get my work done for me then what am I even doing here? Screw it; it's *the Moon*!

"Fffine," I say with a growing grin. My guilt fades as a visual buzz of excitement runs through Dad's entire being. I really shouldn't begrudge his eagerness. He jumps up, clicks his heels together and teleports us to the roof of the next building.

"All right, small confession, Son. I'd already updated those profiles you talked about when I brought you to your boss's office. I hope that's okay?"

I think for a second and say, "I don't see why not."

A visible relief washes over him. "Oh, thank the stars. Well, then, up we go!"

I feel a rumble beneath my feet; the whole building begins to vibrate. Dad looks up over the city, *north-westerly*. Manhattan is buzzing with cars and trains and helicopters and planes, all of which stop in their tracks. And with a small, silent sonic boom, he zooms skyward.

I gather my wits, crouch on top of the roof and repeat as he did. I lift my head, and with some minor strain and in a forceful, uneven motion, I launch myself up into the air.

Dad has stopped just above the city. I drift over to him. "What's up with the traffic?" I ask.

"I'm getting us to the takeoff point. Don't worry." He folds his arms regally as the city begins to slide under us, every street and sidewalk, every house and high-rise. The cars and pedestrians are stuck to the paths they were traveling along.

I look at Dad, a little frightened. "What's happening?" He's concentrating on what he's doing, so there's a small pause before he registers my question.

"Oh," he says with a turn of his head. "I'm moving the Earth into position for us. Freeze time, get the angle right, unfreeze time, and it's one straight shot for the both of us, no trouble at all. You see, Son, to us, the Earth spins as if it's a well-twisted top. All it takes is a hand to snatch it, and it becomes ours for reshaping, as do all things if you can find the reach."

I hold my arms out inquisitorially. "That sounds like it's more trouble than, I don't know—us moving ourselves instead of an entire planet! Can't we just do that?"

The city stops moving beneath our feet. The pressure fizzes out, and the air grows silent.

"Oh...okay," Dad says, his sails losing their wind. "May I ask why? Why would you choose to move only yourself when you can move the world around you? Now, that's a feat!"

I look down. "I feel like I'm interfering. It makes me nervous, you know?"

He smiles, patiently letting go his enthusiasm. "Happens to the best of us, Son. It does take a while to get used to. Okay, then, you ready to fly? The Earth's ionosphere has four layers of gas around it during the day. Once we get about halfway, a fire will cover us both. Don't panic, okay?"

I nod, relieved, my nerves subsiding. That was fast. A one-two-boom strikes the air, and we're off, launching up into the sky like two bottle rockets. I see the curvature of the Earth grow wider. The higher we get, the bluer the sky becomes. A thin ring of light surrounds the land and sea, and the sky darkens above as we make contact with the first layer of the ionosphere.

"HERE COMES THE FIRE!" Dad yells over the rippling echo of our flight.

We bypass the second layer of the ionosphere, and after a few seconds, a heatless fire awakens around me, unfurling outward like a booming flower. My clothes are still on me, completely untouched by the heat. I guess that's Dad's doing. Then we pass the third and finally the fourth atmospheric layer into complete darkness.

I made it! Here I am, gently gliding through a soundless space. And I can breathe! What is that smell? It's like someone has taken a blowtorch to a raspberry pie. I spot Dad hovering in the darkness of space; he points at a small, gray blob in the distance and then zooms toward it. I follow him, speeding through the tar-like blackness of space, and look back to the Earth; it's beautiful, hauntingly so. I switch the gears in my brain back to the task at hand and continue to fly.

The Earth stays put, beginning to shrink slightly. Conversely, the Moon comes into sight and grows bigger and bigger until I see a splash of dust on the surface where Dad has landed. I zip down, straight toward the crater of his impact. I'm flying at a high speed, gaining and gaining on the satellite, until one of the small holes becomes my entire landing zone. I kill my speed mere feet from the surface; sand cascades all around me as I adjust my stance. I'm now upright and still. A whirlpool of moondust swirls around me like wind around a roaring jet engine. Silence falls, and we're here.

"WE'RE ON THE MOON!"

Chapter 7

BEAUTIFUL. That's the only word that comes to mind. Dad looks more excited for me than himself. I descend to the Moon's surface, stretching my feet down to the ground. "That's one small step for—Ow." I fall flat onto my face. Dad laughs to himself. His laugh is incredibly loud within the vacuum of space: for some reason, our voices seem to travel through that which sound cannot.

"Watch your step," he says, cackling at my misfortune. "I thought you'd be prepared for the lack of gravity?"

I spit the moondust out of my mouth in disgust. "Sorry, It seems I was...overexcited," I say sarcastically, while struggling back up to my feet. Readying myself at the edge of the crater, I jump and slowly drift down into it. It's daunting at first; the craters look a lot smaller from Earth. As soon as my feet hit the bottom, I bounce high into the air, like an unsure basketball leaping out of its hoop. I land on the outer rim and then lose my balance once more and tumble back down into the crater, stopping just before I hit the floor. Dad lifts me back up telekinetically, and I see small puffs of chalky powder getting patted off my knees and elbows.

"Do you know what this crater is called?" he asks as he slowly sets me back on my feet. I shake my head. "Copernicus. Turns out he was wrong. The son *is* at the center of the universe—mine anyway—and he needs to be more careful."

I nod, embarrassed, and blow my nose. A small collection of stones flies out comically and floats in front of my face before falling to the ground without a sound. "Have you been here before, Dad?"

He doesn't answer but kicks the dust off his shoes and starts to float up, out of the crater. I follow him. We're higher now and can see our pale, blue home locked in its vacuum—right where we left it.

"Beautiful?" Dad asks.

"Absolutely!" I reply. I pull out my phone and hold it up to take a picture. Dad swings into a pose in front of the lens, his tongue stuck out and one eye closed like a poor attempt at Michael Jordan's dunk-face. I snap Dad's picture and look at the result. He is the biggest thing in the image, with his finger under the giant globe as if he is balancing it like the aforementioned basketball. I put my phone away.

"So, what do you think of your parents' *home away from home*?" he asks, quietly contemplating to himself.

"You and Mom? What was this, like, a vacation spot?"

He holds out his arms. "Yep. You were conceived right on this patch."

I lurch back and lift myself off the ground. "That's just great, thank you, Dad."

"You're welcome. Have *you* ever had sex on the Moon?" he asks sincerely as if he's forgotten I haven't been here before!

"Obviously not," I answer.

After a beat, he says, "Well, you should."

"I will, Dad, thanks for the advice." My words are laced with sarcasm, but he doesn't seem to take the hint. He's in a deep state of reminiscence.

"It wasn't just here, Son. We went everywhere—did everything."

Please stop talking. "That's nice, Dad," I say through a shudder-inducing cringe, really hoping he is done.

"Different planet for every mood."

"Okay, Dad!"

There is an even longer silence, then, when I think he's finally got the message, he declares proudly, "Mercury was my favorite!"

"ALL RIGHT, DAD!" I shout, red-faced and uncomfortable, and he finally snaps out of his little mind-vacation.

"Oh, sorry. I was rambling again, wasn't I? Well, what do you want to do? Do you want to stay here, or do you want to go to Mars or something?"

I have no idea why he would ask such a question. "Why don't we stick to the Moon for now?"

He nods. "Whatever you want!" He pushes off the ground and bobs along the surface, squealing like a delirious schoolboy. No matter where we are, he's still a dork. It sure looks fun, though. Okay, I give.

"WOOO-HOOOOOOOO!" I shriek, launching after him.

The steps propel Dad across the Moon's powdery surface. I try to mimic his movements, stay upright and on-course for our destination. We're surfing the Sea of Tranquility—I am so excited! We're going to the first landing site, where Armstrong and Aldrin touched down and made history. I guess, in our own unique way, we're repeating their feat, except no one will ever know...I think?

"Dad!" I shout. "Is there any chance we could be on the news right now? Flying around the city."

He slows his pace. "No. I made sure no one could see you. I lost my focus during the helicopter scare, but I think we'll be fine. Just know that I'm not going to be able to shield you forever, kiddo. I already have a full-time job!"

I laugh. "Well, you're on a break now, so you can chaperone for a little while!"

Dad turns his jumps into a glide and increases his elevation. I copy him and see the Moon's body bend into a horizon. The Earth rises behind it like a morning star. It's strange not having any breeze to get in your way, nothing to tie you down. A weight is missing from my shoulders; I can push myself off the planet's surface and choose whether and when I come back down. It's freeing.

After leaping for what seems like minutes, I see something in the distance, a small metal object flashing ahead of my eyes. Dad turns his head as he bounces to shout to me.

"You see that strange shape over the next hill? That's the first Lunar Orbiter. It was basically the gateway module used to find a landing spot for the first human lunar mission, and naturally, it's the first thing we'll see on our way to Apollo 11's Lander. It's the first of many modules out here in this area!"

I nod and lose my balance but quickly get it back. Note for the future: no nodding on the Moon. We make it over the hill, and Dad draws nearer to the surface. It's smooth; no wonder this is where all the machines congregated. I can see them from up here—different metal pieces, legs, boxes, dishes, antennae of gold, silver, and bronze—all scattered across the same stretch of dust creating a vista resembling a monochromatic Christmas decoration.

We swing down to the surface, and there it is: Tranquility Base, the 1969 landing site! It's a lot bigger than I'd thought.

"Keep yourself hovered above the surface, Son. We don't want to mess with history...metaphorically speaking." A big grin fills Dad's face. I get the joke. It's okay.

The flag, stretched out as if by wind, is held up by a horizontal rod through its back. Once a symbol of how much work it was to get it here, it now gleams as white as a summer cloud. The red, white, and blue have been washed out of the fabric. If more people knew Earth was waving a white flag in front of its face then I expect there would be less excitement over ever being visited by an alien civilization. It looks as if it was left here to greet us, whose backs are without rods. I almost feel sorry for it. There is stuff everywhere.

"Yeah, the flag was bleached white by the sun."

Solar panels stretch out from small, metal boxes; a silver plaque hangs behind the metal ladder attached to the Lander. It's inscribed with signatures of Armstrong, Aldrin, and Michael Collins—the third astronaut who piloted the command module. The plaque also has the name of the then-President of the United States, whose signature is a lot larger than the others. That seems unfair considering they did all the work. He really was a dick.

Something behind the Lander catches my eye, glinting in close proximity. A small crater. I hop on top of the module, which rattles soundlessly as I land…on the Lander and look down to catch my balance so I don't fall backward. A huge amount of moondust puffs around the module as I kick out before resting my foot on the higher portion of the roof rack. I barely miss the small dishes that decorate the top and the weird, short parasol thing that points up at me accusingly.

I look back down to the crate from a moment ago. "Dad, what's that?"

"That's the site where the astronauts dump their space-trash! You can go down there if you want, but try not to touch anything, or someone will eventually notice, and that will start all sorts of crazy shit."

I leap down into the crater, hovering above the space-junk within. I will look, but I won't touch. It's dusty as hell. There are countless random pieces of disconnected machinery: solar panels, dishes, copper cylinders, and food containers. I can't blame the original astronauts, but I hope that if we ever do set up something habitable here, we don't create the first off-planet landfill.

Let's see, what else is there…ah. I see some poofy, white cushions that look like they're from the Lander. They're big enough for my arms—still not touching! There's also a bunch of small, clear, vacuum-sealed packets, and inside, what looks like…oh God.

"Dad!" I call, horrified.

"What is it?" he replies, concerned.

"You said it was their trash pile, not their toilet!"

"Well, I don't know everything!" He chuckles to himself. "But that is *one large shit for mankind* right there!" He's lucky I'm leaving everything where it is; otherwise, I'd be tempted to throw it at him. And, with that, I exit the trash pile, leaving my dignity behind with the lunar droppings.

I slowly drift back over to the Lander's remains and lay my hand on its golden heat sheeting. It's freezing. My handprint stays where it is, framed by the dust that covers its metallic miniskirt. I smooth it down, wondering what it's made of. As I peer closely at it, the first layer disappears in front of my eyes, as if my vision is travelling, but really, my mind's eye is solving the puzzle of the sheeting's creation.

Sensing Dad watching everything I'm doing, I lose concentration, and the shapes fade. I shake my head to refocus, ignoring him, ignoring him and bam! The image I have of the material breaks open. Inside, I see a honeycomb web of metal and wool. It looks cozy. I rip a long piece of it from the module and wrap it around myself like a cape.

"What the hell are you doing?" Dad shouts.

"What?" I ask, expecting his question. "It's a replica!"

He looks back at the module to see that the sheeting is still there. I reformed it back onto the module without a scratch. Now I have my own golden fleece, I'm not freezing, but I still feel a chill.

"You're not feeling the cold, Daniel. That's in your head," he scolds. I guess I really frightened him for a second.

I pull at the corners, so they stretch out like wings. "I think it's cool!"

An impatient look descends on his face. "Okay. If you like it that much, you can keep it, but that's all, understand? Now, are you getting in or what?"

I ignore him and shoot off into the air. My cape flutters behind me like a rattling tent on a windy night. I zoom around the Moon in perfect silence, speeding faster and faster until I have circumnavigated the whole thing. When I reach my starting point, Dad is in the air, waiting for me.

"I see you're still full of energy. Want to go somewhere else? We could go and see China's landing site. It's basically the same except their flag is in color, or...we could even visit somewhere farther out in space if you want?"

I hold my thumbs out in front of my cheesy grin.

"Where to? Mars, Mercury, Saturn? Any planet you want!"

I remember what Sam said earlier. "Farther than that! Pluto, I want to see Pluto!"

"Pluto it is. We can loop around some of the other planets on our way there if you'd like?"

Unable to contain my excitement, I launch past him and into the darkness, accelerating faster than I ever have. I speed past Mars, and it's a lot brighter than I envisioned—a huge golden ball of sand, a small mimic of our mother star. Then, from the shadows, Jupiter rears its massive form out of nowhere. Its colossal, cloudy body greets us in a mix of oranges and blues, like an autumn painter's palette has been dropped into a gasoline spill. I see the red spot at its navel; like Mars, it isn't as red as it appears in images, and I'm tempted to get a closer look at it, but I remember it's a giant storm. That doesn't appeal to me, and besides, I might lose my cape.

Off we zoom, past the giantess of the galaxy, arching our way over a large field of asteroids and onward to Saturn. We follow a bright, curving plume of blue light that bounces off a nearby moon like a deflected laser. We use it to track our route to Saturn. It's beautiful, iconic, like the Central Park of space. I look back to Dad and point down to the luminous ring which encircles the planet's beige body. He stretches his thumb out to me like a deep-sea diver without a radio.

I tilt my body over and speed down directly into the rings, slamming into a sea of dust, ice, and rock. As I swim through the heart of the inner layer, its larger rocky pieces pass me, spreading the sea of salt-like smut about like a broom does dust. I feel safe, however, as gigantic chunks of ice are scattered across the horizon like islands, all waiting to be plundered for secrets. I dip in and out of the ring like a dolphin, repeatedly breaching the surface, glowing dust particles flying all around me, as if to mark my territory, but when I turn back to inspect my work, there's no trace of me ever being there. I look over to Dad, who has inscribed his initials into one of the large stones. They're lowercase and curly. He then strikes a line atop the first "h" turning it into "ℏ." It's an unnecessary affix, but who am I to judge? I barely made a splash. Dad flicks the rock, which bashes into a group of its friends like a stricken pool ball, and directs my attention to a whirling cauldron of glistening ice shards which reflect the sun's light right at me, making me feel as powerless as I was before I found out who and what I am.

The rings behave in a very specific way that echoes human biology. Each piece of ice of every size is in a constant state of motion, flowing around the body like cells in the bloodstream. They form, break apart and reform themselves, in a state of constant refurbishment, held in place by a number of segregated moons. I gaze down at the planet itself. You'd think it would be dull in comparison to its jewelry, but no; its size and depth overpower every sense. Strokes of methane decorate the surface in imperfect stripes, from the brightest yellow to the darkest gold.

"This is the spot where I proposed to your mother," Dad says, and I look slyly at him. "What? I know it's a cliché, but you would have done the same thing. As I proposed, I unhooked the rings from the planet's orbit, shrank them down to the size of a wedding band and slipped them onto her finger. She couldn't take her eyes off them. I could tell how excited she was because the rings started spinning on her finger." He laughs at this, and it slowly dissipates into silence as his mind wanders for a brief moment. He chokes his sorrow down and arches his neck so his face is upturned. I spot an errant tear float off into space. He catches it in his hand, squishing it against his palm. It changes shape but remains whole. Dad wipes his hand on his coat and shoots me a camouflaged smile. And with that, we start to fly again, zipping speedily away from Mom's precious trinket of stardust. No matter how powerful my father is, no matter how much he can lift, how fast he can fly, no matter where he goes in time and space, the memories of my mother will follow him forever.

Desperate to pry myself from the situation, I hurry down toward the planet and around its atmosphere. Its colossal, collaring contours grow into almost intelligible landscapes. I glide closer, eager to get a look at the surface. An immense amount of white cloud plumes around me, cutting off my vision like an impromptu blizzard. I glance over my shoulder to see if Dad is following, but the gases congregate behind me, blocking my view of the icy rings and star-filled space. It looks like the sky is on fire, only without any heat, and my clothes are still fine, exactly the same as when I took off from Earth. Dad isn't with me, so it wasn't him keeping them from burning. My body must be protecting them on its own—I hope it can protect me too. A white, dense fog engulfs me, obscuring the hands in front of my face.

I'm still going, although it takes a lot more energy to stay upright. I can't rely on floating anymore; I have to keep my head down as I dive. Well, I guess I can cross skydiving off my bucket list!

As I fall faster, my panic rises, and my heart rate escalates. I don't need to breathe, but I really want to. I hold out my arms like I've seen skydivers do—it's a lot harder than it looks. My golden sheet is billowing wildly from my back. It's completely vertical, rattling in the wind. The pressure is too much; it rips itself from around my neck, and I look up to see it flying away. There's nothing I can do. I have to let it go.

I turn back to the planet. The white clouds have darkened now to a thick brown, which continues to darken the farther I fall. Suddenly the noise picks up, growing from barely there to eye-wateringly loud. The storm-like wind is becoming unbearable, slowly tipping me into a roll, but I can't let that happen, I'll never find my way out. I add more weight to my left arm; it begins to inflate with solid fat and splits the sleeve of my sports coat, creating a long flow of checkered cloth that dances around my inflated arm. The effect reminds me of the drapes in my bedroom flapping in the wind. *No, concentrate!*

I slowly drop back to my original leveling and with just a thought shrink my arm back to the way it was, reasserting my balance and gritting my teeth to face the wind head on. If this is a gas giant like Jupiter, I may be able to pass through without even coming into contact with a surface at all! I mentally take hold of the stitching in my torn sleeve and weave it back together; it's tight, but it will hold. This gives me an idea!

I feel for the molecules in my clothes and my body, and once I've established what's what, I shift my focus until I can physically see those molecules in my mind. I hold out my hands toward the colorless circles, and with a flick of my wrists, they separate, and I change from a solid to a gas-form. My body breaks apart into the smallest particles, passing through the threads of my threads as a pink-colored gas. My clothes drift in front of my gassy eyes and fall way down through the dark clouds of which I am now a part.

My socks, shirt, jeans shoes, and underwear are torn apart by the winds, and in a flash, I revert back to my original state and grab my coat as it starts to split in two. I stop the rip before it reaches the top of the coat, creating an "Λ" shape with flapping sleeves. Conjuring up a couple of dense metal bars, I thread them through the coat as if it were a tent.

The wind cuts at my skin like razor wire despite there being no visible evidence to show this. Blinding pain rushes up from my toes to the ends of my ears as I repeat what I did to my molecules with the jacket and the metal. In response, it puffs around me in a cloud of gray gas. Before it completely passes me, I turn it back into a solid, and my arms are in the sleeves. That was...weird.

With my arms extended, the jacket becomes wings, and I'm sent skyways in the updraft. The pace of my fall has been lessened significantly, but the wind has now turned into a full-on thunderstorm, yellow streaks of lightning lining black clouds.

I take each end of my wings and furl them around my body. Like a diving hawk, I missile through the squall, forcefully smashing through the frozen storm clouds, each direct burst roaring like canon fire. I pass the area of the storm only to find I'm being crushed under the atmospheric pressure. Heat rises and my pace slows as I splash through a hot swamp of hydrogen and helium. Pure liquid humidity engulfs my naked body, bringing that *feeling* back to my stomach. Claustrophobia hits, and my ribs barely keep my heart from breaking through my chest. I lose my grip on my wings, leaving them to collapse in on themselves, burning up in a ball of molten flame. I shake my head, grit my teeth and plunge farther, applying additional force to my fall to push through the sickness. The swamp grows hotter and brighter, too hot, too bright. I can't take it anymore. I grow dizzy; even my senses are on the verge of throwing up. I...I can't keep...

...

...

–

–

–

In my eagerness to pry myself from the situation, I hurry down toward Saturn. A hand snatches my arm. It's Dad—

Wait. What? How did I get back here? He isn't crying anymore; he looks angry more than anything. He gently lets go of my arm and reins it to his side.

"Don't go anywhere without me, Son, not out here. It's dangerous!"

What the shit? Saturn? I *was* somewhere. I was falling through Saturn, and then...I remember darkness...and I was here. Wait a minute. The manual Dad gave me said I could manipulate time.

"Dad, what the hell is going on? How did I get here?"

"What do you mean?" He seems somewhat startled by my question. "You don't remember? We flew here from the Moon."

"Yeah, I remember that part, but I was falling through Saturn and got lost, and I closed my eyes and...suddenly I'm back here."

Dad strokes his unkempt chin. "I see. Did you...want to come back here?"

"I think I did." I irk.

"Then you had your first time-jump! Congratulations, buddy!"

"What happened? Where did I end up?"

"You tried to pass through the gas all the way, but it's more than gas. You hit the layer of metallic hydrogen. I tracked your heartbeat—easy to sense since we're the only ones out here. I followed it for a few years, and there you were, just floating there, naked and alone. If you'd gone any farther, I don't know if I could have found you." Dad's words are fearful and weak. He floats over and gives me a great big hug. If I needed to breathe, I wouldn't be able to. He finally lets go and calms down. "Right, where to next?" Adjusting himself, he gives a couple of manly grunts to show me he's tough.

"Uranus?" I suggest hesitantly.

Dad scrunches his facial features together, trying to contain his laughter, and his eyeballs freeze over from the suppressed tears of joy. I sigh and head toward the next planet.

We're flying in silence through the darkness, and the farther we venture toward the outer rim of the system, the darker it gets. Now, only a dim light remains as we meager deities drift through the circular abacus that holds our home, carefully keeping it locked in the temporary dance of night and day.

We arrive at a cluster of celestial bodies, at the center of which we spy the ringed turquoise marble that is Uranus. It's covered by a single, bright shade of greenish-blue. Even though the planet is surrounded by massive moons, its atmosphere is a lonely one, as if the thin rings are there to keep the moons at bay. Its smooth, glassy finish bounces the minute amount of light it receives back to our eyes. Innocently, it spins on for us, a god's unfinished project, blank but not uninteresting. There is humility to this swollen, pale-blue sphere that stares like the featureless face of a drowning man. I look over to Dad, who is waiting for me to finish ogling the blue world, his body framed by the decrepit gray of Titania—Uranus's largest moon. Dad's mood has shifted; his patience has all but disappeared. His arms are even folded, and he is tapping his foot against nothing. He turns to me as if he felt me looking at him. That's his cue to move on.

"Come on. Evidently, it's dangerous to let you dawdle," he says, drifting past me and glowering into the darkness. Noiselessly, he flies off. I follow and see him in the distance. Ahead of him lies a small field of asteroids.

"Dad?" I shout through space. "Shouldn't we be going over this asteroid belt like we did the first time?" A small ball of white light shoots from his hand, and the closest asteroid explodes into smaller pieces. He sends a rapid fire of light bolts, decimating the rest of the large, brown space rocks into pieces until they resemble harmless pebbles scattered on a black beach.

I speed to his side. "Are you all right?"

He smiles. "Yeah. I made the asteroids myself—felt like shooting something. It helps me relieve stress. What can I say? My hobbies are unusual. Sometimes I take my frustrations out on bits of space rubble. Other times, I simply go for a run...on the sun."

I laugh as if he is joking, but I guess by this point I look a little foolish.

"So, were they rockets you were firing out of your hands? Or lasers or…?" I wait for him to interrupt me.

"I call them brightbolts. They're fun to make and easy to control. What you do is you conjure up a handful of visible heat energy, and then you form a shell of solid light around it, send it to where you want it to go, and boom!"

"The asteroids were destroyed, but there was no *boom*," I point out.

"Ah, no. Not up here." He twirls his hand in a circle. "Vacuum… no *boom*, but still…*fun*. You try!" he says in a much more pleasant tone of voice. He stretches out his arms, and a large boulder forms far ahead of us.

I hold out my hands, cupped. A dim light flickers in my palms. It feels extra warm in the icy cold of space. My arms shake under the weight of the conjured energy as I move the light into my right hand and curve my left over it. A small, bright orb now covers the energy, glowing a luminous white. I look over to the asteroid Dad made for me.

"NOW!" he yells, and I stretch my arm, hurling the bolt of energy, which disappears in midair.

Confused, I look to Dad, who seems totally relaxed. "Did I do something wrong?"

He points to the rock, and it quietly shatters into a million pieces. "BOOOOOOM!" he cheers loudly and holds out his hand. I give him five and then shoot more bolts at the smaller rock fragments, turning them into a weak dust. When I stop shooting, I'm grinning.

"Atta boy, Daniel." Dad pats me on the back as a soundless, sonic boom propels him back into motion faster than the speed of tachyons.

I follow once more, and we speed toward Neptune. Dad dips his body, finding a low path through the rings and under the planet. He spins around so he is flying backward, looking up at Neptune, and I do the same. It's so weird; it feels like going backward on a train. My stomach rumbles from the orientation, but that won't make me turn away from the beautiful sight. Neptune launches over us like a giant, rotund tidal wave crashing over a glass ceiling. It can't touch us, but it still takes bravery to withstand its visual force. It flies overhead and away from us; I wave at it and spin around. In no time at all, Pluto comes into view. We're finally here. Yes, we have made it in record time for Earthlings, but travelling can still zap all of your energy. Strange, it looks different somehow, something is missing…

"Where's Pluto's heart?" I ask Dad, and he chuckles.

"That's Charon, Son. Pluto's moon." He curves up and over the imposter with ferocious speed. As I do the same, another sphere passes above the first: Pluto, the bespeckled, brown beauty, carrying a large heart on its chest as if it is offering us a warm welcome.

Dad stops and faces me, panting like he is out of breath. "So, here it is. What made you want to come here? I don't mean to question you, but there isn't anything here. It's pretty, I'll give you that, but still…was it just the distance?"

We've come a long way, true, but that's not why we're here.

"It's something Sam said a few days ago. You remember Sam, right?" He shakes his head. "The guy who lives with me—tall, a little angry looking?" Still nothing. "Hamster-guy." I add.

His eyes widen, "Oh, the Algerian?" he exclaims happily.

"Yes…Algerian…I…Sam…his name is Sam. Anyway, he has this protective instinct for smaller things, like animals or people.

"Hence the hamster?"

"Hence the hamster. So, the other day, he mentioned Pluto. It was out of the blue, but he thought it was unfair that it doesn't get to be a planet when the other eight do. He sees them as kids in a schoolyard, and the bigger boys won't let Pluto join their gang because it's smaller than they are, like it's being bullied and it's too small to defend itself." I can't believe I'm telling him this. I almost regret making him come all the way out here, but Sam's feelings resonated with me in some strange way.

Dad hovers there, thinking to himself, staring at the dwarf planet ahead of us. "You want to turn it back into a planet?" he asks. "How?"

"I don't know…grow it?" I suggest tentatively.

"And turn it into a target for its gravitational neighbors? That will only hurt it more."

Okay. So that won't work.

"Any other ideas?" he says, tilting his head.

I think for a second, trying to find the logic. "Rid it of its gravitational neighbors? Their existence is the only thing stopping it from being a planet."

"And that's fair? Trading two whole worlds so one can be awarded a promotion?" He looks at me with a small amount of pity. At this point, it is welcome.

"I guess not."

We both grow silent. It's like we've blown a tire in the middle of a road trip.

"Don't take this the wrong way, Daniel, but that's a very, very human problem, not one you should share with Sam. His feelings of powerlessness aren't really your concern—at least, not so much that you make it your mission to stop him feeling such powerlessness by destroying other worlds. Look, there are multiple groups all arguing their own set of rules. They struggle with the same problem as Sam—powerlessness. Again, it's very *human*. Why stop at finding worlds when you can give them structure and ruling? No one knows how the universe operates. Some will try to mold it the way they see fit, but, Son, they don't even know we exist. If we did anything this far away from their perspective, the people in question would never know, just like Pluto. It doesn't care—it *can't* care. Sam does. Humanity does—"

I interrupt him. "You said we're gods. Not human. Whose idea was it to call us gods? Was it yours or Mom's?"

He raises his hand, tracing a line around Pluto's heart. "It was your mother's. I admired her confidence. She convinced me with a single question."

He's still tracing, but he's grown quiet.

"Which was?" I press.

He stops and turns back to me "If they are human and we aren't, why should they get to tell us what we are?"

His answer doesn't exactly fix my problem. I feel a melancholia wash over me. The way he speaks about Mom, she sounds like a completely different person to the mom I knew.

I feel Dad's eyes on me. He clears his throat. "So, no, you don't get to make Pluto a planet. However, I do have something else to show you." He puts the backs of his hands together and in one motion separates them as far as his arms can go. Then he stands, shaped like a crucifix in front of the bright, blaring hole that has opened up. A *crack* in space. Inside, a cascading spectrum of colors rises and falls, drifts left and right, moves backward, toward, across from and within itself.

"Beautiful!" I say, gulping my wonder back down my throat. My dry mouth produces echoes of what would usually be words. I ask, still gazing into the hole, "Dad, what are we looking at?"

He answers with a struggling smile.

"The interstice of everything, memory made material, my greatest creation."

The words hit me like hailstones. I'm unable to look away from the mesmerizing whirlpool of color. All I can do is emit a small whisper, hoping for Dad's response. "What is it called?"

He stares into it, as do I, with a contemplative awe, the colors dancing in his pupils.

"Forever."

Chapter 8

U GH. I haven't even opened my eyes yet. When Dad showed me *Forever*, I suddenly became dizzy. He assured me it was natural. I didn't faint or anything, but I needed to get back to Earth. So, here I am: back home in my bed, nursing the worst hangover of my apparently eternal life. My memories are surreal. Simply looking at Forever was like being a cat in a laser-light show; every new color and shade snatches your instincts. It's difficult to focus on anything when a million more lights are vying for attention. Dad's formal explanation was brief; all I know is that he created it and it is a memorial. Could that be literal, like some kind of shrine perhaps? It isn't like any shrine I've ever seen before—not a single incense candle in sight. Then again, I don't know *what* I was looking at. I could barely keep my eyes from rolling back into my head. It was beautiful, but also kinda terrifying.

Shielding my face from the harsh morning light, I peek at my bedroom window, discovering it's been shut all night, and the heat isn't helping me find any reprieve. I slide up to my headboard like I'm trying to escape my grave. The only thing I hear is the thumping of my pulse. The last time I saw Dad, he'd teleported me back to my doorstep, and when I turned around to thank him, he'd disappeared. What time is it now?

Oh, my clock lies face down on my floor. I must have knocked it off when I collapsed into bed. I scoop up the clock and see that it's— shit, it's 8:32 a.m.! Goddammit, I'm going to be late.

I attempt to wriggle out of my bed, only to flop back down onto the covers. It takes all my energy to drag my body over to the edge of my mattress and swing my legs around. I lower my feet to the floor, wobbling as I get a feel for the warm, scratchy carpet below. I put pressure onto my toes, and without warning, I tumble faster than I fell on the Moon. I barely lift my hands in time to shield my face from the impact. Rolling onto my back, I hold out my hand to my phone. Thankfully, it jumps its way into my palm.

I dial Dad's number. A voice comes over the phone.

"Hello?"

"Oh...sorry, Wallace. I didn't mean to call you."

"Hey, how long has it bee—"

I cut him off and dial Dad's actual number.

"Hello, Daniel. Is everything okay?" Dad answers with the energy of a first-grader.

"I can't walk, Dad!"

After a small pause, he lets out a huge laugh. *"Ha-hold on. Can you move your legs at all?"*

I lift my right leg; it barely makes it a few inches off the ground.

"A little," I say, struggling.

"Then, yes, I was right to laugh! It's fine, Daniel. It's just your body getting used to your powers. We did travel to almost ten worlds yesterday. If you think your body hurts after a long walk through the city, imagine how much of an effect fluctuating gravity levels have on your muscles! Don't worry. You'll be fine in an hour or so. You should get more exercise, or at least mold your muscles more. I get instantly beautiful in a couple of seconds. No pain, all gain. All right, Son, I gotta go—oh, wait! After work, we'll go back up and take a look at Forever, what do you say?"

"Okay. Thanks, Dad."

"And remember to say hi to your Ana for me."

The phone clicks dead. *Oh, no! Ana!* I ran out on her yesterday without a word!

Hoisting myself up from the floor, I flop backward onto my bed, not sure what to do for the best. I can't fly in a closed public space, or not without Dad's help, and he's clearly busy. I have no choice; I have to call Martin's cell directly. I get up out of bed, successfully propping myself up like a weeping willow, swaying about in the breeze of my own bullshit.

"Hello?" Martin answers with a low and broken whisper.

"Hi, Martin," I say, groggy and uncomfortable.

"Dan! Where did you go, yesterday? You were seen early on, and then you had disappeared."

"Yeah…about that. I-I've come down with something…Something bad. Since yesterday. I had to leave early. I don't know what it is—"

"You can't just take the day off whenever you need to, Daniel." His tone grows stern, and he has a point, but *it was the Moon!* If only I could tell him. I rub my eyes with my free hand. Sandy flakes fall out of them onto my fingers, and I almost lose my footing again but stop myself. That was close…

Okay. This next part will not be without embarrassment. I can't even keep my eyes open for this.

"I— Sir, there's shit everywhere."

The other end of the line goes silent for a second.

"Hamster?" he asks.

"Unfortunately not." I sigh.

"O…kay, Dan. Say no more. For the love of God, say no more! Just get whatever you ate out of your system and get back in as soon as you can, okay?"

"Can you see if Ana can cover for me?"

"She isn't here either. We're short-staffed today. She's at the hospital. You were with them when her mom collapsed, right? Is she going to be okay?"

"I don't know what I can even say about it. We shouldn't really be discussing it at all. Isn't there a privacy rule against this?"

"You're right. I…I need everyone back here as soon as possible, okay? We've seen a large dip in activity lately—mainly in our department—and I've been summoned downstairs to 'explain things' to management. Can I count on you to get your shit together, both literally and figuratively?"

"Yes, sir, and sorry—again and thank yo—" The phone buzzes that high-pitched tone, telling me he has already cut the call. I need a shower. I smell like...well, nothing, but still. I obviously don't feel right. Hold on...I wonder what happens if I...I think clean thoughts. From nowhere, a warm, white light surrounds my body for a second, then fades, leaving my skin with a thin layer of moisture, which quickly evaporates. I run my hand through my hair and sniff. It smells fruity and refreshing. I sniff under my arms and...it worked! I'm clean! The yellow crap has even disappeared from my eyes, and I look better than I have for a while. Awesome! I take a step forward... and collapse again.

With a sigh, I resort to levitation and hold out my arms to receive my clothes, which fly out of the closet and onto my body—dark jeans and a blinding-white T-shirt. Dingy as my room is, it looks unusually bright outside, so I beckon my D-frame sunglasses, which zip out of the drawer and snap right onto my face. With that, I can get going. I teleport out of my room, then out of the house and into the sky. In a flash of potent energy, I soar toward Gesond Hospital, where Ana should be, and teleport into the main waiting room, landing with a thud on the same seat as when I was last here, up against the gray wall. The room isn't as empty this time, and everyone looks up from their phones in confusion.

"What?" I say. "My butt itches!" Their confusion turns to disgust as they go back to their phones. Conversely, Ana stands up in shock at the sight of me. I wave her over because I can't walk.

"What are you doing here?" she asks with artificially energized concern. I take off my sunglasses, showing my tired, bloodshot eyes. I guess it's story time.

"Despite how I look, I'm only a little...hangover...hungover, sorry. I was out all night with Dad—enough for me to want to skip work. Nebrezza wasn't happy. He told me you were skipping too, but 'due to your *circumstance*,' he understood why. I was worried about you and your mom, so I came to keep you company."

She lets down her guard, releasing an exhausted smile, and collapses onto the chair next to mine. Her head comes to rest against my shoulder as she lets out a massive sigh.

"That's sweet," she whispers, closing her eyes.

"Have erm...have you been sleeping?"

"Of course I haven't." Ana yawns right on my question's cue, and tears flow down her cheeks. I panic until I see that it's only a reaction to her yawn...and now I really want to yawn...it's gone.

"We're different people, me and Mom." Her warm words heat my hoodie. "She can cope. If I was the one in the hospital bed, she would be sleeping just fine. We're not the same. My dad...that's not who I mean...he was always the nervous wreck, depressed and sullen, but at the end, even he found a way to help someone. Even with his fear of every living creature, he still went to war. He said he was going to fight for *me*. He told me it was okay to keep away from the chaos. And so, I was left behind to tend to the war machines...you know them? I know you...I love you...war machines..."

Her breathing becomes slower and heavier, and when I look at her, she's fallen asleep on my shoulder. Cupping her head with my hands, I ease her down onto the chair. Her soft, unwashed hair unfurls like the red rays of evening sunlight. I wipe my hands on my jeans and step away from my seat, leaning against the wall for balance. My legs shake with the pressure, lowering me into a squat against my will, and I remember Sam asking for the chaise longue a few days ago.

I replay the conversation, ignoring his words and focusing on his actions. He waved his hands like he was controlling a puppet. If he could get me to do his bidding, then I can get my body to do what I want now. I envision strings affixed to my legs, arms, and shoulders, lift my hand from the wall and snap my fingers. The energy in the room evaporates, showing me exactly what I wanted to see: a still room, sound and motion-free. Time has stopped for every human in the hospital, thankfully. I need the space if I am going to work.

I adjust the structure of the walls and ceilings that entomb me, altering their refractive properties to those of water. The walls become windows that only I can see through. I spy Lillith above, lying still on the second floor, amid a row of other patients laid flat-out in their clinical cots. I take hold of my exhausted body and float upward. Then I phase through the surprisingly dry water-walls like a ghost and drift over to Lillith's bedside. I take her cold hand. She's practically skeletal; the orange hue has disappeared from her skin. Gently, I lay my other hand on top of hers and close my eyes.

I picture the pain Lilith would have experienced during the accident. I see a red fog among shadow. It's too abstract; I need a shape. I concentrate, and the fog clumps together into a tiny, red spiral shining dimly. No, it's not enough. As much as I know Ana, Lillith is a stranger. Maybe if I change subjects. I picture Ana's pain in my mind's eye. Suddenly, the spiral shivers, and from its top sprouts a red tree, its branches covered with red leaves. I may not know Lillith, but I know Ana. I know how she thinks, how she feels. And if Dad could drop my dopamine levels, then surely, through Ana, I can reverse-engineer my way into Lilith's mind.

The tree that sits in the abyss begins to split from the center. The leaves and branches bloat and connect together, changing their form from a broad-leaved neon tree into a comprehensible red scan of Lillith's brain. The red hues shrink, burying themselves in the now-forming blues and purples of Lillith's vegetative state. In the mindscape I've built, I safely launch a figurative bolt of electricity, which lightly strikes the flickering brain scan. A flash of greens and yellows are infused into her brain, only to dim after a second of activity. The image fades.

I concentrate harder, picturing Lillith's sleeping face. I then picture Ana's face next to it. Slowly, I move Ana's familiar visage over Lillith's, covering it like a mask. It turns transparent, revealing an abstract skull, which soon fades from sight, leaving only the image of Lillith's brain again, dormant and cold in the shadowy mindscape. Let's break philosophy, shall we? I strike it with a larger bolt of imaginary energy, and it fires up like a combustion-engine, with streaks of greens, yellows, and reds dancing around inside the brain image, which now glows ferociously in my mind's eye.

Synapses fire, thoughts process, and a loud gasp of air fills the room around me. I open my eyes to see Lillith sitting up in her bed, her eyes open almost as wide as her mouth, staring up at the tiled ceiling. She stays like this, inactive and unable to move due to her being frozen in time like everyone else in the hospital. I teleport out of the bedside chair and back down to the waiting room, where I scoop the still-sleeping Ana into my arms and teleport her to her mother's side. Laying her on the chair I have just vacated, I teleport up and out of the hospital.

Above the rooftop, I hover, looking through the walls at the scene I have set up. I snap my fingers again, and time instantly restarts. Ana wakes up, peering around, lost in such a familiar place, and finally takes notice of Lillith, alert and staring. A second of thought will pass through Ana's mind; she'll compute the situation, ease into a change of environment. *Is this a dream?* she'll wonder—no, wait. She leaves no pause for confusion. Ana leaps out of the chair and puts her hands on her mother's face, trying to help her focus. Lillith peers around the room with vacant eyes. Ana grabs her attention, and with a struggle, she mouths something I can't hear. Tears begin to stream from Ana's eyes—joyful tears. She stands up and calls for someone. A lone nurse races over to tend to Lillith, and Ana spins around, a smile on her face. It's as if she is looking for me, to tell me the good news. However, I can't share in this moment with Ana or Lillith; it belongs only to them. I turn around and fly up through the sky, into the darkness of space. I have needs of my own, answers that I seek. And in order to get that information, I must have business with Forever.

It's still there, the celestial tear in the fabric of space: *Forever.* It calls to me, and in response, I speed toward it. The seams of the crack shine as brilliantly as they did before, as if every color inside the hole has merged to form the most startling shade. Suddenly, I feel a familiar presence behind me.

"I knew you'd be back before your day was out. It's intoxicating, isn't it?" Dad says, smiling at me.

"I'm not sure that's the word I'd use. More like, *overpowering*," I say, candidly, still uneasy about all of this.

"You'll get used to it. Like riding a bike or walking the sun, all it takes is the courage to know you can do whatever you set your heart on doing."

I smile, reassured. An excitement begins to build within me. "You walk on the sun?"

"Well, I *jog* on the sun. I don't need the exercise, but it's a good way to relax. It provides thinking room. Just you and a path of bubbling-hot, gassy plasma for company. No distractions, no burdens, just movement."

"I'll have to try that sometime."

"Try Forever first," Dad suggests encouragingly.

"I will, but before I so willingly give myself to this...thing, I obviously need to ask—what is 'Forever,' and where did it come from?" I'd normally avoid such a blatant question. However, Dad relishes being the informer, so I'll call it a gift to him.

He puts his hand on my shoulder and moves next to me. "Forever is the result of a little experiment of ours—mine and your mother's, I mean. When you can do as much as we can, you get a little curious as to how far you can go. One day...or night—yes, I think it was night—we took two hydrogen atoms and broke them down into their subatomic nuclei. We broke the nuclei down, and after some searching, we found the protons and neutrons that make up the nucleus. So, we broke those down into what would be called quarks and gluons. If quarks are the bricks of the nuclei, gluons are the mortar. We only needed the quarks."

"...Okay," I say, giving him time to breathe between his monologues.

"Normally," he continues, "quarks only exist within protons and neutrons. They are naturally contained within those particles and can't be separated in real time. However, we, like you, had the ability to control time. So, we stopped it, and there they were.

Quarks. Subatomic particles preformed, isolated from their little particle cages."

"...Okay," I say again.

"So, once they were free, albeit invisible to our sight, we could alter properties of the particles in which the quarks resided. This allowed us to make them visible to us by force. The next step was the scary one—breaking down the quarks. And it looked as if we were successful. Together, we managed to do something that shouldn't have been possible, but then, as soon as the one part became two, something else happened. Time was taken out of our control. It restarted itself as we split the quarks, almost like what was beneath had taken charge. And in an instant, without a sound, Forever was formed—a gateway between dimensions, a crack in the fabric of space, which can be moved and used.

"That's the best I've got, Son. Anyone who can interact with Forever can see every second they've lived. The colors are a collage of their entire being. I'm sorry for that mouthful, but I couldn't help myself. I'm such a proud papa!"

I take his answer in. Throwing it over in my mind a few times isn't necessary, as immediately, one thing sticks out as a problem to me.

"So, if you can only look at your memories, how do you control where you go? How do you actually get to the memory physically without getting lost in a maze of the constant flow of time? Surely it has to be on a whim?"

He puts his hand to his chin. He's clearly wondering whether I am already out of my depth before he answers. "Well, every action is on a whim. Time is a dimension—we already travel through it. Humans can only travel forward, but we can travel backward through time. We just have to separate ourselves from the forward-flowing stream, and this is only possible by shaping it. Time is both relative to you *and* the forward flow, so you take advantage of your own relative flow, and you make it so your body and mind travel forward *through* the backward. That's what Forever allows, it being a plane of existence so traversable that time has no choice but to play by its rules, as time exists on all planes. You can take a journey in your timeline and enter the time-space of the Peach Epoch, where the universe was condensed to the size of the aforementioned fruit, and you exist both in that time and in your own. Therefore you're able to perceive the universe the same way you do now, like you're in your own tailored *time-suit*."

"You could have told me this in the document you gave me," I say, folding my arms. In turn, Dad puts his hands together like an excited realtor.

"Ah, but I wanted to see your face when you found out organically. Okay! Daniel!" He's excited now. "The floor is yours, figuratively speaking. All you have to do is look inside Forever, find the memory you want to watch, and there's your evening's entertainment, figuratively speaking. But beware, Son. It can be emotional. You don't need to worry, though. I'll be back when you need me." He says this as he disappears behind a wave.

I turn back to face Forever, which opens out to me like a diamond with the brightest light in the universe shining through it. Carefully, I peer inside the blinding gateway and am hit with a violent pushing force. It takes all of my strength to keep myself from flowing backward into the darkness of space. I clench my eyes closed, bracing. After a minute, Forever stops exerting the force, allowing my mind the necessary freedom to occupy its space. As I get closer to the whirling whiteness, I have a flashback of myself as a child. I'm sitting in front of the TV in our living room back at our old place in Jersey City, and I'm doing that stupid thing kids do—moving my bare eye closer and closer toward the flashing TV screen in front of me. My forehead touches the glass, and with bare, dilating pupils, I see the clear images that were once discernible break down into the pixels that make them. This is how Forever seems to operate: the closer you get, the more the colors are broken down into image tiles made up of every shade and shadow.

The images speed in all directions, existing in a perpetual state of chaos. I have to concentrate on what I want to see to corral the desired memory into my focus. I think of my mother, smiling contently, a dear target. Her face appears in front of me only to be shattered into splinters by a falling mortar shell. My view speeds up…the side of a familiar high-rise of New York…the roof of the center structure explodes violently in a flash of fire, and I black out.

After a while of nothing, my eardrums begin to vibrate with the distant sounds of a chaotic scene: the screeching of tires, the striking of ballistic ordinance, and the screaming of helpless people. Desaturated sunlight shines above me. I'm back in New York, that same high-rise looming over me, untouched. It's packed. Crowds of bustling pedestrians flow in and out of the city like a river made from personality and perfume. Each and every person here wears the same wonderless look, but I'm here for something long sought-after: a job interview for a staff position with Adno Architecture. It was a misread vacancy, but I guess this was fate or something, as Dad helped me put my presentation together and taught me the basics of arcades, braces, and colonialism. "Start small and grow with time, like a tree," he said.

The meeting starts off surprisingly strong, considering the situation, but toward the end I'm bouncing around questions as if I'm giving my thoughts on a book I forgot to read in elementary school. I lean on subjectivity long enough, but I'm choking. The interviewer says nothing, but his darting eyes are enough, and I practically jump down the steps and onto the streets of east Harlem. Bloomberg finished what Robert Moses started; the place is now a stark, brutalist collection of shapes, something only a control freak would find whimsy in. As my feet connect with the pavement, strange noises make themselves known, and loud crackling echoes fill the daytime air. Suddenly, a huge line of people pushes me back up into the building.

"Hey, I've just left…" I say to the man in front, whose hands line my back.

"Get to the roof!" he shouts at me, panicked. This is enhanced by the force with which the crowd behind shoves, bottlenecking me back into the building. I unwillingly lead the stream of people up the stairs like the head of a very confused mother duck.

As I'm pushed through the fire escape doors to the roof, the line breaks, and some of the people behind loop their way ahead of where I stumble. After catching my breath, I peer over the shoulder of the dark-haired woman in front of me. There's a thick trail of smoke rising from the upper half of the distant Empire Building. My heart rumbles violently. *An accident or an attack?* I hold out my cell phone, activate the camera, and with a pinch of my fingers, I zoom in to the scene ahead. The building grows on my screen, after which a blurry explosion bursts out of the lower side of the building. This is no accident. Three more explosions follow, and the most iconic building in the whole city comes crumbling down, filling the whole of midtown with an ashy river of smog.

As we watch on in horror, swift shadows pass over our heads, the dark spots flying toward the lower parts of the city. They look like jets, but they aren't making any noise. More explosions follow; the layered crown at the top of the Chrysler Building shatters when a missile fired from one of the jets strikes it perfectly, decapitating the building. Debris rains down from the now-splintered spire, an eruption of screams sound from the streets below, then more bangs rumble from the city without a break.

This time, the missiles miss the buildings and hit the streets. Flashes of fire rip up the sidewalk and the pedestrians below, who are hurtled cruelly through the air like stones in a hurricane. No one within earshot can say any more than a couple of spaced-out expletives to contain themselves. The curses grow louder as the silent jets turn and come toward us. Before we can know what's going to happen, the dark-haired woman turns and pushes me down onto my back, and my phone smashes next to my head.

"GET DOWN!" someone screams a split second before a loud crash sends up a blast of smoke that engulfs her. Red bricks fly across the roof, pelting the crowd above me down to my level. Instinctively, I jump up in fear and scramble to the fire exit, not thinking about who is under my feet. A high-pitched whooshing joins the screams that ring in my ears. I push through the door and run; the door blows off its hinges as another missile strikes the roof. The force of the blast sends me tumbling down the stairs, alone.

As I look up, I realize I'm on the beach in Greece, back in the arms of the Valkyrie. I snap out of the memory and I'm back in silent space, staring at Forever. Dad quietly appears next to me.

"It's okay, Son," he says reassuringly. "You're doing okay. Just try to keep the memories separate."

Yesterday's lunch climbs its way up my throat, and I slap myself in the face and lean back into Forever, looking closer at the dancing colors. I try to focus, separate the memories as Dad said. I think of my mother, her smiling face. She starts to sing, and I feel a hot wave of embarrassment rise up to my head. After a dizzying swirl of abstract shades, I see a large, carefully decorated sheet cake in front of me, sixteen bright candles flickering on its face—*my* face to be exact. A fuzzy old picture of five-year-old me with a cross-eyed, gap-toothed grin covers the cake.

I recognize this memory now. It's the morning of my sixteenth birthday, and Mom and Dad are singing merrily. Their harmonies embarrass me, but it will be worth it when I get my money. I wave my hand around, signaling them to pick up the pace. Dad gets louder in response, tapping Mom in the side with his elbow. Her laugh overtakes her surprisingly professional melody. Exuberant, Dad comes around the table and hands me an envelope. Before I rip it open, Mom plants a large kiss on my cheek as my grandma, who sits across the table from me, snaps a picture with her new digital camera. I never knew my grandpa, nor would I know my grandma for many years more.

Disgusted, I swipe the moisture from my cheek and rip into the envelope viciously, searching for the cash inside. The envelope is empty. No card, no money. This is bullshit! I shake the envelope, letting loose a small photo caught in one of the folds. Curious, I dump it out onto the table, where it lands face up, literally. It's a photo of a woman's face. Blond hair and brown eyes—a pairing which, now that I think about it, I don't recall ever seeing on anyone before. No, wait, I have. It's L.Cpl. Albrier, the woman who saved me in my dream.

Confused, I look up from the table to see that I'm back on the beach in Greece, only there is no war. There isn't anything but the sand and sea. I stand up from the wooden chair I have apparently been sitting on, step around the empty breakfast table and slowly head toward the sea. I'm back to my old self, no longer sixteen and angry. I hear a calming rendition of "The Birthday Song," source unknown, but the music comes from all directions. The sand crunches under my feet; the guarantee of friction comes and goes with every step. The gray, lifeless ocean waves spreading foam over the dull, stoneless beach.

All of a sudden, two predator drones fly over my head at an alarming closeness. I jump into the sand, covering my head with my hands. After a second, I peer back up; they weren't drones, after all, but a pair of seagulls. They dance around the muted sky in perfect harmony. The brighter of the two birds flies down toward the beach and lands on the sand, picking up chunks of grit in its beak, searching for a living bite to eat. The second gull follows, landing behind the first. It stamps its little webbed feet, causing a long, wiggling worm to burrow its way out of the sand. The first seagull—I think it's a female—picks up the worm and drops it in front of the male, who pecks wildly at it.

Suddenly, they both stop and turn, staring at me with wide, frightened eyes. The first bird flies up into the sky; the male follows it excitedly. The female turns around and starts to peck at the male, pricking feathers away from it in a furious rage. The male strikes back, pecking hard at the female's wings, and they both fall into the murky sea. As they land, a large wave forms and makes its way toward me. I turn to run but have nowhere to run to on the open beach. "The Birthday Song" is getting louder, deeper. It turns from a pleasant melody into an unintelligible hum of horror. The pallid wave smacks me, throwing me to the ground, soaking wet and shivering.

When I look back, the tide is pulling out, farther and farther away from the beach, and above the beachhead hovers The Valkyrie, waving its arms like a conductor, transforming the sea into its symphony. More waves zoom toward me, dashing me against the sand. My mother's murderer hovers there, playing with the waves as if it hasn't even noticed me. I hear a giant crash behind me as a furious explosion rings off. The shifting sand freezes at its greatest possible height into a grainy pillar. I look past it and see the ref center from my dream. It's on the exact opposite side of the beach. That must mean…

I turn around and notice directly behind me, a Chinese soldier stands, frozen, where he wasn't standing before, a lingering muzzle flash lighting his fearful snarl as he fires. The shells his weapon is dispensing are not moving nor is the battle scene around him. It's only me and the Valkyrie, who is still hovering over the sea, swishing his hands around without a care. The sea, however, has stopped obeying his commands. I turn and skirt the sandy explosion, but as I pass it, the sand obelisk bursts open, knocking me down painfully to the ground. In an effort to save myself from further shocks, I jump to my feet. Another explosion goes off in front of my face. I instinctively raise my hands to shield myself.

There is no impact. Like the first explosion, it seems as though time is frozen until I make my move. I gulp and ready my legs for a long-haul run down to the ref center through a field of carnage and debris that will likely start up as soon as I move. And that's exactly what happens. Small pockets of sand jump up around me, reacting to the mortar shells being fired from the beach-landing soldier. I serpentine, avoiding every bullet and miniature sandstorm that comes my way. The noise of war has dampened the celebratory singing from before. I put the palms of my shaking hands over my ears, and the sound becomes a muffled mess. I pick up the pace, sprinting frightfully across the battlefield.

The rocks that Albrier and I used for cover in my dream are no longer there; they all must have taken shelter inside the building. I swing my arm like I'm swiping at the PLC unit with an imaginary sword. In its place flies a violent gust of wind. All the sand from the beach is ripped up behind me like a flowing cape that irons itself out into a thick layer, separating me from the bullets. I make a fist and feel the molecules of every grain smash together, creating a solid wall of stone. The wall takes the impact of the bullets, but it quickly crumbles with every hit. I race forward, almost at the "safe zone." My steps turn into a jump, which sends me flying through the ref center window and into the building. I tumble into the back wall and crash to a halt on the floor. Dazed, I look up to see several muzzles from guns held by a very confused American Marine troop, and there's Albrier. She looks as confused to see me as the rest of the 32 Pantheon regiment. I hold my hands up in surrender.

"Don't shoot?" I ask with a cheeky look of fright plastered on my face.

Albrier lowers her weapon and holds out her hand. I reach for it and am plunged into darkness. I spin around, looking for a sign of life, but there is nothing but the slight glow of stars. I am back in space, back behind Forever, back in the present. I know what I have to do now. I know what I want.

Chapter 9

FOREVER pulses vividly in front of me. Inky shadows caress my body while the white of my T-shirt bounces the light back to its source. The odor of burned steak skims the walls of my nostrils. The smell of space isn't exactly that of overcooked foodstuffs, but it's the only comparison we *astronauts* have to work with. Accompanying this aroma is a peaceful nothing that helps hold my eardrums still. I look down at the small hairs on my forearms, which hover charmingly above my skin. In fact, all my hair is aloft; even my eyebrows are spiking slightly. I am in the company of nothing but this crystalline crack in space, and that is only a part of the plan I've laid out in my head.

I leave Forever where it is and zoom off in the direction Dad went. I close my eyes and send psychic feelers out into the galaxy, hoping to find a small echo of Dad's heartbeat. After a few seconds, I find him; he is on Titan—one of Saturn's moons. At *whatever times the speed of light*, I make my way to him, then speed up, setting my pace faster than that of a neutrino. If there was any life on the closest moon to me, then I'd resemble a shooting star. The thought of this soothes me greatly. Slowly, my body drums out a vibrant light as I soar through the vacuum of space. I'm lighting my own path like a mobile nightlight—a beacon to a galaxy that is ultimately indifferent to my presence.

On my way to Dad, I spot a large field of asteroids like the one we saw when we first came out here. They're inviting targets for me to test my arm. I pick up speed, and with a mighty fist, I strike one of the gigantic space rocks. It zooms through the lack-of-air and far away, striking one of its distant neighbors like a prodigious pinball. The impact reverberates throughout the mass of asteroids, breaking the boulders to pieces and hitting the next row over. It's like that ball-and-string toy you see on an executive's desk—a Newton's cradle—except it's completely soundless and only a god can play with it. The asteroids don't actually stop moving; there is no friction to keep them together, no strings tying them to one another, so I start blasting. Sizzling streaks of energy leave my hands as I send heat wrapped in hard light in the direction of every one of the boulders, splintering the asteroid field into a fine space dust. Dad's right. That was satisfying. I turn back around and launch myself upward; one of the best things about flying is that I can turn my thrust off and still soar through the void.

Reaching Saturn, I'm overcome by a distinctive, fearful feeling at the sight of the ringed colossus. As my eyes focus against the shocking impact of Saturnal light, I notice a strange, cloudlike mist pulsating from the inner-most layer of Saturn's rings. They're not pieces of floating ice but an enveloping, circular cloud that's recently opened up to shower the beige gas giant with a cool but violent rainstorm. Dad's heartbeat has grown louder; I'm almost there. I put my arms to my sides, increasing my flight speed silently. I slice through the barely lit boundaries of space between planet and moon. As I move farther in, I spot Titan in all its golden glory, taking in its view with literal bated breath. Following the beat of Dad's halcyon heart, I thread down past the southern half of the equator and through the atmospheric ring, taking the slight heat of the entry fires. The flames dissipate, revealing a hazy blanket of orange clouds, which swiftly part as if to welcome me into their world.

I thunder down and crash-land on a jagged bed of golden ice. Giant shards scatter around me, propelling a dense fog of snow into the air without disruption. This—the heat of my flight energy combined with the splintering water ice around me—causes spontaneous shoots of stalagmites to form, creating a clear, cold crown in the center of which I stand, unshaken by the rough impact of my landing. I hop out of my icy playpen and see a small figure walking back and forth a short distance from my landing zone: it's Dad. He is slowly moving large, uneven balls of ice around the ground. He doesn't seem to have heard my landing; maybe the snow muffled the sound.

For the first time in days, I shiver from the cold; it's warmer up in space than it is down here. I raise my body temperature to the highest level it has been since my travels began. Considering the gravity of this moon is weaker than that of Earth's moon, I'll have to adjust my footwear. I concentrate on my lightweight, civilian shoes, and after a second, the density of my rubber soles increases from their original $0.11g/cm^3$ to that of iron, which is $7.75g$ higher per cubic centimeter. This makes a dramatic difference, weighing my feet down nicely. No more face-planting for me!

I take my first actual step on Titan. A sizzle sounds from underfoot. My raised heat melts the ice beneath me, but I'd rather not risk the structural integrity of a piece of land I've only just arrived at. Instead, I lower my thermostat and open out my arms. Suddenly, an arresting light surrounds me, weaving a fresh new layer onto my person. My sports coat flows out from the light, rolling down from my shoulders to my butt. The coat buttons itself up with a mechanical precision...except for the button at the top, which goes in the hole below. I fiddle with the collar, exchanging the two top buttons, glad that no one was around to catch my blunder. With a long sigh, I flip the collars of my newly formed sports coat upward and slowly make my way toward Dad.

The smooth, glittering orange snow crunches underneath my feet as I traverse the rolling slopes. I can't seem to adjust; the whole area is a visual paradox, orange like the warmest desert but colder than the densest tundra. I'll call it the anti-desert if I get naming rights. The closer I get, the clearer it is Dad is working on the bank of an unfrozen chemical lake. The methane that fills it would be gaseous if it was back on Earth, but Titan is so cold that it lives as a gasoline.

My teeth chatter viciously beneath the sound of the arctic winds. I sound like a cymbals monkey on a sugar high. If Dad didn't hear me land, he will certainly hear my molars. Or not, as he keeps rolling his ice balls back and forth. He's making some sort of body for a snowman, and it's not his first. A large, almost featureless one stands to his right. Protruding from its mouth is a crude corncob pipe that looks like it's made out of a shaped shard of ice. In the center stands a smaller, more intricately built snowboy with a face full of icy smiles and a pair of small, wooden arms, one of which reaches out toward the daddy-snowman urgently, only the daddy-snowman has no arms of his own. It looks like the newest boulder Dad is rolling is for the snowmother who, at this point is only made up of a single ice ball to the left of the other two. Dad is lost in thought; his teeth are clenched behind tight lips.

The noise of the wind disappears as I reach the lake.

"Cute," I say, disrupting his Zen.

"So, how was it?" he quizzes, focusing on his project.

"Where did you get the wood from? I don't see any around here."

"I conjured it. Easy-peasy. Are you going to answer me, or do you want to help me finish these up first?" He rolls the unfinished ball of ice away and into the methane lake in front. It sits on the surface for a second before it sinks into the chemicals. Dad straightens up and turns to me. He stretches his arms as if he's going for a hug, but a stretch is all it is. He's waiting for me to answer.

"Forever was...weird."

"That's hardly a surprise. What did you see? Oh, oh, oh, no, let me guess! You saw that time where I fell through the ceiling when I was trying to rearrange the attic?" He says this with an all-knowing smile. I shake my head, and his eyebrow twitches for a nanosecond. He tries to hide his disappointment from me. "Oh, well, that's what I saw. Funny stuff, right?" His laugh tapers off quickly.

"I saw the morning of my sixteenth birthday. You and Mom were with me. I had my cake all candled up and ready. Grandma was there—she took a picture of us with that digital camera we got her. First time I ever saw her use it."

A train of thought hits Dad hard. His mind drifts, and his eyes glaze. He sticks his tongue in his cheek and not in a funny way. It looks painful, as if it's about to burst through.

"Dad...can I ask you a question?" I ask sheepishly. I know I'm bringing back solemn memories for him, but everything is different now.

"Was Grandma like us?" Dad guesses. I nod quietly. A strange tingling flows up my spine—a fear. How far does our story go? The concept of a god has existed as long as instinct, but in the form of human defense mechanisms, tools of power and the effects of illusion.

"If she was," Dad says, obstructing my thought locomotive, "she never told me. I can't imagine her dying if she did have our strength, and yet die is what she did." I sense not sadness, but a seething anger beneath his words.

"It could have skipped a generation?" I theorize.

He shrugs. "If there is someone or something godlike out there that came before the four we know of—the Valkyrie included—then it has kept its presence a secret. So, no, Son, to answer your question. Grandma wasn't like us. She died of natural causes, something we are evidently impervious to." He holds out his hands to the blowing snow.

I don't want to create such a weight for Dad, but I have more I need to know; my plan depends on this talk.

"Can't you bring her back? Or Mom, or anyone we have lost? Is that not something a god can do for himself?"

"No, I wouldn't dare, and neither should you. What's dead is dead, and what is done outlasts godhood. The past is not a playground that provides the hopes and dreams of children. It is final. You can look into Forever, but you cannot touch—"

I interrupt him this time. "So, the iceberg you collected from 1912, from the berg that the Titanic hit...that was a forgery?"

"No, it was inconsequential. A tiny piece taken from a prominent human event. I am trained in the use of Forever. At first, it messed with my powers and sent me to places I didn't want to be. I didn't understand what I was trying to manipulate. Time is a myriad of lines and dashes that flow out endlessly in each direction—up, down, left, right, in, out—shake it all about, right? Lines change to squares, squares to cubes and cubed cubes for each of the measurable dimensions—first, second, third, fourth. Forever seems to be the fifth. Its own line in between these shapes." Dad pauses briefly.

"What's your point?" I ask.

Dad sighs. "Just because Forever is there doesn't mean it needs to be used. Do I want to go back to see if those 'figures of legend' were like us? No, I don't need to. Have you ever seen the real Thor's hammer? The one in all of those interlaced stone carvings? It's a peculiar, tapered shape, wouldn't have been useful as a weapon at all. That's why they sell so well as souvenir pendants for tourists. The artists always illustrated the thing upside down. My guess is that the artists never changed anything. 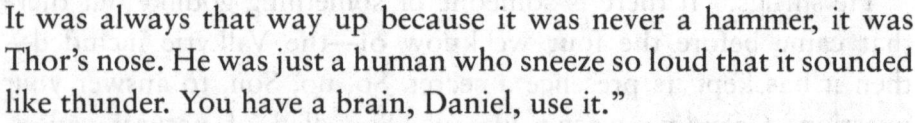 It was always that way up because it was never a hammer, it was Thor's nose. He was just a human who sneeze so loud that it sounded like thunder. You have a brain, Daniel, use it."

As his monologue comes to a close, the world around us seems to grow even quieter than it was, like the entire area has fallen asleep from boredom.

"Lillith is out of her coma," I say to break the silence. Dad's face clouds over as he searches his memory banks for the context of my statement. His eyes widen when he finds something.

"The orange lady?"

I pretend to scratch my forehead to shield the annoyance I have on my face. "Yeah," I say with my tongue between my teeth. "The *orange lady*."

"Well, that's great! How did you find out? Phone call from Ana?"

I see he remembers her.

"No I...kind of brought her out of it myself." With a fizzing crunch, the ice ball family Dad spent so long building shatters into small, see-through smithereens next to us. Dad reaches out to stop them, but it's too late. Their salt-like fragments are blown across the lake in a stream of white wind that dances into the air and out of sight.

"I see," he says, prodding the snow with the nose of his shoe. "You're a lot more like your mother than I thought. That was her talent and hers alone. Once. So this is why you were asking about resurrection. Well, skeletons don't have such a good quality of life."

He looks out across the lake with yearning, as if he wishes to submerge himself below the depths and never come back to this conversation.

"Are...are you mad at me?" I ask.

"I should be. You did take a while to tell me, but I won't be. I'm soft like that. But you need to be more careful. I take it you froze time to prevent yourself from getting caught?"

He wasn't always this soft. He was the rule-maker in our house. Mom was the "stern one," but Dad had the last say. Little did I know that they were putting on a show for me, letting me find my own way to godhood, allowing me to have a normal childhood filled with middle-class delights and happy memories. I wonder why they kept up the façade for so long. They told me the truth about Christmas when I was ten. I cried my heart out when they did—maybe that was an unsuccessful test? Anyway, it doesn't matter now; I was always going to be like them.

Through the frosted windows of my eyes, I notice Dad staring right at me, waiting impatiently for my confirmation. I sniff the air hard to take in nitrogen I've forgotten to breathe. I shake out of my daydream and raise my thumb to him in an attempt to claw trust back, maybe even some admiration.

"Good," he says. "From now on, I recommend you refrain from playing god and stick to being one...in secret."

"I will, sir." I haven't called him that since Mom was around.

"That's my boy," he says happily, rubbing his hands together to break the newly formed skin of ice that has covered them. I look at mine and discover they're the same, frozen from the cold, but with a simple shake, they're released from their icy sleeves. "So, anyway, is that all you wanted to tell me or was there something else?" he asks me with half a smile.

A flash of Albrier's face emerges in my mind. I guess my mission will have to be a black-op.

"I wanted to see what you were doing down here. That's all," I say, feigning nonchalance.

"Oh, no. I won't let you get away that easily. You're only here to avoid that meeting in work. Well, you've been off-planet for about two days, so you're safe for now, but I expect your boss won't be too happy."

A nervous chill shakes me as it travels down my entire spine. "What meeting?"

"Oh, come on! The memo, in your boss's office. I saw it when I visited you. He's weird, you know? Keeps a shabby old service pistol in his top desk drawer. Bottle of Scotch too. Bad combination if you ask me."

"Forget all that. Just…tell me who the meeting is with?"

He paws at his head, knocking the residue of snow from his styled hair. "It's the…erm…Taiwanese tenancy meeting. *The renters meeting, eleven a.m.*"

Now the *chill* has turned to full, horrific frostbite.

"Why didn't he tell me about this?" I ask, spinning in slow, panicky circles in the snow.

"Because your boss is an idiot. Now, Daniel, turn yourself around."

I do what he says only to see that the view of my landing zone has transformed into a wall of fluctuating color.

—

—

—

The colors merged into a blinding white, and for a second I could hear all sorts of random noises, what sounded like a baby crying, the sound of a crashing wave or explosion, the buzzing of a bee and then nothing for a few seconds after.

Now, out of the silence, a loud, distorted force attacks me on all sides. A hard wall of wind has taken hostage of my every sense. I'd have a panic attack if I needed to breathe. The pressure isn't unlike that of the protesting crowds I had to push through earlier in the week—claustrophobic and full of cold air. I spin around hoping to find some stability. The blinding sight of sun and sea becomes clearer as my senses readjust to the picture of the world, and after a few blinks, I see I'm back, way above New York City. I would have been better being left farther down; I'm too small to be detected by anyone monitoring the city's airspace. I shrug a shoulder and attempt to fly away, but I can't. It's like something has hold of me, gripping harshly onto my shoulders like football pads. I look above me. It's Dad. He's lifting me psychically.

"I SAID TO YOU TWO DAYS FROM NOW THAT FOREVER CAN SCREW WITH YOUR POWERS!" he shouts over the noise like a chopper pilot at a nightclub. "I'M GOING TO HAVE TO CHAPERONE YOU FOR A BIT. I DON'T WANT TO TAKE ANY CHANCES! ANYWHO, KNOCK 'EM DEAD, DANIEL!"

I wave up from below. A flash of light shines, and then I'm left waving at the ceiling in the Montage Tower locker room. I put my hand down to my side and spin around to check for witnesses: thankfully, I'm here alone. I transform my space clothes into my work clothes and psych myself up for the meeting. Renters: easy-peasy. Price is all they want to talk about, as everything else is on display. I check the time on my phone. It's still the same date and time as I left: *10:30 a.m., August 13th*. He sent me back accurately, thank God. Thank Dad. My phone bursts to life in my hand. It's Martin.

"Hello?" I answer.

"Hi, listen. I know I've just told you to take the day, but...shit or no shit, I can't let that happen anymore. You're going to have to get down here. There's an email I...forgot to send out, and it's a huge deal—a renters meeting. ARTificial Light, the huge Taiwanese prosthetic limb company, want to stake their claim in the building, and they're on their way from their hotel as we speak. You need to be here as soon as you can. Use a towel as a diaper or something—"

"I'm here. I'm in the building. Now can that be enough poop talk, please?"

"I thought—"

I interrupt him; he's starting to stress me out with his flappy questioning. "I know what you thought. It went away. Now, can you meet me in the locker room?" Even though I can't see him, I can hear his smile coming through his end of the phone line.

"Okay, see you in a few." He hangs up. He sounded exhausted.

As I take my first step, the locker-room door slams open. Martin! He was outside the whole time. I look him up and down. His gray head of hair is disheveled, his clothes are creased, and he can barely stand upright.

"You're looking a little under the weather yourself, boss."

"I haven't slept. I had a guest staying at my house—Ms. Scotch. She's twenty-five years old, tastes like putrid death, and I drank every last drop."

I try to keep my voice low. "Okay, well, you've really screwed the Scotch on this one!" I keep my ears open to access how alone we are on this floor. I suspect not very.

"That's nothing. It wasn't even mine. It was a gift for our guests." A repressed smile almost claws its way onto his face. I try to keep my noise bottled up, but at this point it might not even be worth it.

"What the hell is wrong with you?!" I whisper furiously.

"Hey, who's the boss here?" he drunkenly snaps back.

"Who's sober here?" I retort.

"I'm perfectly fine...audibly. I just need someone there I can trust, who can help keep me...focused. You sell things for a living. You should be there anyway! In fact, you should be the only one, but I can't send someone so young to engage these guys. That's not how they play business. Just keep this whole thing from turning to shit, and I'll get to keep my job for longer than the six months I've had it. I've done you enough favors, dude!"

I put my hands out to calm him down. "We'll be fine. This won't be the only meeting. They already know what they want—be their safety rail, and they won't fall from the path they're already walking."

"Yes, we will, won't we?" The words drain thinly from him like the weak trickle of a broken fountain. He moves over to the sink and splashes cold water on his face and head and roughly smooths his hair back into an executive's parting. He looks like a post-middle-aged child at a casual wedding.

"Only if we actually make the meeting," I say, gesturing toward the door. "Shall we?"

He shakes the water from his head like a dog after a light rainstorm, the droplets narrowly missing me. I hold out my hand for a high-five. He ducks under it and out of the door. In exchange, I give him a quick, reassuring pat on the back, and he goes flying through the adjacent wall.

Chapter 10

CRASH! That was all it took to royally send me into a panic. The collision thunders through the building at the scene of which the proceeding smoke quickly dissipates to reveal a stunned but conscious Nebrezza, sitting ass-deep in a pile of broken wall, the debris cradling him like a half-intoxicated baby. As of yet, no one has rushed into the corridor to investigate, unless I'm somehow stopping them from doing so without realizing. Whatever the reason is, it's both the best and worst thing that could have happened at this point. I scramble over to Martin, who sits dazed and confused.

"Are you okay?" I whisper, peering into his eyes, which spin around in his head like plates on sticks. He looks up at me, and in his shocked state, he starts to swing punches at me. I close my eyes and allow him the retaliation; his limp flurry bounces off my cheeks painlessly. He bats out at my solid skin like a cat would a bowling ball. The frequency of his flailing dips as he takes hold of his mental bearings, processing what has just happened. He seems to be coming back to his senses somewhat. I carefully help him to his feet.

"I'm so sorry, Martin, I really didn't mean for that to happen." I'm such a moron. Why did I touch him?! What possessed me to do something so stupid at such a time? Excitement? I'm *not* excited for a business meeting...am I? *Goddammit, focus!* Martin has just entered *another room* without the use of a door! "Martin," I repeat, "can you hear me?"

He is still wide-eyed but together. His pupils dart about the room, then back to me, then the room and then me. Finally, they stay fixed on mine.

"What...just...happened?" he asks without breath. I quietly walk him out of the crater that I made with his body, and he slips on the chunks of wall strewn all over the corridor floor. I have his arm, so he stays upright, but he begins to panic again. I lift him high above my head and away from the accident. I then pat him down, smacking the wall dust and debris from his expensive three-piece.

"Nothing," I say. "You tripped and fell."

"I did no such thing!" he growls and kicks at me. I put him down but keep a hold of his shoulders.

"Says the *drunk*! Look, if we don't make the meeting, we're both screwed, as is any possibility of making a deal with the Taiwanese. I'll take the lead, improvise a bit, and you come in when you feel ready. It won't take long, and then we can talk about your *accident*."

"But—"

"Please, Martin. Just keep moving. What happened once could happen *again*."

That line hits him like he hit that wall. I know. I sound like an asshole, but I didn't mean anything by it. Really, I didn't! I'm just sure that fifteen minutes of awkward stumbling is better than disgracing the whole company to a potential international partner. I'm being objective.

I forcefully lead him down the corridor. "What room are they in?" I ask, quickly twisting my head around the corners of the hallway like I'm playing a three-legged game of tag.

"Six-ten!" He's all hunched over, refusing to lift his head up to me. I look down and see that his feet aren't even touching the ground anymore. This is quickly turning into some sort of misunderstood kidnapping. I release his shoulders, and he leads me to our meeting.

We soon arrive at the office door: 610. I've never been in this room before, but the hall it sits in is fully furnished with dark-gray leather chairs and publicity photos. Alongside these are dog-painted art pieces in triangular frames that line the matt-blue walls. I peer though the frosted glass to see the blurry outlines of a young man and an older woman standing like dolls in a collector's case. As I go to open the door, Nebrezza moves my hand away and pushes in front of me. *Good thinking, boss.*

As we enter, the frosted shapes transform into real people. The older woman wears a gray skirt suit and has her hands crossed in front of her. The one on top is clearly shielding what looks to be a hard, white-and-blue prosthetic. At least she wears what she works with. She takes the seat at the head of the conference table and smiles in our general direction, eyebrows raised as if she's expecting bad news. The younger man I recognize because he works here. The head of HR—Willard Roberts! He must be an emergency translator Nebrezza sent for. He speaks Taiwanese Hokkien as well as Afrikaans, Arabic Hindi, Japanese, Korean and most annoyingly English with a side of smarm.

"Nice to meet you," he says. "I'm Willard Roberts. I'm part of Mrs. Peng's translation team." Every word of his comes out in a thick, familiar, transatlantic London/Californian (he's from Minnesota).

"We know who you are, Willard," I say with a fake giggle at his ridiculous joke.

"I know, but I thought it would be fun to pretend," he mutters back. *I'm pretending not to hate you right now, Willard.* We each plonk down on the nearest medicine ball available. Martin and I take the left side of the table; his deflates slightly as he sits on it. Willard sits directly across from us, with Mrs. Peng in the center. Oh God, Peng Leikela. That's who we're meeting with!

Okay. I get it now. The formality, the silence, Martin's flop sweat, HR! She wasn't always in prosthetics; she was a majority shareholder of the biggest power plant in Southern Taiwan for a while. But there was a literal boom in the need for prosthetics after the war, and she sold her shares and moved on to pastures new and lucrative. I don't know whether to be impressed or disgusted. I wonder if she'd even be in this line of work if she wasn't physically forced into it.

As I snap out of my internal rant, I realize Nebrezza hasn't said a word since we arrived, so I guess I'm taking the lead early. Martin sits rummaging through his pockets for something, probably to see if he's gotten all of the wall pieces out of his clothing. While he's on mental vacation, I pour him a glass of water from the dish in the middle of the table and move it in front of him. He doesn't seem to have noticed, but I've done all I can—wait. I flashback to my first day of godhood when Dad calmed me down chemically. How did he do it? Dopamine? That helped me then, but it would be unhelpful in this situation. No, he needs endorphins!

Placing my hand on Nebrezza's shoulder, I concentrate, picturing him in my mind's eye. My mindscape is a dark, hollow void that surrounds a floating figure of Nebrezza. He has a pained look draped across his face. Pieces of drywall form around his body—a recreation of him crashing through the office wall a moment ago. Time then reverses in my vision, and Nebrezza is flipped backward through the hole he made, which rebuilds itself as he lands on his feet, facing the dry, spackled slab. He runs directly at the newly rebuilt wall and charges straight through it, smashing it to pieces with his own strength.

I open my eyes, and Nebrezza lets out a loud, regurgitated cough. This surprises our guest and her imp. I lightly pat Nebrezza between his shoulders, and he coughs a little more.

"Is everything okay?" Willard asks with visible concern.

"Better than!" I answer smugly. I'm ready for a show. Martin isn't the boss for nothing! "Hi there," I say to Mrs. Peng. "This is Martin Nebrezza. He oversees everything that goes on in the building—technologically, personally, uh…reputably—"

"Then why isn't he telling me this?" Willard asks, cutting me off. What is he doing?! Playing devil's advocate is a theoretical practice. Field tests won't do shit for us! Mrs. Peng can't say anything without backup, so why would I let Martin go it alone? Okay then, if he had a question ready that early, I guess he won't mind if I give him what he wants. I don't respond; I lean back and wait for Martin to insert himself into the situation. This will hopefully knock Willard off Peng's shoulders. After a second, the silence of the room snaps Martin out of his self-exploration, and he tries to get a grip.

"Oh, pleased to meet you, Mrs. Peng," he shouts wildly. "It's a pleasure to find you in my face rather than my computer screen! Ha-ha, HYUK!" A loud hiccup lunges from his mouth, completing his first ludicrous sentence of the meeting.

Willard looks as if he no longer wants to *pretend* that we haven't met. He clears his throat and repeats what I assume can only be a very formal version of what Martin said to Peng, who sits and listens with her eyes closed. They shoot open when he finishes, and Peng gives an enormous laugh, which bounces about the boardroom. Martin and I look at each other like *she* is the one acting insane. Peng says something back in unintelligible Taiwanese that perks Willard right up.

"Mrs. Peng returns the greeting happily. I assume this is due to my intervention. Speech impediment, isn't that right, Martin?"

What Machiavellian bullshittery is this? Martin slowly, pathetically nods his head, hiccupping loudly as he does so, much to Mrs. Peng's amusement.

Martin continues on. "So, obviously I apologize for the state the building is in. It means that, well, a tour is basically off-limits at this point, I'm sure you understand?"

Willard translates once again. Mrs. Peng concurrently nods. She carries on with her speech but this time for at least a minute without any stoppages. Willard obliges.

"Manhattan is a recovering island, obviously like many islands on the planet. I wanted to give our company a running start—pardon the pun. However, you understand that you are not the only...large business building that's being erected. You're just near enough to completion to have caught my attention, but keep this in mind. I am not here as a courtesy, I find it easier to do business face-to-face and, ugh...surreptitiously? Solitudinous...ly!"

Looks like Nebrezza isn't the only one choking on his words.

"Solitudinously?" he asks with a not-so-subtle, shit-eating smirk. *Yes, that's it. Get yourself off the ropes!*

"Does it matter?" Willard asks, slightly embarrassed.

"I just want to be clear. She's illustrated that she is in need of a strong, location in 'pre-mint,' and she knows full well that if you throw a stone in the city, you're bound to hit a newly installed window of a semi-constructed high-rise. However, it seems we share a boat. There are as many interested renters as there are buildings for rent. Surely, our meeting couldn't be as random as she paints it to be due to her own situation being so loose and disorganized.

"I say this with all due respect. As chaotic as the last year has been for us, we're building not changing. You, Mrs. Peng, moved from one company to another, from nuclear power to prosthetics, and when I consider this, I can guess that at this moment, you don't know what you want. Am I correct?"

Willard looks paler than usual, but I'm ecstatic. Martin is a pretty disorganized guy, but he is where he is for a reason. Is this how he operates? Lulling people into a false sense of superiority? If so, Willy was helping set the scene without even knowing what the scene was going to be.

"You're right," Mrs. Peng says in fully intelligible English!

"I am?" Martin says, shaken by her unexpected question.

"Oh, please. Willard is intermediately familiar with our language, but he isn't quite as versed in our customs. You're right, Mr. Nebrezza. Now, why am I unsure about the move? It's simple really. You're coastal. And to put it delicately, so is Manila. The difference is that your city has had a two-year head start on your reconstruction. Entire countries have been left on waiting lists. Meanwhile, the grand utopia that's being built here has been filling up quickly. I was set back by my...own business, and other medical innovators got a head start on me. I don't like being late, and I like competition even less."

What the hell does that have to do with anything? It's a high-rise not a Midwestern cottage.

"So, you want me to help you figure out how far behind in the transition you are compared to other companies?" Martin asks flippantly.

"Why not?" she says with a smirk.

I'm getting frustrated now. Is she deliberately wasting time?

"With all due respect again, Mrs. Peng, that's not part of my job description. The world has been through hell, yes, but the survivors of war are at a point in their lives which begs assessment. PTSD cases are at their highest since records began, as well they should be. I'm trying to ask if you're feeling all right, Mrs. Peng."

"Ugh, sir, maybe we should get back to the issue at ha—of importance?" I say, stumbling in my flimsy attempt to not offend.

"I agree." That's the cleverest thing Willard has ever said.

The squabbling pair glares at the two of us as if we've jumped the barrier of their football game. Mrs. Peng puts one of her royal-blue, carbon-fiber fingers up to her lips and shushes Willard back down to his place. And while she doesn't frighten me particularly, I choose to sheathe my own tongue to give the newly reinvigorated Martin some breathing room.

"Grief still runs rampant in our minds. We don't know ourselves at this point in time and we know our neighbors even less. There's danger there," Peng says, continuing from where they left off. She's trying to break Martin down to his emotional data, not just as a negotiator but as a person. This is all a game to her. She's not traumatized; she's having fun.

Oh, Martin's talking again...

"You can read where the country is headed based on who is in charge. Our president isn't any different from the mountain of moderates who came before, but the difference is, the current president brought America through World War Three—even if they were in a bunker at the time. The next few years will be a brave new start for all, thanks to the miracle of human survivability. However, time will go on, and the memories of the war will start to lose their vividness. America will be right back where it started, and evidently, your country will behave the exact same way if only a little later."

It looks like that made a mark on her a little. I don't even know if Martin remembers where he is. Peng has retreated into her head, and I don't blame her. It's grown so quiet now that it's almost like I'm back in the vacuum of space. I have the same chill flowing through my bones like a burrowing beetle.

"I love the theater!" she yells patronizingly.

Willard buries his face in his collar, but his eyes are made wide with his concealed smile.

Irritated, I press my hands onto the desk tightly.

"All I wanted was to discuss your knowledge of the area in which you're located. There was no need to launch into such an emotional tirade, Mr. Nebrezza. I can abide poetry but nothing this precious."

The varnished wood under my palms splits, causing a large crack, which upends the glass of water in front of Martin, spilling it over the cherrywood. The room goes still, and three sets of eyes stare at me in disbelief. Martin wobbles free from his dipped medicine ball, takes me by the collar and drags me toward the exit. As I look back, the table collapses completely in half, loudly crashing to the carpet.

"Don't you walk away from me!" Peng shouts in a tantrum tone. Nebrezza doesn't listen; he doesn't care about work at this point. I'm too much of a distraction. I have to get us away from here. As we turn the corner out of the office, I close my eyes, and we teleport out of the building and up into the sky. I take Martin's flailing weight while I create one of those clear bridges Dad made for me. I drop him onto it, and he falls down on his knees screaming into the wind. To him, his life is over, but I obviously know better.

"Martin!" I shout over the screaming. "Get your shit together!"

He stops and then slowly shuffles himself around to face my shins. He shakily attempts to get to his feet. However, he can't gage his footing, so he falls to a knee like a knight's squire. I'll take it.

"Ask away." I sigh.

"What the hell are you?" His voice has a prominent chattering whisper—a mix of the adrenaline and the cold air that's flooding his system.

"I am a god, apparently. I haven't always been one, but I am now. I can teleport, shoot heat from my hands, carry whole buildings, fly, and more. Do I have your full attention now?"

He glares at me as if I am an apparition of a half-remembered dead relative. I sigh, and with a flash of thorough movement, I take him by the scruff of his neck and pull us both through the sky, transporting him all the way to Senegal. I place him atop The African Renaissance Monument—the first of the Eight Wonders of the *New* World—and drop him on top of the child's head, 160 feet from the ground. I land slightly lower atop the father's head. It's strange to be up here, and for a second, I forget what I'm doing, drink in the view and feel the newer, warmer climate caress my skin.

I look up and see Nebrezza wobble to his feet. The metallic curls of the giant bronze child create almost no friction that can hold his flat-soled work shoes. He puts a pointed tip into one of the spaces between the hairs, keeping his balance. He looks over at me, the fear in his eyes begging me to end this. He's still a-nestling; fear isn't good enough. I'm not trying to hurt him, nor do I want to threaten him, but I need to create empathy in him. That way, I won't be burdened by unnecessary guilt. I jump across the chasm between father and son. In one swoop, I snatch Nebrezza up by his shoulders, and we zip off again back to the sky bridge I left high above New York City.

We both hit the clear pathway. The air leaves Nebrezza's lungs and joins with the furious wind that surrounds us both. Nebrezza lies on his back, looking up at the great gray yonder above. The clouds look down on him like the amateur sky-dweller he has become. One stray glance and his entire world will tumble around him. I've taken a wrong turn. I need to get him back on his feet. This can't all be for nothing.

"WHAT DO YOU WANT FROM ME?!" he screams. His eyes have shrunk to basic lines in his face, clenched so tight they've almost inverted in his skull.

"I WANT YOU TO TRUST ME!" I yell back.

A small shard of bravery pierces his heart—the nerve of what I have just said to him. He thunders back up onto his feet, his arms down by his sides, fists rolled up, ready to show me what an ass I'm being. If he swings, I'll have to dodge; breaking his hand on my face will only serve to emasculate him further. He changes his mind and turns one of his fists into an accusing finger.

"I DON'T EVEN KNOW YOU!" he says with a deep, hurt rage.

"Yes, you do," I say softly as the wind ceases around us. My words hit him perfectly. The familiarity of my voice helps bring his mind back down from a shocked anger and into a more sensitive and accommodating place. "I just want you to understand," I say. His focus is now entirely on my words, not with the great height at which he stands.

"So, what can we expect from you, Lord?" he asks as if this is what I want to hear. He's being glib again. As the words fell from his mouth, I could almost see his teeth carving their way through his tongue.

"I...I've never been called that. Look, you didn't do your job, Martin!"

"My job?!" he asks in disbelief.

"Yes. A series of events, dominoes falling into place—that sort of thing—and you've inspired me to be better."

"The Peng meeting? Do you want to speak to her again? After that display in there, she probably won't even come back to the city, never mind our office." I scoff at his ridiculous interpretation. "I...I don't understand," he says, frustrated.

"At the moment, I can make anything I want out of thin air—like this clear pathway we're on. Not only do I build, but I can also destroy." I wave my hands up to the sky, and a hole is cleared in the clouds. "I may be able to travel back in time, but it doesn't mean that my own time can't be wasted if I have *work*. I have *god shit* to do. So, can I go now…boss?"

He kneels, entranced by my display. "You can control that much?" Unexpectedly, he doesn't look shocked anymore. He looks happy, full of a pure, childlike joy. "You're going to the war…to my son," he says, shuffling to his feet.

"Uuuuurgh…yeah. Your son *is* where I'm going, yeah. I'm going to save your son!" I exclaim.

Martin jumps high up on the sky bridge, clacking his heels together like a Dickensian paperboy getting his weekly shilling. I roll my eyes, and with a flash of light, I send him back down into his office. He puts his palms together and raises them to me from the highest floor of Montage Tower. He's approached by construction workers, who escort him back into the building. I turn around and fly up and away from the city.

Chapter 11

RELATIVELY, I feel unsure. All I have to lean on is my curiosity as I dart through the darkness of space, thundering away from Earth. Despite my speed, I can easily see where I am going. Evidently, it's not just my body that has adapted to godhood but my mind as well. The mysteries of space are not so mysterious anymore, as each passing sector is alive and legible to me. I don't have every piece of this super-powered puzzle; I don't even think I am halfway, but at least I know where to go next.

I thread through the solar system like a sentient needle, watching the many planets and moons gently glide past from every direction. For the meantime, we're locked in an interplanetary dance that could only be accompanied by slow piano. That's how space feels, when you're a distance away from every piece of solid matter. That soft, free feeling is preyed upon the closer I get to the planets, and I have to shake off the shivers that I feel down my spine caused by the repeating gravity spikes that try and fail to claim me as part of their world. It's nothing too discomforting—a couple of speed bumps I must occasionally slow down for.

Out of all of Earth's celestial neighbors, the sun moves the slowest, glaring at me like a colossal warning light, a bright omen of the danger I am flying into. Tingly fingers of heat pepper my front while my back carries on it a cloak of prickly cold. Eventually, they switch places as I ignore the sun and continue on my flight. I feel a small piece of panic rise inside, and in an effort to suppress it, I speed up, passing the rest of the planets and moons at a brisker pace. All light is then replaced by darkness, and inside that darkness sits a pinhead of color that glints farther out in front of me. Forever is right where Dad left it.

I stop in my tracks and face my quarry, the whirling pool of interdimensional light that is Forever, blurring in full-frame like a camera flash trapped in time. Earlier, Dad pitched it to me as a mixing pot of endless possibilities—possibilities for analysis, for breakthroughs, for calamity. I must remember to watch my footing. I move closer, toward Forever's opening, and déjà vu takes hold of me in the form of an immense pull. It operates on its own level of physics. It isn't a drain through which all life will be swallowed if left long enough. Everything surrounding it remains still; even the space dust near it sits almost calcified. I'm the only thing that Forever seems interested in.

I close my eyes, and separate, yellow light surrounds my body, leaving only my head bare. I open them and find I am clothed in all of the appropriate military gear I will need. My outfit is a replica of the one Corporal Benson wore in my dream. I check my shirt sleeve and see the "Pantheon" has copied itself from my memory. I rip it off, splitting the sleeve in two, which quickly re-stitches itself. I drop the logo, and it silently floats out of sight. Slowly, hesitantly, I peer into Forever, searching for my target. I see no image, light. I move farther in, holding on to the sides of the void. Strangely, this 3D hole in space has an edge, yet there isn't anything to indicate that other than what I am clutching. My arms ripple from the pressure, but I need to keep my grip. Farther in, small parts of the warping sea of light attain some rigidity, and it almost begins to pixelate. Like before, the more I focus on these pixels, the more colors, shades, and shapes appear, and inside every one of the tiny fractals is an image of a scene I can't quite make out. I need to get a closer look, but that would mean letting myself go.

Taking a deep breath of nothing, I peel my fingers from the unseen edge of the 3D hole. As I do, my eyelids instinctively slam shut, and I cross my arms to block whatever horror could be waiting for me inside Forever...but nothing happens. My body has gone completely numb. I open my eyes to an endless vista of plain white light; no edges or corners, just a light without a source. The forceful pull from outside has left me alone; I'm back in that relaxing, zero-G state.

As I make my first move, the light around me flickers and projects upon me all the colors of all the spectrums. It's a lot to process. I feel like I'm caught in the gaping maw of a rainbow-gargling unicorn, and I need to become accustomed. I spin around, analyzing the noiseless space I now inhabit. I look to what I think is below me at what appears to be a surface, but when I move lower, I discover it isn't something that can be touched, and my finger passes right through it. As my skin connects with whatever it is, a sound echoes all around me, like footsteps trotting back and forth, except they don't fade with distance. It's just one step forward, one step back.

I withdraw my hand and place it back at my side, which causes me to spin slightly. I correct my orientation to what I hope is upright. Then, out of the blank space, a familiar image appears like a ghostly apparition. It's an isometric projection of my bedroom back in New York. It looks warm and safe, bathed in the golden glow of bedside light. Another sound chimes in on top of the footsteps. It's a woman's voice.

"Why can't we just meet at Justine's?" The words bounce off whatever counts as walls in this place, adding an atmosphere to the image of my bedroom. The sounds fade out again, bringing back the silence.

After about thirty seconds of me staring, the shadow moves about my bedroom. It belongs to a small version of me, and the strange view startles me slightly, but I calm myself. After all, he is me, so, logically, I'm *just* as scared of me as...*I'm* scared of...*me*...or something. I stare closely as my duplicate steps away from my open bedroom window, stretches, and approaches his bed. As he tucks himself in, I take note of the clock next to him. It reads 12:04 a.m.

Oh, wow. I think I get it now. This isn't me at this moment; this is a memory of me in the past, at 12:04, the last thing I remembered before I woke up as Corporal Benson on the beach.

I sense a paradox, an overlapping worry. Logistically, according to some theories, to control time as a dimension inside a 3D space, the user would have to ignore the strict laws of physics of that space because time always has to exist. This is what Dad meant when he told me that we "swim the laws of physics." We can because Forever exists *between* the laws of physics, like an error in a once-functioning computer system. Maybe the paradox can be fixed? I'm here, after I returned from seeing Forever for the first time, after the kitchen light bulb exploded above my head. If I can see my past, why would I allow that last part to happen when it will ultimately be an inconvenience? What is important about that event that allows it to exist?

Oh, shit...I think... Yes, I have an idea. The only way this paradox exists is if something happened that hasn't happened, so this must be where it happens. He-*me* at 12:04 didn't *dream* the war, I think I sent myself there, and I'm seeing this moment in time, here in Forever, because this is where I do it from.

I slap my palms together with a distorted clash and proceed to push them out toward the image of myself asleep in bed. I open my arms wide like Dad did earlier. Out of the shadows, a small, glowing tear forms above the sleeping Dan. I drop my arms when it reaches a length of around seven feet. In my vision of my past, Forever hovers over my sleeping body. However, physically, the opening is a lot less disorderly than this one, and it has no effect on anything in my room. My blankets still cover me, my bed hasn't been lifted, and my alarm clock, phone, and lamp stay on the nightstand without any fuss.

After a couple of seconds of waiting, a fragile, transparent copy of my body peels away from sleeping Dan and is sucked up into the Forever portal. Forever then slams shut, and the room returns to its former still state. This...actually explains a lot! How I—or a projection of me—managed to find its way into the body of a random soldier fighting in a war years earlier. I couldn't send myself back entirely; I wonder why. Would my being in Forever lessen the effect of the Forever I conjure in the past?

Unfortunately, this makes way for a whole extra list of distracting questions: how many times will I do this? Is this my first attempt at time manipulation or my first *successful* attempt? Is this why I used to wake up on the floor? No, I can't think of that right now. I just need to find her. I concentrate on my target time, and the colors around me begin to shift like a cartoon funhouse. I fly deeper and deeper from blues, to pinks, from reds to a shade between red and yellow—the shade of wet sand. I fly forward, and the walls of color pull away from me, tapering at what I perceive to be the center like a shrinking corridor swallowing a door. I speed up into the center of the shape until it stops stretching, leaving me with a precise fractal of the scene I am looking for. I see a dark tide lapping at moist sand. Foam piles up softly at the ocean's edge.

As I stare blankly at foreign surroundings, I realize the image from my past has taken me without my knowing, and now here I stand, sole-deep in dull, beige sand of a Greek beach. The wind howls around me, carrying the smell of tide and charcoal with it. Plumes of smoke rise in the distance; this was a recent war zone. I notice the refugee center at the end of the beach where grain touches the grass of a green hill. A concrete path leads from the hill all the way up to a large castle on the edge of a cliff. Out of every place on earth to hide, why didn't they choose the castle?!

Confidently, I lunge forward to fly over to the ref center and instead fall face-first into the sand. What the hell? I stand up and try it again. I gently hover over the sand for a second, hands reaching out toward my destination, and then WHAM! I'm dragged back down onto the sand. What's wrong with me? I try to conjure a brightbolt in my hand, but all I can produce is a small flicker of light. It's like ten percent of a camera flash and quickly flickers out, overpowered by the dark of night. Dad warned me that Forever could mess with me, but this is way more than a prank! Is it because I don't have my powers at this point in time? Or did I short-circuit somehow? There's only one person I can ask, and he's thousands of miles away in New York, plus he would kill me if he knew I had directly disobeyed the future him. Maybe this was a bad idea. I pick myself up, dust my costume off, and start walking to the ref center. From the lack of scorch marks, I would say that I am at a time before the boats landed. Who knows, the Pantheon may not even have arrived here yet.

As I hit the "t" of that "yet," the door of the ref center bursts open. There she is. Albrier, Lance Corporal... Ahem.

"Lance Corporal Albrier." She doesn't see me. She slams the door behind her and takes in a deep breath of the night air, then sighs it back out and walks around the center toward the hill beyond it.

"WAIT!" I stupidly yell. The alarmed lance corporal pulls her pistol out of its side holster and aims it in my direction.

"Identify yourself!" she shouts, surging her way toward me with an angry determination in her eyes. A light at the end of her pistol turns on, blinding me on the dark beach.

"SPEAK!" she yells.

I can do this. I've done it before. "I'm...Dan Hardacre, Private, 33rd regiment! Lower your weapon...please?!"

"Where are your tags?"

Shit, shit, how could I forget the tags?! You moron.

"I lost them back at camp," I say. "The blood...it was everywhere..." Panicking, I improvise, fall to my knees and collapse onto the sand like a startled goat on its first summer vacation. I keep my eyes tightly closed, waiting for something to happen. She could quietly kill me, not take any chances, or she could leave me here to be taken by the tide. Albrier starts moving, her boots crunching on the sand like a rubber pestle meeting a grain-filled mortar. The noise makes the hairs on my neck rise to attention; the adrenaline of an unwatched touch sends a shiver down my vertebrae.

"Shush, now, let me get you inside," Albrier whispers, putting one of my arms over her shoulder. I am hoisted to my feet. "Come on, get stepping," she says under the strain. I pretend I'm struggling to find my footing, which turns into a limp as I'm slowly guided along the beach. "It's Albrier!" she shouts just before she violently bashes open the door to the ref center.

"What the hell is going on? Who's that?" an unfamiliar voice calls from the bed closest to the door.

"I don't know, Ben. I found him on the beach. He collapsed when I approached him. Nebrezza, ugh, sir, what should we do with him?" The shapes of the troop flail about behind my eyelids like shadow puppets.

"Well, he's wearing our colors. Even if his shirt is on the tight side, he's unarmed. Benson, help him onto your bed."

Hold on. *Tight side*? I haven't eaten in a week, asshole! After a pause, I'm pulled up by my arms and moved to a recently warmed cot. I stare up at the white light of the center, rolling my eyes as if I am a dizzy cartoon. Lowcroft then enters the discussion.

"Are you kidding me, sir? We don't know who this guy is." I cut her off before her seeds of doubt can be sown.

"Boats...enemy boats...headed this way," I say groggily. "Three of them."

"Hey, hey, did you say boats or drones?" Alvarez asks.

"Chinese," I answer, looking up at Nebrezza, who is standing over my "lifeless" body. He slaps me abruptly in the face, snapping me out of my stupor.

"You're going to have to be clear with us, okay, kid?"

I shake off my trance and with confused fear, as if I have just come to my senses, stare at each of the faces surrounding me.

"Yes, three Chinese boats, all with heavy machine guns, also, they're each carrying this...digital...mortar...thing. It'll tear through here like paper. I came to warn you! You have to get out of here... the castle on the cliff! We can go there...or something."

"That castle is a black market," Alvarez says. "The storeowners will open fire on any armed group that approaches."

"We're on a beach," Nebrezza interjects. "A dawn landing makes sense for a quiet, open space like this."

"And if they *don't* show?" asks Albrier.

"Then we have the night to ourselves," Nebrezza retorts.

"This is bullshit, Sarge," mutters Lowcroft.

"Well, my orders aren't, so get your shit together and set up at that window."

He points to the center-most window of the building. I have a horrid flashback of Lowcroft's bloody machine gun falling out of it.

"NO!" I yell at the group, who frown in unison at my outburst. "It's too open. She'll be hit before the second boat even beaches. They outgun you, remember? You need to be smarter than this!"

"Ha!" Alvarez shouts from behind everyone. "Look who he's talking to. Do you know who this is, son?" he points at Nebrezza.

"Yes, I know his father, Martin. Martin Nebrezza." The group looks straight at their leader, who is as surprised as they are. He rubs his eyes with his thumb and forefinger, trying to push the stress of the situation to the back of his mind.

"Lowcroft, take your SAW, put it at the center-most window!" he repeats.

"But—"

"BENSON!" he hollers, interrupting my interruption. "Albrier, you two roll those boulders either side of the building to about six or seven feet away. You'll get behind one each and lay down some covering fire when I give the signal. Alvarez, *pop smoke* when the last of the boats has landed. No one fires a shot before that time. And you...Daniel, is it?"

I cringe "Dan. Private Dan—"

"Yeah, whatever, you stay here. I don't know who you're with or how long you've been with them, but you're clearly green, and green can turn red at the drop of a shell, so you get in the corner and keep your mouth shut until I say so, understand?"

I nod quietly and do as he says. He begins pushing the cots together into a sniper's nest like he did in my dream. Lowcroft gets on her giant LMG. Albrier takes a knee behind her boulder. Benson takes his to the far right. God help them all.

I would if I could.

A few minutes go by.

"Got anything, Sarge?" Lowcroft whispers.

"Yeah...YEAH, I see a dingy, coming around the southern cliff. It's coming straight to us."

"Tell me when," she says, adjusting her weapon's bipod.

"I see a second...and now a third. Green-boy was right."

"Duh!" I shout back. Nebrezza shushes me back down.

"Remember—on my order, not on my fire. Alvarez, get ready with that smoke."

Alvarez heads out back behind the building. How is he going to throw smoke that far?

The squad sits patiently, no shots fired so far. The third boat has landed, and the PLC soldiers are hopping out one by one, heads on a swivel like a traveling passel of heat-packing penguins. They know they're being watched, and there are only two buildings in view: the castle and this overused shoebox.

Nebrezza slowly lifts his finger to his ear. "Fire smoke," he whispers into his earpiece's microphone. I hear a familiar *plomp* as Alvarez launches a smoke grenade from out back. It flies overhead and lands right inside the enemy group like a comet hitting a forest. Either he has a throwing arm like mine, or he used a mortar cannon like the ones the Chinese have. Regardless, the ambush has begun. Nebrezza fires the first bullet, hitting a captain square in the forehead. As he goes down, the confused boatmen start firing in all directions. Some lucky-guessers hit the ref center, but they're immediately fired upon by Albrier and Benson, who pop out from behind their boulders and, in tandem, launch two grenades out of their rifles, dispatching the two soldiers closest to us. Nebrezza gets off a few more shots, taking out a crouched rifleman, followed by a soldier hurrying back to one of the boats, who takes a round to the back and slumps over the landed craft. Finally, Lowcroft opens fire with her large LMG, finishing off the group before they have time to set up their mortars.

The pandemonium turns into peace. The fight is over.

"All clear?" Nebrezza asks, pushing on his earpiece.

"Clear. No, wait, one left. No, just a wriggler. Now it's clear." Benson breathes heavily as if to rope his adrenaline back inside himself.

"Well, looks like the kid was telling the truth," Alvarez says joyfully as he reenters the building. Lowcroft lifts her gun down from the window and places it like a holy relic on the ground.

Nebrezza still has his eye down his scope. Trust isn't ever a two-way street for this guy, even with his own marines. "Albrier, Benson, regroup," he says quietly into his comms, satisfied. The pair comes out from behind their rocks, and together, they hurry back, barely making a sound.

Abruptly, Nebrezza cuts through the silence with a stern question. "Benson, which one was the wriggler?"

"The one on the boat, why?"

"They're still moving."

"Well, put another one in him," Benson says just before

PLOMP

A grenade shoots off from the boat. A mortar shot screams up to the sky and plummets with hot rage. Albrier pushes Benson, but his weight keeps him from budging. He shoulder-barges Albrier back, and all at once, the grenade strikes the ground in front of him, flinging him onto his back. Nebrezza opens fire, emptying his magazine into the shoulders and head of the mortar operator, finishing him off.

I jump up from the corner, but the rest of the squad pushes me back into it, making room for Albrier, who bursts through the door dragging Benson into the ref center. Lowcroft runs over to help carry him, but Albrier just drops him. He has deep cuts all over, and as warm as his flesh looks, there is no life left in him. Lowcroft tries to restart his heart with CPR, but it doesn't do him any good. He was gone as soon as the grenade hit. Albrier sits on the edge of Benson's cot, her brown eyes stuck in one place, disconnected from her brain as if it needs the extra space to process what happened. She lowers her head down onto the cot, staring blankly at me the whole time, then slowly closes her eyes and passes out on her side.

Alvarez walks out of the back door, whispering something angrily in Spanish. Lowcroft continues to push on Benson's chest as if he's just playing possum and will spring back to life with a grin on his face and a high-five ready. Nebrezza clutches his head at the loss of his friend and underling. His hands make way for his angry eyes to find him a target. He takes his rifle and begins striking the wall next to him, smashing a deep hole into it. It grows larger as he hits it again and again. In the end, he throws down his rifle and sits against the wall. That's when he sees me, cowering in the corner like a cowardly fool, idiotically twirling my fingers until I can find the courage to speak up. Nebrezza jumps to his feet and pulls his pistol out of its holder. I can't help but notice the small scratches in its side, lines and crosses like you'd see on the wall of a prison cell. This is before he shoves the gun in my face, crushing it against my cheek.

"Why?" he asks through gritted teeth. "Why did he die?"

"H-he *didn't*!" I say through squashed lips.

"WHAT DO YOU CALL THAT?!" he screams, pointing at Benson's body. I don't know what to do. This didn't happen before.

"He wasn't supposed to!" I whimper back, the cold barrel of the pistol stabbing into my cheek like an ice pick.

"What do you mean 'supposed to'?" Lowcroft says, exhausted yet trying to remain calm in the chaos.

"I...I...I saw you. I saw you all die."

Lowcroft looks at Nebrezza as if I am insane, naturally, and strides over to us, adding to the chaos she pointlessly tried to contain.

"There is a pile of dead Chinese soldiers out there being swallowed up by the tide. I have no problem putting you there with them, limbless but alive enough to drown."

I try to ignore her imaginary threat and keep my attention to the man with the real gun. I guess I have to tell them the truth. I can't be sure that his bullets won't kill me in the state I'm in.

"Nathan Nebrezza, I know your father. He's my friend—my boss. I work for him! I saw your name on a postwar epitaph along with everyone else's here, including Benson's. Ever since then, I have been drawn to this beach, to this war zone. I don't know why, but I knew I had to come here, to save you, to save Albrier, like she saved me!"

A shaken voice comes from the other end of the room. "Do I know you?" Albrier is awake, sitting up over Benson's body. The calmness of her voice is either a refreshing change or a sign of broken patience.

Chapter 12

Predictably, the Pantheon didn't believe me, so after a long stand-off with the grieving group of strangers, I finally "came clean." They saw me as a weakling and a coward, so it wasn't difficult for them to believe that I was a private who went AWOL, hiding from enemy soldiers, finding refuge at a *refugee center* filled with armed allies. My story disgusted most of them, although Pvt. Lowcroft defended me, which came as a surprise, defending my status as *part of the draft*, which in war translates to *part of life*, I guess.

I don't know why she helped me. Maybe it's because she's a private, like I'm supposed to be. Or maybe she didn't want to see another person—even a cowardly stranger—die in front of her. Before the war, Martin Nebrezza worked for a company called CyberGem. To win over Nebrezza Jr., I told him that I too worked for CyberGem, calling our meeting a "blessed coincidence." The war took its toll on a lot of small companies—well, those that weren't swallowed up by larger conglomerates, anyway. This made the people a community of sorts. To the Pantheon soldiers, my regiment is the 480th—which doesn't exist—a *newer* regiment that forwent the usual military tropes. We don't do nicknames; we don't have any tattoos. These revelations don't surprise them.

I peer around the room. Alvarez has his head stuck in his journal again, scribbling away without saying a word. He pushes his pencil down hard, scratching letters deep into the paper. He shakes

161

his writing hand in an effort to rid himself of a cramp. He catches me staring.

"What are you drawing?" I ask.

"My dead friend." He scoffs back at me. I take the hint. "I'm serious," he says, sketching away. I make an apologetic mumble and leave him to his coping mechanism. Looking around, I see the other members of the regiment are also in their own worlds, grieving in the quietest way they can. The only noise among us is the wind, howling eerily through the hole in the wall Nebrezza made with his rifle-butt. The corner with the hole is the place I have been given to sit like I'm a misbehaving child in a timeout. I look through the hole at Albrier, who is outside on the beach, sitting in the crater left by the shell that killed Benson. Without my powers, time drags laboriously on. The fighting was hours ago, but it feels like weeks. Benson was buried on the hill where the beach ends; I wasn't invited to the funeral. I stand up and approach the door.

"Where are you going?" Nebrezza angrily asks me.

"I need some air," I say quietly.

"You have a hole!"

I ignore him and head out the door. As it closes behind me, I hear him sighing. What? I'm not under his command. Now, I have to be delicate with this, but I can't take being cooped up in that broken room any longer. I stand on the rim of the crater where Albrier sits and let the silence have a few jabs at the awkward ice in the air before I open my mouth. She stays as she is, hunched over with her arms around her knees, which are up under her chin, ignoring me.

"Urm...excuse me, Lance Corporal Albrier?" I say prudently.

She doesn't answer.

"You don't have to say anything. I just want to thank you for finding me on the beach—for taking me in."

She doesn't answer.

I stay at the crater for a bit longer, staring out at the ocean, wishing I could take flight and never see this beach ever again.

I...don't do well with this stuff. I have been in an entire world of grief for over two years now, and you would think I'd find it comforting, but I don't. In fact, I don't feel relaxed at all. I feel flushed and scatterbrained.

But what about her? What is she feeling? Why can't she tell me?

"I—Albrier, I also want to apologize…for everything. If it wasn't for me, then none of you would be in this situation."

She still doesn't answer.

"Anyway, I just came to tell you that. I understand why you're not talking to me. Please don't feel guilty."

"I'm not talking to anyone," she says as I am about to leave.

"I don't know what to do for you all," I mumble.

Nothing, she mouths, her voice kept in to prevent tears from coming out. I hop down into the hole and attempt to hug her. She stands up and walks away from me, climbing out of the hole and stomping across to the ref center, wiping her hand across her face in a rage before almost pulling the door off its hinges. She enters and starts waving her arms at Nebrezza, who looks up from his book, concerned and uncomfortable. I hurry over to the building and catch what they are talking about.

"…said the intel was solid. And we can't stay here," Albrier says stiffly to Nebrezza, whose brow has started to furrow.

"I know, but we're all shaken up, you especially, even if this anger conceals it for a few easy seconds."

"We were going today, anyway!" Albrier protests.

"We were, and now I've lost a trusted gun in exchange for a deserter!" Nebrezza snipes rudely. He knows I can hear him!

"And this will be his punishment!" Albrier says. "Anyway, we don't know how loose Nestor's lips will be about this thing. We have a small window, and we need to head out ASAP!"

"Head out where?" I interrupt.

"Are you kidding me?!" Nebrezza yells.

"I'm guessing you aren't here on vacation, Sergeant. What is it you have to do?"

"I'm not telling you of all people, deserter. You shouldn't even be here!"

"And neither should the sub, Sarge! Keep that in mind. You agree, right?" Albrier yells over to Lowcroft, who nods. Alvarez shrugs, not wanting to get dragged into another fight.

"It's what we're here for," Albrier pushes.

Nebrezza frowns, irritated by the hard truth of Albrier's argument, and points at me.

"And you, *deserter*, what exactly were you shipped out here for?"

"We were told to hit an enemy supply drop not far from here. We went to intercept but were cut off on the road by an unexpected group on patrol. I exited the Humvee, which was riddled with bullets seconds after. I saved myself from a quick death, and no, I don't feel good about it. So whatever Albrier's talking about, I want in."

"You forgot the part where you led the enemy to our location," Alvarez interjects.

"We were on the road, not in the sea. I spotted the boats from the cliff before I got here. They were already on their way."

A long silence follows. Alvarez and Lowcroft look away from the awkwardness of the scene. I don't blame them. Nebrezza unsnaps from his thoughts and throws me an old backpack from underneath one of the cots. It hits me in the chest, knocking the wind out of me.

"Private Dan, we are involved in what we're calling a 'minor military occupation.' Each of the world's superpowers is converging on the center of Europe, staking claim to as many untethered nations as possible. Land was always the goal. However, America underestimated the value of the sea, and that's where we're being pounded by the enemy's Smart-Subs. Their stealth technology is ahead of the curve, and it needs cracking. That's what we're here for. We got word from a trader in the castle of an abandoned sub right in the middle of this island. This is a search-and-secure mission. If the latter part isn't a possibility, then the sub needs to be destroyed, got it?"

I nod breathlessly with a wide grin on my face.

"Stop smiling," Albrier adds sharply. "This is serious. If shit gets heavy and you try to turn tail and run, I'll put a bullet in you myself. You understand?"

I nod again, only without the grin.

"So, what good will finding this sub do?" I ask.

"See that mortar Alvarez has with him? The cool thing about that is it's connected to others like it. It scans the environment, and other mortars appear as dots on its HUD. The sub should have a similar feature since it's owned by the same company. That's what Command theorizes, anyway."

"And where is Command now?"

Lowcroft clears her throat. "Well, the bird that choppered us in was taken out with a CloudKiller missile. We took as much as we could when we parachuted into the sea, but we left our comms onboard. Now it's at the bottom of the ocean."

"What about the pilot?" I ask.

"For a drone?" Alvarez asks sarcastically.

"Maybe you should have stayed on board?" I say back with a smirk. He gives me the finger and begins to pack. Each member of the Pantheon does the same, folding their cots into soft rolls and stuffing them into their bags. I try to roll up the one Benson won't be using, but my hand is swatted by Albrier, who carefully bags up Benson's dog tags. I guess it will serve as an epitaph of sorts. The whole group approaches me and turns me around, filling the bag on my back with random junk they don't want to leave behind—a book for Nebrezza and Alvarez, a spare pair of boots that Lowcroft found in the changing room, a bunch of extra ammo, glow sticks, ration kits, and every one of their filled canteens. I'd make a joke about them adding the kitchen sink, but I don't doubt they'd try if they could.

Whatever.

We've been walking for a half hour. "One point six clicks north," Alvarez said as we left the ref center. At first, it seemed like a short distance, but I underestimated how much of a bother this anvil on my back would be, and without my powers, I am in a state of cold turkey. My arms and back are shaking with pain, my legs cramp with each step. I haven't done this much walking since before my re-birthday, and the hilly terrain we're crossing isn't helping at all. The rest of the crew is equipped with these ridiculous *bouncing bags*, which bob up and down hydraulically with each step they take. They're supposed to make the carrying easier, but they just look idiotic.

And yet, I can't help but feel left out, being the only one who isn't "bobbing." I used to "bob" in and out of buildings, on and off planets, and now I'm struggling to carry a bunch of crap for ungrateful strangers. It's selfish of them to do this to me if you think about it.

As we clamber up the steep, muddy hills, we catch sight of a smoke pillar. After climbing a bit more, we see it's from the front of a dilapidated farm out to the far left of the stone path we're using to mark where we're heading. The barn has been torn down, and the equipment is strewn all over the place, probably ransacked for fuel and supplies by the enemy soldiers. There are tire treads like alien signals all over the crop fields. The plume of smoke comes from a scarecrow, which stands burning ferociously as a visual cry for help. Fatigued, I stop walking, and the weight of my bag drags me down onto my ass. I hit the stones with a painful crunch. The group stops and turns to see me on the ground struggling like a newborn... erm...a newborn... Oh, who cares?

I sit and catch my breath, staring over at the Pantheon, waiting for one of them to rush to help me, but they just stare back impatiently.

Nebrezza rolls his eyes and asks half-heartedly, "You okay?"

I point over at the farm. "Should we go and check that out?"

"Ugh, I'm not sure that would be such a great idea. Sarge, what do you think?" Lowcroft says, wiping her forehead on her shirt sleeve.

"We stay on the path," Albrier says from in front of Lowcroft before Nebrezza answers.

"But there could be enemy soldiers in there," I press. "If they've seen us, they could follow. Do we want to risk them ambushing us from behind?" If nothing else, I'd get a break from this backpack.

"There aren't any enemies in there," Nebrezza mutters quietly.

"How do you know?" I shout back. He stares down at his feet, which kick at the gravel.

"Because we captured this sector a long time ago."

"Oh," I say, not quite understanding what he means. "*Oh*!" I get it now.

"Yeah," Alvarez says solemnly.

"Every country has psychopaths," Lowcroft adds, a wall for her conscience to take cover behind, and I don't really blame her.

Albrier starts walking again. Bypassing the rest of the crew, she storms away from the desecrated farm and down the path toward our actual target, if it is still where the trader claimed it would be.

As we head into a small, wooded area, we see that some of the trees have been torn up from their foundations. Something big and heavy forced its way through.

"You say a *submarine* did this?" I ask.

"That's why it's called a *smart* sub. They're built for nautical combat but they're amphibious. Looks like this one strayed off its path." Albrier steps over one of the felled trees.

"It's clearly gone haywire," Alvarez adds, hopping quickly over a tumescent tree stump.

"It might have been searching for a water source. Our intel says they're programmed to seek it out if they find themselves lost, scanning for moisture in the ground."

That's sounds sadder than it is," Alvarez says as we shuffle our way through the forest, following the wreckage the sub left in its wake. After a few minutes, the space opens, and the widest tire tracks I have ever seen stretch up and over a grassy hummock. The crew begins to climb on all fours; I reluctantly follow, using the treads as a ladder. Splinters of dirty grass pull away as I dig my hands in and haul myself up the steep hill.

As we reach the top, we're greeted by a wide, open valley. At the base is a giant lake, at the center of which sits the Smart-Sub. It's completely still. Its chassis is a little banged up, and by the looks of it, it lost one of its treads before it reached the water. How the hell did it get here?

Nebrezza looks through his sniper scope at the motionless machine. "Its tracks lead into the water. It must have confused the lake for the sea."

"What an idiot," Lowcroft declares sarcastically.

"Oh, shit." Nebrezza twists the magnification wheel on his scope.

"What is it?" Albrier asks.

"It's surrounded by bodies—ten of 'em, maybe."

"What the hell does that mean?" Alvarez asks.

"It means we have to be careful."

"Well, I'm leaving this bag up here," I say, attempting to shimmy the backpack down my shoulders.

"No, you're not. Everything goes with us." Nebrezza starts down the hill toward a large boulder at the edge of the lake. The rest follow him, and I follow them. After a couple of wonky steps, the descent gets steeper, and the weight of the bag pushes harder against my shoulders, causing me to lose my footing. I tumble violently down the hill, passing the rest of the Pantheon like misshapen tumbleweed, and crash at the bottom, landing on my right arm. I push up with my left, only for the pain to strike me hard, and cover my mouth to stop myself from screaming.

"You okay, Private?" Alvarez calls as the entire group jogs to my location and stares down in horror at my twisted limb. Lowcroft takes my arm in her hands and applies pressure. I scream into my hand.

"That's definitely broken," she says.

"YOU THINK?!" I yell back at her.

Suddenly, the Smart-Sub roars to life. A large, metal funnel pops out of the top of it. It loudly spins up like a tumble dryer and launches a small drone into the sky. Its propellers spin, twisting it slowly as it scans the area, looking for the source of the noise. The Pantheon runs away from me, taking cover behind a boulder on the lakeside.

I have to keep still. Maybe it will confuse me for one of the dead bodies surrounding it. I see that Alvarez has unpacked his mortar from his backpack. Is he going to shoot the drone in the lake or the drone in the sea? It has a fifty-fifty chance of actually helping, but I have to have faith that he knows what he is doing. He stands the mortar up and starts typing into its screen. The rest of the squad cover their ears.

And

PLOMP

The mortar shell flies into the air and strikes the flying mini-drone in its left rotor. It spins out of control, all over the place. Albrier rushes out from behind the rock to help pick me up, but as she does, the recently shelled mini-drone corrects its course and fixes its sights on the pair of us. It isn't only a camera; it's got mounted sub-machine guns. It opens fire, striking the mud around us. Albrier grabs me by my backpack and drags me over to the boulder, from where the team lends cover fire.

The drone spins turbulently, dodging their shots. It doesn't waste its time firing back, focused instead on tracing our path with a line of bullets that pierce the ground along our intended route. We won't make it at this pace, but as I try to clamber up, my limp arm strikes Albrier's knee, tripping her. She growls and, with both arms, lifts the bag on my back. In a painful swing, I'm thrown into cover and out of danger. However, the force of her throw buckles her knees, and she crashes to the ground. She is wide open.

As the mini-drone turns, it sends streaks of dirt upward right next to were Albrier fell. Out of nowhere, instinct takes over my body. My broken arm SNAPS back into place, and I reach out and take the drone in a psychic grasp. The squad continue to fire at it, but before they can get a clean shot, I fiercely hurl it down into the water, under which it detonates, causing a huge wave to form and curl over where we're taking cover. I throw my other arm up and take hold of the wave. Closing my eyes, I picture the molecules the water is made up of and clench my fist, forcibly dragging them closer together. At once, the whole lake freezes, the wave included, forming a large, arcing shield of ice which hangs over us. The Pantheon gazes up at the huge, frozen wave, their mouths agape at what the hell just happened. But Albrier isn't looking at the frozen wave. She's looking at me.

Chapter 13

CAUGHT red-handed, or should I say *broken-handed*. Albrier saw me use my powers. However, everyone else is still in the dark, and for the life of me I can't figure out why she hasn't told them. The sun has set now, and we've taken refuge under the wave I solidified.

According to Lowcroft's readings, the Smart-Sub launched a drone that doubles as an explosive device. It's programmed to launch itself at a target if its damage levels become too high and/or after its ammo depletes. The mini-drone can only learn of a target from the sensors of the fully grown sub. Thankfully, this particular sub is aware of our presence, but without the ability to move, it can't be sure what it's hearing or seeing behind the frozen wave, under which Nebrezza has ordered us to stay for the night. We'll make our move on the machine when dawn gets here. Hopefully, we can get close without having to fight it again, although that doesn't look likely.

We sit, covered by a pale, orange light coming from a small pile of tactical glow sticks—an artificial campfire. Its light should last until the morning sun. The Pantheon members are trying to keep themselves together. Lowcroft, wary of the drone's presence, is as tensely guarded as if she has a camera pointing directly in her face. It was kind of funny for a while, watching her robotic movements play out, but now it's making me nervous. Nebrezza is sitting in silence, curled up like a folded blanket in the back of a cubby. Alvarez sits with his legs crossed, scribbling in his notebook, and keeps peering up at us like he's studying our every move.

"So, is this the weirdest thing you guys have ever seen?" he asks, pointing to the wave with his worn-down pencil.

"Obviously," Nebrezza answers sharply.

"Do you resent it for replacing you as the weirdest thing here, Al?" Lowcroft mutters.

I look to Albrier, whose chestnut eyes are fixed on me. She's not even blinking. As our lines of sight clash, she quickly rises and, in a surprisingly relaxed way, silently steps over the pile of glow sticks, making her shadow grow to that of a giant behind her. I don't know why she's so at ease, but I'm becoming more worried with each slow step she takes. With a thud, she takes a seat right next to me and leans back, propping herself on her hands, looking up at the frozen wave above us.

"So, we haven't really had a chance to chat, have we, Private?" The subtext is so heavy it almost drags her words from my ears and down to the Earth's core.

"No...we have not. War, huh? *Madness*!"

"Where are you from?" she asks my faux-visage of soldierhood as it gently slides from my very being like the wax from a burning candle of lies.

"New York," I say quietly.

"Ah. And *when* would that be?" she presses, putting a grubby, unkempt hand on my shoulder.

"Two years."

"*Ago?*"

"From now," I say, both correcting her and, strangely, myself.

"Wanna know what the weirdest thing I've ever seen is?

"Me?" I mumble. As I do, all the blood in my body converges on my head. It doesn't help that I can feel her intense stare burrowing through my temple.

"Well, it was a surprise. It shouldn't have been. Lord knows I've seen enough movies to be at least a little desensitized. But no, still a surprise. Anyway, I've relaxed my position on the situation, since I remembered you already said who you were and where you were from, and we didn't believe you. Obviously, it's not that crazy on our part to call out the deranged ravings of a traumatized soldier as simply *madness*, like you said." She continues to glare, slicing through me with a precision only someone with a clean, focused anger could do.

"Why haven't you told the rest of the squad?" I ask. I could probably take her apart atom by atom, but I'm at her total mercy at this moment.

"It's not really my place to *out you*, is it?"

"Look, when I arrived—"

"*When Benson was killed*, yes," she says, clueing me into her grief at such speed that even my sense of self-preservation feels for her.

"Again, I am so, *so* sorry. That wasn't *supposed* to happen." I pick at the badly sewn-on Pantheon badge on my sleeve.

"And what *was* supposed to happen?" As she says this, her hand moves from my shoulder, up my neck and onto the back of my head, and she plays with my clumping, unwashed hair. I'm waiting for her to grab a fistful of it and throw my face into the hard ground, but she doesn't. And, of course, the closeness sets my senses off. I tingle, my brain firing the wrong signals around my body, raising goose bumps like tiny beacons of idiocy. She notices and leans in closer to my ear. "Well?"

"I don't know what I thought was going to happen…but I dreamed I was in a battle on a beach with all of you, only I was Benson. When I woke up as myself, my dream became lucid. I was on the beach, in this time, halfway through a goddamned exchange of fire, shooting with a gun I've never used at enemies I never had with friends I didn't recognize. It was fun for the first few minutes. But then my lack of soldiering led to me getting all of you killed, horribly. Before you died, however, you…kissed me and then sacrificed yourself to take out the last of the enemy."

"You came all the way to a war zone because I kissed you?"

"Can you repeat the question?"

"You need to get laid, dude," she says.

"No shit! Would you let me finish?" I snipe, visibly flustered. "We fought together. I *was* Benson, and I was *playing* Benson, like...my mind in his body. The body was who your kiss was for. Not me. And then you died, saving the person you loved, the person I invaded. And I—*Benson*—was supposed to die with you, but he couldn't die because Benson was me, and I can't die, *apparently*. Now, in the real world, that's not how the scenario played out."

"Putting aside how creepy all that is..."

"I didn't choose to—"

"Are you human?" she interrupts me again.

"I don't know," I admit. "I have been called a *god*. Just let me give you all of the information I can, and we can go from there, okay?"

"Well, hurry up! I can't sit like this forever."

"After you all fell in the dream, a dark, metallic figure scooped me up and brought me out of the war, off the planet, and back into my body, which was still in my bed in the time from when I left."

"And it was flying?"

"Yes!" I shout, expecting a follow-up that doesn't come. She turns her head almost 360 degrees to face Alvarez.

"Alvarez, can I have your diary, please?"

"It's a journal!" he shouts from his side of the wave.

"Your *book*, give me your *book*!" Excitedly, she pulls her hand away from my head, ripping a few hairs out of it in her hurry. It didn't hurt physically, but it did emotionally...that it might not grow back! Oh, wait, no, yes, it might. I squeeze my eyes together and feel four dark hairs sprout from my scalp.

Alvarez tosses his very used, coverless notebook over to Albrier, who snatches it out of the air like a Mets fan would a tossed hotdog. "Please be careful with whatever you want to write. There's private stuff in there, you know!" he says with uptight, childlike apprehension. Albrier flicks through the creased, dirt-decorated pages as if it were a wrapped gift.

"There!" she exclaims, holding out a two-page spread of the New York City skyline. Above it, two small figures fly away from a small boy clutching a toy robot. Could that be me? I don't remember any toy robot.

"What is this, Alvarez?" I ask.

"This was October 6th. The day of my seventh birthday. My mom and I went to visit my dad, who was working in the city. It was the second time I'd been there as a kid. I'd just picked out my present from that store—you know, Incognitoys? Where was I... Oh! The trip was kind of my *main* gift and then any toy I want—"

"You're thirty-three, not seven anymore. Tell the story like an adult!" Albrier shouts over to hurry him along with his ramble.

"Anyway, it was my seventh birthday...*twenty-seven years ago*, which makes me thirty-four and makes Albrier bad at math. I had just left the store, and I saw a huge flash of light in the sky. Out of it flew two guys, speeding up into the clouds."

"What did they look like?" I ask, as curious as a dead cat.

"I couldn't see their faces." This strikes a cold, needling pain along my vertebrae.

"That was it!" I say. "The faceless, flying man. I saw him in a dream!"

"Well, I saw two in real life, so bragging rights are mine, Private! So anyway, after I saw them, the bush next to me exploded."

"And?" Albrier asks with the last of her patience.

"And that's it...*boom*!" His journal swiftly flies back into his chest, thrown extra hard by an unsatisfied Albrier. "Careful!" he yells, lovingly clasping the book.

"She's sorry, Al," I say, probably *lying* on her behalf.

"So, what are you planning to do now?" Albrier asks me.

"I don't actually know. We're in a stalemate with the sub. It can't see us, so it can't kill us, but I can kill it, easily. But that's the problem. You don't want me doing that in front of everyone. So, I guess we're gonna have to sit it out until the sun comes up like Nebrezza wanted."

Albrier clicks her tongue loudly and spins around, moving back into the position she was in earlier: chin to knees.

Some quiet time goes by. Lowcroft and Alvarez are sleeping side by side, unconsciously cozied up together like two boxed kittens in the cold. Nebrezza is a different story. He is hard-faced, slowly moving his hand over the bottom of the tent-like tidal wave.

"Strange," he whispers. I stare up at him, awaiting his explanation. "Well, strange goes without saying here, but I don't mean *just* the wave, something deeper. It's cold like ice."

"Well, it is frozen."

"But it's not melting. Regardless of how cold the night is, we're enough of a heat source to make this thing sweat, and yet it's dry as the mud you're sitting on."

"What do you think caused it, Sarge?" I ask Nebrezza, testing him.

Albrier looks up from her floor space with half a grin. Nebrezza puts his hand on his chin as if that activates his brain.

"At first, I believed it was something the Smart-Sub did. The explosion from the mini-drone caused the sub to rock, which moved a lot of water our way. The freezing effect might have come from a device or mixture that the sub sent out in self-defense. We have intel on these things, but like I said before, it's not much. Anyway, the fact that the wave is still in this form may mean some kind of freezing gelatin compound that mixed with the water, giving it the cold texture but allowing it to keep its rigidity. Yes, that's most likely what has happened here. Maybe it was a device, a compound, or maybe the explosion disturbed some chemical under the lakebed, causing it to leak out from the earth."

Actually, it's not melting because I keep refreezing it every few minutes. Nice try though, Nebrezza. Albrier barely manages to stifle a laugh before rolling into a fetal sleeping position on the ground. I lie back down on the cold, dry bed of mud, looking up at the wave I made, my outsider art. While I examine it closely, something catches my eye: a strange wobbling silhouette through the ice, but it disappears when I blink. An eyelash or a trick of the light, I think. just being paranoid. Besides, the sub hasn't made the slightest movement or noise since we've been under here. Nebrezza slinks off into his own area, puzzling over his "mystery," and Albrier comes and sits next to me. Goddammit, what is it this time?

"You should get some sleep," I try.

"Sleep's not working." We sit without a word for a few minutes. She's obviously not going away. I guess small talk is better than awkward silence.

"So...where are you from?" I ask, nervously trying to keep up my team-player appearances.

"Alaska."

"What part?"

"The state capital. And no, it's not Anchorage, before you say. It's—"

"Juneau," I interrupt with a sense of overwhelming nostalgia.

"Yeah...how did you know?" Albrier asks with some surprise. Her eyes dart about, waiting for me to answer. It takes me a second.

"My mother was born there. She grew up on the edge of the city. She didn't stay long, though. She moved to Jersey City when she was a teenager."

"I can't say I blame her." Albrier shrugs.

"She always wanted to go back, but life kind of kept her restrained."

"Is that so?" Albrier says and retreats into her own memories of home, her family, friends...whether any of those things still exist at this point in time. Another second of silence goes by.

"What's it like?" I ask.

"Well, last time I was there, a glacier was seen headed down the Gastineau Channel. It was disrupting the path of the fishing boats."

I look at her, confused.

"It's as fun as it sounds," she says sarcastically.

"That's a shame," I say with a glum retrospective, Albrier spots this as clear as the ice above our heads and shuffles uncomfortably with guilt.

"She still has time, doesn't she?" The air grows somber.

"No. She died when I was a teenager."

"Oh."

My solemn look sends her into a long-haunted train of thought, of Benson. Her grief is fresh, so no matter how many distractions she clings to, it will always find a way to make its presence known. Her eyes fill with tears as she gulps hard, trying to suppress her discomforting memories. It's a smart move. Keeping sentiment locked up can help a soldier on a battlefield, but it's been too long. The prison bars have rusted, and a tear is free. It falls from her eyelashes toward the ground. I point at the droplet, stopping it in midair, and show it to Albrier. She collects herself to get a closer look. A perfect sphere of sadness lingers atop my finger as I display it for her, spinning it like a basketball for a bug-sized player.

"What are you doing?" she asks with a sniff, swaddling up her sorrow.

"What would you like me to do?" My words flow softer than the gentlest breeze. She slowly points a finger and jabs it into her levitating teardrop, I telepathically move it from my finger and onto hers, back where it belongs. A smile fights its way onto her face, and her eyes swell with more tears, now of pride, at the little drop of water bouncing on top of her index finger, bobbing like a pet in need of attention. She moves her hand over to the frozen wave and wipes the tear on its surface. The droplet instantly freezes as it touches the arching ice.

"How cool was that?"

"Yeah!" I say in celebration. We both look to Nebrezza, who stands there almost white-eyed with shock, watching us.

"Sarge, how long have you been—"

"DID YOU FORGET I WAS STANDING HERE?!" he yells breathily with perfect comedic timing, causing the sleeping pair of Alvarez and Lowcroft to stir. Albrier hushes him angrily, dragging him down to the ground next to us.

It took a while to run Nathan—ugh, I mean *S.Sgt. Nebrezza*—through what had happened, but he refused to keep it hidden from the rest of the team. There are no secrets in the Pantheon, he says, so we'll let the other two in on the details when they wake up. Then we'll formulate a plan on how to complete their mission. It shouldn't be long now; the sun is up past the horizon, which makes it about 6:28 a.m. Eastern European Standard Time, which I hope is still a thing.

Nebrezza hasn't really been himself since our discussion. He's twitchy, fiddly, and unnervingly distracted. Now he is the stranger in a strange land as opposed to me, and I'm back to my old comfortable, powerful self. It feels good not to have someone constantly keeping an eye on what I'm doing. I mean, they're all looking, but it's out of curiosity, not out of worry. It's like the whole troop has been demoted.

We watch the sunrise. It's beautiful, casting a rainbow over the newly awoken Pantheon and me. Rations are consumed in a hurry-—I pass on having any, as I don't feel the need anymore. I would have killed for something a day or two ago, but now I am completely energized and ready to continue. The morning is cold, just like I remember from the upstate camping trips my parents would take me on in a faux-display of normalcy. No matter how warm the weather was, the morning always had a chill after a rigid two hours of sleep in a flimsy pyramid of polyester and pesky insects.

I study the before-battle brigade as they get ready. L.Cpl. Alvarez is toying with his mortar, its tiny screen displaying the Smart-Sub's presence as a tiny blinking light. In this microcosmic form, the sub reads as being right on our backs. Pvt. Lowcroft has stripped her LMG and is cleaning the parts, getting it ready for its curtain call. She finally removes the huge box of ammo from my once-cumbersome pack and snaps it into the bottom of the gun. Threading the long belt of bullets through the open feed tray, she slams the top shut, locking the ammo in place. The noise echoes off the icy wave above, adding urgency.

L.Cpl. Albrier has been a literal trooper, rallying the group, and a plan comes together in no time at all. The Smart-Sub is still out there. The Pantheon members have their orders: relocate the disabled sub and gain access to its interior. From there, they will try to break down its various systems before gathering evidence to take back to HQ. I am relaxed, the weight having been taken from my shoulders in more ways than one, as now my powers are back, I have no need to struggle under the might of an overstuffed bag. I don't feel out of my element anymore; my godhood both elevates and grounds me. In fact, everyone seems more relaxed. Nebrezza has recuperated emotionally, and his confidence is back. I even detect a bit of cheeriness to his delivery.

"So, before we pluck the heart from this mystery, are there any questions?" he asks the group.

"Can we get on with it?" the rest of the squad answers in unison as if they were expecting his question. The banter laces their familiar comradery, a bundle of last-minute joy.

I look up through the wave and notice that dark spot is back—the secret shape—but with the sun out, it appears it was a trick of the light after all. Then it moves. Arms and legs sprout from both sides, and a smooth, featureless head bursts out of the top.

A sickness slowly flows from my stomach to my brain and then back down. Albrier stands next to me and looks up to see what has me transfixed. Her brown eyes blink rapidly behind long strands of her golden hair, a smirk grows on her face, and she starts to laugh, loudly, manically. As beads of terror-sweat fall down her face, I realize she is laughing against her will.

The Smart-Sub activates, aiming its external machine guns up at the shape, and sends a volley of glowing red sabot-rounds directly at it. The bullets bounce off its body in all directions, causing thin strings of light to extend from the dark figure like rays from the sun. The bullets pelt the landscape around us like lead rain. Suddenly, the figure thrusts out one of its arms, guiding the bullet stream to its palm and ricocheting it into the frozen wave above us.

Our tidal tent shatters violently into icy splinters, revealing the Valkyrie in full form, the finger at the end of its outstretched arm pointing directly at me. The Valkyrie hovers over the dry lakebed, in which sits the now-agitated war machine, which continues its assault, pelting the newly formed intruder with useless machine gunfire.

The Valkyrie forms a fist, and the sub-machine-gun barrels fold in half as if they're nothing but rolled-up newspapers. The guns stop firing.

Thinking quickly, I send the sharpened ice shards from our now-shattered shelter back up at the Valkyrie, who lets them bounce off its armored skin. A booming, mechanical roar comes from it, sucking Nebrezza, Alverez, and Lowcroft toward it, sending the trio rolling into a small cluster on the ground. Just before the Valkyrie can strike the troop, a gigantic crashing shockwave sounds, and another flying figure streaks down from high above us, grabbing the Valkyrie by the shoulders and launching it right up into the stratosphere. It's Dad! He found me! And he doesn't look the least bit happy.

Dad's now the only flying figure above us. I look over at the Pantheon, all of whom are completely speechless. However, Albrier hasn't been able to stop her laughter. Purple-faced and gasping for air, she collapses onto the ground as the rest of the team race to her aid. I look to Dad; maybe he can help. But before I can shout, he lunges at me, grabbing my ankle. He flies up from the battlefield with me in tow, distancing us from the carnage.

Then he stops suddenly and stretches his arm in the direction of the immobilized Smart-Sub, which slowly lifts from the lakebed. Hauling the machine over his head without laying a finger on it, like a weaponized bolt of lightning, he launches it down at the Pantheon. The soldiers quickly disperse in an attempt to get out of its path, but there's no time. As the sub hits the ground, the CloudKiller missiles it's carrying detonate inside, causing an immense explosion, which sends a fiery storm of carnage outward, completely engulfing the Pantheon in a cloud of smoke-flame.

The sounds of their pained screams strike my heart like a perfectly aimed arrow. I look down my leg at my upright father, who wears a lifeless expression. He starts his flight upward once more, up and away from the burning hilltop. I am witnessing death, up-close and personal, while being dragged, helplessly, upside down and into the sky. A tear falls from my eye and rolls up my forehead. It tumbles alone to the newly created crater of corpses below.

Chapter 14

Life as a whole flashes before my eyes as I'm pulled through Forever and back out into space. All the thunderous noise of our exit was extinguished as soon as it started. Dad and I have been in total silence since. We're launched out of Forever, flung through a large spread of blank space and back down toward the surface of Titan. I spot where the line of the equator would be just before Dad hurls me down at the moon. Like a softball hitting glass, I break through the atmosphere, the incandescent flames dancing around my tumbling body.

I hold out my hands and project a psychic force to slow my descent. As I burst through the orange clouds, I'm ambushed by the sight of the biggest mountain I've ever seen. I've fallen about 10,000 feet since I was level with its peak and I'm still going. Like a landing helicopter, the force of my sudden presence causes the film of freshly fallen snow to rise from its icy bed and swirl all around my floating body, but the kinetic force that cocooned my body is swiftly overpowered by Titan's gravity and disappears on touch.

Dad arrives soon after me in a feverish fashion. I could see the red flash of his anger long before he came through the clouds and into proper focus. He gently lands on the stretch of ice I found in front of the looming cryovolcano.

"I told you, Daniel," Dad says—his first sentence in literally years. His words are shaky. There is a control to them, but it grows thinner with every syllable, pain rising through his almost musical lecture. "I told you, and you completely ignored me. I am your father. I am your guide in this dangerous universe. I am your experience. You listen to me. It's what I am for!"

I step closer to him. "Dad, just listen—"

"No, you listen!" he says, stomping a crack in the ice beneath him, which stops me in my tracks. "I warned you, Daniel. If you scale the walls of time, you need to be certain there is going to be a place to return to."

"Will you just—"

"As long as the past is accessible, then so are you, your loved ones, and death itself. That...monster who stole your mother from us, that thing that could rip a precious life from the hands of two gods! It was the hardest fight of my life, Daniel, and I barely stopped it from taking you. My only son. My only family!"

I grip onto my nerve. He's just mad I ignored him, but as long as I stand my ground, he'll know he's speaking to an adult.

"Why did you interfere?" I ask bluntly.

This stops his frustrated shaking. He studies the cracked ground below his feet, fighting a misplaced smirk that is trying to distract him from the difficulty of my stubborn stance. He shoots a barbed look to me, and a rush of wind whips through my body, knocking me onto my war-torn backside. As I land on the ice, I feel it begin to rumble, and there's a huge, incendiary crunch behind my back. I quickly corkscrew to my feet and land with the mountain in view. The titan of Titan starts to vibrate, shaking huge piles of snow loose from its pointed peaks, mounds of which slam to the ground in slow succession. Countless tons of ice, water, and methane splash down and detonate into foggy oblivion. The liquid instantly freezes in midair and becomes large shards of frozen danger that rains down all around us.

And then, after a moment of silence, the mountain known as Doom Mons shatters into a deluge of jagged offcuts of ice, which crumble and tumble down to Titan's surface. All at once, we're struck by an enormous shockwave like that of a nuclear bomb, which rips all the snow and ice up from around us until we're floating above a giant, sloping crater that stretches for hundreds of miles. Inside this crater are thousands of jagged mountain pieces, each one sharper than the slickest of stalagmites.

I look to Dad, whose crimson face is marked with now-frozen tears. "YOU MADE ME A MURDERER!!!" he screams. His words bounce off the frozen ground and the walls of my heart. The rubble beneath him fragments to smaller fractals, which hover all around him as if he is the star at the center of a system. He floats toward me like a shark on a natural hunt. "You were told, Daniel. You can look but you cannot touch! And touch you did! So I looked for you, I fought for you, and I rid you of the mess you made at the expense of real human lives!" It's a surprisingly suppressed yell, but it doesn't make his hurt words sting any less.

"Dad, I didn't know—" I say, trying to calm him down.

"You *did* know! You knew because you were *told*! I *told* you, remember?! You made yourself an enemy to the universe as we knew it, and I had to pay massively to bail you out, you nepotistic little asshole!"

"That's not fair!" I cry as my tough exterior crumbles just as Doom Mons did, and I collapse into a pathetic, splintering mess in midair. I need to keep myself togeth—

"There is no such thing as 'fair,' Daniel!" he says, defiantly cutting me off mid-thought.

"What can I do? What can any of us do? I'm new at this!" I try to find any graspable straw.

"You can stop *lying* to me!"

Found one!

"What?! I didn't *lie* to you!" I scrape the frozen tears from my cheeks. "I didn't include you in my business—that's 'lying' now?"

"Daniel...you don't just have a god body. You have a god brain too. It's physiologically impossible for you to be anything other than the *genius* you are. So when I catch you being an idiot, I can only assume you're doing it on purpose. And if you're an idiot on purpose, then I can only say that you're lying."

"Oh, please! You don't get—"

Dad stamps his foot onto the air with a sonic boom, the force of which causes the field of ice blades beneath us to quiver violently like sand on a subwoofer.

"If I know that the thing you're going to say is wrong, then you don't need to finish saying it!" He growls. "The universe is a binary entity, the two halves of which are at war with one another. We have to keep out of their way. You're trying to force a paradox to choose a side. So that's why I'm taking the choice from you."

"What?" I blubber, astounded by his bluntness.

"I lost your mother. I won't lose you too. I'm transporting you back to Earth at an earlier time. It's been a considerable number of years since you left—that's how time works out here."

This rings a bell in my brain. How could I have missed that?! How could I have been so stupid? As I look up, Dad's anger is still present, but it's different. It's sharper, like its morphing into righteous assurance.

"Goddammit, Daniel. Not once did you stop to think about how much I've done for you. It's not difficult. Okay, once you're back on Earth, I'll put a barrier around the planet. You won't be able to leave. You won't be able to access Forever, and time will be safe from you. When you can comprehend the seriousness of your actions like an adult rather than a spoiled, twenty-four-year-old child, you can have your privileges back. Do you understand?

"Wait! Dad, please!" I beg with the confidence of a guilty man being sentenced to hang.

"Turn around," he commands, opening his arms wide.

I feel a wall of numbness push against my back, clawing at me like undead hands from an icy tomb. The colors shimmer in the reflection of Dad's eyes. It's Forever. I slowly turn, shaking as I do. Prey in the eyes of a predator, it swallows me whole.

I lie in the atmosphere, my back to Earth. It's been days since we had that conversation, and not just because of the time travel. I'm depressed, deflated. I feel a familiar drag I haven't felt in a long time. Stillness. Nothingness. A paradox.

Darkness dances above me; brightness beckons below. I'm flanked by life and death, held close by the known and unknown, sandwiched between substance and...

I don't want to leave.

I haven't done much since I got back to the present. I did talk to Martin. I watched him for a while, waiting for the perfect time. I didn't want him to have any alcohol in his system, so while he was asleep, I removed the alcoholic content from the bottles in his fridge. I sat in his living room waiting for him to wake. I had nothing to keep me company apart from a dark reflection of myself that stared at me from his dormant 8K television. When he found me sitting on his couch, he was startled, but more in an excited way. An aura of hope and impatience danced around his whole body when he hopped into his living room wearing a bathrobe that he didn't bother to tie properly. He refused the couch. Instead, he sat on his tiny glass coffee table to listen to my story.

While I was telling him about what happened during the war, he kept looking over my shoulder toward his apartment door, waiting for his son to burst through with a bottle of champagne and a long-awaited embrace. But before my story was over, Martin stood, tied his robe, and collapsed onto the couch silently. I moved away, giving him space, and he just sat there in a broken heap like an abandoned wooden puppet. The worst part was the way he kept on looking toward his door. No longer was it a means of ingress but a practical joke with hinges. It broke my heart to see him like this.

Against my better judgment, I told him everything that had happened with his son, the Pantheon, and the Valkyrie. I left my father out of it. He already had enough of a headache from my actions, and I couldn't loop him further into this than I already had. I'm not a parent, but I know faith plays a big part in the whole mother-father thing, and if a child dies before the parents, then I guess faith is the only thing that remains.

That's what I had taken from Martin. I'm a god, yet I have no knowledge of an afterlife. I didn't tell him it was an accident that he found out about me. Maybe a lie would have been better for him. Instead, I projected the rules of time Dad devised for me onto Martin's TV. I thought that the true, objective explanation would act as some sort of bandage for him, but it didn't. He asked me to go back again, to stop him from finding out about my abilities, but he already knew I couldn't. I don't want to change time anymore. I only want to watch. After that, he never said a word. He went over and opened his living room window. The cameras in his building didn't see me come up the stairs because I didn't, so I was to leave the way I'd come.

From there, I decided I'd fly to the Moon for some solitude, but Dad's barrier was already up, stopping me for reaching it. I wonder where he is now. Dad has all of the freedom he needs. He's probably out running track on the sun or swimming through Jupiter's red spot. He can never just be where he is. Even when I was younger, he would always be out the house on some errand for hours in the day on the rare occasion he wasn't working. Confined spaces really agitated him. You would think I'd feel the same way now, needing a plan, a way to break out of the box I have been put in, but I don't. I don't feel anything.

I thought I had a plan for saving the Pantheon—a blueprint to a better tomorrow—but in the end, that plan became a vague idea. And from there, it faded into failure. Goddammit, I came up here for the silence. Instead, I am constantly followed around by bad memories and reverberating words of shame. Memory, that's a dimension of its own. A powerful space which can take hold of a person's soul without intruding upon the physical realms we perceive. It cannot be measured in light, energy, or electromagnetic forces because it exists beyond them. This is evident by my being up here, in Earth's sensory deprivation tank, and this hasn't made the voices go away. Another paradox.

The stars flicker dimly in the darkness. Those visible aren't the only ones there; they're the only ones that can be seen with any clarity from this particular place in the system. The rest are shielded from your sight by random bumps in the road, a moon or a planet taking their place, warping your perspective. You know they exist, but they've been demoted from plasma giant to ambiguous data as far as you're concerned. This is how it's going to be for a necessarily long time. You know, if I was allowed out now, I'd probably go and have a look at some. Compare, contrast, rename. I'd compile a detailed description of the ones I saw so you could know what you're missing.

It was a simple task, one fit for a god: Save lives in war: another paradox. Check three on the tally. The only way to save lives is to end the lives of others, easy to grasp, right? When those lives have already expired, the choice is even easier. It's not even yours anymore; it's already been made. And yet, their faces haunt me. All this time, I thought I was missing something: a coward's fate; excused from a sworn duty to fight on behalf of those who can't stand up for themselves—the weak, the ill, the rich, objectivists paying with privilege. That is the group I fall into. A trust-fund kid, blessed with a celestial currency that never runs out. And what did I do with all this powerful freedom? I created my own time loop and went back to the chaos my nepotism saved me from.

I can tell myself the world was scarred long before the war, but that's the big picture, too broad to sting. It's not pain; it's a sick feeling in my stomach, one that's easily gotten used to.

The world is ultimately doomed, not unlike Doom Mons. But I guess it had it coming.

Doom Mons, a place my god brain abduced into legibility, no longer exists. The titan of Titan was brought down in a fit of rage and disappointment, but those with any sentience won't be aware of such a change for a while, and by the time they are, the formulae will remain a mystery to them forever. Will anyone notice when Earth changes? When humanity comes to an end? Furthermore, will that change be suicide or murder? If Nebrezza is right and it's the former, will mourning the dead even be appropriate when the world was run, up to the end, by the ruling hand of those without empathy? Not a secret cult or an exclusive cabal but a disconnected group of men and women, strangers to one another but all with the same agenda in mind: the acquisition of money, power, and comfort at the cost of international stability.

Holly's cruise-jumping donkey story wasn't unique to our time. When the war first hit Europe, puff-piece editorials were everywhere, written and released onto the popular news sites, internationally. Each of these stories contained European facts and trivia to help "educate" and "lighten the mood." One of these stories detailed how, genetically, everyone living in Europe (at the time) was descended from a Roman emperor born in the 740s. Geneticists traced European family histories back thousands of years using binary: one person, two parents, four grandparents etcetera. This all led them to the same ancestor every time: Charles I or "King Charlemagne."

Obviously, if you were to measure international influence in the same way, you'd need more than people to help with the calculations. You'd need to measure the very concept of societal influence: wealth, credit scores, personal relationships, land ownership, the worth of general currency, recorded business dealings, laws written, political donations, individual reputations, and more. Follow the tree of influence using binary and there has to be a beginning, like there was with Charlemagne. Not an individual but a lot of similar people.

Based on where they are in society in terms of class, it stands to reason these particular people got there due to their ability to process logic. They are, however, blind to the influence of emotion and sentimentality; they'd fail to reach such a height otherwise. These people are the reason why humans incorrectly believe that "the world is a cruel place." It isn't. It's a habitat, shaped by the behavior of immoral human beings with too much money, too much power, and too much influence. The world is almost entirely a capitalist one, and people say capitalism can only exist if everyone has something to aspire to. And these people, by simply existing, break this rule and continue to warp that capitalistic system, setting humans on a path to ruin. Now, I ask you: how is that the fault of the world? Tornados ravage whole towns, sure, but these humans have bankrupted entire countries, and yes, you read that right, they're humans, just like you. What if I tell you they were a necessary line of code in an early build of humanity, one that expanded, grew complex enough to delete its own expiration date? Would this help sweeten my thesis?

This is how lives are shaped, not by a "cruel world" but by immoral humans making self-serving decisions that collaterally affect the lives of everyone below their level of influence. They aren't gods. They might think themselves divine and are treated as such, but if they were in my position right now, their bodies and minds would fail them. They are humans with too much power, influence, and control, and the world they control is the one you live on. I preach, but I can't judge, after all. I've not always been in control of my life, that's for sure. I close my eyes to the sight of the stars.

When I was a junior in high school, the theater group I was a part of was tasked with putting on a performance of *The Golden One*, a folktale from Michigan about a dying boy and his golden pony friend. I was chosen to read the part of the eponymous Golden Boy during the first script read-through. He was a blond-haired, blue-eyed beauty whom the whole town adored. It was the first time I had been chosen for something important at school, and I was determined to do a good job. I took the reading seriously and held on to my one chance with all my might. I wouldn't just be The Golden One; I would be the *only* one.

By the time rehearsals started, I was given my real role, not the boy who everyone admired but the ass of the horse he called his best friend. I pleaded with the teachers to change their minds, that I would do a good job. They always said the same thing: "The Golden One can't be a brunet, can he?"

The role was recast, and in the end it wasn't even given to a boy but to a girl who always wore a hairpin badge of a bow in her ponytail. It was a little childish for her age, but she was never called out on it. She couldn't act. She just read the words aloud with lofty tones, but like the boy in the story, everyone adored her. She was admired both onstage and off. I wasn't really surprised. She was a kind kid with good grades and respectful of both teachers and classmates. She left our school before we got to our seniors. She was never a friend of mine, but the place still felt darker after she'd gone. However, her entire family became a focal point of rumor as soon as they'd left town. Apparently, one of her parents was the vice-chair of a drug company, and they were caught embezzling money. They had to pay huge fines to avoid jail time. After they'd paid off their punishment, they no longer could afford to live so close to the city. Then again, I only heard this through word of mouth in high school, so it could have all been bullshit.

Still, I never knew why I was passed up for a girl. Why was being a brunet a problem but not being a boy wasn't? Anyway, after all was said and done, I stood there night after night, hunched over in my horse costume, kicking my feet when prompted. I heard every noise the crowd made—every laugh, every gasp, and every cheer. I knew none of them were for me. I was on stage in front of all of the parents and family friends, yet I was completely invisible to them.

Mom and Dad came to watch on the last night we were performing. From behind the curtain, I saw them take their seats before the show. They were both wearing identical scowls, and they sat together, but it was only their chairs that were close. They were disconnected, probably from a long argument they were having as they were leaving. They argued a lot when I was a teenager. I wasn't any help for either of them. Any time they started up, I closed my bedroom door and let them have at each other. Their fights would be short: the longest probably lasted about ten minutes before loud bangs could be heard and they both left the house. Regardless, they came to the show. I had complained to them about my situation. They were disappointed, but they were going through a lot themselves; it was during the *Purple* stage of their marriage. At the time, I judged them for not helping me out. I should judge them more *now* for putting up with that whole situation with the powers they had. I never knew why they didn't help me, but I do now. This was the world being the world, functioning as it should, free from the control of gods above. And I was what I was meant to be at that time: a horse's ass.

I wonder if I'd had my powers—if I was a god at the time of rehearsals—would I have gotten the part? I could have changed things, rewritten the teaching staff, the students, even the play, but would it have come out in my favor? Could I have taken back my role without making the nice girl disappear from all existence? I, like everybody, have always wished for the ability to change events that don't go my way, but now I have that power, I don't think I want to. I wouldn't trade my life for peace of mind. I probably wouldn't be able to, anyway. I know it would end like the war did for me: with Dad pulling me back through time like a pet owner dragging his misbehaving mutt from a frightened child. He'd have no choice.

I am alone up here, out of the path of all satellites, and no one can see me. There are billions of lives down below, yet none of them are watching me. My blood stirs with anger. Memories of my time as a non-golden boy eclipse my guilt from my forgoing failure. The cheering, jeering crowd's voices are drowned out by music, music in my mind. It's not a grand score but a soft, melodic piano, like the one I heard when I flew to Forever alone. The song softens my spirit, and my anger changes to a strange excitement. The music swells slightly, and I am overcome with a surge of energy that runs through my whole body, riding my pulse from head to toe.

I open my eyes and look out into space. Slowly, I spin my whole body around, cartwheeling at my leisure like a twirling star in the sky. The little lights in the dark swirl above me, twinkling as I move, like the flashes of a trillion cameras. I flip over, kick out with my right leg and punch with my left. These faux-fighting moves flow freely with the lack of gravity. I twist around, performing a perfect pirouette as high up in the atmosphere as Dad's barrier allows me to be. As my elbows bounce repeatedly off the invisible field, it warps, refracting light from it. This shows up as polychromatic points wherever I apply pressure, negating the need to see those lost stars beyond. Like a lap swimmer, I push off the barrier and corkscrew noiselessly through space, the brightness of the earth below skimming past my eyes forming a ying-yang pattern in constant flux.

I'm high above the Earth, and I'm dancing, dancing like no one can see me, because they can't. Out here, I am free from judgment, free of disappointment. I can dance all I like, and no one can stop me. And if you were here, would you tell me that I'm dancing poorly, that my dance is bad to behold? If so, why? Why would you try to make a paradox pick a side? That didn't work for me because it *doesn't* work. Anyone telling me or anyone that they are unable to dance is like saying there's a right way to speak, laugh, or love. I don't know what my dance is trying to say, but does it really need to say anything?

I finish up, taking in Earth in its blue beauty. I have explored our solar system and envied that ability as soon as I lost it, but Earth has been here. The great wonders of a broken world have been at my disposal from the beginning; I don't need to see stars. I speed downward, an unseen comet screaming back to my home, heading for America, and then New York. No, this won't do. I don't want the feeling from up above to end. I don't want company. I am perfectly fine without it. All I want is stability. My feet have missed the feel of solid ground.

I curve my body to match the shape of the horizon and then, with a flick of my legs, I turn to take a detour. There are many places on Earth that are uninhabited. Be they places of danger or religion, not a soul can be found. I will go to a place which is a part of neither party.

Fire comes and goes as I zoom through the sky and slam down on an uninhabited volcanic island close to Iceland. Yep, *that* island. Its name is Surtsey, and it's still a child. A volcanic eruption brought it to life in the 1960s. Ironically, it's an unassuming little place—no mocked-up drywall in sight. Humans are only allowed to visit in order to study it, and those visits are infrequent. However, they say nothing about gods stepping foot on its black beaches, so step foot I will.

Chapter 15

RECALLED back to Earth on nobody's orders but my own, I'm hovering over the mid-Atlantic at the southernmost point of Iceland—one of the first countries occupied when the war broke out. America took control of the land and government in a matter of weeks. There were mass protests and even a riot or two in the center of Reykjavík, but it didn't matter. Indifference and the bloated American military budget won the day for the invaders in the end. America then used Iceland as a hub for its forces, sending some up to Denmark and others across to Norway and the United Kingdom. The whole thing went on from there, similar situations in three different directions: protests, riots, and death, all until the three occupying superpowers collided at the center of Europe. When they did, the forces splintered, directing stealth drones past the "collision point" in Germany. America sent theirs to Russia, Russia to America, and China to both of them. The latter could afford such a split since they had the most soldiers and made everything themselves—something remunerative outsourcing *prevented* America and Russia from doing.

I finally see it, the small shard of the Vestmannaeyjar archipelago… that's a funny word, *shard*. Increasing my speed, I reenter to get to a place I've never been. The sea is shipless and without expression, no one for miles in three different directions. Behind me, however, lies the sleepy Heimaey harbor, which seems as dormant as the volcano that shares its space. Comparatively, the island of Surtsey is a lot smaller and beautiful in its minimalism. It and the larger siblings it sits between form a sturdy path of stepping-stones fit for a giant. The dark, craggy rock is gently lapped at by colorless foam, giving sustenance to the moss that has formed along its back like the fur of a land-mammal. In the center of the large lava mounds that make up most of the island, I spy an unexpected surprise: a small, cubic structure, a building high up enough to be used as lighthouse. But that doesn't make sense, not with how low the clouds are overhead. I'll have to check that out later.

I have to confess that I don't know why I'm here. Maybe it's because I know those protesters back home would tremble with anger at the sight of me desecrating the sacred land they have no shares in. If only they were here, then I'd for once be in their presence without a violent sense of claustrophobia gripping my nerves. I wonder what they're up to now as the "brave face of patriotism." That's the way the surviving countries went after the war—one day a year they mourn their dead and the next 364 pretend the war was their victory in order to forget the losses. The truth is that no country was victorious in the war; even the survivors died in some way. Another paradox.

No, no one won the war because they couldn't. Only time had that power. As the weeks went on and the death tally rose, people grew bored with the conflict, numb to the unpunished atrocities they were seeing on the news twenty-four seven. The booing grew louder for all the wrong reasons. And then everything just stopped. The Berlin Treaty was signed by all three superpowers. They went into the negotiation halls to divide European countries among them "fairly." They still haven't come out.

I think boredom is a powerful force. I think it, like fear, is a defense mechanism all humans share. It has evolved into a reaction against strange philosophies, those which are hastily cut down into simple, grotesque mimetic imagery to keep people engaged. Selfishly, I think about Holly, my one tie to the *news world*. As long as a collective boredom can flex its form, her life will be her work, and companies like Huble who profit from excitement will continually scramble, swinging a million bats around in the hopes that one finds a ball that can be sent smashing through the glass pane of "peace."

Nebrezza was right. There will be no personal backlash for these profiteers. Vandalism is only a minor offense. I don't know if Holly can make it past that world. She has the ambition, she has the routine, but she has the clamp of faux-professionalism keeping her in a place where she can do no "damage." Another paradox.

Sam's the opposite. He is the biggest of all of us but enjoys comfort and security. This wasn't so apparent when I first met him. I took the opportunity after the war to get into the previously out-of-reach haven of New York. Sam had the same idea, but his lack of ambition made him entirely reliant on his parents...and I feel *I* can judge him for this. Yet another paradox.

And then there is Ana, someone who refuses to *leave* her own headspace...like I'm one to talk.

I do hope she's okay. She's been through a lot, but I would never know if I wasn't there. She isn't the *sharing* type. I am, though, so contrary to how quiet and down she was, she always had the energy to help me out. I saw this the day we met. Ana showed me around when I was accepted for a position at Hourglass, high up in Montage Tower. The first thing I saw of her was the look of dread she gave me when her name was called out for her to "volunteer" an office tour. Offices were bad places for a lot of women to work for a long time. I hope I wasn't a problem for anyone.

Once the tour began, I tried to get Ana to leave me to wander by myself, I said it to appear "independent," but really it was my reaction to her reaction. Well, it didn't matter anyway, as after a while we seemed to settle each other's nerves, and the tour became what would be our first hangout session, just the two of us circling the halls of the tower, floor by floor. Me: a claustrophobic concoction of angst, and daddy issues, and Ana: a bundle of anxiety, depression, and mommy issues.

I slow my pace for a gentle descent, and after a few seconds, my feet come into contact with the island, its soft-looking surface rock hard to the touch. The north spit of the island protrudes and tapers like the tail of a sting-ray. I balance as I walk the edge of it. Tenderly, the tide caresses the black, grainy tail as if it's calling it back below its depths. The harsh, Icelandic waves have pushed a large amount of misshapen, lead-colored pebbles up the land and under the feet of the lava domes. This leaves an almost untouched black beachhead for me to meander along, hands in my coat pockets, head down, eyes up over the stiff collar around my neck—a stance suitable for a late-twentieth-century album cover.

After a couple of steps, I come across the sound of flapping ahead of me. I squint through the Icelandic wind to spy a small, shabby nest of seagulls farther down the shoreline, their beaks as bright as buttercups. Graying feathers fall from their dirty-white bodies as they shake their heads, nuzzling one another. It's just past mating season for the lucky bastards. This pair looks happy to stay attached, a rare sight. I try to quietly shuffle past them, but the crunching of the black sand beneath my shoes alerts them to my presence the second I take my first shifting step. Both birds make a squishy-faced scowl at me. Territorial, they hop up and out of their nest, flapping their sharp, lengthy wings, their spiky screeches piercing my eardrums like fishing hooks. I heed their warnings and go about my business. One of the birds jumps down and pecks at the footprints I have left behind. With a wave of my hand, moving sand into them, I fill in my prints as if they were never there.

The sight of those birds brought the clouds over my head. Their paranoia is as justified as the humans'. All it will take is the right personality disorder and the world will once again fall into chaos because that's who thrives in chaotic environments: the morally insane. We saw it on Wall Street before it was re-regulated, we saw it in the highest offices of the highest lands before they collided headfirst into one another, and the collateral damage of their crash resulted in the deaths of millions. The world is different now, but can it evolve under the rule of decent people, or will the evil ideas corrupt the seemingly incorruptible? Can humankind really project itself into the darkness of space without the bad apples that lay in its midst using their lack of conscience to take over the new, new world?

As I think this, I tune in to a low hum, which buzzes from beyond the beach. At first, I mistake it for the hum of anxiety produced by my bad thoughts but no, it sounds like the boat used by the soldiers to land on Greece a couple of years ago. A burning energy tracks through my arm, and instinctively, I conjure a small brightbolt and take aim at the intruders. Peering past the angrily spinning ball of light in my hand, I sight the source of the noise: a large, yellow dingy. If my eyesight were worse, I'd swear I was staring at a giant rubber ducky. In it is a group of humans dressed head to toe in blood-orange waterproof clothing, not combative camouflage. Their vessel is headed directly to where I am standing.

Goddammit, it's the sand patch. I'm standing on the only place on the island that their boat can dock. Are researchers really a threat to me now?! In one angry stroke, I close my hand, causing the brightbolt to collapse in on itself and out of existence. What the hell is wrong with me? I swiftly look for a place to hide, but there isn't one. Cornered, I cover my face with my hands, hoping for the crew to pass by without fuss. The hum of the boat grows louder as it draws nearer to the shore. I see it now, rolling closer with each second. I see it…through my hands. I drop them down to my sides and see nothing of myself. No clothes, no skin. I'm completely invisible.

Just in time. The research boat is close enough to Surtsey that I'd stand out like a…well, an unwelcomed visitor to a private piece of Icelandic rock. The only thing in the guidebook Dad made for me was something about "adaptability"—maybe this is included in that category? Engaging with the panic I felt, my body rid itself of all texture. Now there is nothing left of me to see but the cold-weather breaths that pointlessly vent from my mouth. I cease breathing as the boat's engines cuts out.

The researchers on board huddle together at the back of their bobbing vessel, trying with all their might to raise a smaller dingy out of the lifeboat storage area. After some fumbling, they successfully lug it over their heads and lower it into the swirling sea. A taller female scientist picks up three, pearl-colored plastic paddles and distributes them to the rest of the team, minus the driver, who roughly shakes her hand. I don't think he's going with them.

At once, the leader of the team and what appears to be her right-hand man board the dinghy without a problem, leaving only one researcher to board. The straggler puts his foot over the edge but withdraws it fearfully. The leader waves at the straggler while yelling something in Icelandic. He clumsily leaps and lands inside the smaller boat only to lose his balance. He flails about, almost rolling into the sea, but his team grab the tail of his waterproof coat and drag him back from the dinghy's edge.

After a few rocky seconds, they each start to paddle, stroking aggressively against the circulating current. The wind picks up—they'll never make it to shore at this rate. They continue to drag their paddles to no avail. Suddenly, the waves rise higher than they already are, causing the dinghy to sway violently. This pressure sends the team reaching out for the small, dark cords on the side of the boat for safety. The more effort they put in the farther back they are sent.

I can't watch this anymore. I motion with one of my invisible hands and lift a wave below their boat, launching their dinghy across the sea toward the shore. The lifeboat crashes onto the beach right at my invisible feet. The man who *almost* went overboard now does exactly that, tumbling out of the boat and landing hilariously on the black sand. I successfully suppress my laugh. The crew are shaken but together. The leader of the group pulls the straggler up off the ground. She shouts something in excited Icelandic, gently pawing at the sand with her black, rubber boot. The other two are silent, stuck in awe at the majesty of the island.

I watch the trio quietly. After a few celebratory hugs, the leader points toward a distant lava mound, the one with that little hut I saw when I first got here. That must be where they're staying. They march off together, up the hill in their merry little troupe, dragging their distressed dinghy behind them. I stay down here.

As they disappear into their cabin, I notice that the sky around us has transformed from gray and overcast to cloudless and orange. I've been in my own headspace for so long I didn't notice how late it was. The sun has begun to set in the distance. It forms a unique yet recognizable pattern, a beautifully bulbous hourglass which kisses the horizon like a lover. It's a visual phenomenon called the Novaya Zemlya effect, which comes from the refraction of sunlight when it shines between the layers of Earth's atmosphere. It scares me to think that I will never know where that information came from. I don't remember reading it, nor can I tell if it's something my god brain made up on its own without need for confirmation.

Be quiet and enjoy it, Dan. The Earth has gifted you a timepiece made of precious fire and you didn't even have to leave the planet to receive it. My mind stirs once again, reminding me of the error I see right in front of my very eyes—an error I wish I could *unsee*. The Novaya Zemlya only happens when the sun rises. There shouldn't be an hourglass pattern for me to see.

I think.

I'm sure I'm right.

Aren't I?

Suddenly, a thick, icy panic sets in, layering itself over my spine like cold soup. What is happening to me?

"GODDAMMIT!" I scream at the top of my lungs, and the lapping waves retreat from the force of my noise. The cabin above me stands dark and still, window blinds rolled down to keep the strong light of the sun out of tired eyes. They didn't hear me. However, my scream did scare the pair of nesting seagulls, who sharply spin their beaks to me. After an ugly squawk, the couple quickly abandon their cushy nest, leaving their precious eggs behind. My eyes follow them as they fly toward the sun, splitting away from each other, one high, one low, as each bird makes for their own section of hourglass, keeping to their own space as they fly separately out of sight. Another goddamned paradox.

All of a sudden, out of the *orange* instead of the blue, I'm attacked by a memory of Alvarez's journal. The drawing of the flying men—he saw them.

He saw the Valkyries.

I put my hands together and thrust them out in front of me, making a long shadow over the dark sand like the midnight hands of an analogue clock. I open my arms out, opening Forever just like Dad did in space. Black sand noiselessly blows all around me, and the gray sea ripples sharply, raising zigzagged lines which run in all directions like they're dodging bullets. The crack in spacetime widens into a rotated white smile. It works on Earth just fine. I don't know how Dad would react if he found out I can open Forever like he can. Maybe he'd be proud; maybe it would scare him. Whatever the reason, I could tell him, "I learned it from watching you!" like a teenage smoker.

I know I'm disobeying Dad again, but I'm not going to touch anything. I'm only going to look.

With great joy, I hop into Forever, searching my mindscape for my new destination away from the black beach of Surtsey. The colors inside Forever mix meticulously, showing me what I want to see: New York City, twenty-nine years ago.

In a flash of white light, I'm perched atop the flame in the hand of the still-standing Lady Liberty. After I find my perfect footing, I gaze lovingly out across the bay at New York City, which stands as a palatial postcard of what was a bustling metropolis of opulence and iconography. My childhood TV viewings are brought to life right in front of my eyes. I made sure I landed late enough for the sun to be out but early enough that I have a couple of hours left before the ferry tours begin. I don't have to hide out here.

With a metallic pop, I push off from the statue's iconic nightlight, leaping loftily from the green torch's golden flame, and dive down toward the plinth on which she stands as both a hopeful helper and peaceful protector. A blur of greens and blues passes my eyes as I soar past her colossal flank. I lift my head slightly, setting my flight path. Majestically, I whiz through the air, speeding away from the monument and headlong toward the city skyline. I take myself farther down, right above the shimmering sea, my reflection rippling in the copper-colored waters. The force of my flying sends splashes up high, leaving a trail of foam and bubbles in my wake the likes of which speedboats create. I slow to give my reflection a quick high-five, splashing the bay water up into the air, which sizzles out of existence in dazzling diamond light.

As I pass the edge of Ellis Island, I dip below the surface and torpedo up and out onto the wall below Battery Park. I cling to the brickwork silently, peeking up through the safety rail, soaking wet like a really nervous prisoner. I don't see anyone out; it is six a.m., after all. Hopping over the fence, I gracefully land on the soft, dry grass. The whole place is golden in the light of dawn. I look down at my wet clothes; another disguise is in order. I quickly jump up a lone tree in a secluded corner of the park, and in a flash of yellow light, I transform my old look into one fit for a Saturday morning jogger, sweatbands and all.

Dropping down from the tree like an energized baboon, I make my way out of the park and over to a large, blue truck. As I approach, a tiny, muscle-free man pops out of the back shutters. He's lugging a large stack of hot-off-the-press newspapers over to a closed newsstand. He spits a cigarette out of his mouth and onto the ground. Struggling with every step, he finally drops the stack onto the concrete with a blunt slam, the gust from which puts out the discarded cigarette in one puff. I rip one of the papers out of its plastic cord like a magician would an informative tablecloth and check for the date. YES! I landed perfectly, powers and all!

"Excuse me?" I say to the paper man, who is now perched on the edge of the van rolling up another cigarette.

"Hmmm?" he murmurs in a gruff yet high-pitched way.

"Do you know the way to Incognitoys?"

He stops rolling and looks me up and down.

"Bit old for toys, ain't ya, kid?" he asks with a sharp grin.

"It's my son's birthday," I lie.

"Well, aren't you the father of the year, huh?" he mutters facetiously as he looks around his truck. "Here." The man tosses an unopened phone book at my chest. I take the blow with ease but pretend to be winded. "Ya best keep up the cardio, son, if you wanna grow up big and strong like me." He lets out a grunt, which then turns into an extended fit of coughing for what feels like eighty-nine seconds.

"Thanks, mister," I say, scanning the back cover of the book.

"Now, can you do me a favor?" he asks, lighting up.

"Yes?" I stop reading and shoot him a helpful smile.

"Can you leave me alone?"

I nod, slowly backing away, and cross the street to take refuge in a nearby phone booth. I rip the book out of its package and flick through the thin, yellow pages, speed-reading the names until I get to Incognitoys! The address is listed, and it's close, on the corner of Jay and Houston. I look out and see creepy paper guy standing on the back of the truck with his oversized, gloved hands gripping the grab handles. He stares directly at me through the phone booth glass. I raise my thumb to him and force out a smile of victory. He whacks the back of the truck with his free fist, and it takes off with him.

As the sound of the truck's engine disappears into the distance, I burst out of the phone booth, still in my exercise gear, and quickly jog to the toy store, checking over my shoulder every so often. The streets are unusually quiet: I know work doesn't start until later for most in this time, but I expected to have to bash my way through rivers of people all calling me names and pushing me back.

I finally turn the corner that hides from view a glowing blue-and-gold sign which brightly beams "Incognitoys!" I've never been here before. The whole chain went bust before my first time visiting the city. I carefully cross the analogue asphalt to the other side of the street. This doesn't stop an oncoming motorist blaring their horn at me for wasting half a picosecond of their speeding time with my thoughtless walking. Activity has started to pick up.

I peer in through the store's giant glass doors; it's dark and empty inside. The sign out front says that it opens at ten a.m., which would be helpful, only I don't know what time Alvarez gets here, and I don't know what a seven-year-old lance corporal looks like. I have to sit and stake out the place for as long as it takes, but I need somewhere to hide. I can't just sit on a bench all day watching kids. It may be the 90s, but creepiness still exists.

Turning around, I scan the surrounding redbrick rooftops, hoping to find a perch to sit on only for traffic to pick up on the road. Nothing. That's not my only problem, however, as in an instant, a python of luxury sedans has moved in, blocking the road on their way to the financial district. This causes a jam right in front of me. Horns blare, curse words are thrown, and I'm surrounded by witnesses. I can't fly like this. I can't even turn myself invisible with this many eyes on me while I stand on the street like I'm stoned off my ass.

Concentrating on the noise around me, I stop time and fly up to one of the closer rooftops. The smoky view of the morning city distracts me for a second before I look down and try to read the store sign. If I didn't already know it said "closed," I wouldn't be able to read it at all. It's too suspicious on the sidewalk. I guess I could conjure up some binoculars—NO, THAT'S EVEN CREEPIER! I look about the street across from the store and notice a collection of bushes. I guess they'll have to do. Hopping down from the building, I jump behind a bush, restarting time as the leaves consume me.

Okay. Now I'm all comfy, there's nothing to do now but wait.

It's been hours since I arrived: it's now almost closing time. I've sat through four tantrums, three crying fits, and nine extended bouts of general whining. The drivers are way too boisterous for this late in the afternoon. The kids have been quiet, though—wait just a bush-diving minute! Could this be him? Peering between the passing cars, I spot a small Latino child entering the store with his mom. It's exactly 3:54 p.m. I wait.

He's been in there for six minutes. What's he looking for? Better days?

And out he comes. His little hands aren't empty. That *must* be— it *is* him! Little Lance Corporal Alvarez, dressed in a tiny black waistcoat and blue shirt. His doll-sized outfit looks formal enough to be celebratory. His left hand in his mom's, his right hand clutches a flashy toy robot. He waves the toy in the air, *pew-pew*-ing as if it's raining death from above onto a Turkish village. His mom shushes her noisy child as she presses the buttons on an enormous cellular phone, keying in a phone number. The boy minds his own business, whizzing his robot all around, *whooshing* and *fwooshing*.

Suddenly, Alvarez falls silent as he stares blankly past his robot and into the sky. His shaking hand drops his birthday gift onto the sidewalk, and he points up at whatever he sees, jumping up and down shouting, "Mommy, look-it!"

Even in this era people are still glued to their cell phones, and she completely misses what Alvarez sees, but I don't. It's the flying men, framed up high by the looming, white sun. The figures hover for a second and then quickly speed away from the Earth. I launch my invisible body out of the bush, which explodes onto the street, firing leaves across the sidewalk and knocking the phone from Alvarez's mom's hand. I'm not sure if that's a good thing or a bad thing, but I have to keep these guys in my sight.

I soar higher and higher until the blue of the sky turns black. I'm back in space, twirling my body around to see where the gods went. I see them, across the globe. I'm still invisible, so I won't be caught. They're hovering under Canada. I stealthily drift closer to the silhouetted spacemen. I still have a while to

...go, wait, they're gone! They were just here, and now they're both gone. What the hell happened?!

I speed over to where the figures were, but all that remains is a thin streak of multicolored light that connects me to Earth like a zip line made from rainbow. It leads right down toward the planet, right toward... Oh, shit.

Though a blast of atmospheric fire, I thunder down to Earth, tracing the streak all the way down. As I follow, the line grows larger, widening out until I am taken in by it.

I'm spat out onto an orange frozen wasteland, my face pressed against a sheet of solid snow. I stand and turn, trying to find any sign of life within or on the tangerine-tinted tundra, or any witnesses of my power, at least. I think I'm back on Titan. I turn a full 360 and see that I'm wrong. There's a giant cityscape across the bay from me, and it's familiar—one which holds significance in the very bark of my family tree. I'm standing on the back of a giant icy glacier that sits right in the middle of the Gastineau Channel.

I look across at the stream of fishing boats lining the closest dock. Alongside these is a much larger, decorative battleship, which serves as a memorial to the fallen. All the vessels are dormant, waiting like corralled horses to be taken out. After a few seconds of quiet contemplation, a mighty wind blows from the distant buildings, knocking me onto my back, my arms and legs spread out like a novelty Popsicle of the Vitruvian man. My vision blurs, and something unseen begins to pull me through the ice and down into freezing darkness below, blocking out all of my senses. What can I do but hold on to the last thing I saw: the city across from me. I treasure my memory of a memory.

Of Juneau.

Chapter 16

WAKING to the feeling of pain is both familiar and foreign to me. I haven't felt much of anything in the last couple of weeks. A hard sheet of ice *broke* my fall, shooting cracks away from my body like shadowy lightning. I lay tangled in a twisted blanket of snow. Well, it *was* snow. It's stiffened, making it surprisingly tough to break away from. I'm getting sick of the smell of cold air. How many times must I fight my way through vague constructs of ice and light?

Aggressively, I force my arms out of their binds, bursting through the rest of my coverings, and take my first dim look at my surroundings. From what I can make out, I'm in a long, cavernous tunnel of whirling ice...or glass. Whatever it is, it's reflective. I can see my face in it. I only hear two things, the crunching of the ice under my feet as I take my first, uneasy steps and the distorted sound of my breath as it bursts roughly from my sapless mouth. It makes no fog, however. That shouldn't be all the noise there is. It isn't logical. The wind should be whistling, and the ice above me should be cracking like a lit fireplace as it adjusts to my heat, but the cavern is completely soundless.

My arms vibrate as I collect energy, and in a long, drawn-out flash, I launch two brightbeams up at the curved ceiling above, hoping to create a flight tunnel out of here. The change in light almost blinds me, and the distorted growl of my beam assaults my ears. I can't take much more, so I drop my hands and wait. The dust has nowhere to go, but it clears from my sight regardless. If I did pierce the surface of the ice, it wasn't by much, although the area is a little brighter, as I see now that I'm standing in a large tunnel which glistens almost artificially. It resembles the frozen wave I made two years ago, except it's deeper. Much deeper. No normal ice should have been able to withstand the energy I launched. Whatever it is, I didn't build it.

Looking up at the ceiling, I see my brightbeam didn't get through the surface. Instead, it clings on, illuminating a small area of the tunnel like a fluorescent tube light bulb. I need to see more, so I launch a stronger, continuous brightbeam, painting the ceiling with liquid light like Michelangelo at a rave. Light rains down, drenching me in glowing droplets. I pull up my collar and walk farther into the darkness with one arm out, ready to shoot whatever lurks ahead.

After a minute of walking, I notice something peculiar: the longer I walk down the tunnel, the louder my footsteps become. My boots bang and boom as if I'm stepping on an overstretched war drum. I cover my ears and start to run, my feet sounding like Lowcroft's machine gun as I speed through the darkness in bewilderment. I keep going until, out of nowhere, my feet stop on their own, and I jolt forward, smashing my head into a lukewarm wall of ice.

Half of my face fizzes with signals of pain, something I've not missed feeling, physically. I put a hand to my inflamed cheekbone and feel the thick, bloody slice that underlines my left eye, leaving a long, streak of blood which trickles down my cheek, marking me as a crying clown. I stubbornly try to get up, but I can barely move. My head and arms are free, but I can't get off my back. I shake my head side to side to rock myself up, but it only makes me dizzy.

★

I'm stuck staring at a swirling void of shadow on the cave's ceiling. I close my eyes, but the void remains. I open them again and notice a change: a pinprick of light has appeared on the ceiling. I blink, and another one appears next to the first, dozens more flickering into existence as I flutter my eyelids. They aren't dots of light, they're stars, and their shine gives the shadows of the cave the appearance of crushed black velvet.

The stars dance about, growing arms of light as, in unison, they reach out to one another, linking together into semi-tangible data, distinguishable shapes for my eyes to scan. There's a whale, a snake, a centaur, a wolf, a scorpion, a winged horse, men, women, and shapeless beasts. They collide with one another, creating a cauldron of color above me. They shake hands, lick paws, exchange items and blows. War takes over, an eruption of hate and violence that turns the ceiling into a depiction of purgatory painted in pure starlight. No, they aren't living beings at war but constellations. Together, they make up a map of the known universe.

My back loosens from the floor, and I'm launched right at the map, which grows, consuming me. In a split second, my body levels, and I'm falling through empty space. Panicking, I spread my arms like a skydiver in an effort to slow my descent. It doesn't work. My synapses fire rapidly as I continue to fall, relaying a trillion thoughts around my brain, calculations, deconstructing defense mechanisms and reconstructing any concept I can hold on to for safety. I'm fighting the current just like the paddlers did on Surtsey. But *it* has the power. Why fight against it when I can use it?

I bring my arms and legs together and speed up, rocketing past every swirl of blue, purple, and gray, past the star-forms of stampeding animals and dancing humans, past planet after planet, moon after moon. I'm diving at such a speed that time is following behind, stretching itself toward me, threatening to unravel. I fire a brightbolt at the folding spacetime, but instead of heat in a light casing, its light entombed in the strongest gravitational force I can conjure, that of seven suns. The universe latches onto the bolt, drawing itself back like a raging river. With that done, I turn back. In the distance, there's...something. I can barely make it out, but it's dark and spherical, like a camouflaged crystal ball...or a black hole.

It *is* a black hole—the famous one that sits at the center of the Milky Way, so dense even light can't escape its grasp, hence its famous pitch-black appearance. Around its supermassive form loops a jet of light and dust, contrastingly blinding to behold, but the closer I get to it the less impressive it seems. It looms over me, its enormous body blocking every other piece of matter from sight. I'm still far away from it, on the very edge of its gravitational perimeter, yet I feel it tugging at my clothes, my arms and legs, the hair on my head. It's difficult to keep velocity stable. I have to get farther away.

My flight speed has slowed but not by so much I can't keep my distance, if I push hard enough anyway. I grit my teeth and press on, narrowly untangling myself from the black hole's clinging ropes of pressuring force. I finally am able to sneak by, carefully avoiding catching any more of its attention. I look back with a cold sense of relief.

I'm in familiar territory now: our own solar system. Every planet and moon dashes past me like extraterrestrial traffic. I loop around the Sun, Mercury, and Venus. This tributary I'm traversing torpedoes me right back toward Earth, and I fly for a few minutes longer before passing Mars. As I do, I take a long look out into the darkness, hoping to see the hue of Earth's beautiful blue ocean. I don't see it; nor do I see any of the sturdy greens and browns that make up the land. There is nothing but a faint glow where the planet should be, right next to the moon. Ah! That's the shine from the shield Dad made to keep me grounded. Well, it's safe to say the shield is redundant now. It always was. I lunge forward, slamming my head into it.

I scream, vaulting up onto my feet. I look around and see that I'm back on Earth, back on the icy tundra where I collapsed. There is no wall in front of me anymore, only a bright, blue light which beacons out at me, seemingly from nowhere.

I take trepidatious steps through the light; there is no warmth to it whatsoever. It takes me a few more strides before I finally break out the other side. The sight of what I step into fills me with awe: a large, white, rotund room made of what looks like carved crystal. The floor is completely flat, but the ceiling is perfectly round.

There's an outstanding quality to the crystalline surfaces and a colorful twinkle, which comes and goes, giving it a peculiar feeling of familiarity. It's less like an igloo and more like the relative reverse of a black hole. I find it easy to walk around in here, but it's eerily quiet, almost dead. The circular ceiling is decorated with strange, twisted etchings, each one a completely different design from its neighbors. At the center of the room, I see the back of what looks like some sort of chair. However, it's no ordinary piece of furniture; it's a large, crystal-clear throne of obscure craftsmanship. The throne is transparent, but its thick blocky backrest obscures whatever is sitting in it. I make my way around for a closer look.

Oh, shit.

Seated in the throne is a skeletal, gray corpse with a mess of long, white, brittle hair that cascades down its spine and a gaunt, ghoulish look of shock on its face. Next to the enthroned corpse floats a small, pristine hourglass, not perfectly smooth, but it's without sharp points—a fine-looking piece though almost entirely alien in its design. No laser on Earth could carve this. Silently, I step closer to the throne, bringing the full figure into view. It looks like an ancient ruler of some kind, long lost. It is a fossil of a person, skeletal but not completely bony, as ragged patches of gray skin and tissue fill out the corpse like mortar between bricks.

Turning my attention to the hourglass, I peer inside, at the collection of sand at the bottom. It's a harsh mix of black and yellow grains that seem to vibrate independently, buzzing like bees in a dormant colony. I take the hourglass by the top and pull it close to me, then let go. The hourglass smoothly snaps back into place as if it's strung up by bungee cords. I place my hand back on the hourglass and shift its weight to the side, spinning it on its axis. The room starts to shake and rumble, but I'm not frightened by this cavern's noises. Not anymore.

I flip the hourglass.

Several sonic booms sound around me as the stream of sand passes from one side of the glass to the other, grains of dark and light coming together, melding into a neutral gray. As the sand pours down into the other reservoir, I notice something strange in the glass's reflection—a pair of mercurial, brown eyes staring right at me. A tingle plays the hairs on the back of my neck, and I slowly turn to face that which has awoken. The sloppy sound of shredded skin re-stitching itself tunnels through my ear canal as I meet its gaze, seeing nothing but holes where eyes used to be, circles of shadow. My blood feels like it's crystallizing under the shark-like stare of the seated being. I don't know what it could be, this dreadful being. Human, alien—

Two hands reach out and snatch my collars viciously. The being, though frail and decrepit in appearance, firmly grips me with the shaky strength of its zombie arms, lifting me off the ground and up into the air. All the while, its hollow eyes glare with a fury I have never encountered before, wide with a mix of aggression and shock. The putrid smell of its fogless breath is enough to render me unconscious, but I fight it, averting my gaze as I roll a brightbolt in my hand. When I look back at the creature's face, its pupils have retracted. Staring back at me now are two smooth, hazelnut bagels glazed with recognition.

The being recognizes me…and I her.

Mom?

The sinewy fists gripping my collars unfurl, and I'm taken in for the tightest, warmest embrace. All the cold has disappeared from the room, as has my fear, like my soul is slowly wrapped in the softest comforter. My face presses into the long, satin shroud covering her from neck to toe, though it does little to hide her frailty.

"Mom?" I say, this time out loud.

She struggles to get the words out, like she's being strangled but without the panicked expression that would come with the life being choked from you. She extends her long, cadaverous hand toward the hourglass; she can't even lift her fingers high enough to point. I look in and see that the last grain of sand is about to fall.

And it does just that.

A loud, roaring crash shakes the room around us, causing the hourglass to fracture and fall. It smashes down onto the icy floor, fragmenting into the smoothest, whitest sand I've ever seen. After a second, the whole thing evaporates out of sight.

"He-e-e?" she says in searing pain.

That voice. It *is* her!

"MOM!" I scream, diving in for another hug, almost breaking the poor dear in half. I step back, giving her the space to fall back onto her seat, which she does with a muffled thud. Her head flops to the side like a newborn's would, and she kicks and flails trying to keep herself steady. I take off my coat and wrap it around her pale, ramshackle shoulders, moving her into what I hope is a more comfortable position before I sit on the armrest, which needles the back of my thigh, spreading a chill around my body. With nothing but a blank black-and-white baseball shirt to keep me covered, I have to increase my body temperature to stop my shivering, but I don't want the chair to melt—if it can melt, that is.

I wrap my arm around Mom's shoulders, keeping the coat in place. "Mom, it's me, it's Dan. Your son."

"S-s-s-son," she says, her distorted voice scraping its way up and out of her throat.

"That's right. Can I do anything? Maybe bring some heat into this place?" My mind is empty. I have no idea what I can do. It's not like I can just get her some tea.

"N-n-n-not son!" she splutters.

"I *am* your son."

"N-n-ot just son." Her voice is sounding clearer, but her teeth are still chattering.

"Mom?" I'm unsure who I'm looking at and grow more worried with every silent second.

"M-m-y-my *baby*!" she says, scrunching up her face behind long-awaited tears. I jump at her with another hug, keeping my arms wrapped around her throne to take some of the emotional weight I can't keep back.

She holds me close. Her overgrown strands of dead hair tickle my nose as I'm being reined in. When I move away again, I see her face has started to fill out. Her reinvigorated skin cells shine like gold dust, adding a magical glow to her. All of a sudden, she lets out a pained growl, and the gold flecks on her skin begin to converge and glow fiercely, enveloping her in a shell of light. Her silhouette alters, like she's molding herself from clay made of starlight. Her long, frilly, dead hair returns to its middle-aged gray with streaks of the darkest black. Her skin does its best to hide new wrinkles, but they don't go down without a fight. This is a side I haven't seen before. She is a familiar stranger to me now.

She begins to writhe in excruciating pain and arches her back, pushing herself farther up the throne. Gripping onto my hand, she sends a sharp crack down my bones, and I wince but take it. Then she pushes my hand away, and it flexes back to normal. Her pain continues, however. I reach for her, but she pulls away from me.

"Mom, what can I do?"

Her response is a scream that fills the room, reaching up to the chiseled ceiling and shaking the walls. After a moment, she falls silent and sits there, staring at me through half-closed, gray eyelids which quietly clap together. She does know who she's looking at...I *think*.

"My times or yourrrs?" she asks, slurring her r's like a drunk toddler. Her newly awoken speech pattern aggravates her somewhat. "P-PRESENT?!" she shouts at me.

"It is. Well, the memorial ship is docked at Juneau's harbor, so it's after the war." I say this casually, trying to hide that my heart is breaking, watching her struggle.

"War?"

"Yes. The world went to war...again, but we can talk about that later, okay? Try to not move." I try to reassure her, but she holds a hand up.

"Code, give me the code." She points over her shoulder, and I notice the word "WAR" has been scrawled on the wall of the hollowed-out glacier. She always did like to take notes.

"How is planet…faring?" she asks through clenched teeth. She pushes her fingers against her forehead, trying to keep the pain suppressed.

"Well, it's healing, you know? Before the war, people were angry, disenfranchised. That turned to sadness, which turned to hate, which turned to votes in elections. If you were angry and dangerous then you won by a landslide. This wasn't *really* how the world was feeling but…an *aftereffect* that the *hate-waves* had on humans—the waves of energy produced by Dad's fight with the Valkyrie. Their mutual hatred became some kind of radiation, I guess."

She sits, squinting at me, puzzling over what I've said.

"Everything, not…Valkyrie…BULLSHIT!" she spits, startling me.

I lean in close and paw gently at her newly reformed hair. "Hey, hey, it's okay. It can't hurt us anymore."

"Dan, please, I need everything."

I gulp at her now-well-worded request. Choosing an appropriate start for a long story, I recount the events of the last few weeks—my perspective of them, anyway. I try to include all names, dates, times, occurrences, hospital visits, meltdowns, and nightmares. As I talk, pieces of my story are being inscribed on the walls of the dome, and by the time I've finished, the words are everywhere, the source code that makes up the last few weeks of my life.

Mom studies the writing in a long, retrospective silence, during which the words start to disappear, one by one, starting with "Valkyrie," "Non-Nuclear," "Dad," and "Peace." When those are gone, other parts of the text begin to fade. Connectives, adjectives, whole sentences, and paragraphs evaporate from sight until only the numbers remain: waking times, the date of my re-birthday, and the age I was in my first Forever memory—sixteen. Then those too disappear until, finally, my whole recap has been whittled down to the number 16.

"Oh God. Dan…Dan, I'm so sorry." She buries her face in her hands to hide some sort of shame.

"Sorry? Mom…for what? You're a god. Even if you died, it wasn't for so long," I whisper comfortingly to her, adding a small, celebratory chuckle to help guide her state of mind to a happier place.

"No, Dan, I'm not a god. We aren't *gods*. We *never* were. That was *my* mistake, sweetie. Please don't take it on yourself."

"Is this because you died?"

"Died? This isn't a grave, Dan. It's a prison."

"I don't understand," I say, that fear filling my belly once again.

"You said the first thing you saw in Forever was your sixteenth birthday. Well, that was the last thing I thought of when I was being put in *here*, in this prison…a prison sculpted from Forever. With what we can do, our…*subconscious* sometimes acts without us realizing—my selfish, subconscious desire for a happy place, with you on your sixteenth birthday, the last place we were all happy together. They weren't 'hate-waves,' but they were waves, nonetheless. You've been on a path back to me against your will, and for this I am so, so very sorry."

"But I've had a life, Mom." What is she talking about?

"And you still can," she says incongruously, after which a thick, serious air smothers all noise and she looks away from me as more tears fill her eyes, but she holds them in. She never did like me to see her upset.

"I was supposed to be there when it happened," she says softly, deep in thought. "It was supposed to be a happy occasion—like your birthday was. I even got you a gift, nothing special, just this little… guidebook thing I put together. I tried to make it look nice, gold on the edges, a lace bookmark. You know, to make it easier for you… to teach you."

I reach into the inside pocket of my sports coat and extract the rolled-up book Dad gave to me on my re-birthday, I unfurl it and hold it up to her, front first.

She reads the wobbly text—"For DanIEL, My SoN. HaPPy ReBirTHDay! Love DAD"—and her tears instantly evaporate.

"*You* made this?" I ask.

She sits silent as a deep, stewing rage whirls about her.

"If we're not gods like you say then you're going to have to tell Dad. He's been living as a 'god' for some time now!" I joke, just to get her back to talking to me. She looks up at me with intense heartbroken pity.

"No, Dan, you don't understand. Your father isn't a god. He's the devil."

"I...what?"

"Who do you think put me in here?"

My pulse hammers about my head, causing my ears to ring with a hot screech which oppresses my brain. I can't think straight. I try to grab onto any word I can.

"Why?! WHY WOULD YOU SAY THAT?!"

"It was on the wall. Those two flying figures above Earth you saw." The figures appear on the wall behind her. "They flew, hovered above, then a light flashed, and they disappeared. His final blow to me stopped time for a second. You didn't see me fall, and you didn't see him leave, but that's what happened. Why do you think I said I failed, Dan? I lost. There was no God vs. Valkyrie showdown. You...no...*we* were misled. I surrendered to him, and look what happened!"

"WHAT?! WHAT *HAPPENED*?!" I yell, shaking sweat and spit into the cold air.

"*War*, Dan. It was coming, and I made stopping it my goal. I couldn't let Earth kill itself."

"How could you have known about the war? You'd been gone a decade when it started."

"The conglomerate that bought the company I worked for—they were military contractors on the side. We were brought in to create algorithms for website trends designed to drive a campaign of information warfare not just against the country but against the world, and it wasn't just us. The other superpowers had the same idea—to use social media trends to stir up the masses and keep them angry, afraid, and most importantly *confused*. They asked terrifying questions and deprived the world of any answers. All anyone could do was *react*, and those reactions were usually negative."

"So you saw the pattern that was leading to war. How would you go about stopping it? Start your own website or news program? Your own cable network? You could have done *anything*. Why would you and Dad fight over something so trivial?"

"I'll tell you, but I want you to answer a question first." She takes a long breath. "I am a figure of unelected authority. I set my own rules for others and punish those who break them. What am I?"

"A fascist," I say, disturbed at where our conversation is going.

"No, I'm a *parent*. That was my algorithm. Provide the world with a parent who loved it, fed it, clothed it, nurtured it, called for timeouts when fights broke out—you know? 'I don't care who started it, you will both stop this fighting, right now.' Do you understand?" she asks with a smile, but I can't answer, so she continues.

"You don't elect parents, and we were separate enough from humans to be this *for* them. Yes, obviously, some people would have issues, but we could wait for them cry themselves out. Then we'd swoop in and give them a glass of hot milk and let them sleep it off. This was the only thing I could think to do to save Earth, to make it into a nest in which humanity could grow, then when the time came...who knows? Maybe they could have found a way to leave, fly off and start a family of their own."

"You can't just make decisions on behalf of a planet!" I protest.

"What if it was the only way to save them, Dan?"

"I...I don't know. I'd be worried that I was wrong."

"With so little time to act, we couldn't let the war play out and then go back in time to undo everything that had more risk to it. We could have ended the universe doing that."

"And this is why Dad locked you in here?"

"No. This was our home. We lived with billions of our fellow humans, almost all of whom yearned for a better world. We were 'the Earthlings'—a planet-sized family on a world that wasn't too hot or too cold. It was a home, and it could have been perfect.

That's how I eventually saw it. That's what made your father mad. He didn't care for this world or the people on it. He wanted to leave Earth and never look back. I refused, and when your father doesn't get his way, he strikes. He's emotionally manipulative, controlling, and competent.

"I got my powers first, but I could only use them sparingly to keep him from getting more resentful than he already was. After a few months, he somehow gained these abilities himself, but that resentment didn't leave him, and he took it out on the Earth. He liked seeing the humans at one another's throats, and whenever I protested, he brushed me off and called it 'a human problem.' He sees himself as a pioneer." She raises her fingers to quote: "'With our abilities we could explore the unexplored, Dyani. The Milky Way isn't the only galaxy. We can fly away and leave the humans to wipe themselves out.'"

"I can't believe this," I say.

"I didn't at first, and then we clashed, both ideologically and physically. It lasted for years outside of Earth's time—the constant battering of each other. One of us would have to give in or the fighting would never stop, and in the end, that bastard did what I wanted anyway!"

"He didn't take over the world!" I yell.

"Neither did I, and yet he kept me here!" she yells back. "After our fight, your father couldn't just leave you on Earth alone and let the humans nuke themselves because that would have freed me. After doing everything he said he didn't want to do, he saw that the war was getting too close to you. So, he *parented*, making feuding nations sign a peace treaty without them even knowing it. He manipulated everybody. It's what he does. Think back—when that woman pushed you from the explosion in Harlem, it may have seemed like the selflessness of another, but how do you know she wasn't thrown by the invisible man in the sky? He did exactly what I said we should and in doing so proved how much of a moron I was for thinking such things!"

I don't know what to say to her.

Mom sighs at my silence, squeezes her eyes shut, and forces out a physical thought bubble that floats up above her head. I look to see what it shows.

It's Dad, holding his hand to Mom's chest above Earth, on that afternoon, twenty-nine years ago.

"I'm sorry. But you have to go away now," Dad says sadly.

A small shard of light begins to glow in his hand, but just before it blows up, Mom stops her memory.

Dad's smiling. He's *fucking smiling*! The last physical thing Mom saw was Dad's smiling face as he condemned her to a prison of his making.

The flash of light comes, and the bubble above Mom pops into a faint mist.

I take in what I was shown and compose myself for a hard question.

"Mom...you said you 'let him win.' Why would you do that?"

"I loved your father, I really did. I loved how clever he was, our time on the Moon, how his hair got these blond flecks during the summertime. I loved his happy little smile whenever he knew he'd impressed me in some way." A cloud darkens her trip down memory lane. "I hated seeing him angry—which was frequent—at being stuck designing 'small and pathetic homes instead of towering skyscrapers for people who matter.' Angry with me to the point of disappearing for days without telling me so he could go on tiny trips all over the Milky Way, leaving me wondering if he was ever coming back. He was irritable, jealous, deceitful, impulsive, obsessive, paranoid—but worst of all, he was confused. We were both confused. We couldn't be educated when there was no textbook for what we were.

"So we had to go by human rules. How humans live their lives— their milestones, age, probability, laws—selected signposts they follow to the grave. The problem is we can change our age at will. Probability means nothing to us when we can make things happen. We have no milestones. We were doing our best, and our best was *terrible*—"

"How did he win?" I interrupt without looking at her.

"What?" she asks, for the first time breaking from her monologue. *Now* I look at her.

"You have to answer me. You said you 'let him win.' If so, then why? If you were all-powerful and all-knowing, and if you correctly predicted a world war and that Dad would have no choice but to interfere in its course, why did you let him put you down here?"

I see her shield crack. Her mouth wobbles, and tears of shame dance in her eyes and they want to be free.

"You, Dan," she says at last. "He threatened you."

Chapter 17

HENRY, please don't." That was the last thing she said to me. The last thing she said before she made me put her away. Her tear-filled eyes looked up at me, the shame she must have felt giving in to the monster that lived inside her brain. It's a picture which haunts me to this day. That monster anchored her to a single world, to a lack of ambition.

My feet drum on liquid lava, a vicious concoction of helium and hydrogen that makes up the body of "Sol," the sun of this solar system. An upbeat, summer song drowns most of the solar surge that surrounds me, but I can feel everything—every pop of plasma, each throb of every windswept solar flare. I'm lucky the music is in my head because earbuds couldn't survive out here. Then again, you can't either. Without me, that is. You're welcome.

I know you're wondering why I jog when I can sculpt myself into whatever shape I feel like. Well, it keeps me grounded, so to speak. I used to jog each morning before I ascended. It helped me think. And thinking is everything when you can be anything, do you follow? Katrina's anthemic voice echoes in my ears as the waves of the sun dance in perfect, rhythmic harmony with the energetic sound that has taken refuge in my brain.

It's a little on the nose but I can't help it if the song sets the mood when a mood *needs* to be set. I feel the heat of the star picking at my skin cells, a world war on a molecular level, and my body can't lose.

The whoosh and swish of plasma whirls about my stomping feet; my running shoes glow with each step, fraying and sewing against the wishes of the torrid trail on which I trot. So far I've done 173.5 miles, and I'm still uneasy with my decision. I know he did what he did, but he's still a child. He doesn't know better.

But he *did* know better, because I *told* him. I have to remember that. Forever isn't something to be used lightly. Speaking of which, I'll need to use that when I decide to go back down to Earth...*again*. It feels good not to have it hovering in my periphery like it did when I used to jog on the Moon. Doesn't that tell you a lot? So close to each other and yet the barren one is the only point of interest.

Maybe when we leave, Daniel will help me make Earth *its* moon? That might be a fun father-son activity. I chuckle out loud for no one to hear. Listen to me babbling such nonsense, letting my guilt for grounding Daniel make me forget one of my own rules. It's silly. I can't think like that. It's not very godlike in scale or style. Rivulets of sweat surf down all sides of my red tracksuit, I ball my gloved hands up into fists and pick up my pace.

By now, I'll have fully completed a whole lap and still nothing, but why would I ever expect my muse to whisper when all I can think about is a planet ruled by a generation named after a single letter? X marks the *blind spot* in their self-awareness. I left for a couple hundred weeks, and by the time I returned, they'd started referring to the youngest generation as Z. They didn't coin the phrase, but they used it all the same, molding them in their own lackluster image. Such a tepid group should have never been given naming rights to anything. *Generation X*: The Funky Chicken of humanity.

No, I'm not even kidding. *Generation Z*, as if they were the last one! Despite their manufactured reputation of being laidback, they fear redundancy, and from this came another world war. No wonder the young resent them. "Digital Natives"—that was the name they were originally assigned, but that's too "impersonal." It has to be a "relative" title, a paradox that Banach and Tarski would envy.

As if anything can be considered relative since I discovered Forever. Thank the stars I don't have to be associated with them anymore. I don't even know how old I am at this point—not that it's of any importance.

It's not about anything superficial like the number; I just wonder. If the number is a factor, then do I age backward when I go through Forever—back to the age I was wherever and whenever I land? Does it matter how far away from Earth I go? How many planets with higher fields of gravity have had me aging slower than a normal human?

There has always been this lingering set of questions hovering over my head, and even though I don't want to know the answers to these persistent mysteries, I can't allow myself the luxury of ignorance. It's strange. Maybe I will want to seek those answers one day, or maybe Daniel will find them for me, who can say? With this last thought, I fire myself away from the sun, bringing the darkness of space back into view. Distract yourself all you want, Henry. You'll have to go see him sooner or later.

Later it is.

I soar through the celestial nothingness, discharged like electrodynamic debris, weaving in and out of the gravity pull of each ubiquitous world I pass. The first time I made this journey, I nearly slammed into the sun. I was moving at such a speed I couldn't see where I was going. That was a lesson learned, one I could teach to my son, not that he doesn't fail on his own from time to time. As a matter of fact, he fails a lot. I can't believe he went down into Saturn when he knew it was a gas giant! Maybe he is an idiot, after all? No, he can't be because that would make me mistaken and, again, lying to myself. I gaze out at the open ocean of shadow as I tear through the system to destinations unknown.

Now I think back, that particular screw-up on Saturn didn't *technically* happen, so I can't *technically* still be mad over it. What *did* happen, though, was his little trip to Greece. Back to the war—

and for what? To save a random group of soldiers who came to him as apparitions in a dream? I can't wrap my head around what happened there; it's not like anything we do is ordinary. But *really*, he went all that way back in time just to pick a fight with a Russian sea-drone?

What a wonderful use of my wife's work: automated submarines designed to take control of the sea by attacking any passing ship that came within mere feet of its state-of-the-art sensors. Little does the world know, the main purpose of those subs was to reduce the population of war refugees by a genocidal amount. Traumatized and terrified, the last thing the pilots of those rickety old vessels of hope saw was the cold, dead eye of a computer. I wonder how many people knew of this plot. I wonder how much money they were given to stay silent. Probably not that much; vultures are happy with scraps. What a shit-show that war was.

Where was I? Oh, yes…after Daniel defied my strict orders to keep out of the affairs of the past, he went back to a war and revealed his abilities to a group of humans he never knew only to get his ass kicked by a washed-up submarine. What would possess him to do something so reckless? After all of the hard work I put into keeping the war from him. Initially, the countries weren't even going to declare their conflict as a world war; there wouldn't have been a point. They were going to have at it nuclear style: may the best superpower win. So, like a responsible parent, I went hopping around the Earth, redrawing the paths of far-reaching conflicts, dismantling *every single* nuclear weapon. I gave the humans a gift that night. I'm just like Santa Claus.

Obviously, it's more complicated than that. Their military forces built more nuclear warheads, and some even hit their targets when fired. All I needed to do was travel back through time, locate where the missiles were to be fired from and shut them down. I know there's hypocrisy to this, but I had to do it for my family. If the detonation was close enough, the energy dispersed by one of those warheads could have gotten to my Dyani, all alone in that icy cave.

Her body would have absorbed the radiation, giving her enough energy to break free from her punishment.

By the end of the whole charade, the superpowers were spending so much money on nuclear development that a change of plan became a necessity. Additionally, the news of their constant failures started to leak, showing their obvious vulnerabilities to an angry public, many of whom were already starting to hate the idea of the conflict. So, instead of endlessly trying and trying again, they gave up. I was coming back from a silo in Nevada when I caught word that they'd drawn up a *denuclearization treaty*, and with that, the rest was history for them.

Oh, yes, my wife's name is Dyani. We named Daniel after her as she won the coin toss. Not that it was entirely fair; the side that's facing upward from the hand has a 51% chance of reappearing when flipped. Even with this knowledge, I gave Dyani what she wanted because, you know—"happy wife, happy life."

I don't know when to go back to him. I can't time it. How soon is too soon? How late is too late? I've never had a good grasp of the tiny details that make up relationships. Most of the time, they're pointless to consider, but you know what people are like these days with their personality profiles and PTSD.

My mind flashes back to Dyani sitting on her throne in Juneau. I laughed when I first saw that chair, not because I was happy to see her dormant in it but at the thought of her making it. Even in her final state, she managed to conjure a *throne* to rest in, perfectly reflective, though she wasn't always alone in her keep. I used to visit from time to time to give her degrading body a dust and to fix her hair up all nice. I even decorated. She couldn't see the stars above, so I brought them to her, in the form of carvings in the ceiling.

I think she would have been happy with where I put her. Well, if she wasn't, then she'd have missed the gesture. She did, after all, yearn to go back to Juneau for a while. Not that she ever relaxed enough to give herself the chance to get there. "It's not the right time," she used to say to me, a thin veil over her guilt for leaving her mother, who tragically died a few weeks after we eloped to New Jersey. "Broken heart," they said. Why Dyani felt guilt over a natural passing is beyond me. Maybe it was her mother's way of letting her go? I think that's noble.

I'm at the edge of the system now; time to teleport.

In a silent flash, I zip over to another happy place of mine: *HD 189773-B*. No, that wasn't text-speak—a "B" marking bucked teeth on a really long face, LOL. No, it's another world. One in desperate need of a new name. Let's see...I won't call it "Daniel" or "Henry" due to how confusing that would be. Hmm...uncommon English letters...uncommon figures... Got it!

I zip over to *Xevioso*. It's located only sixty-three light-years from the Kuiper Belt, the area which marks the edge of your solar system. I found this cosmic wonder deep in the heart of the Vulpecula constellation; this was *my* pale blue dot. It's larger in scale than even Jupiter and spins so close to its own sun that the solar flares actually erode the atmosphere, creating a gigantic gaseous tail so that it resembles a blue sperm cell. It gets its color from magnesium silicate particles in its atmosphere; they're just what I need.

I teleport down to Xevioso's surface, and at last, the storm hits me, winds seven times faster than the speed of sound. You'd be dead in nanoseconds, but to me, it's similar to how a deep tissue massage used to feel. I look off into the distance, and I see it: a larger-than-life storm cloud as dark as space itself. Remember the silicate I mentioned before? You should, it was in the last paragraph. I turn to face the cloud as a thunderous crack of lightning sounds from deep within its swirling vortex of a body. Mighty forces shake the ground beneath my feet, both of which are gripping tighter than the grip of love on the heart of a human. Here they come!

A deluge of rain screams toward me, flying at a speed of over a mile per second, each droplet a shard of pure glass. Don't worry; this is fun for me. I throw a punch, striking the first shard and shattering it to pieces. I repeat the process as fast as I can, throwing a billion fists at a billion glass daggers, which detonate into a sparkling mist. I strike the rain so fast it looks as if it's moving far slower than it really is.

In a furious flurry, I punch and kick my way through another wall of silicate, decimating each piece with pure precision. I kick a leg skyward and spin into the air, corkscrewing as I fire long beams of energy from my hands with chaotic aim, slicing and dicing every section of the supersonic storm. Each of the bright, yellow energy beams connect with thousands of deadly drops, instantly evaporating the glass up into the clouds. And with that, the storm passes. I slam back onto the ground.

Has my muse spoken to me?

Yes, yes, she has. I know what I must do. I must reconnect with Daniel ASAP.

I fly up from Xevioso, bursting through its silicate atmosphere in a ball of fire. I stop, however. I can't simply fly all the way back to Daniel. To reach him *as soon as possible*, I'd need to fly at speeds that risk tearing the fabric of space and time, although...I'd love to see that in person, and I *am* a fair distance from Earth—oh wait, I've already torn it.

I open out my arms and conjure my Forever in front of me. In a blink-and-you'd-miss-it dash, I leap inside, spinning mid-flight to seal it behind me. I search the colors for my memory—the backup image I saved next to the International Space Station, as it's in a convenient spot above the planet.

I morph out of Forever on top of one of the station's solar arrays, those wing-like panels that keep it powered up. I look down at my clothing, which seems out of place for a reunion, so I change. In place of my red tracksuit glows a white dress shirt, which buttons itself smoothly and the sleeves roll up to my elbows on command. Dark pants and waistcoat follow—no silk for the back; I'm not a waiter—and to finish the ensemble, my favorite dress coat, which falls past my knees. Wool has a nice weight to it. The tail of my coat floats elegantly in the lack of gravity as I gaze out at the boring view below.

I adjust myself properly before leaning into what will become my exit jump from this man-made monstrosity. No. Stop! Not with so many prying eyes about. I know it's a shame for them to miss me in this form, but it must be done. I can't let the humans see me. I conjure a light-reflecting barrier around my body, which keeps me from being detected by most nearby satellites. I've had to do this for Daniel so many times, and he's not thanked me once.

No, no, again...*happy thoughts, Henry! He's your only son. Keep it light.*

Something over Earth catches my eye or, should I say, *doesn't* catch my eye. The barrier I erected—the one to keep Daniel grounded—is gone. Did he break through it? No, he doesn't possess the strength. Did I go back too far? I couldn't have. I put it up days ago when I was last in this time. Listen to how paranoid I'm being! I haven't made a barrier like that one before. One quick slice with Occam's Razor, and I find the answer. Like the solar arrays on the ISS, I must be its power source and therefore the farther from Earth I get, the more it fades away. Yes, that must be it. I'll keep this in the back of my mind for when I see him.

I zoom down, stabbing through Earth's atmosphere. The same old boring landscapes bid me welcome, a palette of dull grays, greens, blues, and yellows, which lie there without purpose or dignity. I half-circle the globe, find the Americas, and in a flash, I'm back down above the city. I look around until I spy the Hudson, then speed down to it, skimming the surface that smothers the Lincoln tunnel, using the rippling water as a conveyor belt of sorts. Like a soft autumn leaf, I float down and land on the pier. A fitting place to make port, wouldn't you say? This dock is the site where the *USS Intrepid* used to be before it was bombed in the war. The drone that did it thought it was an actual warship! Stupid machine.

After a small, invisible chuckle, I take off again for Daniel's brownstone, built on top of the foundation that was laid out for that hideous penthouse in Hell's Kitchen. It's near the theater district—a hollow gesture on my part but a gesture, nonetheless. Daniel was thrilled when he got it. He always thought I was oblivious to his little "theater" aspirations. I liked letting him believe that; it made him feel safe.

I land on the street beside the house. The sky above is a shade too dim for it to be an appropriate time. I cross the street and stop. I won't go in. Sitting on the small, black fence that frames the steps to his building, I wait for him to come out. The bulbous metal spikes push up into my butt cheeks.

It's not long before I hear some commotion from inside the house. A door card is scanned and beeps quietly from behind the imperial-red, wooden door. I picked that color myself. As the door slowly slides open, a young woman steps out wearing jogging gear. It's one of Daniel's roommates—Holly or Hailey or Stephanie or something. Her tired eyes have more bags than the Pacific Ocean. Not a good look, and it's even worse when highlighted by the glare of the phone screen she taps at silently. I heard that her generation had a habit of staring at their screens too long, but she hasn't even noticed I'm sitting here.

I clear my throat but still no reaction from her. She turns her head, and I see she's wearing small, wireless earbuds. I jump off the fence and stand at the bottom of the walkway. Rescanning her card, she turns to jog down and finally sees me as her foot hits the first step. The shock causes her to fall backward on buckling legs—lucky for her, it's a slow fall, and her head misses the door. She's shaken but uninjured. I let out a small laugh, she a small growl, as she drags herself back up and onto the ugly shoes on her feet, her face pointed with irritation. She picks an earbud out of her ear.

"Are you all right?" I ask pleasantly.

"Why were you standing there!" she hisses.

"I always thought these steps were a hazard."

"And you wanted to warn me?"

"No. I'm here to see Daniel."

"Dan... Oh! You must be his father. Good to see you out of those frames." She points at my eyes. "They aged you, clearly." Again, pointing at my *bag-free* eyes. "Dan is...do you know what time it is?"

Aged me? I hold in my own irritation and fire back through a fake smile, "Time to answer my question."

She stares up at me, the impatient thing. "It's six a.m. He's probably asleep, like you should be, sir." She stares at me impatiently as if she's waiting for something. An answer to a question I wasn't asked?

"What?" I ask, a little disturbed by her rudeness.

"You're in the way."

"Back at you." I let her pass.

"You have your son's wit, sir." Those are her final words to me before she jogs off into the distance.

You see, this is the problem with being a parent. I know she's Daniel's friend, so he'd be crushed if she was hit by a car, but does he really need that sarcasm in his life? The boy is under enough stress as it is.

When that door first opened, I hoped it might have been that Ana girl doing a "walk of shame." She's a little timid, but she doesn't get in the way. Maybe I can get them together. I know she'd be happy; he may not have noticed, but I see her gazing longingly at him. I mean, why wouldn't she? He's awesome. It would do him some good to *hit* that—temporarily, of course. She can't leave with us, so he'd be gone before she morphed into that disrespectful mother of hers.

On second thought, that's a bad idea. I can't see Dan being the "love 'em and leave 'em" type. Not yet, anyway. There are always lessons to be learned.

Back to the task at hand, I continue up the steps and push the door. It doesn't budge. Oh, that stupid bitch locked it after herself! I twist the doorknob violently and pop the door off its hinges. Entering the house, I'm met by a dark, poorly decorated hallway with a wide, carpeted staircase which rises up to an open second story. Unopened mail which dates back weeks is the only welcome mat here. I scoop up the mess of bank statements, advertisements, and overdue bills and head for Daniel's room. The ground floor is a strange place for a bedroom—weirder still when it's right next to the front door, but now I think about it, he'd be the first person visitors would want to come over to see, and why leave them waiting?

Leaning close to the pine-wood door, I give it three soft raps with my knuckle and ready myself for a crushing hug and... Nothing.

I knock slightly louder only for the door to topple onto the carpet with an echoing thud. I stop all motor functions and listen out for any reacting commotion. I hear a bed creak upstairs; someone heavy, stirring in their sleep. After a few more seconds of silence, it's evident I haven't woken them. That will be the tall, stocky guy with thin legs, more like an upright deer than a man. He's lazy, but I suppose that's better than harmful.

I look into Daniel's room to find his bed empty. I explore the space. It's completely without identity—nothing on the walls, no fanciful decorative touches—which is good. Less shit to pack when he leaves this place for good. Speaking of which, I'll go too—I'll stick a note on his fridge notifying him I was here.

His kitchen looks like it hasn't been cleaned for quite a while. There are breadcrumbs, broken pieces of dried ramen, and some unknown yellow liquid covering the main table like settings for rats. Behind me, a filled dishwasher gurgles from beneath the microwave. At least something is being cleaned, even if it takes a machine to do it.

I pile the old mail neatly onto the counter and get on with my inspection. That swirling dishwasher noise is grating on my nerves; I press the off switch on the wall next to it. The microwave beeps loudly as it powers up. I turn the microwave off, but the noise problem persists. I hold out my hand and fry the washer's circuits. This kills it stone dead. I'll bring him a new one later, gift it to him myself. That will be nice.

Out of the calming silence comes a small drumming from up above me, like a tiny pattering of fingers across the second floor. Accompanying it is the tinkling of the type of bell a cat would wear around its neck. I follow the noise with my eyes, tracing it over to the staircase. The pattering turns into slightly louder bumps, one after the other, something hopping down stair by stair like a heavy-duty Slinky.

Curving around the staircase at top speed is a tiny animal—a gerbil or a hamster or something. It runs over, sniffing at any free nook it can find. After it's finished its investigation, it slowly looks up at my unfamiliar face and stares with wide, button-like eyes.

"Hello," I say, crouching down to greet it. It stays put. "Have you seen Daniel?" This gets it moving again. It darts between my legs, and I turn to find it running over to the fridge. It squeaks, indicating to the top door with its head. The bell around its neck jingles incessantly as it nods. I look to where it wants me to: on the door hangs a small picture of myself, Daniel, and Dyani. It's a snapshot from his sixteenth birthday—the one that was on his guidebook. I didn't know he had his own copy already.

"Yes, yes, that's Daniel. That's my son. Have you seen him?" I plead with the creature. It continues to squeak in response, burying its tiny nose in a small paper bag tucked between the fridge and the wall. "What is that?" I pick up the bag and tear it open in a hurry. A flood of brown pebbles burst out of it and rain down onto the patchy linoleum floor. I pick one up and sniff: it smells like burnt meat, similar to how space smells. I drop it back to the floor, and the gerbil runs over and gobbles it up in one bite. I see. It was just hungry. What a waste of time. With a slow wave of my hand, I lift the gerbil into the air and toss it over my shoulder. It hits the wall behind be with a soft splat. It slides daintily down the wall in a smear of its own blood and lands in the trash. I wish everything was that easy. I could just stop the Earth on its axis and sweep the surface of this exhausting world, but here's the thing: if I did that, Dan would never talk to me again, and I can't have that. My son is all I have in the universe now.

I dust off my hands and look back at the snapshot on the fridge. It's crooked, held on by four souvenir fridge magnets, each one a piece of Algerian architecture. I'll have to visit Algiers before I leave. I'd quite like to see the Maqam Echahid, a memorial built to honor those who fell in the Algerian war for independence. Oh, look at that: more war. But why am I even surprised? This species only has the ability to evolve by orchestrating conflict. No, now I think about it, the magnet will have to do as far as a sightseeing goes.

I look past the token collectables and catch a glimpse of my own stupid face smiling back at me. I hate the way I look in this photo, nothing but a dull, sweater-wearing dork grinning with his beautiful wife and perfect son. I like the way Daniel's grumpy face looks in the glowing candlelight, though. And to think, the little shit just wanted to stay in bed all day. As for Dyani...my word, she's a far cry from this now, all *decaying and lifeless* in her throne room. I may go and check up on her while I wait for Daniel to return. Better to be there than here when Sam finds his gerbil in the trash. That'll bum me out.

I picture the Juneau glacier, an ice barrier shielding the Forever form from human view. It glistens in the chill of the morning light. In a jolt and a flash of light, I'm there and...

And so is Daniel. What the hell is he doing here?

Chapter 18

Finally, Dad has found me. I guess he couldn't track my pulse properly, what with me being surrounded by so many beating hearts. He hasn't moved a step from his landing zone. Instead, he's staring at me, eyes wider than a full moon, his brow twisted into a confused roll. He's clearly lost in his mind, probably telling himself a story, weaving an alibi. His vacant look, however, saps none of the fear I feel for what I'm about to do. He looks taller, wirier in his build. His tanned skin resembles hardened clay, and the blinding shine of the sun bounces off his thick head of multi-layered hair, which blows wildly in the frozen breeze.

I take a step toward him; the crunch of the snow causes him to snap back to the situation at hand. He forces a thick imitation of a smile on top of his bewildered expression, smashing it down into a thought that's imprisoned at the back of his mind.

"Danny...what are you doing here, bud?" His words barely pierce the raging wind that blows between us. I try to keep my head straight. I can't look down at the ground—where Mom is. Not now. I have to keep my composure.

"Well, I couldn't leave the Earth, so I thought I'd explore it. Do you know, I've never been here—the place where Mom was born and raised—can you believe that?"

"Well, you're here now. Look, about the whole 'grounding' thing...I think I may have been a bit too hasty."

I keep my eyes focused on his. There's only one thing I can say now, if I can muster the words.

"I'm sorry—when you grounded me or when you grounded Mom?"

His sun-kissed face loses all its color.

"What are you talking about?" he asks, knowing exactly what I'm talking about. He scans the area, checking to see if an ambush has been set up for him. "I know you're down, Danny, but please don't joke about your mother." His tight lips wrap thinly around clenched teeth, trying to hide a scowl.

"I know you're scared, Dad," I mimic his tone, "but please don't lie about Mom. Not anymore. I saw what you did to her, and I heard what you said to give yourself the opportunity."

He closes his eyes slowly, trying to keep something at bay—anger or excitement, I can't be sure. "Your mom...she wasn't well. Remember that monster I was talking about?"

"The one you made up?" I ask rhetorically. "The Valkyrie—the unstoppable monster trapped in time."

"No...okay. I admit I took some creative liberties—"

"And then, after betraying Mom and lying to me, you ended up doing exactly what she thought she needed to do. You can't lie anymore. She showed me everything." I take another step forward.

"You're worrying me now, Danny. Your mother has always been calculating. What lies has she been telling you?"

"I said she *showed* me everything—both your words and your actions," I spit back at him.

"She *showed* you? Oh, that thought-bubble thing she does! She puts on a juvenile display and you believe her? That doesn't surprise me."

"Dad, you told me she was dead." I almost take pity on the poor, lying idiot.

"I was trying to protect you from her!" he yells.

"No, she *protected* me from *you*! You said you would never stop fighting with her, even when she tried to call a truce with you— a truce you wouldn't ever need to accept because you already had your trump card ready. A week before Mom surrendered, you secretly went back to Earth for a break from fighting. When you got there, you noticed the effect of your battle, how society was as angry as you were, how protests and public disorder were on the rise. You studied them, then you went out into space and released your anger on passing asteroids and the suns of far-off worlds, which collapsed ahead of their time. *That* was you. This indeed had an effect, not a baseless astrological one but from energy transference. You proved your hypothesis."

"That's what this is about, Danny. I was right before she was—so what?" Dad's trying to sow petty ego grievances into the situation.

"So, you blackmailed Mom with the consequences. You said if she didn't give in to your demands then you were going to keep fighting her out in the far reaches of space, letting the hate-waves of your combat infect the planet I was living on, pushing the inhabitants into committing an end-of-the-world event! That's what you said!"

"And how was that a slight against you?"

"Your exact words were, 'Daniel will survive, but his friends, his lovers, his colleagues, and acquaintances will be gone. Humanity will turn on itself, and the planet won't be able to withstand the pressure. And then you'll leave me drifting through space, unable to die, lost and alone.'" I can almost see the cogs turning in his head as he listens. They suddenly stop.

"Son, unfortunately, parents fight. It's a way of life, and sometimes one of them goes too far. I'm not proud of what I said, but if you come down from your high horse, I can actually explain to you what I meant."

"It's not about what you meant. It's about what you are, and you—you're a demon in dad clothes. You can't lie your way out of it, not this time."

Dad stands his ground, formulating a way out of the verbal trap he's set for himself. His silence is a different tactic, but I have all the information I need. He may have deceived me with his words in the past, but now that pressure is being applied, his guilty expression marks his lies clearer than any polygraph.

"What do you have to say for yourself?" I ask, taking another step toward him.

Dad doesn't answer; he just stares straight down at the snow beneath his feet. Silently, he lifts his arm from his side and points it eastward, at the city of Juneau, right at the center of the bridge that connects Juneau and Douglas. He clamps his shaking hand into a fist and squeezes tight in thinly veiled rage. A violent tremor starts below our feet. The whole river has begun to vibrate. All of a sudden, the water beneath the bridge fizzes, and the riverbed splits. The crack grows into a hole of immense size, loosening the foundations of the surrounding land. In no time at all, the city breaks apart at the center of the connecting bridge and completely collapses, folding in on itself, crumbling into a sinkhole. It swallows up the area into a smoky oblivion. Rushing water follows it in a sadistic swirl, smashing what remains of the city below its own weight.

"What...what did you do?!" I ask, completely thrown off my guard. So many lives extinguished in one angry gesture.

"Where is she?" Dad demands.

"I...I...I..." I take a small step back.

"No, not *you*! Where is *she*?!" he repeats, smashing his foot into the ice below, splintering a large sheet with his dark, dress shoe.

"I...sent her away," I say, trembling. I don't know whether I'm scared or angry. All I know is I'm about to explode. Dad takes a step toward me; instinctively, I step away from his advance.

"Oh, Daniel, you don't have to be scared of me. I'm not angry with you, I'm just dis—"

I lunge forward and launch my shoulder into the side of his head. Looks like I was angry. He goes skidding across the glacier.

"WHAT IS WRONG WITH YOU?!" I scream.

He rises up like smoke, his fancy coat muddied and tattered from his rough landing. Lifting his arms, he stretches his spine, and his coat fragments, breaking down into thousands of woolen particles. He cracks his neck and knuckles. Veins line his muscular arms as he readies for a fight.

I inspect him for a weak point. I don't remember his cheekbones being so sharp. It's like his body is sculpted to defend itself against anything. Any area of it could split my hand open with one punch. He pushes one foot deep into the chipped ice beneath, like a track star awaiting the starting shot.

Nervousness sets in. It brings extra weight down upon my shoulders, as if the burden I'm carrying isn't already heavy enough. I remain still on the ice; I've not had much experience of fighting, but that can't be helped now. I just have to use my head. Without warning, Dad speeds toward me, grabs me by my neck, and hoists me up in the air. I manage to tag him in the face with my knee; he grins and slams me down onto the glacier headfirst. He lets go of my neck, but before I can turn to look at him, he's laid his foot right into my ribs, sending me tearing across the large shards of ice, scorching the surface.

I didn't think I could feel pain again, but the pressure his foot applied gifts me an unfriendly reminder. I get back up onto my feet, raising both fists with me like a ring-side bell has just rung. This amuses him greatly.

"My, what a pampered life you have led!" he shouts, hopping up and down like a boxer with a jump rope. I run at him, and he slams down, readying himself for my strike. But mid-flight, I realize. I don't need to hit him when I can outsmart him. I get as close as I can before *snap*, I stop the flow of time, like I did at the hospital. Dad stays in his defensive position, his eyes looking directly at where I was running from. I approach him, inspecting the frozen figure closely. With all of his strength, his experience, his power, I've beaten him. Now I need to figure out where to put hi—

Dad grabs me by the collar of my sports coat. His thumbs stab right through the fabric. Before I can catch my breath, he flings me up into the air and hits me with a mighty uppercut that somersaults me through the cold Alaskan clouds. Then from below, in a huge flash of light, he blasts me with a brightbolt, which slams into my chest. The impact pushes me even higher into the air. I see his tiny figure zip up from the glacier below, all the way up to my face.

"Nice try," he says before punching me again, straight up and out of Earth's atmosphere. I'm spinning at speed as my body enters the frictionless space. I see nothing but the fleeting colors of the planet as it skims past my vision. Over and over, the blue streak whizzes past, disorienting me. I blast jets of air from my hands to steady myself, but I'm going too fast for them to take effect. Then I feel a vise grip on my ankle, and I stop spinning but flail like a flag in the wind. I look down my body and catch sight of Dad's grinning face before he hauls me around like a child with a sparkler, except he's turning at the speed of a NASA centrifuge.

My face seizes up. Dad chuckles at this. I push past my dizziness and kick him square in the jaw. As my foot makes contact, he lets me go, and I plummet unimpeded through space, whirling toward the target Dad picked out: The International Space Station! The ISS grows larger as the seconds tick down. I have to slow myself. Carefully, I fire the biggest brightbeam I've ever fired, right past the hull. It doesn't matter if anyone sees us now; confusion is better than pain. This slows me dramatically, but I'm too late to dodge the station. I'll just have to land as gently as I can.

I stubbornly push out my arms and legs, and in one lucky attempt manage to grasp the docking port at the back of the ISS's main body. I climb as quickly as I can, all the way up to the main antennae protruding from the top of the center of the station. I yank myself up, beads of sweat floating off my hands as I try to get my composure back. I successfully find my footing and look around. Dad is nowhere to be seen, but when I peer into one of the solar panels next to me, I spy a faint shimmer of strange light hovering right behind me. I fire a brightbolt over my shoulder, and it hits the shimmer with perfect accuracy. Dad reappears. He'd shielded himself from my view, but he's here now, as clear as day.

"Nice trick," I shout.

"Watch this one!" he yells back, flying away from me. I'm not stupid; I'm not going to follow him. I'll wait until he gives up this dumb charade.

He stops about a mile away from me. He *did* expect me to follow him. How gullible does he think I am? As I think this, he extends his arm toward Earth. His hand begins to glow, and I see a brightbolt forming. Don't you dare! I jump off the station, propelling toward Dad at a mighty speed. Dad calmly closes his hand, extinguishing the bolt, and flies at me. Father and son are on a collision course, and the harder we hit each other the more energy we will release, which will cause a lot of suffering for both the people on Earth and the astronauts aboard the ISS. I'll hit him, but I'll hold back. I swear!

I reach Dad just out of Earth's low orbit. Quickly, I thunder up with a readied fist, and with a great swing, I hit...nothing. He's teleported again. But to where? A loud whistle sounds from way behind me—from the space station—and I spot Dad, hanging off one of the solar arrays. He crushes his hands into it with ease and after positioning himself, pushes it with his feet as if it were paper.

The station tumbles right toward me. Small pieces begin to rip from its hull as it hurdles out of the thermosphere. I hold out my hands to stop it, but with the force it's dragging behind it, I can do nothing but bounce off it. I reorient myself to see the fruits of my idiocy in full bloom. I've altered its trajectory like a paddle would a pinball. The fully manned station is now heading straight for Earth. Some of it will be absorbed into the atmosphere, but the rest... I...I have to...Dad, you son of a bitch!

I fire a small bolt at the side of the station to change its course, but Dad fires a bolt of his own, deflecting it away. I see him behind the arrays smiling at me, spurring me into falling for his trick. He wants me to blow up the station before it breaks off into too many pieces.

He holds his hand up once more, but this time he's not aiming at the Earth; he's aiming at me. Thinking quickly, I get the first shot off, launching a large brightbeam straight at him. It passes through a gap between the arrays. This will distract him while I pull the station away from Earth. But before I can, my beam bounces off Dad's bare hand, and it's headed straight for—

A flash of silent light rips the station apart. The burning metal pieces quickly dissolve deeper in Earth's atmosphere, fragmenting out of existence.

Out of nowhere, Dad appears, bathed in the glow of atmospheric fire.

"Look what you did," he taunts me. "That station wasn't empty, Daniel!!" This applies firm pressure to my conscience. Dad twirls, immensely pleased with himself, but the longer he puts on this show, the less stage fright I feel. I dash at him with great, vengeful speed, driving my boot into his stomach. He lurches forward in agony. I grab his perfect hair and lay a fist into his jagged jaw, and another and another. The force of the final strike sends him flying backward out of my grip.

"You didn't need to do that!" I say, teleporting to where he is headed and elbowing him in the spine. He winces but spins out of my grip and hurls a punch at me.

"Don't blame me for your screw-up!" He hits me in the side of the head. The impact makes me do quarter of a cartwheel, my head falls down onto his rising knee—

I see the orange glow of Jupiter, its foggy form moving into focus like a dusty basketball heading right for my face. The knee I took to the head must have knocked me out. I look up and see his hand gripped tightly around my wrist.

"So, you're finally awake," he says. He didn't even need to look at me to tell.

"Where are you taking me?" I ask groggily.

"Look, Son, I didn't want to do that, but I have something to show you. After we get there, you'll see the error of your Mom's ways. Yes, you will see."

"Why did you do this?" I try to wrap a mental rope around my composure.

"I've just told you," he answers in a snide tone. A minute of silence then goes by.

"Why do you hate them so much?"

"Hate *who*? The humans?" He continues to pull me along by my weakened wrist like the wind would a leaf. His grip tightens slightly, and his useless breathing grows more forced. Tonally, however, he is nonplussed. "I don't hate them. Hate is their thing, remember? They carry it with them. This animalistic animosity travels down the stream of their DNA, from mankind's earliest ancestors all the way down to the newest of their breed. It's a necessity for them. They can't seem to evolve without the use of violence. On their planet, no good deed goes unpunished, and that's exactly how they like it. They've evolved from a naïve non-issue into a more competent evil. They've...*evilved*. Get it? 'Evilved,' Daniel?"

I don't answer.

He sighs. "The most powerful humans obtained power through violent means, be it physically, mentally, or philosophically. The latter is the most common practice. And now you want to stay with them, to keep them safe from themselves?"

I pretend to ignore his question while bundling my fist up tightly. I have my role to play, and that's what I will continue to do. I feel my strength gradually returning.

Suddenly, Dad stops flying and turns to me. His fingers clamp down harder around my wrist. "You know that the wars aren't over, don't you, Daniel? I created some order for now, but its only temporary. It'll end when we leave them. And then what's next for the humans? *Patriotism, parochialism, pauperism—*"

"*Pessimism, predatism, and paroxysm,*" I say, interrupting his smug speech. "I remember answering that leading question."

Then, to Dad's surprise, my sports coat flops lightly in his grip. I've teleported behind him, out of his hands. He spins like a top, throwing his gift back at me. This gives me the cover I need. I teleport behind him once more and grab him around the waist. With a quick heave, I flip us upside down and teleport us both.

The change in atmosphere from silent space to thunderous storm discombobulates Dad. We both spin violently into a swirling sea of blood-orange clouds. Lightning fizzes and flashes with great frequency. We're in the dead center of Jupiter's Red Spot—a colossal, counterclockwise cyclone. I kick out, sending Dad spinning a short distance from me. The gravitational pull of Jupiter dramatically slows him, like bullet struggling to travel through water. I feel the pressure of the density too. The weight on my shoulders is far greater than anything I've felt before, and as I try to recuperate, I find that Dad's already "upright" and glaring at me.

"Was I wrong to ask such a question, Daniel?" he shouts over the noise of the storm. "Is *world peace* possible in the hands of less moral men, men who are incapable of change? No, the best thing for you is to be far away when their tiny, blue bubble bursts." As he finishes, he catches a bolt of errant lightning and heaves it at me. I dodge it before it disappears back into the clouds, causing a crack of thunder to bellow behind me.

"A moral world was growing until you and Mom had your *fight*. Don't blame humans for your screw-up!" I yell back through the storm, firing my own bolts of lightning at him.

"No war in a world where there is no cure for—" He backhands the bolt away with ease. "—psychopathy, sociopathy, and other vilified personality disorders? You're being silly now!" He fires back, shot after shot of pure, white heat. I take the hit, blocking my face with my arm.

"Yes, evil people are rewarded for their strength, but this paradigm was changing. People were losing too much!" As I say this—almost pleading from behind my guarding arm—I see that Dad used his attack to get closer to me. His sudden reappearance startles me. I lower my arms to block a gut-punch that he doesn't throw. The noise of the storms clears as we reach the eye of this irritating hurricane.

"Only a god can enact such a change, and you have already said you aren't one." As he speaks, he draws all the lightning from the storm clouds and merges it into one fizzing ball. He ferociously slams it down on me. The loud, distorted sound of its force rattles me, and its harsh light fills my vision, blinding me. And then silence.

As my eyes readjust, I spy a familiar sight through the blurred vision Dad left me with, whizzing in and out of view. I'm spinning out of control right toward Pluto. He must have teleported me when the lightning hit. But before I fall any farther, I fly straight into Dad, who wraps his hand around my neck, catching me mid-spin. "Remember this?" he says.

"I—" Before I can utter a second word, he launches me at the dwarf planet. I speed toward Pluto's heart, and there is nothing I can do to stop myself. The silence is overtaken by my screaming as I crash through the atmosphere in a ball of flame and collide like a meteor with the planet's surface. My body takes the impact, twisting and ripping through Pluto's many layers of ice and rock. I burrow helplessly all the way through its sheltered core and out the other side. As I flop through space, watching Pluto break apart before my eyes, I can't believe it. He just destroyed an entire wor—

The area changes again, and I collapse onto what feels like another rocky surface. After a few agonizing seconds of dry heaving and tinnitus, I sit up in a deep trench the shape of my own body, outlining me like a murder victim. As the dust clears, I peer around for clues of my whereabouts; I could be anywhere in the galaxy, and I seem to be here alone. The only thing moving is a large gathering of thunderclouds far away. They are gray and filled with a hateful fury, much angrier than Jupiter's were. They clash with the landscape, melding into one giant blanket of darkness. I see a glint from below it, a diamond-like sparkle that quickly grows, taking the form of a trillion shards of glass, which barrage me, an attack so sudden my mind digs up a sensation of stinging pain. My clothes and skin repair themselves as quickly as they're hit, but it doesn't stop the torture of this assault. Opening my eyes as wide as I can, I psychically take hold of the storm clouds ahead, and with a mighty rip, I tear the source of them apart. The last of the glass rain flies in all directions, and a slow clapping fades into being. It's Dad, contemptuously cheering on my false victory.

"Where are we?" I yell up, tired with his games.

He doesn't answer and instead swoops down and dropkicks me across the craggy floor. Large chunks of rock splinter around me as I catch sight of Dad's expensive dress shoe making its way for my head.

I'm awake...again, this time floating in the darkness of space.

"How many times are we going to do this, Dad?" I ask, dazed.

Dad hovers across from me, a blinding light reflecting off his damp skin. "It was obvious a physical attack wasn't keeping you down for long, so I had to disorient you to keep you out long enough for us to reach our destination."

I turn the right way up, so I'm level with Dad. At least, level according to my eyes. It's difficult to stand perfectly upright in a place where upright doesn't exist. Without solid ground, the best I can do is copy.

"And we're here?" I ask, seeing only darkness on both my flanks.

"Not yet," he answers cryptically and gestures with a hand. "Turn around."

I turn and am greeted with a familiar, frightening sight—one I've only seen in what felt like a dream. It's the black hole from my vision in Juneau.

"It doesn't matter that you failed your earlier test, Daniel. The powerful always get another chance."

Chapter 19

MYTH and legend have affected everything they touch. There is no concept out of its reach, except for black holes. They are the outsider, completely without mention until a few hundred years ago. Silent space is no longer silent as I stare, shaken, at the sight of the monster spinning ahead of me: a supermassive black hole, completely invisible to the naked eye if not for the colossal accretion disk wrapped around its three-dimensional body. The disk itself is composed of a violent combination of gas, dust, plasma, and anything else this thing has swallowed in its lifetime. The light that the shell produces rivals that of the Sun.

"What are we doing here?" I ask, eyes fixed on the black hole.

"I've arranged a little meeting," Dad says, "between you and Saga."

"Saga? Who is Saga?"

"Watch your pronouns, Daniel." I can't tell whether or not this is a joke to him, but he's playing it straight enough that I'm a little more afraid of him than I already was.

"Wait a minute!" I shout.

Dad stares vacantly at the hypnotic disc that spins in front of his eyes, reflected in his dilated pupils.

"Saga...Sagittarius...Sagittarius A*. Is that what you dragged me out here to see?"

"Hmmm?" He snaps out of his trance. "Yes, that's it."

"That's the name of the area we're in, not the name of the black hole itself!"

He shrugs nonchalantly. "Well, we're in the area. Names are weird. New York is called New York and that's a city built in the state of New York. I think it's cute."

"*Cute* is not the word I'd use."

"Of course *you* wouldn't, Daniel. You're still under the impression that you're something you're not. Do you think I'd have been able to tame this beast if I'd thought as little of myself as you do right now?" He makes fists to accentuate his usage of the word "beast," melodramatic as ever, then bursts away from me, flying right down onto the accretion disk, setting his feet upon it as if it is one of his own sky bridges. He's lost his mind! I can't let him go down there alone, I can't. So I follow him, right into the screaming swirl of light and dust.

As I touch down on its hollowed surface, I fall to my hands and knees. The pull is immense. I was shocked on Jupiter, but at least I stayed upright. Here, I can barely stop myself from vomiting into the spinning gases below me, and there is nothing for me to hold on to because the thing I'm trying to use as a floor isn't one at all. It's barely corporeal. I feel like a bee trying to keep a pneumatic press from overpowering me. We're spinning as fast as the accretion disc is, but we don't feel the effect of its movement, just the extensive pull of Saga's gravity. It's so strong that it's actually pulling the breath I don't need out of my body, and my skin has started to sizzle under the intense heat from the friction the gyratory disc is producing.

"Dad, please, we have to go back!" I shout, my jowls flopping all around. My body has started to move against my will; my lips and eyelids spring forward, thinning as they elongate, followed by the skin on my face, neck, and fingers—and any other place where bare flesh is exposed. It stretches away from me in the same direction the warped disk is spinning. Luckily, my powers keep it from snapping, and ribbons of my loose flesh reach out toward Dad, who remains perfectly composed on two feet. I can see in his face he's under pressure, but you'd never be able to tell with his stance. The best

I can do for myself is to shrink the clothes on my body, using them like an elastic band to keep my strands of skin bundled together.

"You know, I used to feel guilty about underestimating your problem-solving abilities," Dad says, cringing as he clearly struggles to remain as collected as he has been. "This was long before you had even attempted my test."

"What is that supposed to mean?" I blubber loudly.

"You've been here before. You *had* to come here. I made sure of it. And did you do what you were prompted to do? No. You idled by, petrified by the size and shape of a naturally occurring phenomenon. On that day, not only did you prove yourself a failure, but you also showed yourself to be a coward as well. Have I taught you nothing in our time together? What possessed you to retreat from such an inviting new realm?"

"New rea— Are you talking about the vision I had in Juneau—at the cave entrance?" I struggle to enunciate my question properly.

"You *know* I am! What the hell happened, Son?" He holds out his hands like an inquisitive juggler, waiting for his balls to drop.

"You thought I'd fly straight into a black hole?"

"WELL, IT'S WHAT I DID!" he shouts viciously.

"Whaaaaat?" I yell, confused and disoriented.

He looks back at Saga, disappointed or embarrassed, I can't really place which one. "Nothing. It's not worth it."

"DAD, PWLEEEASH," I beg through elasticized lips.

He doesn't answer, merely stands there, looking deep into Saga's heart, lost in thought but steady. The only parts of him that are moving are his tailored clothes and his hair, which shakes in the light like barley in the morning breeze. Pathetically, I crawl over to him, the hot dusk burning my palms. I'll drag him away from here by force if I hav—

Without warning, Dad spins and snatches me up off my knees by the throat. I lurch back trying to escape, but he has me. A deep red fills his face. Is it anger or the gravity? I can't be sure, but I am at his mercy.

"I've had the best idea!" he declares. "When your mom and I had our *disagreement*, we kept it between us. I see now this was a mistake—one which I repeated with you. It's clear I can't rely on you to make the sane choices. I think we may be in need of a third party, don't you?"

I flail and limply punch him in the side of his head, but he doesn't react.

"If you won't listen to me, then maybe you will listen to your friends," he says, and I scream at him to see reason, but it's no use. He's back in his own mind again, formulating a way to see his threat through. Sense will only stifle his effort.

After a few painful seconds, he snaps back to the present and swiftly stomps a heavy foot down onto the disc, which alters the structure of the gas, creating a deviation in the flow like a heavy rock splitting a river in two. He slowly lowers my face toward one of the paths, causing me to wince. Then, without a word, he drops me into the offshoot, and I'm instantly dragged down the segregated path and through Saga's event horizon. As if being taken by a rising tide, I close my eyes and mouth and hug my chest in an effort to keep myself from splitting into a thousand pieces. In an instant, I'm subsumed by the pitch-black behemoth.

The strange, chaotic forces at work within the hole don't allow for a proper, focused flow, so my body is pulled in every direction. My unbreakable skin warps, stretching far and wide, wrapping a cartoonishly thin version of me all the way around Saga's perimeter. Every limb gets longer, stretched out like taffy. My head and face follow suit, darting out like fleshy fireworks. As the bright, burning wheel of energies from which I was pushed falls out of focus, I manage to make out the figure of Dad, who waves from above. After this, he takes off for Earth, leaving me at Saga's mercy.

I pull myself together and then stretch back out again. I repeat the action, adding more strength to my re-ravel, only for the same weak result. Thinking quickly, I invert my body, moving my front to where my back was. I am now facing Saga directly. I have no choice: getting inside Saga is better than being stuck in its periphery for the rest of time. With all the might I can muster, I push forward, bringing my outstretched body deep past the event horizon, the stodgy point of no return, the thing from which nothing can escape, not even light. I can't allow this beast to have its way. If Saga's pull is so strong that something as fast as light is unable to escape, then I'll just have to take that pull away. I snap my fingers, freezing time before I lose any more of it. My branched-out body and constricted clothing spring back into their normal shape, like an animated character escaping a medieval rack. I'm yanked inside.

Within the singularity of the black hole, I gather brightbolt energy in both hands. As I do, my arms become almost weightless, rising on their own like paper lanterns in the darkness. I can't see or hear anything. It's not too bad; there's no pain, no violence, no stress of any kind. Maybe I can stay here for a while? The light of my brightbolts begins to dim, leaving me here alone.

I revert my body and try to locate the entrance above me, but there isn't one. In a slow, lethargic twist, I spin to look around, meeting my doppelganger. It stares back at me in awe, perfectly visible. After a few seconds, I realize it's me that's staring at *it* in awe, and it is copying me. It is a reflection with less form, a ghost of myself. I wave my hands around, watching it mimic my movements. There's something odd about its actions...the timing. It isn't in sync with me. I slump my arms down by my sides. Conversely, the reflection opens theirs as wide as they can. As they do this, they look frightened, in a lot of pain. An abrupt agony takes hold of them, draining them of all color, and their mouth opens, seemingly to let out a scream, but I hear nothing. In an instant, they vanish from my sight, finally free from whatever hell they were trapped in.

Startlingly, a distorted, monstrous roar rages all around me. Like a periscope, I scan my surroundings in a clumsy effort to locate the source; I can't see anything but the flickering light emitting from my hands. The light of my brightbolts starts to grow, not just in brightness but in physical size and shape. They spread up my arms and around my body, creating a shell, and I'm pulled backward into the void.

The darkness takes on a texture of some sort, like something I could touch if it was close enough. As I think this, it grows, drifting farther away from me, becoming larger, grander. It's changing shape too, a shadow taking on three-dimensional form, increasing in visible mass as if I'm inside an expanding black balloon. It continues to stretch, growing so big, in fact, that it slowly disappears, obscured by a shadow of its own making. After a while, tiny white lights appear in the space as if the sheet of darkness has been pierced by a billion pins. The darkness has transformed into the night sky—no, into the vast cosmos, the space outside of all worlds.

Before I can process it fully, I'm on the other side of the event horizon, like Saga has spat me out. I effortlessly sail right past the accretion disk I saw before. It shrinks into the distance as I am hurled through space faster than I've ever flown. Different planets and stars whiz past me, moving so fast they're almost in unison, like the screensaver on my old work computer. As I am riddled by the gravitational pull of each body that passes me, I feel myself slowing down enough to move my arms away from my sides.

I twist my body around to see that I'm being followed, not by a person but a strange, blinding line of colorful light, like a long-form Forever, and it's following my flight path perfectly, marking my trajectory. I look back at where I'm headed and happen upon a giant ball of liquid fire. Sol, our sun! This is amazing! I've been shot straight back to where I came from. Thanks, Saga! Saturn zips past me, then Jupiter, then Mars, I'm headed way too fast for a clean impact; I have to slow down. I send two jets of air out of my hands, but that only slows me a little. If I keep going, I'll crash right through Earth. The thought sends a chill through my bones that goes all the way up to my brain...then it hits me. I *have* to "crash."

Focusing on the tiny Earth ahead of me, I raise my hands, and with an arching motion, I erect a clear-energy barrier, an uneven replica of the one Dad made to keep me grounded. Earth is looming larger now, I'm flying closer, and closer, and closer and
SMASH!

I crash through the energy barrier, splintering it to a trillion tiny pieces, all of which evaporate within seconds. I'm surrounded by re-entry fires, lit up like a falling flare. I can't possibly conceal myself now, although with Dad down in the city, there'll be no need. The impact of the crash dramatically slows me down. I am now able to alter my flight path, but I don't have enough control over my descent for an easy landing. I guide myself to America—to New York. Look, this isn't going to be easy but like it or not, we're doing this.

As I edge closer, I try to angle myself just right, looking for the safest spot. I'm struck by the appearance of the city through the blur of my speeding descent. Something is different. I can't see any details due to my speed, like I'm looking through frosted glass, but still...the shape...this is definitely home, but...I don't know, something about it seems...*wrong*. How long have I been away?

I spot a thick, blue line of padding that runs around the island— the East River—that's the best place! I twist in its direction, corkscrewing toward my target like a sniper's falling bullet. I let my body go limp, landing the biggest belly flop in human history, breaking through the surface of the still, cerulean river like a tossed boulder, spewing a fountain of fizz a thousand feet into the air. What doesn't evaporate soon starts to rush down all around me, quickly filling the huge crater my landing made. The river folds naturally back into place, spreading a blue film across the top of the hole in which I'm submerged. When the river reaches a relaxed state, I swim back up. At the top, I shove my hands out of the water and push down onto its surface, climbing out of and on top of the river. I wobble up onto my feet, to be faced with a shockingly out of place sight.

It's Dad.

Well, not *Dad* per se, but a large, looming bronze statue version of him. It stands triumphantly under the bridge, suspension cables flowing from its arms like spider legs. Bookended on the other side is an almost identical statue, but it's of Mom. Both icons stand strong, showing a rare example of them working together to keep the bridge out of the now-troubled water below. This monument stands in place of the Queensboro Bridge, which would have been hanging over Roosevelt Island, which...I can't see anywhere near here.

What the hell is going on?!

I walk with wet steps downstream, examining all sides of the bewildering bronze bridge. I come across a small golden plaque that sits on a small rock directly under the bridge, it reads:

> *Here stands VALKYRIE (right) and CLOUDKILLER (left). Saviors of our city! Seen here in an architectural reimagining of their first public appearance together, stopping the great Queensboro collapse. We hope you enjoy this idol as a symbol of safety and prosperity. Thank you, our heroes!*
>
> *Signed: The City of New York.*

It hits me like a bolt of lightning from a cloud in the shape of the word "obviously." I *did* escape the black hole, only it wasn't the side I entered. Goddammit, it's a gateway! I am on Earth but...not *my* Earth. This is theirs: CloudKiller's and Valkyrie's. They're Mom and Dad, but not! Out of the blue above, a gigantic sonic boom sounds as two figures soar over the city, headed straight up. It's them, each adorned in thick, armored costumes of different colors. Mom's cape flutters around her excitedly. Her hand is nestled in the palm of her capeless husband, who flies directly beside her, a picturesque pair. They soar into the cloudless, blue distance—probably to investigate the crash I made getting through the barrier I erected. I really want to follow them, but I can't stay, not while my real dad is back on my world, left alone with my friends. I have to go and shut down the playdate he's made for himself. Who knows what he could be doing over there?

I fly away from the heroes of this palindromic place, back in the direction I came from, to the marked line which shows my path back to the black hole, a pleasingly convenient cord that guides me all the way to Saga's cold, staring eye.

LIAM QUANE

This side of the black hole is identical to the one I passed through, even if the universe it sits in is a crooked, uneven view of that which I call home. I take a deep breath of nothing and dive headfirst into Saga's accretion disk. My attempt to stand on the surface is met with failure, and I sink like a wishing well penny. As I submerge, I am compressed into a flat paper cutout of a man, and Saga pulls my body into the same broken state it did before. My bones separate from one another as my form elongates, and my arms and legs become rubber once again.

I resist, reeling my limbs back into their original shapes, but before I give out, I get an idea. My skin is soft and pliable. It's useless trying to solve this problem through muscle strength alone; my skin needs to be strong too. I focus, keeping the chaos of Saga's temper tantrum out of my mind. My skin crawls, so much it's practically audible. At a hasty speed, the cells change form, each one passing the alteration onto its closest neighbor, taking on the physical attributes of the densest metal, the flakes of which fold over one another countless times, strengthening the metal cells and smoothing out a clean, even shell, keeping the bits of my body together against Saga's pull.

I burst, dolphin-like through the surface of the gas, dressed head to toe as a metallic, faceless Valkyrie, jumping out of and onto the halo-like ring that binds Saga. As I land, my feet carve out a shining extension which is dragged through the event horizon like a tie in a paper shredder. I follow behind, surrendering to the pull of the interstellar forces, and breach the event horizon.

Back inside Saga. I revert to Daniel Hardacre, the fleshy human who thought himself a god.

I float here in this cavern, without sight or feeling. After a few seconds, my reflection appears again, staring stupidly at me. I wave my arms, and the other me gently waves in response as if trying to communicate. I do the same, politely copying its every move. I open my arms out, creating the universal sign of a hug. As I do this, I'm completely overcome by a potent pain, and it rises from the tips of my fingers all the way down through my body. I push forward, but an unknown force pushes back against me. It's not a wall I can see,

254

but it's certainly there, in front of me, behind me, above and below; a box of infinite darkness that holds me intensely. I try to move, but I remain trapped, arms akimbo, at Saga's mercy.

I clench my eyes shut to bear the sensory onslaught that Saga is imposing upon me. I'm bombarded with stray images of a broken Pluto, huge pieces of the planet diced up and left spinning as a newly created planetary ring which binds a now-dead world. The diced chunks of Pluto's rocky puzzle smooth themselves out, becoming shiny, sun-blasted pieces of aluminum. Pluto is now the ISS, spinning around Earth in a thin, colorless loop. This image is replaced by one of prewar Manhattan, calm and at ease until a Russian predator drone flies past, launching a CloudKiller missile at one of the buildings. It strikes, sending a bright spark fizzing through the air, which then trails all the way down the damaged skyscraper. The spark reaches the bottom, and the monolithic city transforms into a thousand lit fuses which make their way toward faceless people. As the light of the fuse fire draws closer to them, they're lit up for me to see, and I recognize them: my mom, Ana, Nebrezza, Holly, Sam, and even Shanty. Each one smiles at me pleasantly, blissfully unaware that the fuse ends with them.

I scream. It fills the nothingness around me. I force my body forward, ignoring every violent sensation infused into me, pushing my muscles beyond their limits. I push and push, laboring through the pain when finally...stars appear zipping past me at an astronomical speed. I'm once again soaring through space. I'm free. I do the usual gesture, opening Forever out right in the path of my unstable flight. It catches me. From a cavern of darkness to one of infinite color, I search for the year I left earth with Dad and see myself, taking a hit from Dad which knocks me out cold, He then drags me away by my wrist, leading me to Saga and back to here. A minute or so passes in the scene, and Dad returns, solo. He enters Earth. As he vanishes, I fly forward, reshaping an image of the past into the world of my present. I'm back.

I whistle away the minutes, letting time reconnect, and inevitably, when that happens, Forever opens up right where mine did. I turn to face it as it spits out the Daniel Hardacre from this timeline. He doesn't seem shocked to see me.

"Hi…" I say to myself.

"Are you okay?" he asks, out of breath.

"So you know what needs to happen now. I can open Forever… you can go anywhere you want if you'd like."

"It's okay."

"Are…are you sure?"

"Of course! I expected this. You were first. I'm tired, anyway…" His voice is barely a murmur.

"Me too. But I have to ask for one last favor."

"Anything."

I hold out my arms. He comes closer. I meet him with a warm hug. A flash of light hits us both, and we morph together into one.

I turn back to Earth, empowered and reenergized. In a swift motion, I psychically take hold of the spinning debris of the ISS which orbits the planet; it freezes in place. I open my arms wide, forcibly scattering the debris away from Earth in all directions. Then I take off, back to America, back to Dad. I hope I have enough time. Don't worry, Mom, I'll play my part, I promise.

Chapter 20

Click

Hello?

...

Hello?

...

Audio levels are okay. I'm not doing any of that dumb "testing, testing" bullshit. You either hear me or you don't.

Oh, yeah, shit. Ahem. This is Holly Wood, reporter for *Huble News*.

Well, technically, I'm an intern, but I'll stop introducing myself as a reporter as soon as you start paying me, Meria!

These earbuds are awesome. Birthday gifts aren't tax-deductible, so keep your hair on.

Look, Meria, I know you told me to do a write-up on the mass spike of sonic booms that have been sounding out lately, so I did. It's in your inbox already. That gives me some time to check out one of the Union Workers marches scheduled for this morning. They're at Montage Tower—my roommate works there, so I think it would be a good idea to just, you know...hang around, see what happens, ask some questions, you know. "Reporter stuff." Okay, I'll sign off for now. I'm heading out early. I can't have my morning coffee if I haven't had my morning run. This was just to give you some context before you listen on. I apologize in advance, but consider this…extra credit or something. Signing off…okay, how do I stop this thing?

tap, tap, tap, swipe, tap, swipe, tap

Okay…I think…no.

swipe, swipe, tap…tap, tap

…

BEEP

…

WHOA, MY GOD!

CRASH

…

He-he…

…

Gggggrrrrrr.

…

Are you all right?

Why were you standing there!

I always thought these steps were a hazard.

And you wanted to warn me?

No. I'm here to see Daniel.

Dan… Oh! You must be his father. Good to see you out of those frames. They aged you, clearly. Dan is… Do you know what time it is?

...

Time to answer my question.

It's six a.m. He's probably asleep, like you should be, sir.

...

What?

...

You're in the way.

Back at you.

...

You have your son's wit, sir.

...

Asshole.

tap, tap

Oh, there it i—

CLICK

...

...

CLICK

...

All right, well, things didn't exactly go the way I expected...better, actually. The Union demonstration started, but a bunch of those Surtsey guys showed up and kinda sent them packing. They're a spicier crowd. They already started pushing some guy around as he tried to get into the entrance. One of them sprayed a white line down the back of his blazer without him noticing. Poor guy. They're harsh in their approach, but you never know what could be lurking behind

their public image. You shine a bright enough light at a stream of piss, you can get a rainbow.

Everyone's here—all…I count twenty-eight…thirty-two…a truck just pulled up. I like their signs…"Tradition is our Ambition!"…"Harder to change a landscape than your mind"…"No Pets = No Regrets"?

Oh, the truck from before emptied out some members of the "Animal Palz, the rights protestors for our four-legged friends!" Mouthful, right? They're in the wrong spot; they're supposed to be uptown. He-he, I don't think they've noticed. I'm going to join them, see if I can ask a few questions before the cops arrive.

CRASH

Oh, shit, that was glass. Did someone throw a bottle…excuse me, ma'am? Can I have a few seconds of your time? Ma'am?

"Where's your sign?"

I—I don't have one.

"Okay, well, you better get to the front. Keep your head down so they can read our messages, doll! This eyesore needs as many bodies as we can get in front of it."

I'm not protesting. I'm a reporter. I'm here to maybe get some answers, like what is it that you want?

"WE WANT OUR CITY BACK!"

"YEEEEEEEEEAH!"

Okay, and how do you plan on getting it back? Dynamite?"

"IF WE NEED TO!"

"YEEEEEEEEAH!"

Are you a moron?

"What did you just say to me?!"

"YEEEEEEEEE—Oh, sorry!"

I...want to know if you can give me any more on what your organization's goal is.

"To free us from our chains! Free us, free them, free markets!"

I wasn't asking you, sir. Shouldn't you be uptown?

"Yeah, back off. You're in our spot. Take your hippy shit somewhere else!"

"Hey screw you, lady!"

"I didn't think humans were your type, bro!"

"What did you say to him? Don't make me stomp you, asshole!"

"Leave it, Pamela. I've got this."

"Oh, so you'll hurt humans, huh? You're such a hypocrite!"

Excuse me, can we all just calm—OH GOD, WHY DID YOU DO THAT?!

"She deserved it!"

"Have one back!"

SMACK

Everyone...please...stop...stop...you're pushing... The door is locked...ggggrrrrrr! YOU'RE PUSHING ME AGAINST THE DO—

SWING

WHOA!

[Get inside!]

SLAM

MMMM-MMMMM-MMMM-MMMM-MMMM-MMMM-MMM

[Hey, hey, it's all right. You're safe now.]

MMMM—MMMMMM—MMMMMMMMMM—MMMMM
MMMMMMMM

[Just catch your breath and it'll pass.]

MMM-MMMMMMMMMM-MMMMMMMMMMMM-MM
MMMMMMM—Pheeeeeeew.   Tha—   Mmmmmmmmmmm—
Pheeeeeeeeeeeeeeeew. Thanks…Derek…is it?

[My name is Andrew, ma'am.]

MMMM— Pheeeeeeeeew… Temporary name tag?

[It's…yes, thank you! Can you tell the guys upstairs what temporary means?]

Hmm-mmm.

[It started to get a bit rowdy out there. How are you feeling?]

Pheeeew…I'm all right…all right now. Thanks, Derek.

[It's Andr— Oh, that was a joke. Okay.]

Are you all alone down here?

[At the desk, yeah, but there are more guys a floor up. We've been on alert since I found a window smashed from the back way. Looks like they might actually try something today. You're welcome to stay here until they disperse.]

Isn't this against *protocol* or something?

[Do you always protest without a sign?]

I'm not protesting. I'm a reporter. I wanted to get some coverage of the festivities.

[A reporter from where?]

Huble News.

[Isn't it Hubble?]

Missing a B.

[Pedantic one, aren't you?]

Fancy word for a desk jockey.

[I read a lot overseas.]

You served?

[Front and center.]

Medic.

[Where at?]

Lyon.

[Me too!]

No way! Were you at the Roman Theater?

[No. We were set up in some apartment complex for most of it, broom-closet spaces.]

Sucks to be you!

[Hey, don't feel bad for m— Oh, Christ, they're all fighting now. I'll have to get my guys down here…look. ma'am—]

Call me Holly, _Andrew_. While we're talking…is there any way I can accidentally find my way upstairs? I don't think the cops will be long, but I don't need long. I can slip out after the front is cleared.

[I can scan you through to the elevator—just keep your head down when you're up there. Don't mention my name or where you're from, and you should be okay for a few minutes. That's all I can give you.]

How did you even get this job?

[I didn't say it was free. You can buy me a coffee in return.]

Okay, sure. Is there a machine around here?

[No.]

Oh…OH…erm, listen, I'm kind of…like a date?

[I…was hoping.]

I…can't tonight, I'm…screw it. I can't. I'm sorry, I have a lot on my plate, you know? Work, work, work—that's me. If anyone I knew heard you asking, they'd struggle to keep their laughter quiet.

[Okay. I could give you my number. Maybe…you can call me if you ever want to? Could be a day from now, a month, a year, or never. Your choice.]

Erm…Sur—

CRASH

[Shit, get upstairs!]

WAIT, WHERE ARE YOU GOING?!

[I've buzzed my guys. They'll be down in a minute, but you have to get upstairs. NOW!]

Shit, shit, shit, shit! Okay. I'm running…running…the protesters have breached the doors! They've forced themselves inside! Oh God, oh God…Come on! COME ON, STUPID ELEVAT—

DING
Finally.

TAP

HUMMMMMMMMMMM

Oh God. Someone has pressed from the sixteenth floor. I don't want to go that far up!

HUMMMMMMMMMMMMMMMMMMMMMMMMMMMMMM MMMMMMMMMMMMMMMMMMMMMMMMMMMMMMMMMM MMMMMMMMMMMMMMMM

DING

\There you are!/

SAM? What the hell are you doing here?

\You lied to me! Workers Union protest, my ass!/

I didn't lie. They were here, but then those Surtsey guys showed up, and then the Animal Palz joined in, and they just went crazy. They broke in downstairs, and they're trashing the lobby!

\I know, I followed you!/

You what?!

\To a "peaceful demo," which quickly became a brawl between the lunatics and the phonies! "SAFE!" That's what you told me—you'd be safe!/

I've seen worse. How did you even get up here?!

\I broke a window out back, waited until one of the staffers got buzzed in and tagged along. I followed the paint drips his jacket left when he ran inside./

YOU BROKE THE WINDOW!

\And they'll blame the protestors for it. Look, just come through here—I found an empty office we can lie low in until the shit dies down./

We have to go back downstairs. This security guy—he pulled me away from the crowd, and they broke through the doors. He gave me his ID, and he charged after them. We can't just hide up here. We have to go and help him.

\If the guy you're talking about is the one at the front desk, I think we can trust him to do his job, don't you?/

Shut up. You didn't see the size of the group. It was double what I counted when I came in.

\You're panicking again./

I was. I'm not anymore, assho— Oh, sorry, we thought this room was empty.

(Oh no, sorry. It was. I just came in here to get away from all of the noise. It's distracting.)

\Yeah, we...did the same, didn't we, Ms. Wood?/

Yessss, Sam, we did, and why are you calling me Ms. Woo—

(So, are you new here?)

DING

We were gonna ask you the same thing! Ha-ha-ha! Now we have to ask you to leave, Miss...

(My name is Ana. Nice to meet you. I'll just need a few minutes to pack my system up, if that's not a bother?)

\No, you can stay. You're just the sweetest thing, aren't you?/

Sam, shut up. She can't stay.

\Why not?/

Because the elevator is climbing.

\Oh.../

Ana, we need to move out of this office and get far away from the elevator.

(But why?)

The protestors have started rioting. That was the noise you've been hearing, and it hasn't stopped. A few are on their way up here as we speak.

PING

\Gggrrrrrrrrr!/

Everyone, get down under the desk, now!

(I have to tell my friends—)

I don't care. Nobody is to move until I say so.

\We get it. Shut your own mouth, will ya?/

Oh, don't start with m—

CRASH

(Oh, no. They've moved into my office! You have to let me go.)

STAY DOWN, YOU IDIOT!

(GET OFF ME!)

SMACK

\Holly! Oh, shit, what'd you do that for, lady?!/

(Get the hell out of my way!)

BANG

(Oh, no...Martin...)

Uuurgh.

\Holly?/

Where did she go? I'm gonna kick her f—

\She went through there. It sounded like a gun went off./

...We have to follow her.

\Don't be stupid! Holly, wait!/

Whoa, whoa, whoa, sir...sir. Put the weapon down, sir.

(Martin, please listen to her.)

{Shut up, Ana.}

<She's right sir.>

{YOU KEEP YOUR TRAP SHUT, WILLARD. IT'LL BE BETTER FOR ALL OF US.}

(Martin, this isn't like you.)

{Nothing is like anything, Ana. Nothing makes sense anymore! People especially! We loved people, cherished them. Would have done anything for them, and this is how I'm repaid! With gray skies, thunderstorms, sonic booms! Cities are sinking into rubble, space stations exploding into bits right above our heads! And the chaos is spreading! I called Todd, asking why he wasn't at work today, and like the rest of you, he told me to go fuck myself! Can you imagine?!}

<You have it wrong, sir. You're in a safe place up here.>

{If you open your mouth again, Willard, I'll shoot it closed, am... AM I MAKING MYSELF CLEAR?!}

\Mister, PLEASE, JUST PUT THE GUN DOWN!/

{WHAT FOR? HAVEN'T YOU SEEN THE NEWS? WE'RE FUCKED!}

(Martin...please, you're scaring me.)

{Oh, Ana. No. I don't want to scare people. I'm trying to help them, see?}

(See what? What a bullet can do to a person? I think everyone has seen enough to last a lifetime, don't you? What about your son? Do you think he'd like what he'd see if he was here with you today? What about your wife, your daughter?)

<Ana, shut up. Martin, point the gun back at me, please. I'm the one you're mad at. Keep your focus on me. I deserve it!>

\No, point it at the protestors. They started this shit!/

<You're not helping, big guy.>

\Neither are they./

(Martin…please.)

{You're wrong, Ana. My son would like what he sees if he were here. After all, this was his pistol. Look at the scratches in the side. What do you think they represent? Days past? No, no…no, no, no. He was a hero, Ana, a bona fide war hero. A squad-leading, calculating corpse with a pistol in one hand and a book in the other. That was my little boy, my little soldier! Now, what are we, Ana? Can we be called the same? Huh?}

(I just want all of this to stop.)

{So do I. Cowards always do.}

BANG

(WILLARD!)

GET THE GUN FROM HIM, QUICK. KEEP HIM PINNED. SAM, I NEED HELP OVER HERE. I NEED PRESSURE APPLIED TO THE CHEST, NOW!

\I…I…I…I…/

NOW! Ana, come here, I need your help. You see this? It's a voice recorder. Take it out and run it over to my office at *Huble News*. Use my pass to let yourself in. Get it to a woman named Meria Kieta. She'll want to hear this.

(I…don't think that's—)

Call it an exchange. I help him, you help me. Got it?

\Holly…/

I SAID KEEP PRESSURE, GODDAMMI—

CLICK

So, that's what happened? Here I was thinking that you'd finally devolved into the apes you were born from, hmmm?

I hover over a kneeling mass of onlookers. In my hand wriggles Daniel's little friend, Ana. Her struggle is admirable, but all for naught. In my other hand sits a digital sound recording device. I drop it to the ground, hoping to hear a crack. It indeed cracks. I look out at a sea of bright, shiny faces, all transfixed on my very person. My faceless façade cuts into their day quite a bit, I imagine. There were a lot more of them; the streets were crowded with their usual bustling masses and security, but after I made my presence known, most of them dispersed like rodents under a bright light. Some had to be exterminated, particularly those with big, sharp fangs and tiny pistols trying to "serve and protect" their useless nest. And now, here I am: Henry Hardacre on site, reporting to the world for the first time.

All that fighting and arguing...nothing but a mere id-driven overreaction to our combat. Maybe it wouldn't have hit them so quickly if I'd left Juneau where it was, but could you really blame me for doing what I did? You shouldn't. The dead can't, so why should you? Daniel is nice and cozy in the other universe, and now his friends can be my friends for a while. I translocated them out of the office after one of them started shooting. The guy who was shot is still up there. He's probably bled out by now. I tossed the gunman across the city. Typical, isn't it? The one time I need to speak to the humans and one of them goes insane and starts shooting up the place. Again, nothing more than an id-driven overreaction. It's funny—I could say that about their entire species at this point.

"Hey, faceless freak! Put her down, right this second."

"Are you talking to me?" I ask the reindeer boy and wonder if he's found his pet yet.

"Excuse me, young man," I continue. "Did you by any chance check the trash can in your kitchen before you left your house this morning?"

"I don't know what you are, but can you please put down my friend and we can arrange some kind of peace deal? You like trash?

We have plenty for you—check the ocean. There's a ton of it just floating there, all for you if you want it."

I float down to the ground. I'm not completely surrounded by men and women on their knees. Some have their heads buried in their hands, either out of fear or respect. Ironically, the tallest one is standing, speaking to me as if I'm some sort of...alien trash compactor.

"Are you an idiot?" I ask.

"I have been called such a thing," he says back, completely serious.

"Well, then. I'll start with you. You're friends with a man named Daniel, yes?"

"Dan?" he stutters back. "Yes. He's my roommate—one of them. We haven't seen him in a few days. Do you have him back at your ship, Mr. Alien?"

"No, you dolt." I stifle a laugh. "He's—

I hear a faint sonic boom off in the distance. He can't be back already.

Suddenly, as I divert my attention, an empty soup can bounces off my metallic head. As I turn to see where it came from, the reindeer boy jumps onto my arm, trying his hardest to force Ana out of my grip. I move the girl away from his reach and grab him by the neck. Now I have two of them. This should keep the rest of them in line.

I ascend above the crowd again, layering on the spectacle for the witnesses below.

"SAM!" one of the onlookers calls out, pushing her way through the collection of cowards.

"Oh, I remember you! You're the sarcastic girl, aren't you? You stepped out of line a few times, but I can see you have a brain in your skull. I'll quiz you instead. If you could go anywhere else in the universe, leaving Earth behind, would you do it?

"Probably not."

"But you can in this *hypothetical* scenario. Nothing can hurt you. No obstacle can stop you. Why would you choose to stay here on this boring world?"

"I don't know. It's a broad question, dude."

"It's a what? Look, let's say you're a god. Would this still be your home?"

"I guess so. I'd say my home is where my family and friends are."

"Oh my stars! Turns out I was wrong about you having a brain. After we're done here, I think I might have to—" I feel a sudden swell in my stomach. My grip loosens, and I drop Ana and the reindeer into the crowd as I zip away from them at high speed, no control over my own body. What could this be? As I look over my shoulder, Daniel appears from out of nowhere. He has me by my shoulders. As quick as a flash, he hauls me across the city, through a nearby giant, industrial crane, which proceeds to tumble down on top of me, burying my body. With a great grunt, I force the yellow pieces of skewed metal away from me and into a nearby apartment complex. The screams echo as the metal rips through several floors.

As I get back onto my feet, I see Daniel has left the site, no doubt to go back to his friends. That's probably not the best idea.

Chapter 21

TRAGEDY avoided, I guess. What the hell was Dad doing with them? I waited up high, on the top of the Montage Tower's glass skirt, watching him for a while before I struck. Ana and Sam are okay now. I moved some of the crowd under them to break their fall—no injuries but some pretty pissed-off protestors. I soar back over to them, floating about ten feet off the ground, and peer down at the crowd, some of whom I recognize from the office. The others I recognize from the protests, which seemed to be getting out of control pretty fast. Mom and Dad must have been telling the truth about the hate-waves. I tried to suppress my feelings. I really did.

I'm not wearing a disguise like Dad was, so naturally, the crowd is shocked to see me, especially my friends.

"Hey, guys," I call down to them.

"H-h-hi, Dan!" Ana blinks up to me.

"Dan?" Sam asks in an uncharacteristically sheepish way.

"Yeah, Sam?"

"WHY ARE YOU FLYING?!" Holly screams out from inside the huddle of people. She pushes through, stomping her way to the front.

"It's a long story. I'll tell you later."

"Are you an alien?" Sam asks.

"No, I'm just like you," I answer truthfully.

"Then what's that?" Ana points over at a dot of a man in the distance. It's Dad, walking all the way up to us from farther down

Broadway. He's ditched his disguise for the usual white shirt under a dark vest. His sleeves are rolled up, and his stare is so deep that it practically tunnels through his eyebrows. Completing this look of *evil bastard* is a malevolent grin, streaked across his face. I need to play my part properly.

"Family problems," I tell Ana.

"Oh…okay. What should we do?"

"Run. Get far away from here. Stay away from each other and everyone else." I peer into the windows of the office buildings around me. I see a million cell phones, all aimed in my direction, documenting my every move. Filling my palm with a brightbolt, I hold it up, frightening the crowd away from the proverbial epicenter in which they're standing, and move my focus back to Dad, whose booming footsteps are within earshot. They come with the sounds of crashing rubble and scraping concrete. The gravitational force he's producing is tearing whole chunks from the buildings around him. Giant clusters of tarmac, carbon fiber, and gray brick accompany him as he steps toward me.

Out from between the surrounding structures, a news helicopter rumbles its way above my head. An irritating black ball paints an infrared target on me, perfect for a camera to track. The lens twists, getting my image into focus. I'm not hiding anymore, but this isn't a fashion shoot. I telekinetically grip the nose of the chopper, holding it in place. My eyes meet the pilot's sunglasses as I point a finger at the windscreen and carve a message into the glass. The letters are backward so the occupants can read them:

ꓴ U ꓞ

…and that's evidently far enough. The pilot panics, turning the bird around and whisking the news team away from the scene like the secret service would the president.

The once-filled streets have emptied; people have run the other way from us, Holly, Sam, and Ana included. Civilians have abandoned their cars and whatever they were carrying at the time and evacuated to somewhere they hope is safe. The whole city grows silent as I wait patiently for my chance to attack.

And here it is.

I launch at Dad with a mighty push, fists balled and ready to strike. As I approach, he lunges forward, arms outstretched, hurling the collection of rubble he amassed straight at me. I reduce it to dust with a few well-aimed brightbolts and attach my feet to a flickering soda billboard that lines a nearby wall. Running across the colorful advertisement, I fire a barrage of bolts his way. The force of my attack sends him crashing through an adjacent wall, leaving a dark hole. I land back on the street and listen out. A few muffled crashes sound from inside, each louder than the last, and Dad bursts out of the roof of the building.

Raising his arms above his head, he looks at where they're aimed. He's going to launch brightblasts of his own, and...no, he's not. He stretches out his back, wincing in pain, and brings his arms down to his sides, then he lunges like a diving hawk, speeding toward me. I brace for impact, but before he reaches me, he stops and hovers high above the street and slashes the air with his hand.

Puzzled, I lower my guard and move closer to get a better look, only for the building I ran across to tumble onto my shoulders. I don't go down, however. I stand there, taking the weight of the massive structure. Dad finishes his flight, crashing right through the building, which detonates like a grenade, sending shrapnel ripping through anything close by and burying me in rubble.

After an ear-ringing struggle, I drag myself from the rubble and tackle Dad out of the air. I swiftly teleport us away from the city, to the peak of Mount Everest. The change of scenery is jarring and momentarily distracts me. It's enough for Dad to grab me by my collar, and he starts beating the top of the mountain with me, breaking down the peak layer by layer and causing fierce avalanches to roll down every snowy slope of the landmark. Having happily made his point, Dad kicks me through the air hard enough that I level several Manhattan buildings before I come to a halt. The sound of crashing concrete overpowers the small pops of exploding gas mains, fizzing electrical fixtures, and shattering windows.

I do my best to get some distance, serpentining between the buildings. Dad is not far behind me; instead of swerving like I am, he tunnels through the skyscrapers like a laser through cream. He's quickly gaining on me, but at least he's moved away from the buildings. I reach the edge of the island and crash into a wall of hardened air. I feel around for a source. There's nothing to see but a faint, refracted glimmer. I punch the invisible wall a number of times, but it stays standing. Dad slams into me, pushing my face against the barrier.

"You like this trick?" he taunts "It's similar to the one I used to stop you leaving Earth. Little did I know then that you'd already taken such risks with Forever. It obviously proved to be too weak. Fortunately, this is an upgrade. Your mom's design. She didn't like how I'd abscond during our arguments, so she built this as a way of keeping me around. She warped Forever and built a prison for me, so I built one for her. I think that's fair, don't you?"

"You said...there's no such thing...as *fair*." My words tumble sluggishly out of my mouth. I'm tired, so very tired of all of this shit.

"Oh, yeah." Dad puts his hands together and swings them right into my face, launching me down at the city. Skyscrapers tumble behind me like the world's worst game of dominoes. I spin out of control until I smash right through a roof—the roof of my house—and into my bedroom. I hit my bed, but the room bursts with the force of my landing, and my mattress catches on fire.

I get up, dusting myself off. "Holly? Sam?" I yell up to the top of the stairs. "You didn't come back here, did you?"

No answer. Thank goodness! I clamber over the rubble that now litters the long hallway leading to the kitchen. It's a mess—but it was always a mess. Shanty's food pellets decorate the floor, along with more debris. The bag the food pellets came from lies torn in half on the counter.

The kitchen door has come off its hinges, and our trash can has spilled out onto the linoleum. There's a larger, brown shape resting among the spillage. At first, I think it is an errant baked potato that someone has thrown out whole, but as I get closer, I see it's Shanty. I lift the poor creature in my hands. Fur covers a freezing, hard lump of a body, like a refrigerated giant kiwi fruit. I drop down to a knee.

I brought Lillith out of a coma, what if I can...

I close my eyes, letting my mind go completely blank. I try to ignore the sounds of crackling fire that now fill the air, the smell of charred wood and melting concrete, the taste of ash that sits on my tongue. The house can burn. I need to do this as soon as possible.

I flip my mind inside out and examine a thought at the back of it. An image of Lillith's brain scan appears. As I mentally tunnel into Shanty's brain, the image shrinks and morphs into a tiny, gray blob in the center of my mindscape. I send a jolt of energy up through the lobes. The image flickers like a damaged light bulb. The color fades as quick as it arrives. I send another jolt but get no response. I send another and nothing. I send another, and another and another. As I do this, I feel my cheeks run warm with tears.

I return my focus to the physical world and send a stream of electricity from my hands right into the body of the little fluffball. After a second, the blinding light clears revealing little Shanty, cradled in my hands as nothing but a tiny, charred lump of singed fur and flesh. I fire another, and the whole thing catches on fire. It burns quickly, reducing Shanty to a tiny ash pile. I fall back on my butt, crunching food pellets beneath me. Shanty is gone.

What have I done? I open my hands, and the ash flies from them, spilling out into the world.

I stand, shaking, unable to catch my breath. Suddenly, Dad bursts in through the kitchen wall, demolishing everything left of the house down to its brick-filled foundation.

"Why so glum, pal?" he says, sporting that same grin. A rage builds in me. I let out a scream and ram him in the gut with my shoulder, taking us both up to the sky. I viciously swing a thousand brightbolt-lined punches at him, each one twisting his face, knocking his head left and right.

"That's the spirit!" he shouts from behind my thrashing knuckles. He manages to duck out of my flurry and spin-kicks me high up in the air. I tumble through the top of Hearst Tower, transmitting a ripple all the way down to the base, which shatters the windows, one floor after another. I turn and drift farther down the city, back to Times Square. As I do, however, a smooth, white, low-flying predator drone skims under me. I somehow dodge it through reflex alone. I didn't even hear it coming.

The drone heads straight for Dad, who simply bashes it away, turning it into a giant ball of fire. He spits the dark smoke of the impact from his mouth and doubles back on himself, catching the drone's falling propeller in midair. He then hurls it right at me like a mechanical boomerang. I dodge it and fly back to Times Square, hovering above it. Dad teleports in front of me and flip-kicks me down through the roof of the main building at the center of the square.

I burst out of the rubble and skid to a halt on the cracked road. Most of the screens that decorate the buildings are heavily damaged, flickering violently in a fit of confusion. I telekinetically toss the largest screen at Dad, who has now landed, and it strikes him, launching him into the TKTS steps. His impact snaps a few of the crimson planks in half, throwing him off-balance and onto his back. I follow up that attack with a well-placed knee, knocking the wind out of his chest. The entire stairwell explodes, but I don't stop. I whale him in the face, twice, three times. He catches the fourth and kicks me down the street.

I flip backward, shredding the asphalt as I stall my momentum with a single knee. The glow of the traffic panels paints a section of the road blood red. I quickly regather my wits, just in time for a kick in the face from one of Dad's well-polished shoes. I take the hit with full force, staying firmly where I am.

"Now you're starting to fight like your mom," Dad says as he retracts his arm for another attack. I lean on the sidewalk and perform a quick break-dance flare spin on my hands, dodging a flurry from Dad. I come back to my feet and barrel-roll over Dad's furious roundhouse. With the help of the damaged screens above me, I conjure a cluster of lightning to my palm. A shock of brilliant white light takes me by surprise, blinding me. Regardless, I lunge forward, lightning lariat at the ready, stray streaks of which melt from my hand as I speed toward my...enemy. My vision partially returns, each generous blink tangling the image of Dad in a cluster of light pollution. He raises his arms, and the ground lifts under me. Like a skimming stone, I bounce off his tar-topped wall and let myself fall toward him, electric arm outstretched. Dad hurries under my falling body and runs up his conjured wall like an ant scaling a slice of cake. He somersaults off the structure, and with one fierce kick, he sends me spiraling through the lobby of a nearby hotel.

Pushing away from the lobby's wall, I re-enter the scene through the Dan-shaped hole. The memories of what pain used to feel like haunt my body as I shake away my dizziness. My lightning fizzles out, and my senses return. Suddenly, I hear a loud popping sound. A couple of beat cops are firing their pistols at Dad. He stands there, laughing, as their bullets melt into pools before they even touch his body. He has an arm raised to the sky like a preaching minister calling upon the power of God above, an odd sight to see. Obviously, that's not what he's doing. He must just be stretching. Maybe he feels old despite his immortality? I take advantage of this distraction and dropkick him before he wreaks revenge on the poor, inadequate members of the NYPD.

"Get back into your hut!" I shout, chastising them for interfering. They nod quietly and run back into their little box station and out of sight. As soon as the door closes behind them, the whole station explodes, erupting into a luminous fireball in front of me.

Goddammit.

I turn to see Dad, whose hand glows brightly under the blue of the morning sky.

"I was wondering where they were." He's pleased with himself.

"You asshole!" I shout back.

"Me? You're the one who let them die. You saved your little friends, didn't you? You care enough to help *them*, but when it comes to strangers, you just float there and let them die. You're like one of the drones your Mom encoded, algorithmically fighting in defense for whatever you're personally invested in. To hell with everyone else, right?" His words hurt more than his punches. "No, no, don't get me wrong," he continues. "This is a good train of thought. Stay aboard. It'll take us places…free from guilt. Free from arbitrary ties to arbitrary animals." As Dad finishes his speech, I tackle him and teleport us away, smashing us both into the heart of Central Park. We crash through Belvedere Castle. The park has already been cleared; people must have seen us fighting on the news, probably streamed from one or all of the cell phones inside Montage.

Dad gets to his feet, shaking the dirt and dust from his broad, angry shoulders. "Well, then, if he puts people in danger, I'll bring him to where he can't kill any person, but he can kill trees, rip up the flowers from their beds, shred grass into compost. Sure, they're alive, but they can't talk so they don't matter. Am I right?" He studies the rips and tears in his fancy clothes.

"Stop talking and fight me!" I demand. He smirks.

"Turn around."

A cold, metal grip clamps down on my shoulder. Heavy, deep breathing sounds from behind me. I slowly turn, petrified by the thought of what has hold of me, and see my own face, skewed in the metallic reflection. It's the Valkyrie. Its silver face melts, slowly morphing back into Dad's.

"Who were you talking to, Daniel?" he asks facetiously. I whirl around to find the Dad I was speaking to before has disappeared. He was *never* there! He was nothing more than a copy designed to take my focus.

"Don't get me wrong—" Dad drags me up to the sky, right above the clouds. "—I do feel guilty for sitting back and watching you bang your fists against nothing." His words echo as his mask reforms over his face. "But how else was I supposed to learn how you fight?" Without warning, he throws me, and I dizzily tumble through the clouds, back down to Broadway, crash-landing on several abandoned cars, which explode.

When silence resumes, I dig myself out of the wreckage, coughing the dust from my lungs. I look around for Dad, but the taxi I'm wearing like a turtle shell blocks my field of vision. I flex the car off my back only to be riddled by a burst of machine gunfire as a dozen or more full military Humvees roll in, each containing about five members of the National Guard. They've been sent to stop us, but all they're going to do is get in the way. The pressure of their bullets takes me aback. I shield myself with my arms and notice more military vehicles charging in, filling the streets, each one equipped with large, high-caliber machine guns that would floor a rhino with a single pull of the trigger. They're trying to block us in as a coordinated cluster, but one stomp of my foot and all the Humvees' tires burst in unison. The gunmen atop the turrets let go of the guns in an effort to maintain their balance.

"Cease fire!" A mustachioed sergeant hollers above the noise of the shooting infantrymen. The scene grows quieter, then fills once more with errant screams, car alarms, and the crackling of embers—now the default ambience of the city.

"Look, you guys need to move," I assert. "You're getting in the way here."

With shaky hands, the sergeant aims a pistol directly at my head. I roll my eyes and slap the weapon out of his grip. Startled, the sergeant runs into one of the destroyed buildings. As he does, the rest of it falls down on top of him, his screams quickly silenced by the crash.

"I'm not the bad guy here," I tell whoever is still listening. "The guy I'm fighting is. I'm trying to keep this situation under control."

The guards look up and around at the carnage.

"I'm…I'm sorry but this is a necessity," I add guiltily.

One of the Humvees next to me explodes as the news chopper from before spirals into it. I'm thrown to the ground, along with a couple of the guardsman. I look up from the sidewalk at Dad, who hovers over one of the taller buildings that remain standing on 42nd Street.

"What the hell are you doing?" he calls down, holding two smaller construction drones above his head.

I'm not taking his shit anymore. Let's turn it up a notch.

I jump over to the bottom of Montage Tower, taking hold of the walls that line the ground floor. The unfinished, unstable tower starts to vibrate. Some of the glass panels that make up its skirt crack and splinter like the edge of a melting glacier. Lifting the building out of its foundations, I carry it away from where Dad is situated and stop just past the roof of Penn Station.

Dad stays where I left him, no attempt to follow me or to cut me off before I finish. Curious but unconcerned, he tosses the drones away, dropping them like litter, as with one stretched arm, I lug an entire building high above my head and hold it there like an Olympic javelin. I try to get a feel of the wind brushing against my skin, all the while keeping Dad's distant form fixed in my sights. If I aim far above his head, it will compensate for the drag and drop that will affect my throw.

Closing one eye, I cock my arm back, and with a furious roar, I hurl the tower tip-first at Dad. It screams toward him, easily tunneling over the now-shorter buildings that line its flight path. The whole tower bends and wobbles in midair as it soars right for its target.

The tower reaches Dad perfectly, but it stops abruptly before it can stake his heart. It remains above the city, lying on its side. I fly between buildings, zigzagging back to Dad, who hovers, clutching the tower's spire like a catcher would a loose baseball. With his free hand, he points down to the National Guard, who litter the streets below. They peer up, dumbstruck by the show playing out in front of their very eyes.

Dad emits a sonic pulse, which reverberates through the entirety of the tower, and all I can do is watch as it shatters into a thousand pieces. Chunks of concrete, glass, and metal rain down on the soldiers below, all of whom shield their heads with their rifles.

Well, that isn't going to do shit. Before the guardsmen are crushed, I focus my mind, picturing the molecules that make up the falling material in play. Just like with the wave, I quickly reconstitute the pieces on a molecular level, changing the properties of the falling rubble into those that make up the softest of snow. The pieces burst, changing from deadly debris into a gentle snowfall, which serenely flutters down onto the guardsmen while they peek from below their useless defenses in childlike wonder.

Distracted, I miss the multicolored beam Dad fires from his hands. It's different from his other attacks. It's Forever-based, like his barrier. Time stops around me, and I'm hurled high up into the broken screen of the main building that sits in the southern section of Times Square. I melt into it, my face growing to the size of the OLED billboard. Dad has transformed me into an advertisement! The soldiers stare up in disgust at my stretched face as I share my discomfort with the faint, flickering aftereffect of a soda commercial.

"Dad...what did you do to me?" I boom from my picture-prison.

"Forever is easy to shape when you know how. I just wanted to make sure you had a good view."

"A good view of what?"

Dad saunters over to the National Guard, all of whom turn their rifles on him. The sabot rounds leave only the red streaks of laser light as they ricochet off Dad's metallic armor, which casts sparkles over the ruins like some macabre man-shaped disco ball. He takes a run at the soldiers, smashing through the impact of a digital-mortar shot, and slams into the first Humvee, breaking it in half. Snatching the gunman away from his turret, Dad swings him into three others, pulling the pin on his grenade, which explodes in a gray hail, flinging shrapnel in all directions. I wriggle to free myself from the giant TV screen, but nothing works. The ultra-high-definition sound of my struggle is overshadowed by the violent screams of the brutalized guardsmen as they are sent flying in all directions from the punches and kicks and bolts and beams Dad deploys.

I think back to the black hole—how I managed to undo the stretching effect that Saga was having on my body. Using the same principles, I pull myself together, both literally and metaphorically, and snap back to my normal size and shape, but I'm still inside my fizzy, sugar-soaked prison. Dad continues to reduce the guardsmen's numbers effortlessly, turning the military cavalcade into a mass grave. I need to get out of here.

Taking a deep breath, I pick a spot and rush forward. It works, and I burst out through the screen, bringing its battered shell crashing down behind me. I narrowly dodge the debris, make a fist, and in one swift move, blitz toward Dad.

In an instant, the convoy of Humvees streaks across the ground to the other end of the Square, and Dad uses this newfound space to dodge my attack. I crack the rock beneath the street into a crater. Dad flips again, firing a blast of energy my way. It explodes behind me in a muddy cloud as I corkscrew out of the blast radius. As I land, Dad flies in and catapults me across the city with a vicious uppercut. The wreck of Times Square spins in and out of view. Dad is flying at me again, this time with a whole skyscraper in hand, but instead of throwing it, he swings it like a softball bat. As it hits, the whole thing shatters, pushing me farther up the island, all the way past Central Park and into the side of the Empire Building. I slow my trajectory but not before I hit it about a quarter of the way from the top. Office workers leap from their ergonomic chairs, streaming from their cubicles like startled ponies.

"WHAT ARE YOU ALL STILL DOING HERE?!" I yell.

The frightened workers stampede toward the emergency exits as I look back out to the city to see another building in the sky where it shouldn't be. This time, it's a refurbished Madison Square Garden, oscillating toward me like a rotary blade let loose from its fittings. I fire a brightbeam, blowing the stadium to pieces, which screech off in all directions. There was nothing else I could do. The people on the ground stood a better chance of survival than those left inside the Empire Building.

I swerve carefully out of the entry wound and fly up to the tallest point of the building's spire. I plan on waiting for Dad to show himself, but by the time I reach the top, I see he's already there and is looking out over the city. His head cover is down, his real human eyes free to gaze out over the chaos we've sown.

"Do you see them, Son?" he asks above the heavy, icy wind that burns my nose and eyes.

"Can we stop this now?" I ask, squinting, mentally exhausted from our fight.

"We can, as long as you do what I ask." He keeps his back to me. "This will continue, the suffering, the carnage, the death. If our very presence threatens a planet's existence, then that planet isn't our home. I won't stop...I *can't* stop, Daniel." He's begging, *actually begging* me to listen to his distorted thesis.

"I'm needed here, Dad. I like it here. Earth is perfectly distanced from a star to support the life it has. I won't accept the theoretical over the physical simply to relieve you of your boredom."

"Your 'physical' is doomed. None of what you value will last. If the humans don't nuke the world, then the world will nuke the humans in its own defense!" He's starting to panic; he sounds like Mom used to. He's flailing his arms above his head, shouting at the top of his lungs, still with his back toward me. He lets out a growl of frustration at his lack of self-secrecy.

"Fine, let's say you're right," he says. "Let's assume a miracle happens, and the humans manage to survive. That'll just be the end of one chapter of Earth's story. World peace is a lot easier to maintain than galactic peace. It took the humans hundreds of thousands of years to get a probe to Mars. Do you really think they can move their entire species out past the next galaxy in four billion years? Because that's roughly how long they have before the Milky Way and Andromeda collide. Anything that exists inside these megaliths will *cease* to exist at that very point! If the world doesn't end sooner, then it will end later, and the universe won't care. We shouldn't either."

"We can stop that from happening," I say, shaken by his panic.

"No, we *CAN'T!*" he yells, sweat evaporating from his clenched brow, and all of a sudden, I realize what he's doing.

"Stop deflecting!" I yell back, tackling him from the top of the spire. I let him go, and we both stray from the building, falling, upside down, face-to-face, in complete silence. We fall farther and farther, without a word to each other. The architecture stretches out above our heads as we drop like a couple of lawn darts past the lower third of the Empire Building. Dad holds his hand to my chest; a bright, multicolored glow appears. He's going to do to me what he did to Mom, and I can't let him.

I swing a roundhouse kick into his side, propelling him through the weakened ventricles barely holding Empire Building together. No, that shouldn't have happened. It was a controlled kick, which he saw coming from a mile away. He should have dodged or blocked, but he didn't. Dad lets his body rip through the structure, felling the concrete monolith like a petrified redwood. It crumbles down, covering the smaller building sites around it with an immense landslide of rubble and a crash that could wake a comatose giant.

Dad teleports down safely onto the rubble below, dusting off his metallic suit, while I let myself fall through it. I don't deserve a cushy landing.

"Well, that saved me some trouble!" Dad yells through the smoke and the noise of wailing sirens. I burst out of the rubble, ashamed and angry at my stupidity. No matter how many times Dad has tricked me, I never learn.

I go to scream at him, but my ear catches the noise of cheers from the roof of a shorter apartment block. A large group of people— probably residents—stare over at Dad and me. Some are waving bright, hastily decorated poster boards that read "FIGHT! FIGHT! FIGHT!" and "WE COME IN PEACE!" Others have their selfie-sticks fully extended above their heads, commentating as we both look over in disbelief.

"Outside of, you know, existential terror and the cold inevitability of this galaxy's demise, what remains for us on this world, at this time is...*this*." He points up to the crowd of celebrating onlookers. "If we stay, their gratified cheers will change to screams of fear and pain. If we stay, you will continue to fight me, ending the lives of billions and eventually the life of the Earth itself. You have already proven that you're too self-centered to take care of anything or anyone you don't have personal ties to. I have only *allowed* this life for you because it has kept you relatively happy. But you don't really care about strangers because to you, they're a blurred collection of faces, and to me they're targets to aim you at."

"You could have left them be," I said. "But no, you had to try to...prove what, exactly? That hypocrisy and paradoxes plague humanity? You do this, all the while failing to notice how they're part of the universe's build wherever you go. All we have seen in our travels are the same things appearing over and over again—light, ice, rock, dust, heat, darkness. You preach pastures new, but everything I've seen is something Earth could have provided."

"This is *one* universe, Son! We have access to *thousands* of others. We'll forget about this place soon enough, and we'll be happier for it!"

"No, we won't!" I retort.

"Of course we will. Time heals all wounds!"

"Do you really think our precious 'god brains' will allow us to forget all of this?"

Dad's face twists into a semi-serious curl. His eyes freeze in place. I used his logic against him.

"We'll be haunted by our memories of this place and its people," I press further. Dad remains aboard his train of thought, and then a grin forms. That's the last I see of him before his head is consumed by the smooth, dark titanium of his Valkyrie suit.

Screams resonate from above as the crowd that were cheering us on shriek with tangible terror. Before I leap to take Dad's threat away from them, I realize their screams weren't directed at us but at something off in the distance. The same crowd shuffles down from the roof and into the apartment complex. I rise slightly to get a better look over the plumes of smoke that line the horizon like a toxic forest. I see what has frightened them. An enormous line of bomber drones is headed right for us.

They approach slowly. Leading the charge is a squadron of smaller drones, which fire a barrage of hellfire missiles. Their weapons will have less of an impact on the area than the bombers, which I can only guess are capable of leveling multiple city blocks each. But I can't let the missiles hit. I have to prove Dad wrong. I fire a ground-to-air brightbeam, knocking the missiles out of the sky, then conjure a smaller bolt aimed at the last remaining missile to cleverly redirect it at Dad, but before I can fire, I see he's already begun his own charge straight for me. His strike rockets me up through the air and into the path of one of the drones. It detonates, and I'm thrown backward, ripping away sections of light panels, bursting a fire extinguisher, and flipping a dozen cars farther down 34th Street before my tumble comes to a stop.

I'm stuck again, and this time, the bottom half of my body is enveloped in a glowing shell of Forever. He's got me. I'm trapped. I sit up, struggling to break free, my eyes on Dad, who stands squarely in the middle of the broken street, reaching up with both arms and psychically directing the bomber drones to separate locations in the sky above the city. When he's done, he turns to me, arms still in the air, each one conducting a dozen payload-carrying drones.

"Dad, don't," I plead.

"It's a necessity."

I fire a brightbeam at him, but it bounces off his mask. I stop time, and it restarts. There's nothing I can do.

With a shrug of his metal shoulders, the bombers rain down, covering the city in giant, long-lasting fireballs. Dad's form disappears into the light of the closest explosion.

Chapter 22

MOM, you know I can do this. I'll play my part, *I swear*. I love you." That's the last thing Dan said to me before he left to face his father. Without my son here, I will find it difficult to patronize; for that, I must ask for your patience and, if at all possible, your forgiveness. The explosions that rang outside this space have taken themselves far from here. I barely had the strength to cover my ears while my husband—*ex-husband, whatever he is*—went to war with our only child.

A potent pain runs through my entire body in a jagged, ecstatic pattern, contrary to the emotional torment, which is slowly tracing the lines of my soul, its vicious burn the only thing I've felt since Dan left. Without the comforting hush of the enlightened lad I love, my mind rules in a hell of my husband's and my making. This hell is a land of clouded judgment, an effort on my part to avoid the contradiction within my son's earlier reassurances. He tells me he will be successful in his mission, but he leaves me a keepsake in the form of an "I love you."

My pulse has yet to rebroadcast its presence from within my wrist. I pull at the middle-aged skin just below the crook of my elbow, the point at which my arm is its fleshiest, hoping to see it spring back into place when I let it go. As I free it from my skeletal squeeze, the skin lingers, curled up like a sleeping cat. My son doesn't know if he'll ever see me again, and the fact that this is mutual frightens me to no end.

I stare up at the abstract carvings which mark the ceiling of my prison. This was Henry's goodbye to me, an epitaph composed of incomprehensible streaks and slashes. The muscles in my neck tighten as my head swivels about the glacial cavern. It's evident that I have awoken as a different woman, an older, weaker being who sits as nothing but a stranger to the concept of control. Better to be a stranger than an enemy, if there is any difference in a universe as chaotic as this one. I hope Henry is happy with himself. That's the only positive on which my hat can dangle.

Deep in my mindscape, I question if my plan could be an egotistical arrangement. After much meditation, I can't seem to unearth a satisfactory answer, only another question: will we be victorious in our goal, or have I sent my son on a quest to repeat my past mistakes? I don't have access to sufficient data, so no side can successfully swing the vote in its favor. The questions linger nonetheless, pecking at my conscience like a bird beak on glass.

I pull at my skin. My forearm glows white with the pressure from my pinching. I tug as hard as I can, shaping my worn-down casing into a tidal wave frozen in time. As I release, the skin remains suspended, no elastic to drag it back into place. I smooth it over with my palm, clearing the canvas. The white glow has now darkened to a red spot. I think back to the story Dan told me an hour prior to this pull. I ponder whether his words were truly fit for my ear. Guilt bubbles beneath my breast, taking hold of my lifeless heart. I shake it off with a cold shower of gut-wrenching familiars, memories shuffled out of safe context. The darker memories come first: Dan's tears; my failed mission; Henry's smile. The carvings above my head serve as the opening lines of this memoir of madness. I feel a wave of opposition to these memories of mine, one of love and nostalgia: my grown son; the once-forgotten cold that kisses my nerve endings; Henry's smile.

While I struggle to untangle this knot of cognitive dissonance, I am reminded of a song. Yes, a record of an age long past, a song without a tune, a story…a story within itself. I see them now, the idiosyncratic details of this faceless tale that flashes about my rebooting brain with a prideful dance of glee.

When I was younger, I saw myself as a figure of great importance to the world, a celebrity, a star. Even before my first re-birth, I knew cameras, carpets, and clout were in my future. I saw this not as an obligated debt but as an Everest waiting to be conquered. I was to be someone of consequence. These feelings didn't stay bottled for long. However, their effects could be felt all around me. The world was flexible clay, my mind a tense and tactical toothpick, and this realization changed everything. A swell of fearful excitement took hold of my brain stem with an icy grip. Little did I know this feeling would return to me later in life when I met Henry. But until that time was upon us, I was alone and in need of a vent—a way to cope with the utter powerlessness I felt from hiding what I was.

To relieve some of the pressure, I used to stage fictional interviews with fantastical reporters. The locations needn't be glamorous; a small bathroom with a clean mirror would suffice. The loud, booming announcements were replaced with low whispers as I fielded questions from myself. I would be everyone from everywhere, and we would offer ourselves up to me, out of interest and the need for my knowledge.

I'd ask myself the most obvious question as an opener. "Is this a joke?" I'd say to the *me in the mirror*. This would start the sessions off with a reassuring taste of comedy. More serious queries would follow in slow, sensible fashion—

"How does it feel to be the person responsible for *fixing the world*?"

"How are you not tired all the time?"

"I hear there's a movie in the works, any truth to this?"

—until one day, I came upon an unexpected variable within this fantastical equation.

"What are you?"

That was the eventual bump in the road of my rationale, the tumescent growth at which the rate of my role-play would be reduced.

Apologies for my repetitiveness. The letter has taken a hold of my reforming senses. I'll continue with my recitation as best I can.

Predictably, I latched on to familiar responses for every other question, but this one specific problem required study, so much so that I am still, to this day, mistrusting of the thesis into which my chaotic murmurings evolved. The answer, unlike the others, was neither a constant nor an inconsistency, but a story. The story changed whenever it was told, but the fundamental message still dwelled within its core.

I will now tell that story.

Once upon a time, there was an astronaut—an intrepid explorer, blessed with mystical knowledge and an unbreakable body. Her time living with these gifts molded her into an impulsive soul. She dropped out of high school, eloped with her teenage sweetheart against her parents' wishes and followed a career in a field which, at the time, was as risky as it was puzzling. One day, the astronaut found herself on a mission of great discovery. This was to be a lone voyage, however, as she was the only one qualified to tackle the abuses such a task presented.

Nevertheless, the astronaut was not afraid, having survived everything else. The atmospheric dangers from Earth's moon to the moons that circled Pluto were no match for her. This sense of security helped strengthen the legend she was creating for herself in her mind. So, from Earth she flew, hundreds of light years past the edge of our solar system. After almost a millennium of unimpeded travel across the familiar, she finally entered a celestial system, one with worlds close enough to the heat of a star that life could thrive within them. After floating around the system for a short time, she decided to bring her feet to solid ground. She chose a moon at random, one that was bare but open and welcoming. The thought of crossing the barrier to the great unknown was so overwhelming that she made the journey without any idea of what to do after she arrived, so she walked.

After a few hours of travel, she noticed something as she passed an open crater where the shadow of the moon's dark side began. It was nothing to see or hear, nor was it anything to taste or touch. It was a feeling. This feeling was new, dark—the direct opposite of the empowerment the mission offered her. It was trepidation. The confidence that fueled the young girl was sapped from her in an instant, bringing concentrated apprehension to the forefront of her mind. Before she had time to process this newfound feeling of fear, it left her with her next footstep. This stopped the astronaut in her tracks.

With fear gone from her system, she investigated. She moved backward one pace, to the last, uneven boot print she had made. In a flash, the fear returned in full, dancing mockingly in her brain, mixing potent signals, drumming her heart viciously, wringing sweat from her pores without permission. It was violent and evil, and it was only at this point of contact. Again, she stepped out of the boot print she had left in the moondust and was free from the fear once more. The binary nature of this phenomenon wasn't so: the memory of the feeling followed her, singing an inquisitive tune in the back of her mind; this song took effect and diverted her from her mission. Afraid to venture any farther, the astronaut returned home to Earth as quickly as she could and never spoke of what happened to her on the moon to anyone—not her friends, her family, her colleagues. Not even to her husband.

On that moon, I had come into contact with something small but astronomical. I often hope that the *feeling* was just that: a *feeling*. However, due to the parameters in which the *feeling* operated, I can't help but question the validity of this hopeful assumption. What I had felt was not only alien to me, but alien to physiology itself. A *thought-based alien*—a being which existed in both a random dimension of space and in my own mind, and like bricks need clay, this creature of thought needed material from which to build a sensation. This detail is what brings it into the realm of tangibility.

My fear was not of the unknown star system, of my own impulsiveness, over-stimulated ego, or need to be loved. It was the fact that I had found the limit of my humanity. The thought-alien, the strangest thing I had ever encountered, was also the strangest thing I could imagine. Everything else was beneath it in terms of creativity. Every other form of life that could have possibly existed out there needed to adhere to the basic senses of my humanity: something I could see, smell, touch, hear, imagine, or feel.

And so, with this revelation, I had found that my limit as a human being was that I accepted myself as human. Whenever the concept of godhood crossed my mind, I brushed it off. I saw myself as a peer of the people around me regardless of my actions and abilities. I was limiting my own understanding and therefore my potential. The thought-alien was the end. From then on, I stayed on Earth with Henry, not as a human, but as their god.

I was still loving. I treasured the humans; I cared for them more than I ever could. I couldn't enact too much change too quickly; subtlety was required to keep the humans calm enough to accept any alterations I made for them. Some of my grander acts were called miracles; this did not help my case, as humans became lesser beings with each one declared. I kept my secret human identity as Dyani Hardacre, picking up where I had left off. I used my powers and intellect on a grounded level to help the humans improve their own lives through the use of more advanced technology. I became part of the system, a working wife to a human man, mother to a human child, or so I thought.

A few good years later, after a long and, let's say, "under-dramatic" labor, Daniel was born. A birthday gift we could all share. Despite the far-off places I had traveled, the strange collections of matter I had seen, none of it fascinated me as much as our son. There was an objective reason for that: he was unique. Everything about him—his smile, his skin, his baby sounds—was his alone. To match this, I wanted to name him something unique, something symbolic that needed to be sung, something joyful and prominent, but Henry thought it was better to name him something boring, something similar to one of ours.

I won the coin tosses, all six of them. "Daniel" was a bit too formal for me, I liked "Dan," though. It was quick and to the point. I hope he likes it too. He deserves to like the name he was given, seeing as he was the one thing that made Henry and I fuss in unison. He was our little art project. I fulfilled my duty as the matriarch, meaning I fed him, clothed him, sang him songs, and flew him to his various pediatric appointments. These flights stopped when Henry decided he wanted to drive us like "normal people."

As far as whatever miracles we could perform for Dan, we treated him as any other parent would, but only for things he asked for.

We never gifted him anything out of the blue. This way, the gifts and celebrations were somewhat limited by Dan's mind, which was yet to fully develop. This went swimmingly until his teenage years hit him like a moody anvil. All he ever wanted after that was to be by himself or with his friends. I understood, but I wasn't happy.

Henry changed when Dan was born. He met another person he could actually stand—not that he was much use with him. I used to think him an "idiot father" like so many of his contemporaries, unprepared for the selfless world you have to maintain in order to be fit for a life. Now, I can't be sure that the milk he burned or the clothes he shrank were accidents at all, given it freed him of almost all of his fatherly responsibilities.

A couple of years later, Henry developed powers of his own. I kept *mine* well hidden from everyone—my parents, friends, even from strangers—for *so, so long*. But for Henry, his powers just *set in*. Maybe they were dormant, or maybe he was hiding them from *me*. Maybe this was the reason behind our coupling; I can't be sure. He was always a closed book, and the few pages I managed to skim only revealed fleeting details of his true character. I wonder if I ever really knew the man I loved. I feel the urge to ask you—do you think he ever loved me?

And there it is, the *pathetic* reaching of the double-crossed, the questions that come with the shame, the cognitive dissonance breaking the world down into non-realities.

With all of this family talk, I find I am growing impatient and resentful of both Henry and myself, so I'll have to see if I can muster the will to put in the effort a bit later. I will share more, I promise.

I pull at the skin on my arm once again. It showcases a rerun of its earlier antics, staying upright and out of shape. This is taking too long. I hunger for the sight of a new world, a recovering, affected world eager to make the most out of the little time it has. I look beneath me, at the throne with which I am one. My interpretation of its origins creates traffic inside my palms. The sketched-out sections of my flesh roll over one another, bringing into being a fist of questionable power. In a fit of rage, I bring it down onto the arm of the chair, cracking the ignorant façade down the middle, a meridian strong enough to divide the self-awareness from the shame. The throne's arm splinters beneath my eminent hypothenar, shattering into salt-sized grains of milky crystal. Its destruction is almost rhythmic, rattling like the minor keys of a glass piano.

Danie—*Dan* wasn't always as vacant and kind as he is now. When he was younger, misery was his company. Misery and irritation. Those feelings gave him purpose and drive. I was proud to see him standing up for what he believed, even if his opponents were his father and me. There were so many secrets that infected our household, building a life apart from us was a natural state of progression for his isolated sense of stability.

Henry and I fought and argued day and night. I was trapped by him; he was trapped by this Earth. This lasted until Dan began to emulate our misery. He had grown out of his cartoon-themed sleepers and into messier, less tasteful apparel. At first, I latched on to the warnings I had received from Henry's parents: "Kids grow spines just as they grow pubes." Vulgar, I know, but it didn't come from a bad place. They were overly honest and wild as a couple, but they were accommodating guides for our family, more so than my parents would have been.

Dan's gung-ho assertiveness was pleasing to watch for a while, until I realized: history was repeating itself. Dan was growing out of our house as I did at his age, only my yearnings for freedom were more old-fashioned. Dan wanted solid work and a place within a metropolis to call his own. I operated much differently in practice. It didn't take long for any dreams of mine to appear as delusional, and I put them on hold and sought comfort in the idea of creating a new life with a new family. And it all started with Henry.

We met in high school. He was a transfer student for a summer program that gave applicable children from the lower forty-nine the opportunity to get out of their proverbial Americana and into the thermal-lined boots of young pioneers. Unfortunately for Henry, this was hyperbole and nothing more. High school remained high school, regardless of the temperature. I used to watch him, the lonely little southerner trailing the hallways of Juneau-Douglas, his thin, masculine lips locked tightly together to cover the teeth he continuously clenched. He always had his eyes to the floor, so I could admire for as long as I wanted. The promise of "new" wasn't delivered to Henry, but contrarily, I was a gleeful recipient of such a gift.

One day, he caught me staring from the other end of our usual hallway. Part of me wanted to turn and flee, but I didn't. I never broke eye contact. I stood my ground—solid, traversable ground onto which the boy could cling for comfort. Without thinking, I cast him a lifeline, one I hoped he'd take with both hands. And he did. With those same hands, he held me in place while I openly accepted a lifeline from him. It was magical. We never said a word to each other the entire time; we didn't need to. Love is a universal language.

Obviously, things changed. The boy who never said a word to anyone spoke exclusively to me and only when we were alone together. Can you imagine how special that made me feel? After a short time, I'd find out there was a reason for his vow of silence. It was a lesson he'd learned earlier in life. His parents had once told him, "Son, if you can't say anything nice, then say nothing at all!" He thought dark thoughts; he gave in to fits of rage and cynicism. This led to him feeling nothing but contempt for his fellow human. His parents didn't expect their lesson to stick, but their words held like molasses. But like *other things*, Henry broke their rule for me. His words were murky and hateful, yet the mouth saying them was soft and passionate. He told me I was the outlier in his life, the one who stood out from the rest as something to be complimented, to be admired, to be loved. I realize now that, with what I could do at the time, maybe it was unfair for me to love him.

I used to run away from home a lot. And by home, I mean Earth. Once Henry and I declared our love to my parents, they took him into our house, and we were together until we both outgrew our nest. And yet, that wasn't reality. To my parents, Henry wasn't the sultry, sulking boy in need of saving. No, he was an invader. He came into our lives without a word and ripped up the fortified foundations they built for us. I hated them for forcing this stigma onto our relationship. After a while, they stopped calling him Henry and placed upon him the title of "Cheechako"—a term reserved for outsiders coming into the country to work the mining tunnels. They never realized I was too tall to let their disgusting joke go over my head.

So, when the time came for Henry to return to America, a minor—a child—went missing that day, vanished completely without a trace. I gave up my home, heritage, friends, and family in exchange for Henry. I didn't have a home after that, not until we moved into the one Henry built for us. However, I had no need for food, shelter, warmth, or stability. They were human problems.

My parents died after five years of looking for me, an accident that leveled the house while they slept. The stove was left on late at night; the bathroom light created enough of a spark, giving life to the explosion that would end theirs. It was unquestionable. Still is. I refuse to question it. I don't know if I could bear the weight of another investigation. At the time, I was devastated, a god unable to save the lives of her asshole parents and felt nothing when she found the emergency services inspecting a charred crater where their house used to be. If it wasn't for my infrequent fly-bys, I might have never found out.

I squeeze the remaining arm of the throne. It shatters quicker than its mate, creating a dust so fine it drifts away, disappearing out of my sight.

After finding out about my parents, I sought refuge in my work. I began to experiment, engineering software on Earth and toying with the laws of physics in space. This mission I set myself kept me away from Henry, who, without a lifeline to hold on to, was reverting back into that lost little boy. Even after he woke up one day as a "god" himself, he couldn't keep up with me for long. When he did, it was nice. One of those times ended with Dan's conception. I can't even be sure if our relationship was ever a moral one before that point, considering my power. And so I don't think I'd feel right if it had happened earlier.

Having a child caused further problems between us. My son needed his mother, my mind needed its work, and my soul needed to defeat the enemy I had made out of time itself. Time couldn't be conquered so freely; I found there were rules to it, rules which would prevent long-sought-after emotional reunions and the cleaning of slates. These changes would not heal the painful wounds that infect our own personal timelines, but they might move them, maybe even grow them. The risk to the fabric of time and space was too high. I invested in these rules, preached them to Henry as gospel. It's clear to me now that these rules must be broken.

I pull at the skin on my arm and hold it for a few seconds, pulling and pulling until the time comes, and I let go and magnificently it snaps back into place. I feel the muscles in my face retract, forming a smile. I swing my head backward, smashing it right into the backrest of the throne, creating splits that form all the way down its body. After the clicks count down, the throne completely disintegrates, evaporating before I can even stand. With little more than a glance at the carvings on the ceiling of my prison, I charge up, tunneling right through my epitaph and out of my tomb.

I breach the surface, flying face-first into the cold Alaskan air. The bright sun bleaches my skin back to its original brown pigment. My dark hair flows like a river down my shoulders. I land atop the glacier that formed while I was imprisoned and take my first free breath in over sixteen years. I open my eyes to the new world. As I take in the sight, my smile fades, my heart sinks, and I sink along with it, onto my knees in view of a smoggy crater that sits in place of my childhood home. I wanted to see it again one last time before...

★

Before...

★

I don't cry. I just sigh. And then I fly, high up into the sky.

The glow returns to me, excited. It consumes the tattered burial shroud Henry wrapped me in. Within the light, my powers work wonders. Overlapping shapes of fabric mesh together, pushing their way out of the shell of light. Pressed pants cover my legs, a crease-free shirt wraps my torso, and a pair of smart brown cushion boots pop onto my feet. Finally, a long, purple winter coat drapes around my shoulders. I soar down to the southern states, taking in the sights of fall-tinged Arizona, New Mexico, Oklahoma, Arkansas, Tennessee,

Virginia, Delaware, New Jersey, and as this long-desired flight comes to a close, New York.

I settle back into the realm of natural sound as I come face-to-face with...*not* Manhattan. At least, not anymore. I see nothing but a gigantic, squared-off pillar of charcoal-colored smoke. I shift to the left, examining the shape at close quarters. As I peer at its crystalline make-up, something shimmers out of focus over the city, something shiny and thick...some kind of field. *My* force field, enveloping the city, keeping whatever has happened trapped inside. Henry must have put it up to keep the fight in a populated area.

I speed through the center of the shield, dashing it into a trillion harmless pieces. I cut through the overgrown pillar of lead-lined smoke and gently sink, right into the heart of a smoldering wasteland, a foundation of ruined rubble. The piles sit tall and are as gray and lifeless as a corpse. It's almost moon-like in this form. My now-firm skin crawls. What have you done, Henry?

The smoke the shield housed dissipates as I float quietly into Central Park, welcomed by the blaring of myriad car alarms, the cries of suffering children, and the horror of death itself. The charred remains of the park's once-lush greenery make the place smell like a larger-than-life compost bin. The stink surges up my nose like an unwelcome insect. Seagulls have begun picking pieces of flesh from bodies that now litter the streets. Tourists, villagers, parents, teachers, congressmen, soldiers, celebrities, all dead before their time. Another case of collateral genocide.

Two solitary hearts beat out of step with one another; they require closer inspection.

I leap over, crashing down about ninety feet away from them, my fangs bared.

My boys.

Dan lies in a lapping pool of water drained from a broken fire hydrant. He's chained to the ground by a network of multicolored mesh and...

Henry.

Henry is...

I...

I...

I practiced, mentally. I rehearsed the things I would say to him, every witty entrance line. Paragraphs of cold, scolding vitriol, the longest laugh I would ever laugh, but it's all evaporated from my mind. I look at him, faceless and formidable in his silver spacesuit, the mask of which lowers, revealing the battered visage of Henry Hardacre. I attempt to speak, but an odd guttural noise comes out, nothing else. I can't form the words. Not after this long. Not after all he has done.

"I knew you'd be back, you wicked bitch," he says with a sharp grin on his face.

At that moment, all of my emotions come out in the form of a gut-wrenching scream, one so loud that the water from the broken hydrant begins to boil. Silver sliders slip up the sides of Henry's head, covering his ears. Dan does nothing but wince, stuck in the ground like a tangled Christmas ornament, drowning in the noise of my painful ordeal.

I stop as my eyes flood with wounding tears and attempt to steady myself. Henry stretches his arms up to the sky, struggling to stay silent as he does so. His bones crack like popcorn as he regains his composure.

Actually, reader, if you wouldn't mind, could I ask you to take the next step with me? Could I ask you to turn the page, please?

The calcified Forever ties that bind Dan unravel out of existence, much to Henry's shock. He beams himself over to Dan, placing his cold, lead-lined hand on our son's thick head of hair. I know what he's doing. The visible pain leaves Dan's face as his dopamine levels rise, and suddenly he is free and in a much happier mood. Henry also comes down with a case of a cheerier disposition. He stands next to his little recruit, unaware of the chat Dan and I shared only hours before.

"You were wonderful, Dan," I say to my happy-go-lucky little boy. He grins at my motherly compliment.

"Thanks, Mom." He stares at his battered brown shoes, embarrassed but joyful.

"You've got to be kidding me!" Henry yells after a sudden realization. "Daniel lied. You were never *moved* from your glacier. You were right under me! I should have known. It's where you were the happiest, right, Dyani?"

"It wasn't my doing. You locked me away, shut my body down. It took a while for it to recover. My heart was unable to beat for hours after Dan woke me. By the time it came down to Earth, my heartbeat was blending in with everybody else's. Oh, Henry. Ever the fool."

I push out my arms. Then I part them, north and south. Forever opens up behind me. Henry quickly loses his sense of humor. He knows exactly what I am about to do.

"You can't be serious, Dyani!"

"It didn't have to be this way, Henry."

"How powerless do you think I am?" he shouts, horrified. "You take one step toward that hole, and I promise you, there will be no coming back from what I do next."

"At this point, that's what we need," Dan says, quickly snapping his arms around Henry, who fights his restraints with every muscle in his metallic body. Dan's neurochemicals are back to normal, yet he continues to wear a calm smile as his father tries to teleport himself free, but I wall Henry down onto his knees with a small version of my city shield. The now-trapped pair fizz and spark from within their shared cocoon.

"DANIEL, I ORDER YOU TO LET ME GO!" Henry demands shakily.

"Shhhhh—shh-shhhh, Dad. It's okay. You don't have to fight anymore," Dan says.

"But we need them!" Henry begs.

I know, but still…"

The floor beneath us cracks, and pieces of debris start to rise into the air as rivulets of magma pour from the Earth and lightning strikes dance about the block.

I feel a little ill at the sight of Dan comforting his asshole father, but I guess he can't help it with what Henry has done to him.

"No…no, no! You won't do this. I won't let you!" Henry screams, ramming a robotic hand through the roof of the shield. His arm stretches upward.

The debris floats ever higher into the ashen skies. I follow it with my eyes, only to see what is attracting it. It's Earth's moon. That's what all that stretching was for. Henry was moving the Moon; he means to make it a meteor! He had contingencies for his backup plans. This was always his greatest strength, which is why I asked Dan to help me take the possibility of choice away from him, just as he did to me. This isn't something I see as petty vengeance, but as a formula to bring about the greater good. I need to get moving. Dan can't hold on.

Henry swings his head back, butting Dan away from him. This snaps the elastic of the shield, and Henry attempts to lunge at me, but Dan back-flips down onto the ground, reaching out and snatching Henry's leg in midair. Henry tries to kick him off but misses, unable to properly aim when his attention is entirely on me.

"Dad, stop struggling. It's going to be okay," Dan says with a soft smile.

"IT ALREADY IS!" he shouts, firing a hand-beam at Dan, who takes the full force. Deeper, darker cracks form, sifting some of the chalky remains of the city down into the earth. Furious, Dan pulls himself up to his father and strikes him across the face, sending him rolling ten feet away from us. Dan stands in front of me, arms out wide, his eyes fixed on Henry, who reaches up high, pulling the Moon in closer. He has bound it in an effort to keep errant pieces of it from splitting off in every direction. He doesn't want machine gunfire; he wants a 100% guaranteed extinction event. A blazing ring of fire spreads out from the center of its surface as it enters the atmosphere. With whole, flattened neighborhoods being pulled up into the sky, we only have a few minutes before the ground we're standing on does the same.

"Mom, I have to go," Dan says, gesturing skyward.

"We all do," I reply, trying to keep my proud tears bottled up inside.

Henry stands there, eyes darting about, looking for an escape solution.

"You won't do this. I won't let you!" He seethes with the crushing rage of defeat.

The last time I see my son, he is focused, forceful, heading straight for the body of Earth's misplaced moon.

Henry's path is clear. I quickly turn and fly into Forever with him hot on my heels, snarling viciously, snatching at me like an overeager shark.

Forever's colors merge together.

Light shines.

Life.

Epilogue

IT hits the glass, bouncing off the pane like a hailstone. This noise does not, however, startle Daniel, who lethargically twists off his large, uncovered mattress. His bare feet cross the carpet in a slow, humorless stride. He rips open his closed curtains violently enough that one of the rings on the pole above breaks loose, tumbling to the ground like a dropped donut. Daniel's frustration is met by the image of smeared glass, marking the recent impact of a wayward seagull. The crooked thing now lies, disheveled and lifeless, on the stones beneath the window.

Daniel sighs to himself. Pulling his boxers up over his morning wood, he climbs out of his ground-floor window and into the cold, which hits him like lightning. Images of the CDC and flu sufferers flash across his mind as he steps to avoid the carpet of feathers that now litter the 5x15 square yards of concrete garden space. Taking a large shovel that lies in the corner of the yard, Daniel tucks it under the dead seagull and hoists it high, catapulting the bird up over the garden fence. A car alarm rings out from the distance. He hopes it was just a coincidence and climbs back into his bedroom, kicking stones from beneath his bare feet.

Soon after, as Daniel exits the shower, he notices a note on the kitchen worktop.

It reads: "01000010 01110010 01100101 01100001 01101011 00100000 01100001 00100000 01001100 01100101 01100111 Xx."

It takes him a while to read through it, but it's enough to put a smirk on his face. Returning to his bedroom wrapped in a soaking wet bath towel, he leaves wet prints on the kitchen's cold linoleum floor. Minutes later, an almost fully dressed Daniel opens his wardrobe for one last piece. He reaches high and pulls down a film-covered jacket which was lying folded on the top shelf. He loops the protective sheet from around the neck of the clothes hanger and unbuttons a brand-new sports coat. He throws it over his shoulders, hoping to God it fits; even with his thin frame, it's a little too snug for comfort.

"I'm sure I only need sixty percent of my oxygen intake," he mutters to himself. And with that, he exits, leaving his house with a twist of an old, scratch-covered key.

Standing on the train platform, Daniel patiently watches as a crowd grows around him. Second by second, more pile in, filling what little space the platform has to offer, pushing the already-grouped closer together like a bunch of grapes. After an agonizing seven-minute delay, the train arrives in a disorderly fashion, bringing with it an ear-piercing screech. The crowd tapers in a desperate effort to create a thin enough stream to uncomfortably file their eclectic body shapes into the train car, a car so compact that, if the previously mentioned grape simile were accurate, they'd be drowning in a vat of their own freshly pressed juices.

The journey between Newark and Penn station is not a short one; every time one passenger exits, another two jump on to overfill their necessary space. The warmth builds, and the box becomes as hot as the line on which the train's traveling. Sweat fills the air, setting an uncomfortable atmosphere for the rest of the journey.

Penn station is far busier than Newark was. A lot of lively, angry bodies circle in and out of one another, barely avoiding disruptive conflict. Daniel slinks through, picking his way down to the subway for the other half of his commute. He reaches the turnstile, unpockets his contactless Metro card and scans it on the sensor. The scanner's brightly lit blue corners glow aggressively red. Daniel scans the card again with the same result. He tries a third time and pushes the turnstile, which stays stubbornly locked in place.

Daniel checks his surroundings, hoping to have avoided embarrassment of a holdup. A long line of tired, angry New York faces stretches out behind him like a tail with a temper.

"It...won't go," Daniel says to the next person in line, who stands at a frightening height, dressed in thick, colorful fibers. The man mutters something unintelligible and turns to the closest floor-staff member, who is busy glaring at the screen of his smart phone. The tall man throws an empty fair-trade coffee cup at the staffer's head, shaking him back into the real world. He jumps up, ecstatic to be called upon, and shimmies over to the turnstile with a large grin on his face. He sniffs around the area, seeking out the issue. Like an antique librarian, the man delicately pulls Daniel's card out of his hand and examines it closely. The flashing screen catches the man's eyes, which widen with panic.

"Oh, Nelly, we got a *code red*!" he yells exuberantly at the buzzing screen, chuckling to himself in a swift change of attitude. Flipping the card over, he scans the opposite side. At last, the light box glows a soothing green, freeing up the turnstile. The staffer smacks Daniel on the top of his back to signal it's time to move on.

Flustered, Daniel bashes his way through the metal bars and runs down the crooked, stone steps and onto the second line of the subway system. The car is a tighter fit than the train. With barely any room to breathe, Daniel remains crushed up against the glass for the remainder of his journey, stopping at 125th Street, Harlem, gentrified beyond recognition.

Daniel jogs through the winding streets, his Bouncing Bag jumping noisily up and down behind his shoulders. The people on the street turn and stare at this poor, tardy fool who runs inattentively while following the GPS on his cell phone. He stands out all the way until he reaches his destination just past the starting time for his first day of work.

Draped across the red brickwork in large, silver letters hangs the sign for "Adno Architecture," a small, out-of-the-way database-building company owned by a larger conglomerate named CyberGem. They've bought up a lot of computer companies over the years in an effort to dominate the digital market. Their oligopoly is beneficial to someone with Daniel's qualifications but not so much for those older or poorer.

Daniel hops up the steps and into the lobby, where he is greeted by a hulking security guard.

"Your ID, sir?" the guard says, gesturing to yet another turnstile that sits in Daniel's way.

Daniel rummages through his backpack, in and out of every pocket, until he finally finds a laminated keycard buried deep at the bottom of the first one he checked.

"Here it is, Andrew!" he says, loudly reading off the guard's name tag in a sad attempt to break the ice. He then scans his ID card, this time the right way. The machine beeps welcomingly.

"My name is Derrick, sir," replies the guard, perturbed.

"Oh! Well, I'll try to remember that."

"You won't." The guard moves back to his desk.

Daniel stands at a duo of silver elevator doors. He peers up at the screen, which shows the countdown from the fifteenth floor. As he waits, the security guard's cell phone buzzes in the distance. He answers it. Daniel eavesdrops to pass the time.

"Hey, babe. … Yeah, I told them. … They can't make your debut. … Of course I get it, Hol. … Look, they already said that they won't watch *Hubble*! … Because you know why!" He ends with a nervous chuckle.

Distracted, Daniel is startled when the elevator doors open loudly behind him. He steps in, pressing the button for the tenth floor. The elevator shakes as it begins its ascent. The gentle hum soothes him. He feels protected in a giant shell of metal. It comes to a stop, and with a loud *DING*, it opens up to a gray-haired man, who stands there, tapping his pen on the edge of the clipboard in his arms.

"I've been waiting for you, Daniel," the man says.

"I know. I'm so sorry I'm late, Mr. Nebrezza, I had some trouble finding the place, plus the train terminal went nuts when I scanned my card."

Nebrezza places a firm mitt on Daniel's shoulder. "Calm down. I was kidding—kinda. Don't sweat your first day. I'm your supervisor, not your 'boss.' You can call me Martin."

Daniel, thinking this is some sort of test, silently nods and follows *Martin* through a short hallway and into a large, crowded office with computers all packed together in separate, gray cubicles.

"I know it's a bit old-fashioned, but people perform better when they're free to be in their own space. Your cubicle is down there. Log on and take the tour of the intra..." Martin's top half takes the position of Rodin's *Thinker*, interrupting his flow. "Oh, yeah. Here's a thought!" he announces, getting back on board the thought-train. "You said you got lost on the way here, right?"

"Yeah, very lost," Daniel yells clumsily like a troubled teen to the local sheriff.

"Well, let's tackle that problem internally. Before you start, you can take a tour of the building. That way, you can familiarize yourself. Sound good?" Martin offers a wide, paid-for grin.

Daniel nods again, eyes wide like a bobble head that's lost its mind. He senses a risky freedom in Martin's offer. Maybe he can sneak off to get some caffeine before starting his day.

"Willard, would you mind giving the new Daniel here a tour of the building?"

A man peers up from his cubicle, which sits directly next to the office door. "You can't ask me to comb through the entirety of the BAI setup and then hand me a newbie." Willard's two vastly different accents fight among themselves.

"Okay, how about...Ana. You're about the same age, would you mind?"

A chair squeaks from behind a wall at the far end of the office. Out of the cubicle steps a short woman in her mid-twenties with unnatural red hair and a face stricken with panic, the sight of which makes Daniel nervous. Her already-speedy pace quickens as she makes her way down the side of the cubicle farm.

"Okay," she mumbles, trying to not draw the attention of the other workers.

"Wonderful!" Martin announces. "No more than fifteen minutes, though!" he adds with a chuckle.

Ana humors the man with a smirk and exits the office. Daniel waits for his name to be called, but no such call comes, so he speeds after Ana, who has already crossed the halfway point of the hallway.

The tour goes on for a while. The only words spoken between the pair are office names, staff designations, and technicalities.

"Ugh...look, Ana, is it?" Daniel asks, stopping her mid-door introduction. She turns around, rolling her eyes just quick enough that they're back to where they were as she faces him. "I know this is a bit strange, but do you wanna go get a drink?"

Ana is taken aback. She doesn't seem to want to break out of "work mode" but asserts herself and rolls her eyes in plain view for him to see.

"You're weirdly forward, aren't you? Whatever your name is," she says with a practiced scowl.

"My name is Daniel, and no. If you can point me to the nearest vending machine, that would work just as well."

She thinks for a moment. "Are you trying to play hooky on your first day, Dan?"

"I prefer 'Daniel,'" *Daniel* says, wincing at the odd shortening of his name.

"I prefer Dan, it's *cleaner*," she says, grinning playfully.

"Whatever. Can you help me or what?" He looks around them both for prying eyes and ears.

Ana considers a moment longer, then, to Daniel's surprise, says, "All right."

The pair sit on the roof, blue paper cups in hand. Ana takes her time with small sips while her new colleague throws the whole thing down his neck with painful results.

"So, how did you sleep last night?" Ana asks through a small chuckle.

"I didn't," Dan says, dragging the air back into his lungs.

"I don't blame you for being nervous. I get that way sometimes myself. It'll go after a few weeks in the office. The place is pretty chill. Think of it as a stroke of luck. I heard Martin offered the vacancy to his son originally, but he turned it down to go backpacking in Greece. Lucky him, right?"

"It's not this place that I'm scared of," Dan says, swirling the dregs of his green tea around the bottom of his cup.

"Then what is it?"

Dan looks up, visibly shaken.

"Sorry, I don't want to pry. I just...well, it's not like we're working," Ana says, treading the line of reassurance and shamelessness.

"It's dumb," he says, avoiding eye contact.

"I'm sure it's fine?" she pries further. Dan stays silent. "Okay, just concentrate on your work, and you'll be all ri—"

"I have a play," Dan blurts out. "I'm acting...in a play...tonight." Now as breathless as when he downed his tea, Dan looks like he regrets sharing.

"In the office?" Ana asks.

"I—no. Not in the off—" He cuts himself off with a flustered sigh. "It's in a small, independent box theater way, way off-Broadway. In other words, it's in a room above a convenience store in Jersey City."

"That *is* 'off-Broadway,'" Ana says between sips.

"I don't want to tell people because I don't wanna come off as lame on my first day, but I have to because we can't fill the seats of a *secret* play!" Dan runs his fingers through his hair, bringing his hands over his face in an obtuse attempt to hide his shame.

"What's it about?"

"It's dumb." His words are muffled behind his hidey-hands.

"Please?" Ana asks, dropping her mask of confidence out of an odd-placed sense of pity.

Dan looks up. "It's Shakespeare's *The Tempest*...with...robots," he confesses.

"Sounds fun," Ana says, unfazed. "What time do you go on?"

"I...what's the matter with you?"

"My parents are hosting a dinner party tonight. I need an *out*, and now I have one. What time?" Ana presses, trying to catch up to the freeing relief the excuse will give her.

"Twelve a.m.," Dan says quietly.

"Midnight?!" Ana shouts, quickly regretting her earlier commitment.

"'Midnight-Monday-Madness,'" Dan explains hastily. "It's the only time we could get!"

"Okay. I'll go, but you you're paying for the coffee tomorrow." She shakes her now-empty cup.

"Is there any chance that your parents' dinner party could come?" Dan laughs with rare excitement. "We need the money."

After a lukewarm shift, the day comes to a close. Daniel shuffles out of the train station exit and down the street, past a newly opened coffee shop named The Brown Fountain. It's one of those modern, chainless venues that come and go like broken clockwork. Daniel stops, wondering whether or not to feed his addiction. The weight of a sleepless night hangs heavy on his senses. He shakes his head, recollecting himself. The place is packed inside, but there is a small seating area outside. Maybe a drink in the sunset will steady his stage nerves.

As he's about to go in, the front doors are flung open, and a group of rowdy friends burst out, piling into the seating area. Loud and brash, they sit together as a pantheon, occupying with confidence the only seats left. Daniel yawns, shakes his head, and walks on. At the corner, he turns and catches sight of an unfamiliar woman in a "Ratatosk" postal uniform. She sprints toward him, her blond hair swaying in front of her excited brown eyes. The woman zooms past and into the full arms of a burly man who has just exited the station. He's in a uniform too. He drops a large bag onto the sidewalk. It's fitted with the worn logo of a well-known overseas charity that provides aid to Third World countries. The lovers break away from the station and head over to the group sitting outside the coffee house, who cheer loudly, welcoming the couple into their friendly fray.

Overwhelmed and a little jealous at the prospect of their fun-filled evening, Daniel increases his pace and attempts to hop across the street, but the traffic begins to move again, blocking him under a stop light that hovers over him derisively. While waiting, something catches his eye in a local pet store. In the "Animal Palz" window, Daniel sees the tall guy from the train station wearing an even larger smile on his face. He has a rotund hamster in his giant hands. He carries the creature gently over to the front desk and places it into the arms of a little girl, who cuddles it closely. She rubs her nose against its puffed-out cheeks, under which sits a small, silver bell attached to a flea collar. Her mom giggles, scanning her credit card on the reader that sits next to the register. They exit the store with their new family member and climb into the family sedan parked across the street. The driver is none other than Derrick, the security guard from Daniel's new workplace. *I guess we will have something to talk about tomorrow.*

The room is dark. Daniel pants heavily from behind the scenes, dressed head to toe in twisted pieces of silver-painted cardboard. His scene partner is running through his stage directions with the playwright. This has become a necessity seeing as the director is off in another world in the corner of the room. Each of the players can already hear buzzing from the stands outside. There aren't many voices, mostly the friends and family of the troupe. The size of the group doesn't matter to Daniel as he arches forward, trying not to hurl. To take his mind off his stage fright, he sneaks a quick peek through the poorly attached red sheet that separates him from the audience. Scanning the room, he sees two familiar figures stomp their way in: his mom and dad. His mom is completely without patience, ignoring his dad, who mouths angry words to the back of her head. They both find their seats, uncomfortably close to each other. *They both left for work early, so their argument must*

have continued after that recess, Daniel thinks, filled with even more dread than before.

He sticks his head farther out the curtain, catching his mom's attention. She raps on his dad's shoulder, and he looks up from his cell phone and waves cheerfully. They have both transformed into fresh-faced parents happy to see their child, even if it means burying their problems in a deep, unhealthy hole within their souls. Soon after, Ana steps in out of the darkness and takes the chair closest to the exit, right next to Daniel's parents. She fiddles with her clothes, fidgeting in place until she spots his disembodied head sticking out of the sheet. She chuckles and waves. Daniel cracks an unwavering smile at the trio and slowly retracts his head, slightly calmer at the sight of the familiar faces. He joins the rest of the cast as the director encircles them.

"Right, we have half a minute left until we go out, guys. Don't ruin this for me!"

Daniel stretches, getting ready for wardrobe. He quickly meets with his scene partner and takes his place behind him, connecting his half of the horse to his partner's.

I need to remember. This may be opening night, but it's not our only performance. I need to remember that no matter how bad we are now, it will get better.

And

Curtains.

Acknowledgments

This is weird, isn't it? Well, for me it is. You're just getting on with your day. I'd like to start by saying thank you to Debbie McGowan and Nigel Paice, the alpha and the omega of the publishing world and everyone else in the Beaten Track Publishing team. You eradicated my many typos and idiocies with the fury and precision of the most sober of deities (sober being a metaphor only in this case!).

Thank you to Jor Barrie and Ames Leibowitz for making sure that the words were suitable for human eyes and ears.

Thank you to Jasmine Paice for the introduction to Beaten Track Publishing—without you none of this would have happened at all.

Thank you to Holly Dunn for the out-of-this-world cover design. Like an eclipse, sitting here staring at it so much is probably bad for me, but it's just so beautiful that I can't turn away.

Thank you to Morgan Wright for the stunning animation, that's not in the print version of the book because it's animated digitally. I mean really, what on earth did you think the reason was?

Thank you to Connor Houston and the rest of Pennylands for your cameo appearance.

Thank you to TJ Marbois, Tom Hodgson and the rest of the VERO team for all your help and enthusiasm.

Thank you to Kieron Dixon, Adam Greenall and Tommy Pierce for always being there for me, despite how many times I tell you to go away.

Thank you to Jane Gilmartin, Jack Heath, Claire Holroyde, Sylvain Neuvel and C.J. Tudor for your incredible advice and support, as well as serving as inspiration. You also allowed me to name-drop so I look like a big man in front of people.

Thank you John Earle, for your mentorship.

Thank you, once again, to Adam, for putting up with my nonsense on this project. Anthony, Lee and Rita, as stated earlier in the book's dedication: you're alright.

And finally, thank you to anyone who has read, purchased, looked at or stood next to *Road to Juneau*. You are why I get to do this and I will always be grateful.

:~)

About the Author

Liam Quane is a British filmmaker and author from the working-class town of Skelmersdale, Lancashire. After gaining experience making short films, writing screenplays and editing music videos, Liam turned onto a different storytelling venture in the form of novels. And, after reading six of them, he wrote his own in a hectic hail of key presses and dicey guesses. This bullheaded effort morphed into what would later be called *Road to Juneau*. It may be his first book, but he has more ideas for further bookcentric ventures.

Website: https://www.specificityarchives.com

Social Media links:
Twitter: https://twitter.com/SpecificityA
Facebook: https://www.facebook.com/LiamQuane1
Instagram: https://www.instagram.com/liam.quane
VERO: https://vero.co/liamquane

Beaten Track Publishing

For more titles from Beaten Track Publishing,
please visit our website:

https://www.beatentrackpublishing.com

Thanks for reading!